THE
CHILDREN
ON THE HILL

Also by Jennifer McMahon

THE
CHILDREN
ON THE HILL

Jennifer McMahon

SCOUT PRESS

New York   London   Toronto   Sydney   New Delhi

Scout Press
An Imprint of Simon & Schuster, Inc.
1230 Avenue of the Americas
New York, NY 10020

First Scout Press hardcover edition April 2022

SCOUT PRESS and colophon are registered trademarks of Simon & Schuster, Inc.

For information about special discounts for bulk purchases, please contact Simon & Schuster Special Sales at 1-866-506-1949 or business@simonandschuster.com.

The Simon & Schuster Speakers Bureau can bring authors to your live event. For more information or to book an event, contact the Simon & Schuster Speakers Bureau at 1-866-248-3049 or visit our website at www.simonspeakers.com.

Interior design by Davina Mock-Maniscalco

Manufactured in the United States of America

10 9 8 7 6 5 4 3 2 1

Library of Congress Cataloging-in-Publication Data

Names: McMahon, Jennifer, author.
Title: The children on the hill / Jennifer McMahon.
Description: First Scout Press hardcover edition. | New York : Scout Press, 2022. |
Identifiers: LCCN 2021048425 (print) | LCCN 2021048426 (ebook) |
  ISBN 9781982153953 (hardcover) | ISBN 9781982153977 (ebook)
Subjects: GSAFD: Horror fiction.
Classification: LCC PS3613.C584 C48 2022 (print) | LCC PS3613.C584 (ebook) |
  DDC 813/.6—dc23
LC record available at https://lccn.loc.gov/2021048425
LC ebook record available at https://lccn.loc.gov/2021048426

ISBN 978-1-9821-5395-3
ISBN 978-1-9821-5397-7 (ebook)

For all the monsters of my childhood, real and imagined

I, the miserable and the abandoned, am an abortion, to be spurned at, and kicked, and trampled on. Even now my blood boils at the recollection of this injustice.

Mary Shelley
Frankenstein

THE
CHILDREN
ON THE HILL

The Monster

August 15, 2019

HER SMELL SENDS me tumbling back through time to *before*.
Before I knew the truth.

It's intoxicating, this girl's scent. She smells sweet with just a touch of something tangy and sharp, like a penny held on your tongue.

I can smell the grape slushy she had this afternoon, the cigarettes she's been sneaking, the faint trace of last night's vodka (pilfered from her daddy's secret bottle kept down in the boathouse—I've watched them both sneak out to take sips from it).

She smells dangerous and alive.

And I love her walk—the way each step is a bounce like she's got springs at the bottoms of her feet. Like if she bounces high enough, she'll go all the way up to the moon.

The moon.

Don't look at the moon, full and swollen, big and bright.

Wrong monster. I am no werewolf.

Though I tried to be once.

Not long after my sister and I saw *The Wolf Man* together, we found a book on werewolves with a spell in it for turning into one.

"I think we should do it," my sister said.

"No way," I told her.

"Don't you want to know what it feels like to change?" she asked.

We sneaked out into the woods at midnight, did a spell under the full moon, cut our thumbs, drank a potion, burned a candle, and she was right—it was an exquisite thrill, imagining that we were turning into something so much more than ourselves. We ran naked and howling through the trees, pretending ferns were wolfsbane and eating them up.

We thought we might become the real thing, not like Lon Chaney Jr., with the wigs and rubber snout and yak hair glued to his face (my sister and I read that in a book too—"poor yaks," we said, giggling, guffawing about how bad that hair must have smelled). When nothing happened that night, we were so disappointed. When we didn't sprout fur and fangs or lose our minds at the sight of the moon. When we went back home and swore to never speak of what we'd done as we pulled on our pajamas and crawled into our beds, still human girls.

"Can you guess what I am?" I ask the girl now. I don't mean to. The words just come shooting out like sparks popping up from a fire.

"Uh," she says, looking at me all strange. "I don't know. A ghost? Someone who was once a human bean?" And that's just how she says it. Bean. Like we're all just baked beans in a pot, or maybe bright multicolored jelly beans, each a different flavor.

I'd be licorice. The black ones that get left at the bottom of the bag. The ones no one can stand the taste of.

I shift from one foot to the other, bits of my disguise clanking, rattling, the hair from the tangled wig I wear falling into my eyes.

I love this girl so much right now. All that she is. All that I will never be. All that I can never have.

And mostly, what I love is knowing what's coming next: knowing that I will change her as I've changed so many others.

I am going to *save* this girl.

"When do I get my wish?" she asks now.

"Soon," I say, smiling.

I am a giver of wishes.

A miracle worker.

I can give this girl what she most desires, but she isn't even aware of her own desires.

I can't wait to show her.

"So, do you want to play a game or something?" she asks.

"Yes," I say, practically shouting. *Yes, oh yes, oh yes!* This is my favorite question, my favorite thing! I know games. I play them well.

"Truth or dare?" she asks.

"If you wish. But I have to warn you, I'll know if you're lying."

She shrugs, tugs at her triple-pierced right earlobe, squints at me through all her layers of black goth makeup; a good girl trying so hard to look bad. "Nah. Let's play tag," she says, and this surprises me. She seems too old for such games. "My house is safety. You're it." Already running, she slaps my arm so hard it stings.

I laugh. I can't help it. It's nerves. It's the thrill. There's no way this girl, with her stick-thin legs and cigarette smoke–choked lungs, can outrun me.

I am strong. I am fast. I have trained my whole life for these moments.

I'm running, running, running, chasing this beautiful girl in the black hoodie, her blond hair with bright-purple tips flying out behind her like a flag from a country no one's ever heard of. A girl so full of possibility, and she doesn't even know it. She's running, she's squealing, thinking she's going to make it back to safety, back to the bright lights of her little cabin that are just now coming into view through the trees (only bright because of the low hum of the generator out back, no power lines way out here). Thinking she's actually going to make it home, back to her parents (whom she hates) and her warm bed with the flannel sheets, back to her old dog, Dusty, who growls whenever he catches my scent—he knows what I am.

I have weeds woven into my hair. I am covered in a dress of bones, sticks, cattail stalks, old fishing line and bobbers. I am my own wind chime, rattling as I run. I smell like the lake, like rot and ruin and damp forgotten things.

I can easily overtake this girl. But I let her stay ahead. I let her hold on to the fantasy of returning to her old life. I watch her silhouette bounding through the trees, flying, floating.

And just like that, I'm a kid again, chasing my sister, pretending to be some movie monster (I'm the Wolf Man, I'm Dracula, I'm the Phantom of the motherfucking Opera) but I was never fast enough to catch her.

But I'm going to catch this girl now.

And I'm a real monster now. Not just pretend.

I'm going to catch this girl now because I never could catch my sister.

Here it is, forty years later, and still it's always her I'm chasing.

Vi

May 8, 1978

T HE BUILDING WAS haunted, Vi thought as she ran across the huge expanse of green lawn to the Inn. How could it not be? If she squinted just right, it could be an old mansion or castle, something from a black-and-white movie where Dracula might live. But the Inn was made from dull yellow bricks, not craggy stone. There were no turrets or battlements, no drawbridge. No bats flying out of a belfry. Only the large rectangular building with the old slate roof, the heavy glass windows with black shutters that no one ever actually closed.

Vi stepped into the shadow the building made, could feel it wrap its arms around her, welcome her, as she hopped up the granite steps. Above the front doors was a carved wooden sign made by a long-ago patient: HOPE. Vi whispered the secret password to the monster castle, which was *EPOH*—the word spelled backward.

Vi held tight to the plate in her hands, not a flimsy paper plate but one from their cupboards with the bright sunflower pattern that matched the kitchen curtains and tablecloth. She'd fixed Gran lunch—a liverwurst sandwich on rye bread. Vi thought liverwurst was gross, but it was Gran's favorite. Vi had put on extra mustard because she told herself it wasn't just mustard, it was a special monster-repelling potion, something to keep Gran safe, to keep the werewolves and vampires at bay. She'd centered the sandwich on the plate, put a pickle and some chips on the side, and covered it all up with plastic wrap to stay fresh. She knew Gran would be pleased, would coo about what a thoughtful girl Vi was.

Holding the sandwich in one hand, Vi pushed open the door with the other and entered the reception area, which they called the Common Room, with a tiled floor, throw rugs, a fireplace, and two comfortable couches. The first floor was the heart of the Inn. From the Common Room, hallways jutted to the right and left and the staircase was straight ahead. Down the hallway to the right were staff offices and the Oak Room at the end of the hall, where they held meetings. The left wing held the Day Room, where activities took place and the television was always on; the Quiet Room, full of books and art supplies; and, at the end of the hall, the Dining Room and kitchen. The patients took turns working shifts in the kitchen: mashing potatoes, scrubbing pots and pans, and serving their fellow residents at mealtime.

The second floor was what Gran and the staff referred to as "the suites"—the patient rooms. Divided into two units, 2 East and 2 West, were a total of twenty single rooms, ten on each unit, along with a station in the middle for the nurses and staff.

The door to the basement was just to the left of the main staircase leading to the second floor. Vi had never been in the basement. It was where the boiler and mechanical rooms were. Gran said it was used for storage and not fit for much else.

On the wall to her left hung the latest portrait of all the staff standing in front of the old yellow building, Gran right in the middle, a tiny woman in a blue pantsuit who was the center of it all: the sun in the galaxy that was the Hillside Inn.

The window between the Common Room and the main office slid open.

"Good afternoon, Miss Evelyn," Vi said, chipper and cheerful, her voice a bouncing ball. Children were not allowed in the Inn. Vi and her brother, Eric, were the only occasional exceptions, and only if they could get past Miss Ev.

Evelyn Booker was about six feet tall with the build of a linebacker. She wore a curly auburn wig that was often slightly askew. Vi and Eric called her Miss Evil.

Vi looked at her now, wondered what kind of monster she might be and if the mustard potion would work on her too.

Miss Ev frowned at Vi through the open window, her thickly penciled eyebrows nearly meeting in the middle of her forehead.

Shapeshifter, thought Vi. *Definitely shapeshifter.*

"Dr. Hildreth is dealing with an emergency," she said, as a cloud of cigarette smoke escaped out her window.

"I know," Vi said. It was Saturday, one of Gran's days off, but Dr. Hutchins had called, and Gran had spent several minutes on the phone sounding like she was trying to calm him down. At last she'd said she'd be right over and would handle things herself.

"But she ran out so fast she didn't get a chance to eat breakfast or make herself a lunch. So I thought I'd bring her a sandwich." Vi smiled at Miss Ev. Gran was often so busy she forgot to eat, and Vi worried about her—always putting the Inn first and thinking she could survive all day on stale coffee and cigarettes.

"Leave it here and I'll see that she gets it." Miss Ev eyed the plate with the sandwich suspiciously. Vi tried to shake off the disappointment of not being able to hand Gran the plate herself. She smiled and passed it through the window.

Tom with the wild long hair came sauntering into the Common Room and called out to her, "Violets are blue, how are you?" He was one of the patients on what Gran called the revolving-door policy; he'd been in and out of the Inn for as long as Vi could remember.

"I'm good, Tom," Vi said cheerfully. "How are you doing today?"

"Oh, I'm itchy," he said, starting to rub his arms, to scratch. "So, so itchy." He peeled off his shirt, panting a little as he scratched his skin, which was covered with a thick pelt of black fur.

Werewolf, thought Vi. No question.

Tom threw his shirt to the floor, started unbuckling his pants.

"Whoa, there," said Sal, one of the orderlies, whose neck was as thick as Vi's waist. "Let's keep our clothes on. We don't want to get Miss Ev all excited."

Miss Ev frowned and slammed the little glass window closed.

Vi smiled, said her goodbyes, and headed out of the Inn as Tom continued to yelp about how very itchy he was. She heard Sal telling him that he couldn't have a cookie from the kitchen if he didn't keep his clothes on.

Werewolf or not, Vi liked Tom. Gran had brought him home a few times and he and Vi had played checkers.

"Gran's strays," Vi and Eric called them—the patients Gran brought home. People not quite ready to be released back into the real world. Some deemed lost causes by the other staff at the Inn.

Gran had once brought home a man with scars all around his head who had no short-term memory—you had to keep introducing yourself to him over and over and reminding him that he'd already had breakfast. "Who are you?" he asked with alarm each time he saw Vi. "Still just Violet," she'd said.

Mary D., a woman with curly orange hair, told the children she'd been reincarnated almost a hundred times and had vivid memories of every life and death. (*I was Joan of Arc—can you imagine the pain of being burned at the stake, children?*)

And then there was the silent, disheveled woman with sunken eyes who burst into sobs every time the children spoke to her. Eric and Vi called her simply the Weeping Woman.

Sometimes the visitors came back to the house just for a meal or to spend a night or two. Sometimes they stayed for weeks, sleeping in the guest room, rattling around like ghosts in hospital pajamas, spending hours talking with Gran in the basement, where she tested their memories, their cognitive abilities, and tried to cure them. She poured them tea, played cards with them, sat them down in the wing chairs in the living room and had Vi and Eric bring them plates of cookies and speak to them politely.

How do you do? Very pleased to meet you.

"A hospital, even a fine place like the Inn, it's not exactly a nurturing environment. Sometimes, to get better, people need to feel like they're at home," Gran explained. "They need to be treated like family to get well." Gran was like that; there was nothing she wouldn't do to help her patients get well, to help them feel taken care of.

Vi and her brother were fascinated by the strays. Eric took photographs of each one with his Polaroid camera. He did it secretly, when Gran wasn't around. They kept the photos in a shoebox hidden way at the back of Eric's closet. Paper-clipped to each picture were index cards that Vi had written notes on—a name or nickname, any details they'd picked up. Vi and Eric called the shoebox "the files." The cards said things like:

Mary D. has orange hair, which suits her because her favorite thing is toast with marmalade. She says she ate marmalade all

the time back when she was Anne Boleyn, married to King
Henry. Before her head was chopped off.

The shoebox also had a little notebook full of details they'd gleaned about Gran's other patients, the ones they never saw but only heard about; things Vi and Eric had overheard Gran discussing on the phone with Dr. Hutchins, the other psychiatrist at the Inn, when he came over to sample Gran's latest batch of gin. When Gran and Dr. Hutchins talked about the patients, they always used initials. Vi liked to flip through the notebook from time to time, to try to figure out if any of Gran's strays were people she'd heard them talking about.

•   •   •

JUST LAST WEEK, she had eavesdropped on Gran and Dr. Hutchins while they sat sipping gin and tonics on the little stone patio in their backyard. Vi was crouched down, spying on them around the corner of the house.

"Batch 179," Gran said. "I think the juniper's a bit overpowering, wouldn't you agree?"

"I think it's delicious," Dr. Hutchins said, which was what he said each time he tried a new batch of Gran's homemade gin. Vi guessed that the poor man probably didn't even like gin. More than once, she'd caught him surreptitiously dumping the contents of his glass in the flower beds when Gran wasn't looking.

Dr. Hutchins seemed more nervous than the patients. He had a long thin neck, a small head, and thinning hair that sprang up in funny tufts. Vi thought he looked a little like an ostrich.

They'd talked about the weather, and then about flowers, and then they started discussing the patients. Vi got out her notebook.

"D.M. has had a rough week," Dr. Hutchins said. "She lashed out at Sonny today during group. Took three men to restrain her."

Sonny was one of the social workers. He did art therapy and helped in the clay studio. He was a nice man with a huge mustache and bushy sideburns. He sometimes let Vi and Eric make stuff in the ceramics studio: little pots, mugs, and ashtrays.

Gran rattled the ice in her glass. She poured another gin and tonic from the pitcher on the table between them.

"And there was the episode between her and H.G. on Wednesday," he continued.

"She was provoked," Gran responded, lighting a cigarette with her gold Zippo lighter with the butterfly etching on it. The other side had her initials engraved in flowing script: *HEH.* Vi heard the scratch of the flint, smelled the lighter fluid. Gran said smoking was a bad habit, one Vi should never start, but Vi loved the smell of cigarette smoke and lighter fluid, and most of all she loved Gran's old butterfly lighter that needed to be filled with fluid and to have the flint changed periodically.

"She's dangerous," Dr. Hutchins said. "I know you feel she's making progress, but the staff are starting to question whether the Inn is the best place for her."

"The Inn is the *only* place for her," Gran snapped. She took a drag of her cigarette, watched the smoke rise as she exhaled. "We'll have to increase her Thorazine."

"But if she continues to be a danger to others—"

"Isn't that what we do, Thad? Help those no one else can?"

Yes, Vi thought. *Yes!* Gran was a miracle worker. A genius. She was famous for helping patients others couldn't help.

Dr. Hutchins lit his own cigarette. They were quiet a moment.

"And what about Patient S?" Dr. Hutchins asked. "Things still progressing in a positive way?"

Vi finished up her notes on D.M. and started a new page for Patient S.

"Oh yes," Gran said. "She's doing very well indeed."

"And the medications?" Dr. Hutchins asked.

"I've been drawing back on them a bit."

"Any hallucinations?"

"I don't believe so. None that she'll admit to or is aware of."

"It's amazing, isn't it?" Dr. Hutchins said. "The progress she's made? You should be very proud of yourself. You've given her exactly what she needs. You've saved her."

Gran laughed. "Saved? Perhaps. But I'm starting to think she may never lead a normal life. Not after all she's been through. She'll have to be watched. And if the authorities or the papers ever . . ."

"Do you think she remembers?" he asked. "What she did? Where she came from?"

The hairs on Vi's arms stood up the way they did during a bad storm.

"No," Gran said. "And honestly, I believe that's for the best, don't you?"

They both sipped their drinks, ice cubes rattling. Their cigarette smoke drifted up into the clouds.

Vi listened hard, wrote: *WHAT DID PATIENT S DO? Murder someone???*

She knew the Inn had violent patients, people who had done terrible things not because they were terrible people, but because they were sick. That's what Gran said.

But was an actual murderer there? Someone Gran was protecting, keeping safe?

She scribbled *WHO IS PATIENT S???* in big letters in her notebook.

•   •   •

VI THOUGHT ABOUT Patient S now as she walked back across the lawn and drive to their big white house, directly across the road from the Inn. "Who is Patient S?" she asked out loud, then listened for an answer. Sometimes, if she asked the right question at the right time, God would answer.

When God spoke to Vi, it was like a dream. A whispered voice, half-remembered.

When God spoke, he sometimes sounded just like Neil Diamond on Gran's records:

I am, I said.

And Vi pictured him up there, watching her, dressed in his tight beaded denim suit like the one Neil Diamond wore on the live double album Gran loved to play—*Hot August Night*. God's hair was wild as a lion's. His chest hair poked out through the V of his jacket.

There were other gods too. Other voices.

Gods of small things.

Of mice and toasters.

God of tadpoles. Of coffee perkers that whispered a special hello to her each morning in a bright bubbling voice: *Good morning, Star-shine. Pour a little cup of me. Take a sip. Gran says you're old enough now. Take a sip of me, and I'll tell you more.*

But today, so far at least, the gods were silent. Vi heard birds and the slow drone of bees gathering nectar from early blossoms.

It was a bright, sunny spring day, and Vi settled in on the porch swing, reading one of Gran's books—*Frankenstein*. Each time she went into Gran's gigantic library or the little brick Fayeville Public Library in town, Vi let the God of Books help her choose what she'd read next. He spoke in a thin, papery voice, as she ran her fingers along the spines of the books until he said, *This one*. And she had to read the whole thing, even if it didn't truly interest her. Because she'd learned that, even in the dullest book, a secret message was inside, written just for her. The trick was learning how to find it. But *Frankenstein* felt like the whole thing had been written just for her. It made her feel all electric and charged up.

She read some passages again and again, even underlined them in pencil so she could copy them out later when she sat down to write her report for Gran, as she did for each book she read: *No one can conceive the variety of feelings which bore me onwards, like a hurricane, in the first enthusiasm of success. Life and death appeared to me ideal bounds, which I should first break through, and pour a torrent of light into our dark world.*

She was swinging and reading, and listening to the porch swing creak, creak, creak until the creaking became a song—*torrent of light, torrent of light, torrent of light*—and she closed her eyes to listen harder.

That's when she heard her name being called. From far away at first, then closer. Louder, more frantic: *Vi, Vi, VI!*

She opened her eyes and saw her brother. He was tearing up the driveway, bare-chested. His red T-shirt was wadded up in his hands, wrapping something he cradled carefully as he sprinted toward her. He was crying, his face streaked with mud and tears. Whenever Vi saw him shirtless, she thought her little brother looked like one of those terrible pictures you saw in *National Geographic* of a starving kid: his head too big for his pale, stick-thin body, his ribs pressed up against his skin so you could count each one like the bars of a xylophone.

Eric's tube socks were pulled up nearly to his knobby knees, yellow stripes at the top. His blue Keds were worn through at the toes, his shorts ragged cutoffs of last year's Toughskins jeans. His crazy tangle of curly brown hair bobbed like a strange nest on top of his head. After the long Vermont winter, he was pale as the inside of a potato.

"What happened?" Vi asked, standing up, setting her book down on the swing.

"It's a baby rabbit," he gasped, holding the filthy bundle to his chest, unwrapping it enough for Vi to see the brown fur of the tiny creature. "It's hurt," Eric said, voice cracking. "I think . . . I think it might be dead."

Eric was always saving animals: stray cats, a woodchuck rescued from the jaws of a dog, countless mice and rats from Gran's experiments in the basement—rodents too old to run the mazes, to be conditioned by treats and little electric jolts. Eric felt bad for the animals in the basement and had even freed one—Big White Rat, who Gran thought had managed to escape on his own and now lived in the walls of their house and made appearances from time to time, but could never be caught.

Eric's bedroom had been turned into a crazy zoo full of aquariums and metal cages. He had a whole city of plastic tubes connecting Habitrail cages full of mice running on wheels, building nests with cardboard and newspaper. His room always smelled like cedar shavings, alfalfa, and pee. Gran not only put up with Eric's bedroom zoo but seemed pleased by it, proud even. "You have a way with animals," she would say, smiling at him. "A gentleness and kindness they pick up on."

He knew everything about animals: their Latin names, how they were all ordered by family, genus, species. His hero was Charles Darwin, and Eric said he wanted to grow up and travel around the world studying animals just like Darwin had.

Vi leaped down off the porch steps. "Let's see," she said.

"Is Gran here?" he asked hopefully. Even though she was a human doctor (not even a regular doctor, a psychiatrist), Gran was a miracle worker with hurt animals. She could mend broken bones, do stitches, even minor surgery. She also knew when an animal couldn't be saved and was quick to put it out of its misery with a tiny injection or a rag soaked in chloroform.

"No. She had to go to the Inn."

Vi lifted the folds of the red shirt, put her hand on the rabbit. It gave a twitch when she touched it. She couldn't tell where the blood on the T-shirt was coming from, but it seemed like a lot for such a tiny body. She looked from the rabbit to her brother's worried face.

"Old Mac killed the mama. Got her with his twenty-two. He shot at this guy too, but then it ran into the bushes, and I grabbed him." He bit his lip, more tears sliding down his cheeks. "Mac's probably on his way here right now to finish the job." He swiveled his head around, looking down the driveway, out across the road, at the massive front lawn and gardens that surrounded the Hillside Inn. And sure enough, Mac was heading their way: a stooped scarecrow of a man in a wide-brimmed hat and tan work pants, carrying a rifle. Why Gran would ever let the caretaker at a lunatic hospital walk around with a loaded gun was beyond Vi, but as Gran was fond of pointing out, the Inn was not like any other hospital anywhere.

"What we're doing here," Gran always said, "is revolutionary." And as Vi watched Old Mac, an ex-patient himself, stalking toward them, she thought, *Revolutionary?* as her heart hammered and all the spit in her mouth dried up.

"Take the rabbit into the kitchen," Vi ordered her brother. "Go!"

"What about Mac?" he asked, swallowing hard, eyes wild.

"I'll take care of Mac. Don't worry."

Eric rewrapped the baby rabbit and ran up the porch steps, flung open the front door, and hurried inside.

Vi stood waiting, hands on her hips, watching Old Mac get closer, adjusting the gun in his hands, his jaw working like he was chewing something tough.

"Help you, Mr. MacDermot, sir?" she said when he was close enough to hear.

"Those rabbits are destroying the entire vegetable garden. No more spinach or lettuce left," he said. He spoke slowly, with a slight slur, like the words were thick and heavy in his mouth. *Medication*, Vi thought. Most of the patients at the Inn were on medication. It could make them move and walk funny, have trouble talking.

Mac was a tall man with a weathered face and icy blue eyes. He licked his lips constantly so they were always chapped and raw-looking. "T-t-tell your brother to bring that animal out here. It don't belong in the house."

He took a step forward. Vi held her ground, standing right in the middle of the flagstone walkway to the house, her own roadblock.

She was thirteen years old, tall for her age, but still not even up to this man's shoulders. Gran was always telling her not to slouch, to stand tall and proud, and that's what she did now.

"Mr. MacDermot, I'm sure if you talk to my grandmother, she'll tell you it's okay for animals to be in the house. My brother brings home plenty, and Gran encourages it."

"Does she now?"

"You go ask her yourself. Or, if you like, I can go in and call over to the Inn and ask her to come home, but I hear she's real busy so she might not be too happy about that."

He frowned at her, ran his pasty tongue over his dry lips, clenched his hands around the rifle. "She'll hear about this," he said.

"Yes, sir," Vi said, smiling as big as she could, like the silly smiley face on the *Have a Nice Day* mug Gran drank out of sometimes—a gift from one of her patients.

"It ain't right," he said, turning to leave. "Keeping a wild thing captive." Old Mac shuffled back down the driveway, muttering to himself, cradling the gun.

Vi went inside, her bare feet cold against the tiled floor of the front hall. She bolted the door, just in case. She let her eyes adjust to the darkness, took in the walnut-paneled walls, the french doors to the right that led into the parlor and the huge tiled fireplace, the curved staircase to the left. The house smelled of dust, old books, lemon furniture polish.

She heard soft mumbling coming from the kitchen. Sometimes Eric had conversations with his animals, made them talk back in different voices. He was really good at voices. Vi thought that maybe when he grew up he'd go to work doing voices for cartoons or *Sesame Street* or something. He could do a perfect Bugs Bunny: *"What's up, doc?"*

"Eric?" she called. "You in the kitchen?"

"Yeah," he snuffled. Then she heard a squeaky rabbit voice say, "So scared."

Vi hurried down the hall.

Sunlight streamed through the window over the sink. The Crock-Pot hissed on the counter—they were having sloppy joes for dinner and the kitchen was full of the smell of spicy, meaty tomato sauce. Gran had made Jell-O parfaits for dessert—they were chilling in the fridge.

Eric was still cradling the bunny in his shirt.

Vi cleared everything off the table, pulled the sunflower tablecloth off, and laid down a clean dish towel. "Put him down here and let's take a look," she said.

"Save him, Vi," Eric said as he set the rabbit on the table. "Please."

Vi touched the rabbit carefully. She turned it over and gave it a quick exam. It didn't look like the gunshot had hit any organs, just grazed the outside of its left haunch. The rabbit was holding very still but breathing very fast. "I think it's in shock," Vi said.

"Is that bad?" Eric asked.

She bit her lip. "Sometimes, when you're in shock, your heart can stop."

"Don't let that happen," Eric whimpered.

"I know what to do," Vi said, spinning away from her bare-chested brother. She ran back down the hall, to the enclosed porch that Gran called the sunroom. It was where they played games and did artwork and stored weird stuff that didn't belong anywhere else. It was also where Gran made her gin.

In the corner of the room, Gran's still was set up on a heavy table: a crazy contraption of copper and glass tubes, flasks, and Bunsen burners. Gran was on a never-ending quest to distill the perfect batch of gin. One of the burners was on, and the still bubbled gently. The air smelled tangy and medicinal.

Vi turned away from it, went to the shelves, and found what she was looking for: the battery-powered camping lantern they used when the power went out. She took it down and opened it up, taking out the blocky six-volt battery. She rummaged around in a basket full of odds and ends on the shelf and pulled out some pieces of wire.

"What are you doing?" Eric asked when she brought the battery and wires back to the kitchen. The little rabbit was holding perfectly still under his hand. Its eyes were closed.

"We have to be ready to restart its heart. Give it a shock."

Eric looked baffled.

"Trust me. A body, it's got its own electrical system, right? Gran's explained that a thousand times—how it's all connected: the brain, the nerves. It's what keeps our hearts beating, right? And you know how on *Emergency!* they use those paddles to bring people back? It's like that."

She licked her lips, then attached two wires to the big six-volt battery from their camping lantern. She thought about all of Gran's lessons on circuits and electricity, how Vi had made a lightbulb glow once with the electricity generated from a potato, nails, and wire.

Gran had once said the human body had enough electricity running through it to power a flashlight.

And yes, Vi thought of *Frankenstein*. Not of the book she'd been reading, but the movie. Of Boris Karloff being brought to life in Dr. Frankenstein's lab.

It was her favorite scene in the movie. The storm raging, Dr. Frankenstein lifting the table with the monster up out of the room, into the sky so lightning could strike it, bring the creature to life with a great jolt. Then lowering him back down, seeing the creature's hand twitch: *It's alive, it's alive, it's alive!*

"I don't think I feel a heartbeat," Eric said.

Vi nodded, carefully placed her hands on the sides of its chest.

"Is he dead?"

"Maybe not forever," Vi said. The rabbit was warm under her hands. She could feel it breathing, twitching a little. But she wanted Eric to believe. To believe that she had the power to save it. "We can bring him back."

"Are you sure? Are you sure he's dead?" Eric asked, rocking back and forth, looking smaller than ever.

"Of course I'm sure," Vi snapped. "Now, stand back."

He bit his lip and started to cry again. She looked at him, guilt washing over her. How could she be so cruel? What kind of sister was she?

She turned back to the rabbit and placed the wires attached to the battery on either side of its chest.

"Wake up," she said. "Come back to us."

As if on cue, the rabbit lifted its head, gave a little hop forward.

"It's alive," Vi said.

Eric gave a squeal of delight and threw his arms around her, hugging her tight. "I knew it," he said. "I knew you could do it."

The front door opened with a creak and a thump.

Then the sound of footsteps in the front hall, coming their way.

"Old Mac," Eric whispered, eyes wide and frantic.

The Helping Hand of God:
The True Story of the Hillside Inn

By Julia Tetreault, Dark Passages Press, 1980

In the 1970s, the Hillside Inn was widely considered one of the best private psychiatric institutions in New England.

Located on fifty acres atop a forested hill in the small town of Fayeville, Vermont, it housed no more than twenty patients at a time in an environment more like a country estate than a hospital.

The grounds of the Hillside Inn held five buildings. The director's residence was a white wooden Greek Revival structure with a large front porch supported by carved wooden columns. The stables, which hadn't held horses for fifty years, had been renovated into a large arts and crafts area for the patients, complete with a pottery studio and kiln. Next to the stables was the freshly painted red barn, home to maintenance and groundskeeping equipment, as well as the van the Inn used to transport residents on therapeutic field trips. The carriage house had been converted to an apartment where the office manager lived. And then there was the Inn itself: a hulking two-story building of yellow brick with large shuttered windows and a steeply angled gray slate roof. South of the Inn, a large garden allowed patients to work outside in good weather, helping grow a significant portion of the produce used in the dining room. The staff believed strongly in the curative powers of fresh air, sunshine, and a good day's work.

The Inn was built in 1863 as a hospital for Civil War soldiers being shipped home from field hospitals with missing limbs, infections, typhoid fever. In the early 1900s, it had served as a sanatorium for tuberculosis patients where the afflicted were treated with rest and fresh Vermont air. The grounds were beautifully landscaped. The building itself was on the National Register of Historic Places.

With a holistic, humanistic approach, the Inn helped patients "discover who they truly were, heal all parts of themselves, and realize their true human potential" through a carefully curated program of individual therapy, group therapy, meditation, arts and crafts, exercise, music, and gardening. Patients working in the pottery studio produced pieces (mugs, bowls, plates, and vases) sold in local craft galleries and markets. Pottery bearing the Inn's signature mossy-green glaze and the Hillside Inn stamp at the bottom can be found in homes all over New England and is prized by collectors.

The Inn treated the wealthy, but also took in those who could not pay, as well as patients deemed "lost causes" at other facilities. Its therapeutic approach, thought of as radical at the time, seemed to work. The majority of patients who stayed at the Inn not only improved, but learned skills that helped them thrive in the outside world.

Doctors and directors from other facilities all over the country visited the Hillside Inn to see it for themselves. Articles were written on the Inn's innovative approach and rate of success.

To outsiders, the staff at the Inn were pioneers. It was a place of miracles, giving hope to those who had long ago lost it.

The woman behind these miracles was the Inn's director, Dr. Helen Hildreth. Dr. Hildreth had been at the Inn for nearly thirty years and had been director for fifteen. Short in stature and well past the age of traditional retirement by the late 1970s, she was a true pioneer in the field of psychiatry.

"We must always remember," she wrote in an article for the *American Journal of Psychiatry*, "that we are not treating the illness. We are treating the individual. It is our role, as doctors, to see beyond the symptoms and view our patients holistically. Above all else, we must ask ourselves, 'What is this individual's greatest potential, and how can I help him or her achieve it?' "

Lizzy

August 19, 2019

FOUR A.M. AND I sprang up to a sitting position in bed, the sheets damp with sweat, listening to the noises of the swamp. Something had woken me. I'd caught the tail end of a strange sound—a wailing sort of groan—that jerked me away from sleep, foggy-headed and unsure what was real and what was still dream.

I'd had another nightmare. Another dream about *her.*

I looked around, orienting myself and taking slow, calming breaths.

I was in my van, in the bed I slept in every night I was on the road, parked at the edge of the swamp. And I was alone.

I checked to see if my little .38 Special Smith & Wesson revolver was there, in its holster on the shelf beside the bed. I touched it, felt myself relax.

I'd spent yesterday out on a little metal boat exploring the swamp with a local named Cyrus, searching for signs of the Honey Island monster—a creature who, according to legend, stood seven feet tall, walked upright on two legs, and was covered in shaggy fur. The color of the fur varied depending on the storyteller—some said brown, some orange, some gray or silver. The tracks showed webbed toes. Some said the creature's eyes glowed red in the dark.

I'd been at the swamp for the last three days, recording interviews with locals who'd told me stories about the creature, and I'd gotten some good audio of the swamp's sounds. I'd taken some great pictures of gators, ibis, feral hogs, nutrias, and raccoons. But no sign of the Honey Island monster. Now I was lying awake on the bed in my van, all the windows open, listening to the calls of night birds, splashes, an odd trilling sound.

The air was heavy, humid and thick in my lungs.

I heard it again, the sound that had woken me: a far-off groan.

Alligator? Hog?

Or could it be the monster? I held still, listening, then reached for my digital recorder, mic, and headphones.

One of the benefits of staying in a van is that everything is within easy reach—you're always only a step or two away from whatever you need. And I kept my recording equipment on a shelf right next to the bed.

I slipped on my headphones, flipped the mic and recorder on, held my breath, listening, hoping to catch the groan again. I pushed back the curtain and peered out the window at the starlit night.

I got out of bed, still holding the recording equipment and grabbing my headlamp and the little gun, just in case. I took the two steps to the side door, sliding it open and letting the moist air hit me. I stepped out into the night, walking toward the water. Cypress trees draped in Spanish moss stood out in the swamp like huge sentries wearing tattered, ghostly clothing. Frogs and crickets sang. Something splashed. The air smelled slightly rotten, primordial, like death and life all mixed up together. As I crept closer, a shadow moved along the edge; I held my breath, flipped on my headlamp, and spotted an alligator slipping into the brackish green water. He went under so that only his eyes were visible, watching me.

Eric would love this, I thought, locking eyes with the gator.

But Eric was halfway across the country.

Eric wasn't even Eric anymore.

"Not Eric," I said out loud without thinking, capturing the sound of my own voice on the recorder.

Idiot.

The alligator sank under and swam away.

We'd changed our names after what had happened. Eric became Charles (after his hero Charles Darwin). He didn't grow up to be a naturalist, a veterinarian, or a zookeeper like we'd always thought he would. Charlie lived in Iowa and owned an auto dealership. He had thinning hair, a paunch, and high blood pressure (too much beer and fast food), a daughter in college and another in high school. His wife was named Cricket (her real name, believe it or not) and they loved each other very much. They lived in a blue ranch house on a dead-end street where they knew all their neighbors and held potlucks and backyard barbecues. It made me uncomfortable to visit him there, as if I were visiting a sitcom set, but after all we'd gone through, my brother deserved safety and happiness. I was glad for Eric—no, Charles . . . I was always doing that, thinking of him by his old name. It suited him much better than Charlie, or even worse, *Chuck*, as Cricket sometimes called him, like he was a pile of ground meat or a furry animal that destroyed gardens.

The name I'd chosen for myself was Lizzy. I'd picked it because Gran's middle name was Elizabeth and I felt I owed her that much, to carry some piece of her with me. I needed a last name too, and I chose Shelley, because, well, because of Mary Shelley, of course.

So I was Lizzy Shelley now. I was fifty-three years old, my hair going gray. And I made my living hunting monsters.

I had a blog and now a popular podcast, named for my long-ago childhood project: *The Book of Monsters*. I'd been a member of the team on last season's series *Monsters Among Us* and featured in the documentary *Shadow People*. I'd given lectures at colleges on the role of the monster in contemporary society. I crisscrossed the country hunting Sasquatches, shapeshifters, lake monsters, cave-dwelling goblins, vampires, werewolves—all manner of cryptids and bogeymen. People posted on the forums on my website every day giving me leads, sending photos, telling their own stories of close encounters, begging me to come investigate. Between advertising, sponsors, affiliate links, the TV gigs, book royalties, and the branded merchandise I sold, I made more than enough to cover my expenses and hit the road as often as I liked, moving on to the next town, the next monster.

My mission was to do everything I could to get the message out loud and clear: *Monsters are real and living among us.*

But the Honey Island monster so far had not provided any proof of that. I worked my way along the edge of the water, listening to the sounds my microphone picked up, the chorus of the swamp: another splash, frogs croaking low, two owls calling plaintively back and forth, crickets rubbing their legs together in shrill song. So many creatures, such an alive place. Again I wished my brother—not the man he'd become, but the little boy he once was—were here to listen with me.

I picked my way along the edge of the swamp, sweeping my headlamp back and forth carefully so as not to surprise a gator, until I got to Cyrus's metal boat, moored at a rickety wooden dock. I climbed aboard, made myself comfortable in the captain's seat, and waited, listening, searching the darkness for shadows. At last the sun started to come up, making the sky glow a fiery orange. The monster hadn't made another sound. But I imagined him out there, watching and waiting. Finally I headed back to the van.

The van was my home away from home and had cost a ridiculous amount of money but had been totally worth it. It was a high-ceilinged Ford Transit that I'd paid a custom-van-build company to turn into the ultimate monster-hunting machine. I had a raised loft bed with lots of storage space underneath for clothing and gear and a small chemical toilet. Along the driver's-side wall was my tiny kitchen: a twelve-volt fridge, a sink with a foot pump that pulled water from a six-gallon water container and drained into a bucket, and a one-burner butane stove for cooking. I carried one coffee mug, one titanium spork, one bowl, one plate, a kitchen knife, a can opener, a corkscrew, and a one-quart saucepan. My meals on the road were simple: instant oatmeal every morning and canned soup, chili, or beans for lunch and dinner. I supplemented with fresh fruit and vegetables and ate peanut butter and jelly sandwiches when I didn't feel up to cooking.

On the passenger side of the van was a work zone, a small desk set up with my laptop, beneath it a file cabinet and space to store my recording equipment. There were two solar panels on the roof, two more in a suitcase that I set up outside, and a portable power station with a built-in battery and inverter on the right side of the desk. I carried a small Honda generator and gas can to cover me for the days when the sun didn't generate enough power to keep things up and running. With both Wi-Fi and cell phone boosters, I could remain connected and self-sufficient for days, even weeks on end, no matter how far off the beaten path monster hunting took me.

"You live like a woman on the run," Eric (Charlie!) had told me not long ago. "You're never home more than a few days at a time, always on the move." I'd just smiled, bit my lip to keep from saying, *And you, little brother, live like a man stuck in quicksand.*

I set the recording equipment and headlamp on the desk and turned to the stove to heat water for coffee, which I made with instant powder from a jar. Once I'd downed the first gulp of thick, sludgy coffee, I turned around again, pulled out the stool under my desk, and flipped open my laptop. I figured I'd spend a little time getting the eyewitness interviews and swamp sounds imported from the digital recorder onto the laptop and start editing. Then I'd need to record my introduction, talking about the history of the monster, my own experiences in the swamp. I'd tell my audience about the groan that had woken me from sleep, about how I'd gone out to search and startled a gator. I was good at this: telling stories, building suspense.

My computer booted up and I took another sip of coffee, then clicked over to check my email before starting to work on the podcast.

First I heard the blood thrumming in my ears.

All the hairs on my body stood up as if lightning had struck close by.

An alert had come in.

I clicked through and scanned the article.

Green Mountain Free Press
August 18, 2019

Girl Missing from Chickering Island

Police are searching for 13-year-old Lauren Schumacher, who was last seen at her family's summer cottage on Chickering Island on the afternoon of August 15. Her family believes she may have run away. She reportedly told friends she'd met the Island's legendary ghost, Rattling Jane, just before her disappearance.

Schumacher was wearing cutoff denim shorts, a black hooded sweatshirt, and black Converse sneakers. She is 5'3", weighs 100 pounds, and has brown eyes and blond hair with dyed purple tips. Anyone with information is asked to call the Vermont State Police.

I read the article, then reread it. I searched for any other news about the case, but only came up with the same information.

I opened the calendar to double-check.

Yes.

The little tingle at the back of my neck turned into a buzz.

August 15 had been the full moon.

The girls always went missing on a full moon.

How many girls had it been now?

I didn't need to check my notes: nine. Lauren Schumacher from Chickering Island would make ten. Always in a different part of the country. Always on a full moon. Always from a town with its very own monster. And always, just before disappearing, the missing girl had told someone she'd had an encounter with the local legend.

And always, it was a girl who didn't raise big alarms. A girl from a troubled family; a girl who hung out with the wrong crowd; a girl who skipped school and smoked cigarettes; a girl everyone assumed would come to no good; a girl who had every reason to run away.

A coincidence, some would say: the girls, the monsters, the full moons.

But it was no coincidence.

I was sure that this was the work of one very clever, crafty, shape-shifting monster.

The most dangerous monster of all, the one I'd been chasing my whole life, who always managed to elude me. Except in dreams. She always came back in dreams. In real life, I'd gotten close a time or two. But only because the monster had let me. It was a game we played. Cat and mouse. Hide-and-seek. Just like we had when we were kids.

Me and my once-upon-a-time sister.

THE BOOK OF MONSTERS

Violet Hildreth and Iris Whose Last Name We Don't Know

Illustrations by Eric Hildreth

1978

Monsters are real. They're all around us, whether we can see them or not.

There are two main types of monsters.

The first type know they're monsters. They may not be happy with it. They may loathe what they are, but there's no denying their monster selves. They're in monster form all of the time and are often hideous and scary and people run screaming when they see them.

The second, more dangerous type may not even understand that they're monsters. They can pass as human. They hide in plain sight. They can be charismatic, like vampires. They can be tricksters who change form like werewolves and shapeshifters. This is the far more dangerous type of monster because there could be one next to you right now, one sleeping in your house even, and you might not know it.

Vi

V I HELD HER breath as she recognized the footsteps in the hall. Gran always wore low clunky heels, her doctor's shoes. As soon as she got home, she'd take them off and replace them with slippers.

Then she heard Gran say, "This way. That's right. Come in."

Someone was with her.

Most likely Old Mac with his gun. He'd come to take the rabbit back and Gran wasn't going to stop him.

He'd kill it after all. Vi imagined how pleased he'd be, licking his toady little lips, smiling. *Won't be eating any more of* my *lettuces, will you now, you little devil?*

She stood frozen for a moment, still clutching the wires, then shoved them and the battery under the table. The rabbit hopped forward atop the kitchen table, heading toward the edge, and Eric grabbed it.

"Violet? Eric?" Gran called from the hall.

"Ow!" Eric yelped, jerking his hand away. "He bit me!"

With all the wild animals he'd rescued, he'd never been bitten.

"Crap," Vi said. "Let me see."

Eric held out his hand. The bite was small, barely bleeding. "Do you think I'll get rabies?"

"Maybe," Vi said. "Twenty-one shots in the stomach."

His eyes got huge and he looked like he might start crying again.

"But I doubt this little guy's got rabies," Vi said, giving the bunny a stroke on the head.

"My lovelies?" Gran called. "Where are you?"

It was no use hiding.

"In the kitchen," Vi called. "Eric brought home a baby rabbit. It's hurt, and we're trying to fix it up."

There was mumbling—Gran, talking in a low voice.

"We won't let them take you," Eric whispered to the rabbit, leaning over it protectively. "Old Mac will have to shoot me first."

A minute later Gran appeared in the kitchen, dressed in her day-off clothes: a tan cotton pantsuit with a wide belt that made her look like she was going on safari—all that was missing was the pith helmet. She had a green scarf tied jauntily around her neck; Gran loved her scarves. She held a cigarette. Her gray hair, curled and held in place with Aqua Net, made a frizzy halo around her head. Her fuzzy yellow slippers, which she called her house shoes, were on her feet. "All right. Let's see what we've got."

"Vi saved it!" Eric said. "Old Mac shot it, but Vi brought it back to life! You should have been here, Gran. You should have seen."

Gran stepped closer, looked at Vi with her eyes narrowed through the haze of cigarette smoke. "Is that so?"

Vi laughed. "Not really. We thought it might be dead at first, but it was just stunned. In shock. I'm more worried about Eric. The rabbit bit him."

Gran came over and inspected the bite. While she looked at it, Vi threw Eric a warning glance: *Don't say another word. This is our secret: yours, mine, and the bunny's.*

She kicked the battery farther under the table.

"It doesn't look too bad to me. We'll get it cleaned up and bandaged," Gran said. "Give you an antibiotic just in case."

Then she peered down at the rabbit on the table. With sure hands, she probed at the wound on its haunch. "There's a gash and a burn from the gunshot. She'll need a few stitches."

"It's a girl?" Eric asked.

"Most definitely," Gran said.

"Do I get to keep her?" he asked.

Gran gave him a tender smile. "For the time being."

"If we let her go, Mac will kill her," Eric said, eyes filling with tears again.

"We won't let that happen," Gran promised, giving Eric's shoulder a gentle squeeze.

Then she looked past Eric, over to the doorway. "You can come closer if you'd like," she said.

Vi turned and saw a girl standing at the entrance to the kitchen. She looked to be about Vi's age, maybe a little younger. Hard to tell for sure because of the shape she was in. She had bruises on her face and arms. She was so pale Vi could see the blue veins under her skin. She was wearing light-blue hospital pajamas—drawstring pants and one of those awful smocks that tied in the back. Her brown hair was pulled into a messy ponytail and covered up with a blaze-orange knit cap—something a hunter would wear. She had on a pair of dirty sneakers that were way too big, and Vi was sure she'd seen Old Mac wearing those same sneakers out in the garden.

"My grandchildren found a rabbit," Gran said. "A doe. Come see." She held out her arm, beckoning to the girl, who moved toward them slowly, as skittish as the rabbit on the table.

Eric looked from the girl to Vi, his face a question mark: *Who is she? What's going on?*

She wasn't a patient, surely. The Inn didn't treat kids. Only people over eighteen.

"Children, this is Iris. She's going to be staying with us," Gran said. She gave them a warning look. "Iris, these are my grandchildren, Violet and Eric."

Vi held still, feeling like if any of them moved or talked, the girl would bolt.

It was like trying to get a deer to come up and eat out of your hand in the forest.

Iris looked from Vi to Eric, then back down at the rabbit. She came forward until she was standing right in front of it, her fingers going right for the wound, touching it gently there.

"She's hurt, but we're going to fix her right up," Gran said. "You can help if you like, Iris. You can help us take care of her. Would you like that?"

The girl showed no sign of a response—no words, no nod. She just kept her head down, stroking the rabbit, her fingertips red and sticky with its blood.

•   •   •

"I THOUGHT THE Inn didn't treat children," Vi said when Gran came into Vi's room to say goodnight. She smelled like cigarettes and gin. She'd carried in a cup of tea for Vi, one of her sleeping tonics. Vi sipped at it—there was so much honey it made her teeth ache. Gran hadn't changed into her nightgown and robe yet, which meant that she was probably heading over to the Inn again. Or maybe down into the basement to work. Vi looked at the clock. A little after ten.

They'd gotten the new girl, Iris, settled into the guest room, which was right next door to Vi's. They'd had dinner, watched TV (*Little*

House on the Prairie), and then Gran had poured Iris a bubble bath using Vi's pink bottle of Mr. Bubble and laid out some clean pajamas (an old blue set of Vi's). The girl came out of the bathroom with flushed skin and wet hair poking from beneath her grungy orange hat. Vi wondered if she'd bathed while wearing it. She'd buttoned the long-sleeved pajama top all the way up, but Vi could see the bruises on her neck and clavicle and on each wrist. When Iris leaned forward, Vi saw the ragged edge of a cut, the black whiskers of stitches peeking out just under the V in the pajama top. The girl caught her staring and sat up, tugged at her collar. Vi's face flushed. She looked away.

Iris hadn't said a word all night. But she'd watched them. She'd watched them all intently, with an odd mixture of curiosity and fear, the way one might watch a pride of lions: fascinated, mesmerized even, but not daring to get too close. She took the pills Gran handed over and dutifully swallowed them down. When Gran announced it was time for bed and led Iris to the guest room, the girl followed obediently.

Eric had gone into his own room with the wounded rabbit, which he'd set up in an aquarium next to his bed. Through the wall, Vi could hear him singing to it.

Vi looked at Gran, waiting for her to answer.

"You're absolutely right," Gran said as she sat down on the edge of Vi's bed, fingers smoothing the old quilt. "We don't treat children."

Had the girl come from somewhere else? Gran volunteered at a state-run clinic called Project Hope an hour away. There she treated people who were just out of jail or lived in halfway houses. But Vi had never heard her mention kids at the clinic. It was mostly criminals and drug addicts—people required by the courts to see a psychiatrist.

"Not as a general rule," Gran continued. "But there are exceptions to every rule sometimes."

"Who is she?" Vi leaned closer to Gran, set the cup of bittersweet tea on her bedside table. "Where did she come from? Is Iris her real name?" The questions came tumbling out and were answered only with Gran's sly smile.

"You know I can't tell you that, poppet," Gran said, stroking the hair back from Vi's forehead. She reached for the brush on the bedside table. Vi held still, relaxing, as Gran brushed her hair, carefully working out the snarls and tangles. Gran sang while she brushed, a German song her mother had sung to her: *"Guten Abend, gute Nacht."*

The song ended with the line *Tomorrow morning, if God wills, you will wake once again.*

The quiet lullaby didn't distract Vi. "Will *she* tell me?"

Gran stopped singing and set the hairbrush down on the table. She was silent for a beat. She got a certain look when she was thinking deeply about something: Her eyes glanced up to the right a little, and her mouth tightened into a hard line.

"I don't know, Violet. Right now, as you may have noticed, she doesn't speak."

"Why not? Is she mute or something?"

"There's nothing physically stopping her, as far as I can tell."

"But then why?"

"I can't answer that. I can only say my hope is that she will find her voice again. That here, with us, she'll get better. Now, finish your tea before it gets cold."

Gran leaned in, fluffed up Vi's pillow. "You can help her, you know," she added. "You can help us both."

"How?"

Gran smiled. "You're a clever girl with many talents. I have no doubt you'll make a fine doctor someday. Is that still what you want to be?"

Vi nodded quickly, *yes, yes, yes.* "More than anything." She'd wanted to be a doctor for as long as she could remember. Not a psychiatrist like Gran, but a surgeon like her own father had been. He'd been one of the best in the whole Northeast. That's what Gran always said, her face glowing with pride. Gran had been giving Vi special lessons: how to dissect frogs and mice, how to suture. Gran said she had a real gift with a scalpel and steady surgeon's hands. Before Gran became a psychiatrist, she'd trained as a surgeon, so she knew.

"I'm glad," Gran said now, taking Vi's hand and sliding her own down until she was clasping Vi around the wrist, her fingers resting on the inner side, pressing slightly, taking her pulse, feeling her heartbeat. With her other hand, Vi did the same thing to Gran. It was something they'd done as long as Vi could remember.

I feel your pulse, Vi would say.

And I feel yours, Gran would answer. *Nice and strong. You've got a strong heart, Violet Hildreth.*

"You've got a strong heart, Violet Hildreth," Gran said now. She smiled at Vi, making her feel warm and glowing. "And a strong will to go with it. I have no doubt that you'll be able to help me. And to help Iris."

"How?"

"Find a way in. Be gentle and kind. Include her. Treat her like a sister."

"A sister," Vi repeated, feeling the word move over her tongue. She felt a sense that she'd been waiting all this time and didn't even know what she'd been waiting for. Until now.

A sister.

"And, Violet," Gran said in a serious voice as she stood and lifted the empty teacup from Vi's nightstand. "If Iris does start telling you things, I'll need to know. You'll have to give me reports."

Reports! It all sounded so official. Like something Gran would say to the staff at the Inn.

"Do you think you can do that for me?"

"Of course," Vi told her. "I can type them up!" Vi had a Smith Corona that Gran had given her for her birthday. She loved the clack of the keys, the clang of the bell when she reached the end of the line, the slight smell of oil and ink.

Gran chuckled. "That's my girl. Verbal reports will work just fine, Vi. And I'd prefer if Iris didn't know. When she trusts you, as I know she will, I don't want to make her question that trust. Do you understand, my love?"

"Yes," Vi said, nodding, trying to look as serious and grown-up as she knew how.

"One more thing," Gran said. "I don't want Iris leaving the house. Not yet. She can go out in the yard, explore the woods with you kids, but nowhere else. Not into town yet. And *do not* take her over to the Inn."

"How come?"

"I think it would be too much for her right now. Let's focus on giving her a safe environment here at home."

"Okay."

"And, Vi, it's a secret that she's here. No one else can know, for now. Not even Mr. MacDermot."

Vi frowned. Why keep Iris a secret? But Gran's face didn't look like it'd hold answers. Not tonight. So Vi only nodded, said, "Okay."

A sister.

A secret sister.

When Gran left, Vi turned, looked at her nightstand. At the luminous face of the clock, which slipped from 10:13 to 10:14. The ceramic owl lamp with the glowing eyes, turned off now but still watching her. Beside it was a photo of her parents. Eric had the same one in his room, next to his bed. Gran had another photo in her own bedroom of herself and her husband, both young, standing together, Gran's belly bulging. Vi loved looking at that picture, knowing her father was in there, waiting to come out, grow up, one day meet a girl named Carolyn, get married, and have Vi and Eric.

Vi gazed at the photo now, lit up orange-red by the digital clock. She looked at her mother, dark-haired and smiling; at her father, handsome as a movie star, his long surgeon's fingers resting on her mother's shoulders. She searched their faces, as she did each night, for some trace of recognition, of memory.

She knew the stories by heart, the ones Gran told: how her mother named her Violet because when they first brought her home from the hospital her eyes were such a deep, rich blue, they looked almost purple.

She thought of the accident that had killed them. The accident that she and Eric had somehow survived.

Her father had been driving that night. They were coming down from the mountains, where they spent each summer in a cabin on a lake with water so clear you could see all the way to the bottom, even in the deepest part. You could count the fish beneath you as you swam. Vi had tried and tried to remember that lake, those fish. She'd prayed over and over to the God of Memory, and sometimes she was sure she did remember floating in the water in a little blue life jacket while her mother drifted beside her and shimmering fish swam below.

When she tried to remember the accident, it got all mixed up in her mind. Images of the lake and the fish twisted together with the screeching of tires. The crashing of metal and glass blended with the lapping of waves and her mother's soft laughter, the feel of the life jacket (or was it the seatbelt?) tight around her, keeping her safe.

When she asked Eric what he remembered about the accident, he always turned from her, tucked himself away like a turtle going into its shell, and said, "Nothing." He didn't like to talk about their lives before.

She reached down under the covers now, pulled up her pajama top, ran a finger over her own scars.

And she thought of Iris, of that black line of stitches on her chest.

"Sister," she said, the word full of recognition and longing. "My sister."

Lizzy

August 19, 2019

AFTER A TEN-HOUR drive from Louisiana, I unlocked my front door and stepped through into the entryway. It smelled like home: coffee and wood and books.

I'd bought the house—a little run-down cabin just outside of Asheville, North Carolina—ten years ago and had it totally renovated. I was fond of the sparse look of untreated wood, and the walls were paneled with locally milled tongue and groove. The floors were made of reclaimed floorboards from an old tobacco barn. It was a small house—just over a thousand square feet—but it had all I needed and suited me perfectly. There were a lot of windows that overlooked downtown Asheville to the east and the Tennessee mountains to the west. In fifteen minutes I could be downtown, but up here, tucked away on the ridge and surrounded by trees, I felt worlds away.

I set my bag down and went to the basket on the front table. It was piled high with mail and there was a note from my part-time assistant, Frances. She came once a week to assist with email, the website, speaking requests, and basically whatever I needed help with. When I was away, Frances would come by to bring in the mail and make sure the house was still standing. I scanned the note:

> *Welcome Home!*
>
> *The Monsters of the Ozarks Conference emailed to confirm travel arrangements and dates (September 28 & 29) and they want to know what AV equipment you'll need for your presentation.*
>
> *UC San Francisco wants to know if you're interested in doing a guest lecture in October (details in email).*
>
> *Reminder: Your article for Crypto Cryptids is due next Wednesday.*
>
> *AND . . . Brian's called and emailed about a hundred times. He's threatening to come to Asheville next week to take you to lunch and make you an offer you can't refuse.*

I set down the note and shook my head. Brian Mando was the producer of *Monsters Among Us*. I'd been one of the three researchers on the series last season, and according to Brian, I was a fan favorite. They wanted me back for next season. Brian also said he had a new idea to pitch to me—a solo show of my very own. He wanted to take the idea to the network. So far, I'd avoided talking to him about the new show and said I wasn't interested in next season's *Monsters Among Us*. I loved doing my podcast, writing blog posts and articles, even lectures and talks. But I'd never been comfortable in front of a camera. The lights, all the people telling me where to go and what to do—it all felt so artificial.

I picked up my bag and carried it up the stairs to the loft where my bedroom was. I unzipped the bag, dumped my dirty clothes into the hamper, and started to repack.

I wanted to move fast, get back on the road as soon as I could. I hoped to be on Chickering Island before noon tomorrow.

My bedroom walls were covered in unfinished tongue and groove and decorated with old monster movie posters: *Frankenstein*, *Bride of Frankenstein*, and *The Wolf Man*. There was a bed, a little table, and a window with a cactus sitting on the sill (the only plant I could keep alive, being away so much). The large skylight above my bed allowed me to go to sleep looking up at the stars. I often thought about the constellations we'd invented when we were kids lying in the backyard: the Hunchback, King Kong, Vampires— a sky full of monsters.

Once I'd repacked, I carried my bag back downstairs.

The house had a tiny but functional kitchen (I wasn't big on cooking), the single bedroom, a bathroom with an old claw-foot tub, and a big combination living room and office where I spent most of my time. There were more old movie posters hung down here: *Dracula* with Bela Lugosi, *Creature from the Black Lagoon*, *The Mummy*. I'd also put up a poster of *Shadow People*, the documentary I'd been in two years ago. Brian had sent me a life-size cardboard cutout of myself, Jackson, and Mark—the three researchers in last season's *Monsters Among Us*. We stood in the corner of the living room: Jackson holding a flashlight, Mark with his night-vision scope and camera, and me holding a microphone and digital recorder. The pose was very *Ghostbusters*. At the bottom, beside the title of the show, was the tagline: *They're real and they're here.*

I'd wanted to take the cardboard figures straight to the recycling center, but Frances talked me into keeping them. I looked now at the TV version of myself with makeup, clad in my usual uniform of Levi's, black T-shirt, beat-up leather jacket, and boots. "Fan favorite," I said aloud, shaking my head.

On the wall above my desk hung my degrees from UNC Chapel

Hill, where I'd majored in anthropology and minored in psychology before going back for a master's in folklore—the title of my thesis was *What Our Monster Stories Tell Us about Who We Are*. Beside the degrees hung other photos: a snapshot of me with a group of people dressed as monsters at a convention; me standing next to Rachel Loveland, the director of *Shadow People*; me on the stage doing a TED Talk on the role of monsters in modern society. And last, my favorite, me and Charlie hiking in the Blue Ridge Mountains a couple of summers ago when he came to visit.

The bookshelves were full of books on anthropology, folklore, and monsters. The only thing I'd kept from childhood was Gran's copy of *Frankenstein*, which was tucked in there between *Dracula* and *The Strange Case of Dr. Jekyll and Mr. Hyde*, some passages still faintly underlined: *torrent of light.*

The bottom shelf was packed with copies of my own book: *The Monster Hunter's Companion*, published five years ago. Sales had jumped since my appearance in *Monsters Among Us*—the publisher had done an edition with a TV tie-in cover, and they'd sold ten times more copies in the last six months than they had in the previous five years combined.

I pulled out my phone and sent a quick text to Frances: Trip to Louisiana was cut short. I stopped at home, but have to take off again.

Two seconds later, Frances responded: New monster?

A new lead on an old one.

When will you be back?

Not sure. Can you hold down the fort here?

Frances sent back a thumbs-up emoji. Then: What do you want to do about Brian?

I sighed. Tell him I'm away on an important hunt, I texted. Somewhere without cell service and you have no idea when I'll be back.

You can't put him off forever.

I'm not putting him off. I've already given him an answer—it's just not what he wants to hear.

He's stubborn.

Well, I'm more stubborn.

Frances texted back with a smiley face and Safe travels.

I closed with I'll leave a check for you in the basket, feeling an odd little twinge when I realized that the person I was closest to, the one I spent the most time with on a regular basis, was someone I paid. But this was my choice. Wasn't it? My life didn't leave a lot of extra time for socializing for the sake of socializing. And that was the way I wanted it. At least, that's what I told myself. Because every time I tried to make actual meaningful connections with people, I ended up feeling the way I did when the cameras were on me—like it was all acting, pretending to be something I wasn't.

I set down my phone, sat at my desk, and opened the lowest drawer, pulling out the thick file folder that contained years' worth of research: the printed copies of each girl's face, the carefully gathered facts. Everything I knew about the missing girls.

I might never have discovered the pattern on my own. In 2002, I was in Upstate New York investigating numerous sightings of something described simply as Pig Man. A sheriff I interviewed explained that locals thought the creature was the result of genetic experiments the government was doing to create animal-human hybrids.

I nodded when I heard this. Man-made monsters were their whole own category. I'd investigated many creatures that were the supposed results of government experiments: alien-human hybrids, wolves with human DNA, zombie soldiers who couldn't be killed by traditional weapons. I'd heard plenty of stories, seen some blurry photos, but never collected any real evidence.

The truth was, I'd never found solid proof of any of the monsters I hunted. I gathered stories, other people's photographs. I looked at plaster casts of footprints, jars that held tufts of strange fur. I interviewed eyewitnesses, listening to their stories with a trace of envy and deep longing, always thinking, *Why couldn't it be me?* I captured the occasional odd sound on my digital recorder: far-off howls and moans, always sounding less frightening than sad. I'd spent hours and hours in the woods, in cornfields, in old mines and abandoned houses, at the edges of rivers and lakes, searching, waiting, willing them to show themselves to me. Year after year, I chased the monsters, feeling just behind them, touching their shadows sometimes, but never able to actually catch a glimpse.

Back in New York, I'd listened to the sheriff's Pig Man stories and theories: "The body of a man, face like a pig. And he doesn't speak, he squeals. Folks say he escaped from the government facility on Plum Island and made his way here. We've got a lot of thick woods, perfect cover for him." The sheriff didn't flat-out admit to believing that this creature existed, but he didn't exactly deny it either. I asked him if he'd ever seen the creature himself. "You spend enough time out in those woods, you see some strange things," he'd said, but wouldn't elaborate. I asked him a few more questions, then listened as he told me about Nadia Hill, the back of my neck prickling. "That girl who went missing last year, she went around telling people she'd been meeting the Pig Man out in the woods. The story the kids like to tell is that he's the one who took her. Did it on the full moon because that's when he's the hungriest."

"But what really happened to Nadia?" I'd asked. "Was she ever found?"

The sheriff had shaken his head, looked down at the ground. "No. She hasn't shown up yet. Do I think the Pig Man took her into the woods to be his secret wife and raise little piggy babies, like the kids say? No. Nadia ran away, plain and simple."

I told Nadia Hill's story on my podcast and blog about the Pig

Man. The comments blew up: *Was there really a monster in Upstate New York who took a girl?* Blog visitors left comments sharing rumors they'd heard about other people, mostly children and teens, who'd been taken by various monsters around the country: a boy in Maine who'd been carried off in the jaws of a giant catlike creature; a girl who disappeared after she followed a silver lady only she could see into a cave in Kentucky.

Most of the stories were just that: stories. But some weren't. These were the ones that got my attention, sank their teeth in, and wouldn't let go.

And then the email came. From a user who called herself MNSTRGRL.

Took you long enough to catch on, sister. Nadia Hill wasn't the first. And she won't be the last. Come find me, Monster Hunter. I dare you.

I wrote back immediately: Is it really you?

The email bounced back as undeliverable. No such address.

I dove into new research, spending hours online, and soon discovered a pattern of teenage girls who had gone missing on full moons, all from towns with reports of a local monster.

The earliest match I could find was thirteen-year-old Jennifer Rothchild, back in 1988. She'd disappeared from a little town in Washington State with a lot of bigfoot sightings. And Jennifer had told her friends she'd met a creature in the woods, a creature who spoke to her. She'd vanished on the night of the full moon in September. The woods were searched by police, dogs, and teams of volunteers. Signs were put up around town. The police questioned her friends, her teachers, members of her family. No trace was ever found. No one ever heard from her again.

In 1991, fifteen-year-old Vanessa Morales disappeared from Farmington, New Mexico, after telling people she'd seen the Dogman and was going out to look for him on the full moon.

In 1993, Sandra Novotny in Flatwoods, West Virginia, showed her friends a blurry photo she'd taken of the Flatwoods monster. She went into the woods to get a better picture and was never seen again.

Sixteen-year-old Anna Larson vanished from Elkhorn, Wisconsin, in September of 1998 after telling her little brother that she'd met the Beast of Bray Road, that the Beast had told her she was special.

Each girl disappeared on a full moon after claiming to have met some sort of legendary creature.

Nadia Hill in New York State was the fifth to fit the pattern.

In addition to my online research, I'd visited the towns where the girls had disappeared, talked to locals, friends, and family, always under the guise of monster research for my podcast. I'd walked the woods and fields where the girls had gone missing. But over and over, I found nothing.

The monster, my monster, was too clever to leave behind clues.

I held out hope that one of the missing girls would surface one day and tell her story. But none of them ever did. And no bodies or personal effects were ever found. The girls vanished without a trace.

I didn't go to the authorities. I was sure they'd look at what I had and say just what the local police always did: These girls were runaways.

And why would they listen to the crazy theories of a woman who hunted monsters for a living? Besides, once they found out who I really was and where I'd come from—well, that was a road I didn't want to go down with law enforcement of any sort.

So I investigated on my own. Crisscrossed the country, searching, hunting.

And occasionally, I'd get another email from the same user, MNSTRGRL, at a different address. Always, the notes were cryptic, teasing, sometimes quoting lines from our childhood *Book of Monsters*: They can pass as human. They hide in plain sight.

Sometimes there would be questions: Do you know yet? Why I do what I do? Have you guessed?

And sometimes, just taunting: You were so close, but again, you missed so much.

I'd printed copies of every email from MNSTRGRL and these were in the file too. I flipped through them now and looked at the last one I'd received, about three months ago:

Do you ever get tired of it? The cat and mouse game we play?

The hunter and the hunted. Only, which is which, sister? Which is which?

I shut the folder, shoved it into my bag.

I went into the kitchen, put on a pot of coffee, and got out my thermos. Not that I felt the need for coffee now—I was keyed up, on edge—but I'd need the caffeine for an all-night drive. While I waited for it to brew, I pulled out my phone, knowing I shouldn't, but longing to hear my brother's voice.

"Hey," he said when he picked up.

"Hey, yourself," I said back.

"How's Louisiana? Any sign of your swamp monster?" The words were a little mocking. He didn't believe in monsters anymore.

"I'm not in Louisiana."

"I thought you were there for the rest of the week. Where are you now?"

A lump in my throat warned me not to tell him.

But I longed to tell someone, to confess, and who else would I tell? Who else could possibly understand?

"I'm home," I said. "but I'm heading out soon." I paused, then made myself finish: "I'm going to Vermont."

He fell silent, so quiet I thought the call had dropped.

At last he said, "Why?" his voice a little higher than usual. A little-boy voice that took me tumbling back through time. I closed my eyes, pictured a too-skinny Eric, his tube socks pulled up to his knobby knees, curly hair sticking up at strange angles. A boy who was always cradling an animal, trying to tame something wild, to fix something broken.

"I think she's there." I didn't need to say more. Didn't need to tell him who *she* was. "There's another missing girl," I explained, offering up my evidence. "Taken on the full moon. From a place with a monster. It fits the pattern."

Eric, member of the Monster Club, illustrator of our book, would have understood this.

More silence. But I could hear him breathing, a soft wheeze that worried me a little. He sounded like an old man. Behind the sound of his breath, I heard a TV. A baseball game. His beloved Tigers, no doubt. The sound dimmed, and his breathing got louder. He was walking, moving out of earshot of Cricket and the girls. I heard a door close.

"Lizzy, listen to me," he said, voice sharp and no-bullshit, but still barely above a whisper. He didn't want anyone to hear. "You're grasping at straws. Seeing patterns that aren't there. You've lost all perspective."

"I have not." I prided myself on my perspective. In my podcasts, I was the devil's advocate, playing the role of skeptic when I interviewed eyewitnesses, asking questions like "If this creature is really out there, how do you explain the lack of physical evidence?"

I held tight to the phone, listening. Eric (Charlie!) was the only person I'd shared my theories with. The only one who knew about the missing girls, the monsters, and full moons. The only one I'd told about the emails I sometimes got from MNSTRGRL.

"Lizzy, please. I'm asking you to stop."

"I can't. You know that. She's got another girl."

"You don't know that. You don't know it's *her*."

"Yes, I do. I can feel it."

"It's been over forty years, Lizzy," he reminded me. "She could be dead for all we know."

"She's not dead," I said, knowing it was true. I'd feel it if my sister was dead. I would. "She's out there. And she's the one taking the girls."

"Even if you're right," he went on, clearly exasperated, "it has nothing to do with you."

How could this be the same boy who'd once known everything there was to know about monsters?

"It has *everything* to do with me," I told him, my voice edgier than I intended. "Don't you see? I've got to go to Vermont."

"And what exactly are you hoping to do there?"

My breath caught in my throat.

What was I hoping to do?

Save the girl, of course. Get there in time to save this girl and make sure that no more girls disappeared.

"I'm going to stop her."

As I spoke, I realized: I meant it this time. I'd thought it before, but this, this felt different. The fact that I was going back to Vermont seemed significant. Symbolic.

Do you ever get tired of it? The cat and mouse game we play?

I wanted to say all of this to Eric, thought that maybe he, of all people, might understand. But once again, I was thinking of him as Eric from our childhood, not the grown man known as Charlie.

Charlie feigned amnesia. Often, when we tried to talk about our past, when I asked him a question about a specific memory, he'd shake his head, say, "I don't know, Lizzy. That was a long time ago."

"How?" he asked now. "How are you going to stop her?" His voice was icy cold, dripping with fear.

It was wrong of me to have called him. It was selfish. Foolish, even.

"You know how." The words came out snappish, scolding. "You

know what I have to do. You helped write the book—you know how to stop a monster."

He was quiet. I heard the flick of a lighter. He'd quit smoking, but sometimes I could hear him sneaking a cigarette when we talked.

"Lizzy, this isn't healthy," he said.

I said nothing.

"Please," he said. "Don't go to Vermont. Come here instead. Come stay with us for a while. We'd love to have you. Cricket was just asking when you'd come again, and both girls are here now until after Labor Day when Ali goes back to college."

I doubted very seriously that Cricket had been longing to see me. I knew I made poor Cricket as uncomfortable as Cricket made me. Cricket with her highlighted hair, her Crock-Pot cookbooks, her pretty but practical outfits from JCPenney. And the girls looked at me like I was something they'd scraped off the bottom of their shoe. Their weirdo monster-hunting aunt who came for a visit twice a year and insisted on sleeping in her van in their driveway instead of the guest room with the rose stencils on the wall and the matching rose air freshener that was supposed to make you think you were really in a garden.

"Yeah, that'd be nice," I said at last.

"Good." He sighed a relieved breath.

"I'll drive out just as soon as I'm done in Vermont."

"Lizzy—"

"I've gotta go, Eric," I said, hanging up before he had a chance to curtly remind me, as he often did, that his name was Charlie.

Vi

May 9, 1978

"THE HOUSE CAME with the job, Gran always says," Vi explained as she gave Iris a tour, starting in the kitchen. Here was the special drawer where the cookies were kept, and the freezer with gallons of ice cream, boxes of ice pops in plastic tubes.

"Gran makes us milkshakes for breakfast," Vi told her. "They're special health shakes. I bet she'll make them for you too." Other kids got Lucky Charms and Count Chocula for breakfast, but Gran dumped raw eggs, brewer's yeast, and powders from the health food store into the blender with skim milk, Hood ice cream, and Hershey's syrup. They each got one of Gran's special shakes every morning—"My lucky little hooligans," Gran always said. "No one else gets ice cream for breakfast!"

The Crock-Pot on the counter bubbled away. Gran used the Crock-Pot a lot: She made all kinds of stews and casseroles in it, sometimes tiny hot dogs in barbecue sauce. Tonight they were having Swedish meatballs with boxed instant mashed potatoes, which Vi liked better than real ones because there were no lumps.

Vi opened the cupboards, showed Iris where to find the Looney Tunes jars from Welch's jelly they used as glasses, the plates and bowls with the bright yellow sunflower pattern that matched the kitchen curtains perfectly.

"Gran makes breakfast and dinner, but we're on our own for lunch, which is usually sandwiches. The bread's in this drawer, there's sandwich meat in the fridge, and we've always got peanut butter and jelly. Sometimes Gran buys Marshmallow Fluff! You like fluffernutters, right?"

The girl just blinked at her.

"Between breakfast and lunch is usually work time, except on weekends. We're homeschooled and Gran gives us assignments— reading, research, reports, math problems. In the afternoon, we can read more, do art, go outside. If we've finished our work, we're free to do whatever we'd like. Sometimes we go to town. Gran lets us go to the library whenever we want. In the evenings, after dinner, she checks our work, gives us assignments for the next day."

She showed Iris the latest contraption Gran and Eric had built to try to catch Big White Rat, which involved a bucket, a wooden ramp, and a can covered in peanut butter. "Gran had this lab rat, and she says he's the smartest rat she ever knew," Vi explained. "Anyway . . . he got out and now he lives in our walls. Gran and Eric are always building traps to try to catch him, but he's too smart for traps." Iris stared at the empty trap, and Vi continued, "You'll see him, I'm sure. The other day, I was getting Pop-Tarts from the shelf and there he was! He disappeared into a hole in the back before I could grab him, though."

Vi brought Iris out to the enclosed back porch. "This is our arts and crafts area. It's also where we play games." She pointed to the stacks of board games on the shelves. "And this is where Gran makes her gin." Gran's gin still was bubbling away, and Vi showed it to Iris, but warned her never to touch it. A flask full of liquid over a Bunsen burner boiled gently. From it, a long coil of copper tubing looped like a helix, a tiny roller coaster that went on and on, ending in another flask where it drip, drip, dripped down.

"Distillation is simple chemistry," Vi explained. "Evaporation and condensation."

Next to the still was Gran's gin notebook, open to the latest recipe, number 180. Vi looked at the list of ingredients, the measurements in grams: juniper berries, coriander, licorice. Also, the recipe for the mash she'd made with corn, apples, and honey. Gran was always tinkering with her mash recipe. "Sometimes Gran lets us help her, and we get to measure out ingredients on a little scale that uses brass weights." Vi smelled the botanicals that filled the jars lining the shelves next to the wooden table: juniper, orange peel, cinnamon, nutmeg, frankincense, cardamom, black pepper, fennel, lemongrass. There were others too. Strange leaves, roots, and berries listed by only their botanical names. She picked one up, held it out to Iris. "This name, it's in Latin. Gran's teaching me Latin. I only know a little right now. Gran says Latin is the language of science and medicine. I'm going to be a doctor when I grow up, so knowing Latin will be important."

Iris followed Vi into the living room with the TV and dark wood Magnavox stereo console with a record player, radio, and 8-track player. She showed her the records stored inside it: Chopin, Wagner, Bing Crosby, Julie Andrews, and lots of Neil Diamond. "Gran loves Neil Diamond. She says he's very talented. You've heard his music, right?"

Iris only blinked. It had been nearly twenty-four hours, and she still hadn't said a word. She followed Vi around obediently, watched, listened, and nodded or shook her head, seeming to understand, but her face was unreadable. She was wearing Vi's old clothes: a pair of faded bell-bottom jeans and a red-and-blue-striped turtleneck that she'd put on backward and inside out—the tag flapped at her throat.

She still had the dirty old orange hunting cap on, pulled down over her ears. Vi put on a Neil Diamond album—*Moods*—and dropped the needle.

They listened to "Play Me" for a minute—*you are the sun, I am the moon*—then Vi just kept talking, not able to stand the awkward silence. She wished Eric would come down and help her out, but it was Friday, and Eric cleaned all the animal cages in his room every Friday—a chore that took all morning and a good chunk of the afternoon too.

"Gran has a few pictures from when the Inn was built—soldiers missing arms and legs and stuff. Maybe she'll show you if you ask. I bet it's haunted. I mean, how could it not be, right?" She looked at Iris, who stared back, eyes wide. "Anyway, back then, this house was where the superintendent and his family lived. But now we live here. When Gran retires, which she says won't be anytime soon, she'll leave, and the next director will move in." Vi smiled like it was all very matter-of-fact, but there was a weight on her chest. She couldn't stand the idea of having to leave the only home she remembered. And it didn't help that the next director would probably be Dr. Hutchins. Vi hated to think about it—Dr. Hutchins with his tufty hair and squinty eyes eating breakfast in their kitchen, probably never even sitting on the porch swing because it squeaked and he was unsettled by loud noises. Vi and Eric loved to take advantage—to put whoopee cushions on his chair before dinner, toss firecrackers beneath his office window.

"Let's get some lemonade and go outside," Vi suggested.

She measured scoops of powder into a pitcher of water and stirred, and Iris watched her with wonder, as if she'd never seen anyone make lemonade that way. Iris gulped down two glasses right away, messily, the lemonade trickling down her chin.

•   •   •

"MY BROTHER AND I, we've got a club. You can be in it if you want."

The porch swing chains squeaked as Vi pushed the two of them back and forth, back and forth, with the toe of her sneaker on the gray painted floorboards. It was a hot day. The rest of the lemonade was sitting in two sweating glasses on the little wrought iron table beside the porch swing.

"So . . . do you want to?" Vi asked her.

Iris just stared. She hadn't taken off her orange knit hat, and Vi could only imagine how uncomfortable she must be. Vi could see the sweat forming on her forehead, which was white and shiny and perfectly smooth like marble. The hat was filthy, stained with grease and God knew what else. Vi was surprised that Gran let her wear it all the time, even to dinner last night, which was just plain crazy because Gran had all these strict rules about dinner: always at six in the dining room, show up in clean clothes, hair combed, hands and face washed. Best manners. Please and thank you and no elbows on the table, not ever. And everyone needed to be a member of the clean-plate club, or no leaving the table.

But Gran had said nothing, just let Iris wear the grimy thing. And because Iris didn't talk, she didn't have to say please or thank you, or the other big part of dinner, which was telling a story about your day. When you told your story, you got extra praise for using a new vocabulary word you'd learned. Gran was big on vocabulary and on the idea that they should always be challenging their minds. Last night, Vi had used the word *abhorrent*: "I think Old Mac shooting the rabbits that get into the garden is abhorrent and completely unnecessary."

"It's a monster club," Vi told Iris now. "We talk about monsters. We go to see monster movies at the drive-in on Saturday nights in the summer. We go on monster hunts. And we're writing a book. *The Book of Monsters*. We're putting everything we know about them into it, and Eric's drawing the illustrations."

Iris was listening carefully, biting her lip. It might have been Vi's imagination, but she looked interested, excited even.

"So, do you want to join? You can come with us to the movies. The drive-in opens up in June. We take our bikes. You can ride on mine with me." Vi let herself imagine it—this girl on the back of the banana seat of her red Schwinn, her arms wrapped around Vi's waist while Vi pumped the pedals, taking them all the way into town.

The girl nodded, *yes, yes, yes*. And then—Vi knew she wasn't imagining this—Iris gave the flicker of a smile.

Vi smiled back. "Good," she said. "Want to see our monster book?"

Iris nodded again. *Sure, sure, sure.*

"We've got a secret clubhouse. I'm gonna show you, because you're a member now, but you can't show anyone else, ever. Not even Gran, okay?"

The warning was silly, really. Vi was sure Gran knew about the clubhouse. Eric told Gran *everything*—the kid couldn't keep a secret. Even when he swore he wouldn't tell something, he always went and blabbed.

Iris nodded again.

"Okay," Vi said.

She opened the front door to holler the secret Monster Club call. She cupped her hands around her mouth, tilted her head back, began a low howl that got louder in pitch: "A-woooo!" she cried, blasting it out, then letting it fade. She'd practiced her howl. She'd gotten good at it. But Eric was better. He howled back to signal he'd heard. In five seconds, she heard his feet pounding down the stairs.

"The monster call is like a fire alarm," she said to Iris. "You hear it and you come running. You have to get yourself to the clubhouse as fast as you can, no matter what."

Iris nodded.

Eric was on the porch now, eyes wide. His hair was wild, uncombed, and he wore a yellow-black-and-white-striped T-shirt that reminded Vi of a caterpillar—of the monarchs that they found in the milkweed sometimes.

"Iris is joining the club," Vi told him. "We're going to the clubhouse to show her the book."

Eric didn't ask any questions, he just jumped off the porch and started leading the way around the side of the house, across the back-yard with its neatly trimmed grass (thanks to Old Mac, who mowed it once a week), past the old rabbit hutch and woodshed, past the juniper bushes Gran had planted for her gin, and into the woods.

"How's Ginger?" Vi asked. That's what he'd decided to name the in-jured baby bunny.

"She's good. Doesn't seem to even notice the stitches. But you can tell it hurts—she walks and hops kinda lopsided."

During dinner last night, Gran had said he could keep the rabbit until it was healed and big enough to let go.

"Wild things don't belong in cages," Gran reminded him when he started to argue. She only ever let Eric keep the animals who couldn't go back to being wild: the ones with messed-up legs, or missing eyes, or broken wings, or the creatures who'd been in captivity so long they'd forgotten how to be wild.

Eric, Iris, and Vi traveled along the well-worn path that took them through the trees, down a hill. It was cooler in the woods. The air smelled green and loamy. Birches and maples and poplars provided a dense canopy, shading out the sun.

They walked for five minutes, heading toward the creek. They heard it before they saw it . . . the quiet burbling of water over rocks and sand. It was full of minnows, crayfish, and bugs that walked around on the surface in the still places: water striders. The banks were lined with ferns, thick carpets of moss, a few patches of skunk cabbage that stank when you broke off a leaf. Vi loved coming back here. The air was different; everything felt more alive. And it was theirs and theirs alone.

The clubhouse waited on the other side of the creek. They had to hop across slippery rocks to get to the simple shack, about eight feet by ten feet. They didn't know who'd built it or why, but they'd never asked Gran or anyone at the Inn about it—it had been their secret since they'd discovered it two years ago. The whole building was a little off-kilter, leaning slightly to the left. The boards were warped and faded, rotten in places. Little by little, Vi and Eric had been fixing it up. They'd sneak into the big barn over at the Inn where Old Mac kept lumber, shingles, scraps of plywood, nails, and screws. Taking a little at a time so he wouldn't notice, they'd already replaced a rotten spot in the floor and fixed a hole in the roof.

"Welcome to the monster clubhouse," Vi said, holding the door open.

She let Iris go in first, and noticed that her breathing seemed to change, get a little faster. She was excited; Vi could feel the thrum of energy coming off her.

"It's great, isn't it? And it's all ours. No one knows about this," she said, looking right at Eric. "Right, Eric?"

He nodded, looking Vi in the eye. Maybe he hadn't told Gran after all, which would be a miracle.

The clubhouse was framed with two-by-fours and sided with wide boards. There was a door and two windows, the windows too warped and swollen to open anymore. They had a card table and two folding metal chairs set up in the middle, an old broom in the corner that they used to sweep up dirt and leaves that found their way in. Moss was growing on the windowsills and up on the roof. To Vi, it was like a fairy cottage, a magic house where anything could happen. Maybe it wasn't even real for anyone but them; it only appeared when they came into the woods looking for it.

"We'll have to get another chair," Vi said, "now that there are three of us."

"There are a whole bunch in the barn at the Inn," Eric said. He pointed to the chair he usually sat in. "Iris, you can use mine." He smiled, his cheeks coloring. "If you want, I mean."

Against one wall was a set of wooden shelves that held some provisions—peanut butter, crackers, a canteen full of water—along with all of their monster-hunting equipment: a pair of sturdy leather gloves, a compass, a magnifying glass, a flashlight, binoculars, a Swiss Army knife, wooden stakes (in case they encountered a vampire), and a small backpack to carry it all.

Eric pulled down the pack and started showing Iris their gear. "I bring my camera when we go monster hunting," he added. "I've got a Polaroid. I've also got Gran's old Instamatic, but you have to wait to get your film developed with that. This Christmas, I'm gonna ask for a real camera. A 35-millimeter Nikon. That's what real wildlife photographers use. Like the ones who shoot for *National Geographic*. Gran says I can put a darkroom in the hall closet and learn to develop my own film."

Vi nodded. "It'll be important to be able to get good pictures for proof. We haven't come face-to-face with any monsters yet, but we've seen signs," she explained. "Look at this." She reached for an old baby food jar on the shelf. Inside was a long tuft of black fur. "We pulled this off a tree a little ways down the creek. It didn't come from any animal we have around here, that's for sure." She handed Iris the jar, watched the girl's eyes widen.

"And we've seen footprints, too. Strange ones. Almost human, but bigger and definitely with claws." Iris seemed to shiver. "We've made some recordings too, really weird screams and howls, but they're back at home. We don't leave the tape recorder out here. We can play them for you later."

Iris was staring into the jar of fur, turning it, shaking it a little like a snow globe. Her orange hat was pulled down, covering the tops of her ears.

"There are two nights every month we go monster hunting: the full moon and the new moon," Vi told her. "That's the best time to find monsters."

Iris nodded.

"We should show her the book!" Eric said, voice bouncing with excitement. He pulled the briefcase from under the folding table. It was an old, hard-sided leather case, scuffed and stained. He undid the tarnished brass clasps and opened it up. Inside were the monster book, a big box of colored pencils, some pens, pencils, erasers, and markers.

The monster book itself was in a black three-ring binder Gran had given them from the Inn. The label on the spine had read ACCOUNTING, 1973, but they'd made a new BOOK OF MONSTERS label and pasted that over it. Eric had made a drawing for the cover showing his favorite monster: a chimera—a fire-breathing creature that's part lion, part goat, part serpent.

"Vi does all the writing, and I do the drawings," he explained, flipping through the book, showing Iris the pages dedicated to vampires, to the rules of monster hunting.

"This is a wendigo. They're creatures that were human once. Now they eat people." The emaciated-looking creature had its jaws open, teeth sharp, claws out. It was dressed in rags and had black eyes.

"And this," he said, turning the page, "is a werewolf. You know about werewolves, right? They're humans that transform on full moons. The worst thing about being a werewolf is that sometimes you don't even know you're one."

Iris looked down at the drawing: a humanoid form with a wolf's head, red eyes, teeth dripping with blood. She took a step back.

"You don't need to be afraid," Eric said. "Not in the daylight like this. And there are things you can do to protect yourself. Magic and stuff. We'll teach you. We'll teach you everything we know."

Iris smiled.

"Can you draw?" Vi asked Iris. Iris shook her head. "Well, then maybe you can help me with the writing. You know how to write, don't you?"

Vi handed her a red marker and a piece of paper, like it was a test she wasn't sure Iris would pass. Iris took the marker but held it all wrong, clutching it in her fist, all her fingers wrapped around it.

"Write down your favorite monster," Vi said, laying a piece of paper on the table.

Iris looked at the marker in her hand, at the blank sheet of paper.

Then she drew a rectangle. About two-thirds up, in the middle of the rectangle, she drew another smaller rectangle. Inside the smaller rectangle she put two small circles.

"What's this?" Vi asked.

Iris wrote *MNSTR* in big, messy block letters, then laid the marker down.

"Monster? What kind of monster?" Vi asked, but Iris had turned away.

Vi picked up the monster book, closed it, and looked at the cover where she'd written *THE BOOK OF MONSTERS by Violet Hildreth, Illustrations by Eric Hildreth.* She picked up a black pen.

"Do you have a last name, Iris?"

Iris gave a small shrug, then shook her head.

"Okay then," Vi said, printing carefully on the cover, adding *and Iris Whose Last Name We Don't Know* next to her own name. She held the book up to show Iris, but Iris was busy going through the things Eric had shown her in the backpack. She held up the binoculars.

"Binoculars," Eric said. He turned his hands into two tunnels and brought them up to his face. "Hold them right up against your eyes, and that dial in the middle you use to focus." He shook his head as he watched her. "Not that way—if you do it that way, everything looks smaller and farther away. You want things to look bigger and closer."

But Iris held the binoculars with the large lenses pressed against her eyes, looking at Eric, then Vi, making them farther away.

And she smiled.

She kept the binoculars pressed against her face as she walked around the room, looking at everything: the spongy floorboards, the shelves, the window with its cracked glass and spiderwebs. She was looking everywhere except where she was going. She walked into the table hard; so hard that it tipped, dumping the monster book on the floor. She fell back against the wall, hitting her head and making a little shriek that proved she wasn't mute after all.

The binoculars fell to the ground, and Iris's orange hat came off.

Eric gasped.

Vi clapped her hand over her mouth to keep the scream she felt from coming out.

Iris scrambled for the hat and pulled it back on.

But it was too late.

Vi and Eric had already seen.

The front of Iris's head was shaved, and a thick red scar, raised and raw-looking, ran all the way over the top from ear to ear.

THE BOOK OF MONSTERS

By Violet Hildreth and Iris Whose Last Name We Don't Know

Illustrations by Eric Hildreth

1978

If you suspect someone you know might be a monster, there are steps you can take to get to the truth.

Expose them to holy water, garlic, silver, and gauge their reaction.

See if they make a reflection in the mirror.

Do you only ever see them at night?

Do they disappear on full moons?

Learn what kind of monster they are. Study their habits, their movements. Learn where they live, how they feed, what their weakness is.

Then make a plan to kill them.

Vi

———◦———

June 2, 1978

Y OU HAVE TO hit back," Vi said with an exasperated sigh, after
she knocked Iris's block off for the tenth time. They were playing
Rock 'Em Sock 'Em Robots, throwing punches by pushing the plastic
buttons on joysticks. Vi was the red robot; Iris was blue. But Iris barely
threw any punches. She pushed the head of her blue robot back on and
waited for it to be knocked off again.

They were set up on the little table in the back sunroom. But there
was no sun today. The enclosed porch, with its brown carpet and
mustard-colored drapes, felt dismal. The old couch was covered in a
crocheted sunflower afghan that Miss Evelyn had made. The beaded
macrame wall hanging had been a gift from one of Gran's patients.
And the shelves held pieces of pottery that Vi and Eric had made: mis-
shapen ashtrays and lopsided vases. The landscape with horses that Vi
had painted by number last year hung above the shelves. Gran's gin
still bubbled gently behind them.

It was pouring rain, and nothing was on TV but crappy soap operas:

The Edge of Night, As the World Turns, Guiding Light. After nearly a month, Iris still hadn't spoken. Vi was starting to doubt that she ever would, but Gran said not to give up, to keep trying, to be patient and understanding.

Kapow! Vi pushed the button fiercely and knocked the head of Iris's blue plastic robot off yet again.

This stunk. Winning was no fun when your opponent wouldn't even try.

Vi shoved her chair back from the table and stood up, looked again through the stack of games on the shelves.

They couldn't play Battleship or Go Fish. They couldn't play Clue. You had to talk for all of those.

They'd done a zillion stupid Spirograph drawings and made designs with the Lite-Brite set. They'd already played Operation and Hungry Hungry Hippos and checkers. They'd spent almost an hour hunting for Big White Rat—Gran said she'd seen him when she was making her coffee and that he'd run into the crack between the refrigerator and counter.

"If I catch him, can I keep him?" Eric had asked.

Gran had smiled. "If you can build a cage strong enough," she'd said. "That's one smart rat."

Vi turned from the shelf of games. "What do you want to do now?" she asked.

Iris only shrugged.

Of course.

If anything, Iris seemed more skittish now than when she first arrived. At times she seemed almost afraid of Vi. And Vi found it exhausting to constantly be having one-way conversations. Sometimes, like now, she wanted to shake Iris, beg her to talk.

Iris was wearing the disgusting blaze-orange hat. She never took it off. She probably slept in it, for all Vi knew. She was still dressed in Vi's clothes: overalls and a long-sleeved blue shirt, which she had on inside out. Having this girl, this weird silent twin, walking around in her clothes, following close behind her like a shadow, was unsettling.

"Do you want to go find Eric? See if he'll let us take out the bunny?"

Yes, Iris nodded. *Yes, yes, yes.*

She always said yes to the rabbit.

They went up to Eric's room. His twin bed was shoved against the back wall, covered in a worn quilt. Next to his bed was a small table with a stack of comic books, a flashlight, a windup Mickey Mouse alarm clock, and the same photo of their parents Vi had on her own bedside table. There was a small bookshelf full of nature guides and animal books. On top of it stood the model of Darwin's boat, the HMS *Beagle*, that Gran had ordered all the way from England for Eric's Christmas present last year. The rest of his room was full of critters. Cages lined the floor in rows, were stacked on shelves: wire cages and glass aquariums holding mice and rats rescued from the basement lab; a turtle with a cracked shell that Eric and Gran had repaired with wires, pins, and glue; a squirrel who was missing his left eye; guinea pigs (from back when Gran had a few of them in her lab); and now the baby rabbit. He had a whole plastic Habitrail system with tubes leading from one plastic enclosure to another: a city of mice, all female so that they couldn't breed. He'd bought the Habitrail setup with his own money at the pet store and was often adding to it. The male mice were in their own metal cages. There was a rat running around in a plastic ball on the floor. The guinea pigs chirped and whistled. A white mouse ran on a squeaky wheel.

Vi watched Eric take the mesh top off the rabbit's aquarium as he whispered softly to the bunny, "It's okay, Ginger. You're okay. We're just going to hold you for a while. We won't hurt you."

He picked her up, stroked her, and she closed her eyes.

He held the bunny out to Iris, who took her ever so gently.

Iris loved the rabbit and never passed up the opportunity to hold her, cuddle her, stroke her soft fur. The only time Vi had seen the girl look really, truly happy was when she held the rabbit. And she always seemed sad when it was time to put Ginger back in her cage.

Iris held her now, stroked her, rocked her. After ten minutes or so, Ginger started getting fidgety and nervous. Iris was holding her tight, too tight, clutching her so hard that Ginger's eyes got all bulgy, and Eric had to use his soft rabbit voice to talk to Iris.

"I love being held, but I'm very small and need to go back to my cage to rest now. You can come see me later. Will you let me rest? Will you bring me some fresh clover from the yard?"

Yes, yes, yes, Iris nodded as she handed the bunny over to Eric.

Eric knew how to soothe the skittish.

"Thank you," he whispered to Iris in his tiny rabbit voice, and Iris opened her mouth like she was about to speak—to say *You're welcome,* maybe—but then she seemed to remember that she didn't talk anymore, and snapped her jaw closed as Eric set the rabbit back in her cage.

And just like that, the God of Ideas sent a lightning bolt down right into Vi's head, like something from a comic book: *Zap! Zap! Zap!*

She jumped up off Eric's bed. "Come with me," she said.

Iris hesitated for a second, looking from Ginger in her cage to Vi to Eric.

"Let's go," Eric said. "We can come back and visit Ginger later."

Iris nodded and stood up, and she and Eric followed Vi down the hall to her room.

Vi closed the door. "Sit," she said to Iris, nodding at the bed. Iris seemed to stiffen, looking at the closed door. Vi took a breath, added in a voice as soft as Eric's, "I mean, if you want to."

Eric sat on the bed and patted the spot beside him.

Iris nodded and perched cautiously at the edge of the bed, eyes on

Vi. Slowly she shifted her gaze and looked around the room. She studied the bookshelf, its volumes carefully grouped by size and color, the tidy desk, the dresser with nothing on top. Vi liked to keep things neat and organized. She hated any form of mess or clutter. Her walls were painted white and nothing hung on them, no cute posters or framed paintings; the shadows made their own art, and that was enough for her. Her painted wood floor was totally clear, not one thing on it but the furniture: a twin bed, dresser, desk, nightstand. It made Vi feel calm, this room.

Vi opened her closet door and pulled boxes from the shelf, rummaging through her old toys and books—plastic ponies with tangled manes, stuffed animals, a Holly Hobbie rag doll with a patchwork dress and yarn hair in two braids, a cap gun that smelled of gunpowder—things she was too old to want to play with anymore, things she didn't even remember—until she found what she was looking for.

She turned and looked into Iris's eyes, which were a muddy brown, just like her own.

We could really be sisters, she thought. *This girl and me.*

"This is for you," she said, holding out her gift.

Eric's eyes widened, and he smiled and nodded, *yes, yes, yes.* Vi had gotten this right. She knew she had gotten this right.

It was a rabbit. A soft, plush rabbit, once white and fluffy, now more of a dingy gray, fur matted in places, the plastic eyes scratched.

Vi felt ashamed suddenly—it seemed a stupid thing, to give someone a toy this dirty. She wanted to hit rewind, take it back, but it was too late.

"It's a puppet," she explained. "See?" She put her hand inside the bunny, made its little paws wiggle, turned its head to look in Iris's direction. The scratched plastic eyes stared at Iris, who smiled. Vi took the puppet off her hand and held it out. "She's yours if you want her."

Please, please, please.

Iris reached out, slowly took the puppet, stroked its soft head, ran her ragged, chewed nails over its ears. Then she slipped her hand inside.

Vi smiled. "Hello there, Rabbit," she said. And the little head turned to look at her.

"Hullo," it said back in a voice so soft Vi thought she might have imagined it.

But she hadn't imagined it. Iris had spoken! She'd actually spoken!

Not Iris, she told herself. *The bunny.* The toy Vi had given her, hoping it just might crack open a door.

She looked over at Eric, whose jaw had actually fallen open, his eyes huge like those of a surprised cartoon character.

"What's your name?" Vi asked, looking at the rabbit, not daring to look at Iris, worried she might break the spell.

It was so quiet she was sure they were all holding their breath.

"Don't know," the rabbit whispered, the words like a soft, regretful moan.

Vi kept her eyes on the rabbit. "Where do you come from?"

The rabbit swayed slightly.

"Don't remember," came the voice, soft as the rustle of paper.

Vi nodded. Her throat was dry. She was still staring at the worn rabbit puppet, but she was so close to Iris she could smell her, smell the Prell shampoo and Dial soap.

"What *do* you remember?" she asked.

Silence. Vi watched the rabbit. Its little fuzzy head slumped forward as if it had gone to sleep.

"It was dark," Iris said at last. "And there was a voice."

"A voice?"

The rabbit held still and Iris herself nodded. "The doctor's voice. Dr. Hildreth."

"Gran," Eric said.

"Gran," Iris repeated. She was still holding the rabbit, but she turned to look at Vi. "That's all I remember. Her voice talking to me, asking if I could open my eyes."

Vi nodded. "So you don't know what your real name is?"

"Or where you came from?" Eric asked.

Iris shook her head, the shaggy, mousy-brown hair that stuck out from under her orange hat falling over her eyes. "My head hurts if I try to remember more."

She shook her head again. Her whisper was so soft that Vi leaned in close to hear: "All I remember is waking up in a room with Dr. Hildreth standing over me, asking me if I could open my eyes." Iris's eyes were glassy with tears. "I'm no one," she said.

Vi reached out, then pulled her hand back, sitting on it to keep herself from touching Iris. "Everyone is someone," Vi said. She thought that sounded like a song, like a song Neil Diamond might sing, even. The beginning of a love song, maybe.

Iris nodded.

Vi thought of all the things she couldn't remember: her mother's face, her father's voice, what color eyes her parents had. She didn't even remember where they had lived. In a little blue house in the country, Gran said, but Vi couldn't remember.

"We can ask Gran who you are," Eric said. "She must know something."

Vi shook her head. "No way. She won't tell us. You know how she is about people who come from the Inn. Super secretive."

"There's gotta be something we can do," Eric said.

Vi looked at Iris. "We can help you," Vi said. "We can help figure out who you are, where you came from."

"How are we gonna do that?" Eric asked.

"Well, we know Iris came here from the Inn, right? There must be records. A file. Something."

Iris bit her lip. "I don't know."

"I do. *I know.* I know for a fact that if you're a patient of my grand-mother's, there are notes somewhere about you. Saying where you came from, at least. What happened to you. Some part of your story."

"Gran takes lots of notes," Eric agreed.

Iris nodded, looked down at the puppet, limp and still now.

Vi let her hand slip out from under her leg and lightly stroked the bunny's ears. "We'll help you," she said again.

It'd be against every rule Gran had ever laid out. Vi and Eric were not allowed at the Inn. And they were never, ever to touch any of Gran's papers, notes, or journals. Vi turned to Eric. "And you have to promise not to say a word about any of this to Gran," she said. "It's got to be top secret."

He nodded.

"I mean it, Eric. If you tell Gran, I'll tell her that it was you who freed Big White Rat."

"You can't," he gasped, his eyes getting glassy with tears.

"I won't. As long as you keep all of this a secret. I don't even want you to tell Gran that Iris spoke. Not yet."

He nodded again, face serious.

"We'll find out who you are, Iris," she said. "I promise."

The bunny puppet moved. Its paws opened and embraced Vi's hand, holding tight.

Vi closed her eyes, said a silent thank-you to the God of Puppets and the God of Promises, sure her heart might just explode.

The Helping Hand of God:
The True Story of the Hillside Inn

By Julia Tetreault, Dark Passages Press, 1980

The most tragic piece of this tale is, of course, the children.

According to my interviews, they were quite happy. They loved their grandmother very much and felt loved by her in return. They had a good, if isolated, life there on the hill. They had many pets—guinea pigs, mice, a turtle, a tamed wild rabbit—and spent hours outdoors exploring nature and enjoying the fresh Vermont air. They were homeschooled and excelled in their studies. They had access to Dr. Hildreth's immense library and were encouraged by her to engage their curious minds on a daily basis.

Frieda Carmichael, the head librarian at the Fayeville Public Library, a tiny stone building in the center of town, remembers the children coming in often. "Their grandmother would give them assignments and they'd come in to research all sorts of things: weather, current events, world history, astronomy. They'd take notes and write reports with footnotes and bibliographies. It was quite impressive—

they were doing very advanced work for their ages. And they loved to read! Especially Violet. There was nothing that girl didn't read. She'd sit for hours devouring books on science, medicine, history, and horror. She loved horror novels—Stephen King, Thomas Tryon, Anne Rice. Whenever I got a new one in, I'd put it aside for her. If I read those, I'd have nightmares for weeks, but that girl ate them up."

Donny Marsden, owner of the Fayeville General Store, remembers the children too. "Polite kids, just a little strange," he says. "They didn't go to school, didn't seem to have friends. I never saw them with any of the kids in town, anyway. They'd come in, load up on candy and soda, then head back up the hill on their bikes. The boy would buy comic books. And sometimes they'd play the video games I've got set up in the corner: *Sea Wolf* and *Night Driver*. But they'd never play if other kids were around. They had a funny way of talking too. Always using big words. My wife called them the Little Professors. The girl, one time I remember she said, 'I hope your day is sublime,' as she was leaving. What kind of kid talks like that?" He shakes his head. "I kinda worried about them up there on the hill all alone. Surrounded by lunatics is no place to raise kids."

Irene Marsden, Donny's wife, chimes in with her own story: "Our nephew Billy was about the age of the Hildreth boy. He saw them on their bikes one time and asked if they wanted to play. The girl shakes her head and says they can't. 'We're not allowed,' the boy says. 'Why not?' Billy asks. 'Because,' the girl says, 'we're vampires, and if we played with you, we'd have to bite your neck and drink all your blood.' She bared her teeth and snarled. Poor Billy was spooked. He never asked them to play again."

Lizzy

Billboards were illegal in Vermont, but quirky hand-painted signs were everywhere. The one greeting visitors to the island looked as if the local elementary school had helped with the design: The backdrop to *Welcome to Chickering Island* was a bright blue lake with boats and a cheerful smiling sunrise. Above it all soared a giant, disproportionate crane that looked more like a pterodactyl.

I'd pulled out my laptop and done some quick research on Chickering Island when I'd stopped somewhere in Pennsylvania to refuel and get a cup of crappy gas station coffee and a questionable burrito kept warm under a heat lamp. It turned out it wasn't an island at all, but a peninsula on Crane Lake, the fourth-largest lake in Vermont. And despite the name, there were no cranes this far north in Vermont. The whole thing felt like a lie: not an island, and not a single crane anywhere near the lake. Chickering Island had just over five hundred year-round residents, and the population jumped up to a couple thousand during the summer. There were lots of rental properties. A few farms.

A protected wildlife sanctuary. Two campgrounds (at one of which I'd made a reservation for four nights). An artsy downtown full of seasonal shops. Spotty cell reception. It was a place where people vacationed, renting rustic little summer homes along the shoreline of the lake in an attempt to truly get away from it all.

And the perfect place for a monster to hide.

•   •   •

I HAD TRAVELED all over the country, been to nearly every state and up to Canada and Alaska—even down to Mexico—hunting monsters. But I'd avoided Vermont. Hadn't been back there since I was a kid. Whenever I got a tip about a strange creature in the Green Mountain State, I pushed it aside, made excuses.

Vermont meant Fayeville and the Hillside Inn.

Nothing, I'd told myself again and again, could make me go anywhere near it ever again.

The most terrifying, unfaceable monster of all dwelled in those hills and mountains: the dark, shadowy form of my own past.

But now here I was.

I rolled down the window and inhaled the air.

Breathe, I told myself. *You're all right. You can do this.*

I'd driven right by the exit for Fayeville over an hour ago. I'd felt the pull of it, of Fayeville and the Inn, felt the place reaching for me with dark little tendrils.

Part of me longed to stop, to go see what was left of the place.

Others had, I knew. True-crime junkies who loved *The Helping Hand of God* and wanted to see for themselves where it had all taken place.

But the book, and the movie based on it, had gotten so much wrong. I was never able to sit through the entire movie, but I used to have a copy of the book. A copy I'd dog-eared, written all over, crossed out and corrected sections. I'd thought, briefly, of sending it to the author, Julia Tetreault. But no. Parts of the story could never be told.

• • •

THE BEGINNING OF the peninsula that was Chickering Island was barely wider than the two-lane road, and if I squinted at the glistening water of Crane Lake that surrounded me, I could imagine I was crossing by boat.

After a few hundred feet, the land widened. The road forked, and I bore right along East Main Street, following the signs to downtown. According to the map, Main Street looped along the edges of the island. I slowed, following the 25 mph speed limit as I passed through a quaint New England village. Candlestick Art Gallery, Island Antiques, Tip of the Cone Ice Cream, Apple of My Eye Diner (*Fresh Baked Pie Served All Day!*), Roger's (a seafood restaurant and market), Jameson Realty (*Vacation Rentals Available for Next Season!*), Chickering Island Books and Gifts, Newbury Market, Perch Sisters Coffee, Rum Runners Bar and Grill. A wide brick sidewalk ran in front of the stores, full of tourists clutching maps, shopping bags, and coffee cups. The shops had flower boxes outside, and tourists ate muffins and sipped lattes on metal benches.

On the left was a small town green with a twelve-foot-tall stone lighthouse in the center. A mother was watching two young children run around, tackling each other. At the other end of the park, four women on yoga mats leaned into downward dog.

I stayed on East Main Street, which traced the whole eastern edge of the island down to the tip, where the map showed the Chickering Island Wildlife Sanctuary. Once out of the downtown area, the road narrowed and the island became more forested. I passed houses and cottages, driveways full of cars with out-of-state plates, lawns littered with inflatable tubes and kayaks and beach toys, bathing suits and towels hung on clotheslines. I drove by Crane Farm Vineyard and Wines: a little octagonal building surrounded by trellised grapes, though I found it hard to imagine that you could really grow wine grapes in Vermont.

The woods grew thicker, the road draped in shadow, as I approached the wildlife sanctuary. I pulled over into the empty parking area for a quick look. On a gate at the entrance hung a metal sign:

OPEN SUNRISE TO SUNDOWN

NO MOTORIZED VEHICLES

HORSES AND BICYCLES ALLOWED

NO CAMPING

NO FIRES

The dirt road into the sanctuary was tree-lined and well shaded. I knew from my research that the refuge was over a hundred acres of woods, trails, and waterfront, including marshlands. Bald eagles, loons, and peregrine falcons nested there.

I also knew that most of the Rattling Jane sightings had taken place out here in these woods, along the edge of the water.

I felt the woods pulling me in, calling to me, dark and full of possibility. It was the same pull I'd felt as a kid on our monster hunts; the one that drew me to place after place hunting creatures most didn't believe existed at all.

"Later," I promised myself as I pulled away.

I followed the road around the horseshoe curve and started back up West Main Street, which ran along the west side of the island. More woods. A couple of houses. I spotted the sign: CHICKERING ISLAND CAMPGROUND. The little lighthouse from the town green was painted on the sign.

I pulled into the gravel driveway. The office was a small shack covered in weathered cedar shakes. Beach roses grew along the edge of the building. I parked the van and stepped out. I smelled campfires, heard the happy screams of children splashing in the pool out behind the office.

A man a bit older than me looked up from his computer screen when I walked in. He had close-cropped salt-and-pepper hair and was wearing a green polo shirt with the campground name embroidered on the left side. "Hi there, welcome." He looked out the window at my van. "You must be Ms. Shelley."

I nodded, gave him a polite smile. "Yes."

He pulled out a paper and peered down at it through the cheater glasses perched on the end of his nose. "Reservation for four nights, no hookups."

"Right."

"And just yourself? No pets?" He peered at the van like maybe I had a secret pet hidden away inside.

"Just me."

"Okay, I just need your credit card and signature, and we're good to go. I've got you in a prime site, nice and private, all the way in the back of the campground. There's a trail down there that'll take you into the nature preserve."

"Sounds perfect. Thanks."

He passed me the registration form and the sheet with the campground map and rules and the Wi-Fi login info. The password was CRANELAKE. Of course.

"Your first time on the island?"

It's not an island at all, I wanted to argue, but instead, I smiled and nodded. "My first time in Vermont." The lie came out easily. And it wasn't a lie—not really. This *was* Lizzy Shelley's first time in Vermont.

"Fantastic! Welcome. If I can answer any questions, make any recommendations, please let me know. I'm the owner, Steve. We've got activities going on every day; schedule's on the back side of the map. Tonight, s'mores and campfire sing-along starting at seven." He beamed a pleased *how can you go wrong with s'mores and singing?* smile.

I smiled back. "Thanks. I'm looking forward to taking it easy. Having the time to decompress, you know?"

"You're in the perfect place for that. Give a shout if you need anything. We've got kayaks and canoes to rent if you want to get out on the water. Nothing more relaxing than that."

I thanked him, hopped back into my van, and headed for Site 23, which turned out to be perfect. No close neighbors, all the way at the end of the campground, up against the woods. I backed the van in, pleased at the shade and cover the surrounding trees gave me. The front of the site was open and sunny enough for my solar panels.

First order of business: making a cup of coffee. Then I sat down at the picnic table outside with my laptop to try to log on to the Wi-Fi. I wanted to quickly finish and upload my podcast about the Honey Island swamp monster. I'd decided to leave the *Where's Lizzy now?* field on my website set to Louisiana for the time being. I checked the most recent comments and posts in the forums—strange lights in Utah, shadowy figures with red eyes in Oregon, a large cat that walked upright in Tennessee—nothing that couldn't wait.

I was finishing the final edits to the Honey Island podcast when I heard a small engine coming my way, and looked up to see a four-wheeler pulling up right in front of my site. A teenage kid was driving it, dressed in khaki shorts and a green Chickering Island Campground T-shirt. The back of the four-wheeler had a trash barrel strapped to it and a collection of tools: rake, hoe, shovel. I slipped off my headphones and waved at him.

"No way!" the guy said, hopping off the four-wheeler and practically skipping over to me with a goofy grin. "Lizzy Shelley! I knew it had to be you. I mean, how many Lizzy Shelleys with Ford Transit conversions can there be, right? I saw it on the registration form and just about flipped!"

I sighed. So much for keeping a low profile. I should have used a fake name.

This had been happening more and more often since the season of *Monsters Among Us* had aired. I'd always been recognized and fawned over at conventions and conferences, but outside of that, before the TV show, most people hadn't had a clue who I was or what I did, which was exactly how I liked it. Now I had total strangers approaching me, running up to me in grocery stores and gas stations, feeling like they actually knew me, asking to take selfies with me. It was unsettling.

The kid walked closer. "I'm a huge fan! I've been following you since the early days—way before the TV show, before the podcast even, when you just had the blog. When I was a little kid, I formed this monster club, totally inspired by you! We went out in the woods looking for bigfoot and stuff. You're, like . . . amazing!"

I smiled gratefully, but I hoped not too warmly. "Thank you."

Thought: *Now, be a good boy and go away.*

"God, I can't believe you're here!" He moved closer, looked down at my computer. "Are you working on a podcast right now?"

"Finishing one up," I said, snapping the laptop closed.

"Louisiana, right?" he asked.

I nodded.

"The Honey Island swamp monster," he went on. "Did you see it?"

I shook my head. "No, but I think I heard it."

"Did you get a recording?"

"Unfortunately not."

He shrugged. "Next time," he said as he rocked back on his heels,

smiling at me. Skinny, red-haired, and freckled. I guessed he was seven-
teen or eighteen, tops. "You're here about Rattling Jane, right?"

I smiled. "You guessed it."

"Wanna know what I know?" he asked hopefully. "Interview me?
I've got time right now."

"I'd love to." Though the last thing I wanted to do was encourage
this kid, I figured it couldn't hurt to get a local teen's take on Rattling
Jane. In a place this small, chances were that he knew the girl who'd
gone missing.

"Don't you need your recorder or something?" he asked.

"Sure," I said. I got up and went to the van for the digital recorder
and mics, bringing everything out to the picnic table, where I plugged
in the mics and set them up on stands for each of us. I flipped everything on and did a little test to check the levels.

When I was satisfied, I gave him the thumbs-up and said, "This is
Lizzy Shelley. It's the twentieth of August. I'm here on Chickering Island with . . ." I looked at the campground worker.

"Dave. Dave Gibbs, but people here on the island call me Skink."

"Skink?"

"Yeah, I'm, like, this big reptile guy. I've got over twenty lizards." He
was beaming with pride.

"Wow," I said sincerely.

He nodded excitedly. "Been keeping them since I was a little kid.
The first one I got, Norman, he was a blue-tongued skink. I named him
after Norman Bates in *Psycho*. I guess I was kind of a quirky kid. Lizards. Monster Club. Horror movies." His green eyes twinkled, and a
dimple in his left cheek appeared when he smiled.

I grinned back at him, thinking how much my brother would have
loved this guy. The young version of my brother, not Charlie.

"So, Skink, what can you tell me about Rattling Jane?"

He leaned in closer to the microphone, looking very serious. "Well, there're lots of stories. Let's see, to start with, she comes up out of the lake and is made out of fish bones, driftwood, weeds, and old feathers—she uses whatever she can find in the water to give herself a body to come up on land. When the wind blows through her, she, like, rattles and clatters like a bunch of wind chimes. That's how she got her name. They say you hear her coming before you see her."

I shivered. I didn't like this image, not one bit—a creature with no form of its own, assembled from random bits of detritus. The ghostlike monsters always got to me the most. But I thought fear was a good thing—the day I stopped being afraid and on guard was the day I'd let my defenses down. Fear kept me on my toes.

"If you walk around the island," Skink went on, "you'll see sculptures of her, like scarecrows with sea glass and old silverware and stuff hanging off of them to make noises. And they're all looking out at the lake. It's supposed to be good luck."

"Have you ever seen her?"

He shook his head, looking forlorn. "No. But they say you can call her. Bring something shiny to the water and call and she'll come. And she'll hand you a pebble from down at the bottom of the lake. Hold on to that pebble and make a wish and you'll get what you wish for."

"But you haven't tried?"

"Sure, I've tried! I've tried plenty. I've been going down to the water and calling my whole life practically, but she's never come for me." He kicked at the ground with his tan work boot.

I nodded understandingly. "Do you know anyone who's seen her?" I asked.

"Plenty of people claim they have." He looked up at me, lowered his voice. "That girl who disappeared a couple days ago, Lauren Schumacher, you heard about that, right?"

I shook my head, feigning ignorance. "No. Tell me."

"Well, she said she'd seen her. That she'd seen her a couple of times. She had the pebble and everything. Showed it to people in town, friends."

"So Lauren's local?"

"Nah. Tourist. From Massachusetts. Her family has rented a place here for a few weeks every summer for years, though."

"She had friends here, then?"

"Kids she hung out with. Other summer people, but some locals. She showed them the pebble, told them she'd met Rattling Jane, but I don't think anyone really believed her. They thought it was just for attention. She talked a lot of shit, this girl. Always trying to sound tough and impress people."

"Did you know her well?"

"A little. I mean, the kids she hung out with, they're friends of mine, so I'd see her around with them. We hung out a couple times."

I gestured for him to go on.

"Everyone says she ran away. Trouble at home and stuff like that. But me, I'm not so sure."

"What do you think happened?"

He rubbed his chin. "Maybe a girl like that, in trouble all the time, smoking pot down by the docks, fighting with her parents, maybe she's exactly the kind of girl Rattling Jane would show herself to, you know? 'Cause no one's gonna believe her, right?"

I nodded. Maybe this guy was smarter than he looked.

When he spoke again, his voice was so low it was practically a whisper. And before he said the words, he looked around to be sure no one was listening. "I think maybe Rattling Jane got her."

"Got her?" A lump formed in my throat.

He chewed his lip worriedly. "She takes people sometimes. Drags them back down into the water. No one ever sees them again."

Vi

June 10, 1978

THE BASEMENT WAS strictly off-limits. You had to be invited down, and that only happened when Gran was offering certain lessons. Dissections and chemistry experiments were done in the basement. And studying things under the microscope. But the rule was they were never, ever to come down without permission. The basement was Gran's realm, her workshop and laboratory, and the only place in the entire house they were forbidden to enter.

Vi crept slowly down the old wooden stairs, which let out little warning creaks with each step: *Intruder!* they seemed to say. She held tight to the smooth wooden railing, smelled formaldehyde, bleach, stale cigarette smoke. Her heart was beating fast. She wanted to turn back, but knew she couldn't. She needed to find a clue about Iris. Something, anything to help her figure out who she was and where she came from. And the basement seemed like the best place to start.

Vi stepped onto the cement floor, letting her eyes adjust to the dim light. The fluorescent tubes overhead seemed to pulsate, growing bright then dim. She moved beneath them, listening to their hum until she was sure she could hear words, the God of Clues whispering: *This way, this way, you're getting warmer!*

But behind those whispers, she was sure she heard another voice warning her: *Go back. Get out!*

The truth was, Vi hated the basement. Everything about it frightened her: the darkness; the noises the animals made; the way the smells of formaldehyde, rubbing alcohol, and bleach all mingled and got caught in her nose and the back of her throat, making her feel like she couldn't breathe.

She wanted to get this over as fast as possible. Take a quick look and get out. She drew a deep breath to try to relax herself as she looked around.

A row of shelves on the left was lined with medical books and jars of different things floating in cloudy formaldehyde: animal brains, a fetal pig, the heart of a deer. The tiny pig frightened her the most: its perfect little white body, tiny snout and hooves, all curled up like it was sleeping, still waiting to be born. Every time she saw it, she half expected it to open its eyes, kick out at the glass, swim up to the surface of the jar gasping for air.

Along the right wall of the basement, shelves held the wire cages full of mice and rats used for experiments—all albino, their eyes glowing red like tiny demons. The mice ran round and round on squeaky metal wheels, going nowhere.

Beside the cages, leaning against the wall, was the wooden maze Gran used with the mice and rats, testing how different medications and treatments affected the rodents' ability to navigate.

At the far end of the basement, a lamp and a microscope sat on a long worktable.

In the middle of the room stood the stainless steel dissection table. Gran was fascinated by the brain: not just the thoughts and emotions it engendered, but the actual physical gray matter. She spent a lot of time studying animal brains, taking thin slices of them and turning them into slides so she could look at them up close. Like maybe sickness and insanity touched each cell, like the key to fixing it might be hidden there.

Vi stood frozen, listening to the mice and rats: *Go back, go back,* they seemed to chatter. *We'll tell on you. Tell her you were here.*

She had never disobeyed Gran. Not once. Not ever.

Doing this felt all wrong and made her head and whole body feel all tangled up. But at the same time, it gave her this strange rush. She was Gran's good girl, but here she was doing something truly bad. Something against all the rules.

But Gran wasn't going to catch her. They'd worked out a plan.

Eric and Iris were upstairs, standing guard.

Iris was perched at the top of the stairs, ready to signal. If Gran was coming, she would flash the lights: off, on; off, on. Eric was by the front door, watching. If he saw Gran coming across the yard from the Inn, he'd give Iris the signal, then run and stall Gran before she got to the house, giving Vi time to put things right in the basement and get upstairs.

"Stall her how?" Vi had asked.

"I don't know." He'd shrugged. "Maybe I'll tell her I saw Big White Rat? Caught him even, but he got away."

Vi had nodded. It was a good plan.

She walked deeper into the basement, looking around, unsure what she was even looking for, but feeling there was a clue waiting for her. She also had the strange sense that she wasn't alone down there—that someone was watching her. She searched the dark shadows, knowing it was foolish, knowing she was alone, yet the feeling lingered.

The mice and rats rustled in their cages, seemed to call out, *This way, this way if you dare.* She turned and went over to the rodents, all white, all lined up in wire cages with numbers written on the front.

"Can't you give them actual names?" Eric complained whenever he came down and saw the numbers on the cages.

"Do you think they really mind?" Gran asked with an indulgent smile.

"I would if I were them. Being called Number 212 instead of Eric."

She laughed aloud, tousled his hair. "Thank goodness you're a boy and not a lab mouse, then."

Some of the mice and rats were active. Some sleeping, listless. One was so still, Vi was sure it must be dead, although she was afraid to look too closely. All of them had red eyes that seemed to glow, sharp yellow-orange teeth. In truth, Vi was a little scared of the animals. The way they smelled of antiseptic. Some had shaved patches, and tiny sutures. She held her breath as she passed.

Beyond the cages, Vi paused at the exam table, clean stainless steel. She knew so many of the unfortunate rodents would end up here, victims of Gran's scalpel. Some would end up with their skulls sliced with a tiny saw, their brains cut into thin slivers and pasted onto glass slides. Gran believed in what she called a holistic approach to psychiatry. Brain and body were connected, she always said. If something happened to your hand, it affected your entire body, including your brain.

"We carry all our traumas, all our body memories with us," she explained. One of the things she was trying to learn was how to help people let go of those memories, start over.

Vi turned on the bright surgical light above the table to help illuminate the room. She looked down and saw her own reflection in the steel's mirrorlike surface, wavery and strange as if it weren't her at all, but someone else pretending to be her. Behind it, a shadow seemed to move. She jumped back, spun around.

Nothing. No one.

Squeak, squeak went the interminable metal wheels.

•   •   •   •

VI WALKED OVER to the workbench area, sat down on the stool, flipped on the crook-necked work lamp. Gran's microscope was there, with a slide tucked in. She turned on the microscope's light and looked down, using the knob to focus. Blood, cells, the cross section of a tiny mouse brain. She switched the magnification, pulling back. It looked like a flower.

All living things were related to each other in some long-ago way. Vi knew that. The parasite. The worm. The great white shark with rows and rows of teeth. Vi herself. They were all connected. Vi's skin prickled a little when she thought about it.

She loved it when Gran told her about evolution, how every animal on earth came from one long-ago ancestor. One creature, slick and gasping, that had wormed its way out of the ocean.

We are stardust, like the Joni Mitchell song.

I am, I said, like Neil Diamond sang.

Gran said people were not done evolving yet; that it was an ongoing process. "Think of it, Violet," she'd said to her once. "Human beings are a work in progress. And what if we as scientists, as doctors, can find ways to help that progress along?"

A gold pack of Benson & Hedges sat next to an ashtray full of cigarette butts. Vi ran her fingers over the pack. To the left of the cigarettes was a white metal cabinet that held all the medications Gran used in her experiments. It also held the chloroform and the killing jar Gran used when it was time to put an animal out of its misery. Part of being a doctor, she'd explained, was not letting any creature suffer.

Last month, she'd brought Vi down to the basement and taught her how to use the killing jar. An unfortunate mouse had undergone a treatment that hadn't worked. It was no longer able to eat or drink and was just curled up in the corner of its cage, twitching.

Vi knew she shouldn't feel bad, but she did. She felt bad for every single animal that didn't make it. But Gran said the rodents had served a greater purpose, given their lives so that she could learn things that would help her heal her human patients.

Following Gran's instructions, Vi had unscrewed the lid of the chloroform and squeezed the eyedropper the way she had been shown.

Gran explained that, like ether, chloroform was used as an early anesthetic for surgery—they'd probably used it at the Inn, back when it was a Civil War hospital, for amputations on the soldiers. They'd soaked a rag with the sweet-smelling liquid and held it over the patient's face. But Vi had been taught that too much for too long would paralyze the lungs.

"Careful, Violet, don't spill," Gran had warned as Vi soaked the cotton ball, held with forceps, carefully placing it into the glass jar that had once held string beans or beets from the garden. Gran lifted the animal gently from its cage and handed it to Vi. Vi stroked the mouse's tiny white head, an *I'm sorry* stroke, felt its solid little skull beneath its silky fur, the scrabbling of its paws, the quick beat of its heart. She dropped the mouse into the jar and screwed on the lid.

She'd prayed to the God of Mercy: *Let it be over soon*, then bit her lip and waited, telling herself she'd hold her breath until it was over.

Don't cry, don't cry, don't cry.

Doctors didn't cry. Doctors didn't let emotions cloud their thinking or get in the way of doing what needed to be done.

Vi had never once seen Gran cry.

At first, the little white mouse had struggled, scrabbling frantically at the glass, trying to climb the smooth walls with an energy Vi couldn't believe the poor creature possessed. Then, after about thirty seconds, it stopped moving. Went to sleep.

Vi let out the breath she'd been holding.

"Don't take the lid off yet," Gran had instructed. "Make sure it's gone. Watch for respiration."

Vi watched the mouse, saw its breathing slow. At last, there were no movements.

She was sure it was dead, but she waited another thirty seconds, looking at the second hand of her Timex. *Tick. Tick. Tick.*

She stared down at the jar in her hand, wondering if the mouse's soul was trapped in there, hovering like a moist puff of air. If mice even had souls. Gran didn't believe in souls. She believed in the id, the ego, the superego. She believed living creatures were a complicated mix of cells, chemicals, and neurons. But souls? Spirits? Where was the proof of that? Where was the evidence?

"Well done, Violet," Gran had said, putting a hand on her shoulder and giving it a squeeze. Then she'd dumped the mouse into the metal trash can. Later, when she wasn't looking, Vi had taken it out, brought it outside, and buried it in the garden, marking the spot with a little black stone.

* * *

NOW VI TRIED opening the cabinet where the killing jar and chloroform were kept, but it was locked.

There was an empty martini glass to the right of the microscope. A sunflower plate covered in sandwich crumbs.

To the left of the microscope was a stack of books: a medical dictionary, *Physicians' Desk Reference*, an anatomy book, the *Atlas of Surgical Operations*.

Next to the stack was one of Gran's notebooks: a composition book with a black-and-white speckled cover, a pen resting on top.

Open me if you dare, it taunted.

Gran kept a whole series of notebooks. She wrote everything down: patient notes, results of her experiments.

Vi reached for the notebook as sweat gathered between her shoulder blades, making her whole back feel chilled.

Shoulder blades were reminders that we're not all that far removed from the winged beasts, Vi thought. Sometimes she could almost imagine it, what it might be like to have wings, to soar. In her dreams, she often flew. She opened her bedroom window and flew out into the night, circling over the house, over the Inn, going up higher and higher until everything familiar was just a speck.

She had that same sense now, of soaring and looking down on things from far away. Like she wasn't really attached to her body anymore.

The mice and rats rustled and chewed and chattered little warnings in their cages behind her. Round and round they went on squeaky wheels. Round and round went Vi's thoughts as she looked at her grandmother's notebook.

Do it.

Don't do it.

Do it.

She turned, searched the shadows again. Saw the red eyes of the rodents watching, the eyes of the fetal pig in the jar closed, yet seemingly waiting to see what she might do.

Gran's notebooks were off-limits. Never to be opened or read. Even touching them was against the rules.

But Vi had promised Iris.

And promises meant something.

She opened the notebook to the first page, dated nearly two months ago.

Who are we without our memories?

Without our fears?

Without our traumas?

What does the body remember that the mind does not?
Is it possible that memories exist on a cellular level?
If so, is there a way to wipe the cell clean, to make it forget?

There were drawings of cells, notes Vi didn't understand, some in Latin, with what looked like a chemical formula.

Vi flipped to another page:

L.C. not doing well lately. Sending her down to B West.
May need to consider more extreme measures.

She flipped ahead again and came to the last entry, dated yesterday:

Mayflower Project Notes:
Patient S continues to show tremendous progress. She seems to
have no memory of anything that came before, or of her time
in B West. She is learning new things every day and tests above
level in all areas. I plan to continue medication regime and
hypnosis. She is, by far, my greatest success. Perhaps, one day,
I'll be able to show her off to the world, to truly—

The lights went off, then on again.

The signal!

Vi slammed the notebook closed and put it back where she'd found it, replacing the pen resting on top. She turned out the light by the desk and the one above the surgical table. Scanning the basement, she searched for anything else she might have touched, anything out of place. But there was nothing. She was sure. The overhead lights flickered again, off-on, off-on, faster, more desperate.

Vi took the stairs two at a time. Iris, waiting at the top, gave Vi a panicked look. They could hear Gran and Eric talking on the front porch. Flicking the lights off, they hurried into the living room and turned on the TV, leaping onto the couch. *The Price Is Right* was on, a woman in a flowered dress spinning a big wheel.

Gran walked through the front door with Eric on her heels.

"I'm telling you, Gran, I saw Big White Rat. He—"

"Not now, Eric," Gran snapped. She wasn't usually so short with them. Maybe something bad had happened at the Inn.

"But I—"

"I'm going into my study. I need to make a call and do some work. I'm not to be disturbed. Not unless it involves a true emergency, which most certainly does not include any rodent sightings. Do you understand?"

"Yes, Gran," Eric said.

She walked down the hall toward her study, her feet shuffling along in her slippers. The door closed, and Vi heard the scratch and thump of the brass dead bolt on the other side being slid into place.

Eric came into the living room, whispered, "Did you find anything?"

Vi didn't answer. She jumped up, headed for the kitchen.

"What are you doing?" Eric asked, again in a whisper. He and Iris followed her to the wall phone in the kitchen, where she put her finger over her lips: *shhh.*

Vi waited a second, then lifted the handset of the wall-mounted phone while holding down the metal cradle, keeping it hung up. She covered the bottom of the handset with her palm, held her breath, and slowly eased up the metal cradle.

Gran was speaking sharply. "—don't need this, Thad."

Vi could hear Dr. Hutchins breathing, fast and a little wheezy. She pictured his funny ostrich head, his beady eyes that blinked a little too often.

"She's new, isn't she supposed to ask questions?" His voice was higher than most men's, and Vi thought it could easily be mistaken for a woman's.

Gran sighed. "Yesterday she asked where the charts and records for patients down in B West were kept. Why no nurses were assigned rounds down there."

Eric moved closer, trying to hear. Vi shook her head, took a step back.

"These are all understandable questions, Dr. Hildreth," he said. Gran called him by his first name, but Vi had never, ever heard him call her anything but Dr. Hildreth.

"I know," Gran said, sounding exasperated. "But Patty doesn't ever seem satisfied with my answers."

Patty.

The new nurse at the Inn, the really young one, just out of school. Vi hadn't met her yet, but she'd seen her driving up to the Inn in her little yellow Volkswagen Beetle, her long hair feathered back, the skirt on her uniform a little shorter than the skirts of the other nurses. Patty was Dr. Hutchins's niece, and he'd pushed hard to get her the job. Vi had heard him and Gran discussing it for weeks. Gran was against it from the beginning, saying she lacked experience. Dr. Hutchins said that was exactly what made her perfect—that they could train her, could mold her into the ideal employee for the Inn.

"So what did you tell her about B West?" Dr. Hutchins asked now.

Vi bit her lip. B West! Gran had written about it in her notebook.

There was a pause, while Gran inhaled, then blew out a slow, hissing breath. During important calls, or when she was trying to solve a difficult problem, she paced and smoked, said smoking helped her think. Vi listened hard, pressing her ear against the phone. "I told her we didn't use B West for patients. Not anymore. That the basement is just for storage."

This was followed by silence, another intake of breath, then an exhale. More pacing, the swooshing shuffle of Gran's slippers across the wooden floor.

Eric moved toward Vi again, pulling at the phone, but Vi held tight.

"Then today she decided to try to see for herself. I caught her going down into the basement."

Dr. Hutchins made a funny grunting sound.

Gran continued, her voice rising in exasperation. "I told her she needed to stick to her assigned area. She said she'd heard some of the patients talking. Telling stories about B West."

"What kind of stories?" Dr. Hutchins asked.

"She wouldn't say. But, Thad, I'm telling you right now, you need to put a leash on her, or we'll have to let her go."

Eric tugged at the phone again and Vi shoved him away. He tripped over one of the kitchen chairs, sending it crashing to the floor.

Vi kept the mouthpiece covered, held her breath.

Had Gran and Dr. Hutchins heard? Did they know Vi was listening?

Iris helped Eric up.

Vi kept her ear pressed against the phone, listening. It was quiet. Too quiet. Only a slight crackle in the line.

"I understand," Dr. Hutchins said at last. "I'll talk to Patty. She won't ask anything about the basement again. You have my word."

"Good," Gran said, and hung up so hard Vi jumped.

Vi gently placed the handset back in the cradle of the kitchen phone.

"You idiot," she said to her brother. "She could have heard us!"

"You could have let me listen," Eric whined. "Who was she even talking to? Was it about Iris?"

"It was Dr. Hutchins. And I'm not sure exactly what they were talking about," Vi said. "But I know what we have to do next."

"What?" Eric asked.

"Get into the Inn and take a look around. Talk to the new nurse, Patty."

Eric shook his head. "How are we going to get past Miss Evil?"

"We'll find a way," Vi said, looking at Iris. "We have to."

The Helping Hand of God: The True Story of the Hillside Inn

By Julia Tetreault, Dark Passages Press, 1980

Patty Sheridan was a twenty-two-year-old, hired right out of nursing school at the University of Vermont to come and work at the Hillside Inn.

She's left nursing for good now, she says. She currently lives in Santa Fe, New Mexico, where she waits tables and takes painting classes. She's got a serious boyfriend, and they've just adopted a dog.

We met up in a café on the plaza in Santa Fe. Patty's wearing denim overalls spattered with paint. Her hair is pulled back in a perky ponytail. She's got bright blue eyes that seem to be watching everything at once. But I can see sorrow and regret there, just beneath the surface.

"No way would I go back to nursing," she tells me, fiddling with a turquoise and silver bracelet she wears. "Or even back to Vermont. I had to get away, you know? Go somewhere where no one knew me, where no one had ever heard of the Hillside Inn."

She explains that she should never have been hired there to begin with. Other than a two-week rotation during nursing school at the Vermont State Hospital, she had no experience in a psychiatric setting. "I had no business being there," she says. "This was an elite institution, and I was totally green."

Her uncle, Dr. Thadeus Hutchins, codirector of the Inn, got her the job.

"They offered me way more money than any of the entry-level positions I'd been thinking of taking," she explains. "My friends, the gals I went to school with, they said I'd be crazy not to take the job. And the building . . . it's beautiful, right? Did you know it's on the National Register of Historic Places?"

I nod.

"It seemed like the dream job at first, you know? For the most part, our patients were pretty high functioning. And Dr. Hildreth was brilliant. Totally charismatic. When she walked into a room, everyone just stopped and focused on her. She was hot shit—a woman who wasn't just a pioneering psychiatrist, but the director of a nationally recognized mental health center. She looked like a grandma—real tiny with this halo of gray hair, cat-eye glasses, always in a pantsuit with a pretty scarf—but when she spoke, everyone stopped to listen. The patients and staff all had so much respect for her. I felt so lucky to be there at first."

She fiddles with her teacup, then explains that almost immediately she knew something wasn't right at the Inn. As she speaks, she hunches over, shrinks down in her seat like she's trying to disappear.

"I worked the overnights," she says, voice low, confessional. "Patients would talk to me. Tell me stuff when the doctors and other staff weren't around. I heard rumors." She shakes her head, turns away. When she turns back, there are tears in her eyes. "Honestly, I blame myself. I could have stopped things much sooner. I should have gone to the police, or the board of nursing, someone—told them what I thought was going on. Then maybe things would have turned out differently. My role in it all keeps me up at night."

THE BOOK OF MONSTERS

By Violet Hildreth and Iris Whose Last Name We Don't Know

Illustrations by Eric Hildreth

1978

HOW TO MAKE A MONSTER

Sculpt it from mud, ashes, and bones.

Stitch it together with body parts dug up out of the ground.

Bring it to life with electricity and light.

Do a spell on a full moon with thirteen black candles and the blood of a wolf.

Mutter the words of an ancient curse.

Blend a terrible potion.

Use radiation.

A bite.

A sting.

A kiss.

There are as many ways to make one as there are monsters.

But you must ask yourself: Who is the real monster? The creature being made, or the one creating it?

Vi

June 12, 1978

A S VI WALKED up the front steps to the Inn, she thought of the old photographs Gran had shown her from back when it was a Civil War hospital, and then later, when it was a sanatorium for people with tuberculosis. Vi had studied the images: nurses in uniform tending to patients in wheelchairs on the lawn or in metal-framed beds tented over with crisp white sheets. She wondered how many people had died in that old hospital: soldiers missing limbs, people coughing up blood.

And how many of those who'd died were trapped there still, roaming the halls, stuck forever in the place where they took their last breath?

She'd asked Gran once if anyone had ever seen a ghost there. Gran had looked at her with an amused smile. "It's a psychiatric hospital, Violet. People see all kinds of unusual things. But if you're asking me if I think it's haunted, then, no. I don't believe places can be haunted. Only people, and not in a supernatural way. People are only haunted by their pasts."

Vi walked through the main doors of the Inn and into the reception area, her eye on the door to the basement. Was there something down there? A secret part of the hospital—B West?

The window to the office slid open, and Miss Ev scowled at Vi. "Dr. Hildreth is in a staff meeting," she said. "She's not to be disturbed."

Vi smiled her biggest, sweetest smile and stepped forward. "Actually, Miss Ev, I'm not here to see Gran. I came to see you."

Now the woman's whole face pinched together, her mouth puckering as if she'd eaten something sour. "Me?"

Vi nodded. "See, I've got this idea. A *proposal*, really."

"Proposal?"

She'd already gotten Gran on board. Now she just needed to hook Miss Ev.

Vi nodded again. "I ran it by Gran last night, and she told me I should come talk to you. We both agreed you were the best person here to handle this . . . idea. In fact, you're the *only one*, really." She smiled again, innocently. "I wrote everything out. I've even got sketches. May I come into the office to show you?"

"If you must," Miss Ev said. She got up, pushing herself out of the chair and huffing her way over to the door to unlock it, her feet clomp, clomp, clomping. Vi stepped in.

Vi had never been inside Miss Ev's realm. It wasn't a large office, and a great deal of it was taken up by an L-shaped desk. One side had the window with the sliding glass so she could keep an eye on the Common Room and greet (more like stop and interrogate) any visitors. The desk held a phone with buttons for each separate line so she could patch calls through to staff all over the building, plus a big electric Smith Corona typewriter and a set of wire baskets for paperwork. And on the wall, cubbies served as mailboxes for the staff and patients. Under the mailboxes, keys hung on hooks, each one carefully labeled with a colored tag: STAFF OFFICE WING; DR. HILDRETH'S OFFICE; KITCHEN;

DINING; DAY ROOM; BACK DOOR; FRONT DOOR; SECOND FLOOR MED CABINET; FILE ROOM.

Vi's eyes caught the file room key, and her fingers twitched a little. There were no keys for the basement. Nothing that said B WEST. She flicked her eyes away before Miss Ev could catch her looking.

"Well," Miss Ev said. "What is it you want? I don't have all day, Violet." She dropped back into her chair and drummed her fingers on the desk littered with a can of Tab, an ashtray, a cigarette pack, a lighter, and a book of crossword puzzles. Her nails were long, filed to points and painted candy-apple red.

"See, the thing is," Vi began, "I've been studying habitat."

"Habitat?"

"Yeah, it's the environment an organism lives in, like an animal or a plant, it's where they live, it's got what they need to—"

"I know perfectly well what a habitat is," Miss Ev said. She reached for the pack of cigarettes on her desk, shook one out, and grabbed the yellow plastic lighter. A flick of her thumb and a flame jumped to life, igniting the Pall Mall. She blew the first puff of smoke in Vi's direction, as if hoping to make her disappear.

Vi nodded and smiled. "I knew you would." She turned, looked out the row of windows to the front lawn. In front of each window hung a bird feeder. Miss Evelyn believed that watching the birds was far more entertaining than watching television, and often said so. The woman loved her birds. She had bird sweaters. Bird coffee cups. A bird calendar. Bird pictures were hanging up all over the office. "That's what makes you the perfect person to help oversee my project."

Vi pulled out the folder she'd carried over and laid the papers out on the desk. "A bird garden," she said. She pointed down at the drawing that Eric had worked on so carefully last night. "Bushes, flowers, and plants specially picked out to provide good habitat. We'll have a birdbath, maybe even a fountain. Some benches to sit and watch the birds.

Nest boxes and birdhouses. I was reading about purple martins, they live in colonies. I thought we could build a big house just for them. I found a picture in a book in Gran's library."

Miss Evelyn leaned down and looked at the sketches and notes through the haze of her cigarette smoke.

"We'd do it right in the front yard here, so you could see it all day."

Miss Ev's mouth twitched in what Vi thought might be the beginning of a smile.

"The patients could help clear the area, build the garden beds, do the plantings. They could make birdhouses and feeders. But I figured that since you're the big bird expert, you should oversee the whole project. Gran's too busy. And besides, she doesn't know much about birds." Vi smiled. "And Gran and I thought the new nurse could help too."

Miss Ev frowned. "Patty?"

Vi leaned closer, spoke in a low voice, like they were good friends sharing a secret. "Patty's new, and Gran thought maybe this project would be a good way for her to get to know the residents. That it might help her . . . fit in."

Miss Ev sat stone-faced, not saying a thing.

"So, will you do it?" Vi pointed out the little label at the bottom of the drawing, the icing on the cake: EVELYN'S BIRD GARDEN.

"If I can find the time," Miss Ev said, which, Vi understood, was the closest she'd ever get to a yes.

"Great! Hey, is Patty around? Maybe I could talk to her, take her outside and show her the area? Tell her about it?"

Miss Ev picked up the phone, punched a button, said, "Send Patty to see me. Yes, *now*." She hung up.

There was a rapping at the window. Tom's face was peering through.

"Go back to group, Tom," Miss Ev said through the glass.

"Please, Miss Evelyn. I need calamine lotion and they won't give me any. Please. Have mercy." He was tearing at his hairy arms.

"You go on outside, Violet," Miss Ev said. "I'll send Patty out to you." She pushed a button on the phone and barked, "Will someone please get down here and retrieve Tom. You've got to stop letting the patients wander like this!"

Vi passed Tom in the front hall. "How you doing, Tom?"

"So itchy," he said.

"What do you think it is?" Vi asked.

"Dr. Hildreth, she says it's nothing. But I can feel them."

"Them?"

"They're just under the skin, Violets are blue. They're always there."

In five minutes, Patty appeared outside, looking flustered and confused. "Evelyn sent me," she said. "To talk about a project?" She blinked at Vi as if she didn't know what to make of her.

"Hi! I'm Violet, Dr. Hildreth's granddaughter." Vi held out her hand, and Patty shook it. Vi was good at dealing with adults; Gran had made it a point of teaching her to look them in the eye, be respectful, shake hands, make small talk and always say please and thank you.

"You earn people's respect by treating them with respect," Gran had said. "Be intelligent and well-spoken. Let your maturity shine through, Violet."

Vi smiled at Patty and thanked her for taking the time to come.

"Here's the thing," Vi said in a low voice, because even though the window to Miss Ev's office was closed, she could feel the woman watching. "We have to look like we're talking about the garden."

Patty looked more puzzled than ever. At last she said, "Evelyn told me a little about the garden. I think it's a terrific idea." She smiled, and her smile was contagious. "You're the one who came up with it? The whole plan? And Dr. Hildreth okayed it?"

Vi nodded. "She thinks it's a great idea. Which it is. But there's something else. A secret thing. The garden isn't the whole reason I'm here."

"It's not?"

"The garden is a cover."

She was taking a chance. She knew it. Patty could go blabbing to Miss Ev and Gran and everyone else about what Vi was about to say, but Vi didn't think she'd do that. The gods were whispering in her ear: *Tell her, she'll help you, trust her.* And the gods were rarely wrong.

"A *cover*?" Patty asked, her tone a little sassy, like she was losing patience. She turned and looked back at the Inn. She probably had charting to do, patients waiting for meds. Vi could see how young she was—even in her white uniform, she looked like a college kid, not a nurse. She was wearing mascara and blush and pastel-pink eye shadow. She smelled like bubble gum and hair spray.

"I wanted to talk to you. I thought . . . I thought we could share information. Help each other gather intelligence."

"Intelligence?" Patty laughed, shook her head. "Look, you seem like a sweet kid, and I know you're the boss's granddaughter and all, but I'm super busy. I'm happy to help with the garden if Dr. Hildreth wants me to, but I'm not going to play spies with some ten-year-old."

Vi frowned. "I'm thirteen."

"Sorry. I guess I'm not much of a kid expert." Patty turned, started to walk away. "Nice to meet you, Violet."

"Wait," Vi said. Patty turned back, looking exasperated. Vi knew she didn't have long. "Have you heard of anything called the Mayflower Project at the Inn?"

She shook her head. "No."

"What do you know about B West?"

This got her attention. Patty took a step closer to Vi. "Did your grandmother put you up to this?" She looked around, like maybe this was a test and Gran was hiding behind a tree, watching.

Vi thought of that show they sometimes watched with the hidden cameras filming people in crazy situations, how someone would jump out and say, "You're on *Candid Camera*!"

"No!" Vi told Patty. "She can't know we talked about this. She'd kill me and probably fire you. But there's stuff I need to know. And it sounds like you want to know it too. I think we can help each other."

Patty crossed her arms, took a step back. "What is it you want to know?"

"About Iris."

"Who's Iris?"

"A girl. Gran brought her over from the Inn. She's staying with us. She's one of Gran's patients, but she's young. Like my age."

Patty shook her head, her feathered bangs moving over her forehead like wings. "The Inn doesn't treat anyone under eighteen."

"I know. And that's not the only weird part." Vi had her now. She could tell from the way Patty moved closer, eyes wide, mouth a little bit open. The new nurse was hooked into the mystery. "See, Iris doesn't remember anything about who she is or where she came from."

"Are you messing with me? Because if you are—"

"No, I swear. She doesn't even know her name. She just remembers being here, at the Inn with Gran in a green room with no windows."

"A room with no windows?" Patty said.

Behind them, Miss Ev opened her window, looked out at them.

"And I was thinking," Vi said in an extra-loud voice, "that a fountain in the center would be perfect. I bet we can ask Mr. MacDermot to help run water and electricity out to it."

Patty nodded, playing along. "I think a fountain would be lovely. Maybe we can find one that's got a bird design!"

Miss Ev moved back away from the open window.

"I think maybe Iris was in B West," Vi whispered.

Patty lowered her voice too. "The basement is for storage."

"I want to get down there," Vi said.

"No way! Dr. Hildreth and my uncle are the only ones with keys. I don't know what's down there, but I do know it's locked up tight."

Vi nodded. She knew Gran carried a big metal ring of keys in her purse. Maybe the basement key was on it. But getting the keys out of Gran's purse—that seemed impossible.

"Will you help me?" Vi asked.

"Absolutely not. I could lose my job. And for what? Some kid's crazy story? Sorry, no offense, but imagine you were in my shoes. Wouldn't you do the same?"

Vi pressed her point. "I know you're curious about the basement. I know you were asking my grandmother about it. That you've heard stories."

Patty said nothing.

"So maybe there's not a way into the basement right now, but how about Gran's office?" Vi asked. "Do you think you could get me in there?"

Maybe there'd be a clue. Or—did she dare hope?—a key to the basement stashed away in a desk drawer.

"I don't know. I—"

"I may be a kid, but my grandmother listens to me. She tells me all the time how much she values my opinion. If I go home and tell her how great you are, how helpful you're being with the bird garden project—she'll listen. It'll make a difference. Of course, I could also tell her you treated me like a little kid and didn't seem very enthusiastic about helping with the garden."

Patty frowned.

"Please. I'm not asking you for much. Just let me into the building and get me the key to Gran's office. There's one hanging in the main office. Do you ever work nights?"

"Sometimes. I'm doing the overnight on Saturday—eleven p.m. to seven a.m."

"Okay. This Saturday. Get the key to Gran's office and meet me at the back door, west side, at midnight. That's all you have to do. Just let me in."

"I don't know," Patty said.

Miss Ev was in the window again. "Patty! You're needed inside. It seems they've lost Tom again."

Patty blew out a breath. "I've gotta get back to work."

"Thanks," Vi said. "For agreeing to help with the garden. Gran will be really happy to hear how excited you are about it."

Patty nodded and walked away.

Lizzy

August 20, 2019

I PACKED UP THE recording equipment (throwing it into my day bag, just in case) and hopped into my van to do some exploring. As I drove around Chickering Island, I was struck by its tiny size. It was small and crowded: full of tourists, people who'd come for just the day, a weekend, or maybe even the whole summer; people who sat sipping lattes outside the coffee shop, fishing off the pier, riding rented bikes around town.

As I drove, I went over everything Skink had told me. I was used to hearing strange, unbelievable stories. My job was to listen to them, ask the right questions, sift through the stories for the bits of truth that shone and glittered.

The monster stories I'd heard over the years had much in common. There were no specific names. It was often "this guy" or "my uncle had a friend." Details were usually sketchy, as they were with Skink's story. I'd pressed him for details about the people who had supposedly disappeared, been taken down into the lake by Rattling Jane. He couldn't give me a single name or date, could only say that it was for-sure real and it had been going on for a long, long time.

People loved a good creepy story. The need was almost primal: to hear them, have them chill you, then pass them along, embellished with your own details. Fear was a drug, and these stories were a delivery method.

"Some people say Rattling Jane is the vengeful spirit of a woman who was murdered a long time ago, her body dumped at the bottom of the lake," Skink had told me. "Some say she, like . . . *is* the lake."

As vague as parts of the conversation had been, I'd gotten some good leads. I'd learned which house Lauren Schumacher and her family rented—one of the little cabins out past the winery, in a group of rentals all named for flowers; they stayed in Bluebell. Skink told me that her family had packed up and gone home to Worcester, Massachusetts, sure that that's where Lauren had headed when she ran off.

And then there was the piece of information I'd found the most interesting: that Lauren had told people she'd met Rattling Jane; she'd been given a wishing stone.

What did Lauren Schumacher wish for? I wondered.

◆   ◆   ◆

I PARKED MY van in one of the free public lots, then crossed the street to the clean, wide, brick sidewalk and headed right for the bookstore. It was an old habit: the first stop in any new town was always either the bookstore or the library.

As I walked through the door, I was greeted by a large black standard poodle.

"That's Penny," called the man behind the counter as I scratched the dog behind the ears.

"She's a beauty," I said.

"And she knows it too." The man smiled. "Can I help you find anything in particular?"

"Actually, yes. Do you have any books about the area? About the island and its history? And maybe a map?"

"Absolutely," he said. "We've got a whole local section right here." He came out from behind the counter and led me over to a set of shelves labeled LOCAL.

"If you're looking for something about the island, I'd recommend this," he said, pointing to four copies of *Chickering Island, Now and Then* tucked between *The Angler's Guide to Vermont Waterways* and *Unexplained Vermont*. "There's a map in it. We've also got these." He indicated the free colorful tourist maps next to the door, which listed all the businesses.

I grabbed a copy of the book on local history and *Unexplained Vermont*.

I couldn't help but notice that there, on the second shelf, were three copies of *The Helping Hand of God: The True Story of the Hillside Inn*.

There had been several printings of the book—one with the movie poster on the cover—but this one had a line drawing of the Inn on the cover. The drawing was all wrong. The building looked like a huge Gothic insane asylum with black windows, shadowy figures behind them.

I turned away and went to the register to pay. I thanked the bookseller, said goodbye to Penny, and grabbed one of the free tourist maps from the rack on the way out. Then I made my way down the street to Rum Runners Bar and Grill, figuring I'd plan my next move over food and a beer.

In front of the bar and grill was a sculpture: a life-size woman with a wooden frame and chicken-wire body. She was draped in little pieces of debris—shells, bottle caps, sea glass, pebbles, triangles of cut-up beer cans that sparkled like fish scales—hung by pieces of thin, flexible wire.

The wind picked up, and the objects blew and rattled.

I sidestepped around the unsettling sculpture and through the open door, heading right for the bar. After a quick glance at the menu, I ordered the Vermonter Burger with award-winning local cheddar, island-grown greens, and maple bacon jam, and an IPA brewed in Burlington to wash it down.

"Interesting sculpture out front," I said when the bartender brought me the hazy pale-amber beer.

The bartender smiled. She had short, bleached-blond hair and dramatic eye makeup. "That's Rattling Jane. The most famous resident of the island."

"Oh?" A trick I'd learned long ago—pretend you know nothing, that you're walking in cold to every conversation.

"Yeah. She's our local ghost."

"Really?"

"Some folks say she was involved with rum-running back during Prohibition. She crossed the wrong guy and ended up at the bottom of the lake. The other story is that her sister killed her."

That got my attention. I leaned closer. "Her sister?"

The bartender nodded. "She comes out of that water looking for her sister now and then. Grants wishes to anyone who can help her by giving them a special pebble."

"Wow," I said, reaching to rub at a little tingle at the back of my neck.

The bartender smiled. "That's my favorite of the stories, I think." She leaned forward. "But honestly, between you and me, I think the whole thing was invented as a marketing scheme years ago. You wouldn't believe the number of visitors we get because of Rattling Jane. Who doesn't love a ghost story, right?"

I nodded, took a sip of my beer.

"Your food should be out shortly," the bartender said, heading into the kitchen with a tub of dirty glasses.

"Lizzy!" called a voice behind me. I spun on my stool to see Skink walking in. Great. Was the kid going to follow me everywhere I went?

"You off work already?" I asked as he came bounding over.

"I only work mornings. Clean up the sites before new campers come in. Clean the bathrooms. Cut the grass. All the glamorous jobs. The owner, Steve, he's my uncle."

"Nice," I said. "There are worse summer jobs."

"No doubt," Skink said.

"So what do you do when you're not working for your uncle? You in college somewhere?"

"Nah," he said, settling on the stool beside me. "Not yet, anyway. I just graduated from high school in June. Gonna take some community college classes starting later this month. Do that for a year or so and think about what I might want to get a degree in, maybe apply to a college somewhere far away. Get outta this town for a while."

I nodded. "That's smart. You'll save money doing community college for a year. And I think it's good to take some time to think about what you really want to study."

"That's exactly what my dad says." He smiled at me, then eyed my books. "Looking into local history, huh?"

He picked up *Unexplained Vermont*, flipped through it, then held it out to me. "Look, she's got her own entry. 'Rattling Jane, Chickering Island.'" He showed me the drawing next to the short entry: a woman-shaped figure made of fish skeletons, bird skulls, feathers, rocks, even pieces of trash. In the drawing, she was holding open the palm of her hand to show a small round stone. He read out loud from the entry. "'Where did Rattling Jane come from? What, or who, is she looking for when she ventures out onto the land? Some legends say a lost love.

Some say she's searching for her sister. Whatever or whoever she's looking for—watch out! She's known to take those unlucky enough to meet her back down to the bottom of the lake.'"

"Hey there, Skink," said the bartender, who appeared so suddenly that I jumped. "You here for lunch?"

Skink shut the book. "Nah, just a Coke, please, Sam," he said. When she brought his Coke, he added excitedly, "Do you know who this is?" I shook my head. *No. Don't do this.* The last thing I wanted was for word to spread. "This is Lizzy Shelley. She's got this sick podcast: *The Book of Monsters.* But she's most famous for the TV show!"

"TV?" This got the bartender's attention. "You an actress?"

I shook my head again. The bell in the kitchen dinged.

"*Monsters Among Us!*" Skink said. "You must have seen it—Lizzy and these two other researchers going all over the country. There was one episode where they went into this old silver mine in Texas looking for a chupacabra! Man, that one scared the crap out of me." He smiled at me. "The way you belly-crawled through that tiny tunnel . . . and the scratch marks on the stones—all those animal bones you found. A monster lair for sure!"

I nodded. I didn't have the heart to tell him the scratches and bones had been put there by the production team.

The waitress smiled. "Never seen it, but it sounds cool. Hey, I think your food's ready." She sneaked back to the kitchen.

"Skink," I said as kindly as I could manage, "I appreciate your . . . support and enthusiasm, but I was really hoping to kind of lie low here. Not let people know who I am or what I do."

He grinned. "I get it! Incognito! I totally get that."

"In my experience," I went on, "people can be a little more . . . forthcoming when they think I'm just a regular stranger asking questions. At least at first."

"Forthcoming," he repeated. "Totally. I get it. Listen, I was thinking, maybe you'd like to meet some of the kids Lauren was hanging out with, the ones who saw the stone and heard her stories about meeting Rattling Jane."

"Absolutely," I said, as Sam set my burger down.

"We'll take a walk after you eat," Skink said, stealing a fry off my plate. "I'll show you the exciting sites of Chickering Island."

I nodded and went to work on my food, both bothered and intrigued by the new information I'd gleaned, feeling like it held a secret message just for me:

Rattling Jane was looking for her sister.

Vi

June 17, 1978

IRIS WAS PERCHED on the back of the banana seat on Vi's bike, her arms wrapped tightly around Vi's waist.

Vi called her bike *The Phantom.* It was a red Schwinn Sting-Ray, one-speed, with chopper-style handlebars and a long white banana seat.

Eric followed on his Huffy BMX bike that he'd named *The Hornet.*

Gran didn't let them ride into town very often, which was okay because there wasn't much to do there. They didn't go to the public school. Gran said they were better off learning at home because the school in town was *abysmal* and "no place for exceptional children" like they were. She'd sent Vi there for one day back in kindergarten, not long after she'd taken them in, and the teacher had yelled at Vi for already being able to read and write and for asking to be allowed to read on her own. Vi didn't remember any of it, but Gran got outraged all over again each time she told the story. She'd never even tried to send Eric when he was old enough, she just taught him at home the way she'd been teaching Vi. Gran took a hands-off approach, mostly letting them explore their interests and work independently. "You, my lovelies, are clever enough to know what you need to learn and how best to go about learning it," Gran said. They read a great deal, wrote reports and essays, did experiments, and filled out pages in math workbooks. Each night Gran went over their work, making corrections and suggestions, and helping to plan out the next day's studies. Gran told Vi that she was reading and writing at a college level already. Vi planned to go to college when she turned eighteen: premed, then medical school, just like her dad and Gran. And Gran had promised her she'd be well ahead of the other students by then.

◆　◆　◆

THEY WERE ALLOWED to ride to the library whenever they liked, as long as they promised not to do anything else, not to talk to anyone but the librarians. Sometimes they'd sneak over to the general store after the library to buy candy or soda with their allowance.

Gran took them into town sometimes too, driving down the hill in her old Volvo, to go to Fitzgerald's Supermarket, Ted's Hardware, or The End of the Leash pet shop. Sometimes they'd see other kids, and Vi wished she could talk to them, ride bikes with them—wished she could have normal friends like kids on TV did—but Gran forbade it. She said the townie kids weren't worth the trouble.

Gran took them to Barre or all the way up to Burlington when they needed something that they couldn't buy in Fayeville. They went to Sears to buy clothes, to Woolworth's, and even to bookstores, where Vi would buy horror novels and Eric picked out books about animals.

And sometimes, as a special treat, Gran would bring them all the way to the Howard Johnson's in Barre. It was a forty-minute ride, but when they got there and saw the orange roof with the blue cupola, they'd jump out of the car, practically run to the door. They'd sit at the counter on spinning silver stools with turquoise vinyl tops, and Gran would let them order whatever they wanted. Plates of fried clams, cheeseburgers, french fries, and ice cream. Oh, the ice cream! Twenty-eight flavors to choose from, and Vi wanted to try them all: maple walnut, pineapple, fudge ripple. Eric always got the same thing: chocolate in a cone.

Gran was predictable as a clock: She ordered coffee and a grilled cheese (which Vi didn't understand—she could make the same exact thing at home!) and maple walnut ice cream in a dish. "I know," Gran would say when she caught Vi giving her a *not again* look. "I'm a boring old lady."

Vi and Eric would shake their heads, laugh, tell her she was anything but boring.

"One day, my lovelies," Gran promised, "I'm going to surprise you. I'll order something completely different. A BLT and a banana split. Or maybe I'll be a real devil and ask them to make me something that's not even on the menu."

◆   ◆   ◆

AND THEN THERE were the Saturday night drive-ins. Gran had taken them a few times in her old Volvo, but she found horror movies ridiculous. "Completely implausible," she'd complain as a man turned into a fly or a werewolf, as a vampire showed his fangs and sank them into a beautiful woman's neck.

So she allowed Vi and Eric to ride their bikes to the movies by themselves. But there were rules: They had to ride the back roads to get there (too dangerous on the main road at night), they weren't to talk to anyone while they were there (Gran had given them endless warnings about pervy child molesters and drug pushers eager to get young kids hooked), and they had to come straight home after. Gran even gave them ticket money, but Vi and Eric never paid to get in; they'd discovered a loose section of the chain-link fence that ran along the back parking area and sneaked in each week—leaving them with more money for popcorn, Cokes, and candy.

And now there they were, just like each Saturday night of the summer, careening through the darkness, heading for the Hollywood Drive-in.

Only this time was different. This time, they had Iris with them. Gran had been hesitant. She'd instructed Vi to watch Iris carefully, and if there was any sign that she was uncomfortable or overstimulated, they were to come back immediately.

"Have you ever been to a drive-in?" Vi had asked Iris. But Iris didn't know. Couldn't remember.

"What about a regular movie theater? You've been to one of those, right?"

"No," Iris said, and shook her head.

Vi couldn't imagine what it must be like to have no memory of anything; of any part of your past.

She had been "giving reports" to Gran every evening. Gran knew that Iris was talking now—she'd started talking a little more each day, and Gran was very pleased with her progress. And Gran had explained a little about why people sometimes didn't remember things. It was called amnesia, she told Vi, from the Greek word for forgetfulness. Vi nodded. She'd seen characters with amnesia in TV shows.

"What causes amnesia?" Vi asked.

"Sometimes it's physical, like a head injury or taking a certain kind of drug. Sometimes, a deep psychological trauma."

Vi wondered what had caused Iris's amnesia. If Gran knew, she wasn't saying.

And now that Iris was talking, Gran wanted to know everything Iris said. Vi told her some of it, but there were still a lot of things she kept secret.

She'd told Gran that Iris didn't remember anything, not even her own name, but Vi left out the part about how she had promised to help Iris figure it out. She also left out the fact that Iris had been helping them with their monster book, because the Monster Club was top secret. "She can write," Vi reported. "Her writing is bad, kind of like someone just learning, and she can't spell at all, but she knows her letters and stuff."

Someone must have taught her, Vi knew. She imagined a family somewhere, Iris going to school, having friends, even a real sister maybe.

Gran had nodded as she absorbed all this new information, then leaned forward and clasped her hand around Vi's wrist, fingers feeling her pulse in their familiar way, their own secret handshake. "You're doing a wonderful job with Iris," she'd said, giving a gentle squeeze. "And it's making a difference. I'm proud of you, Violet."

◆   ◆   ◆

THE HOLLYWOOD DRIVE-IN was pretty much the most exciting place in Fayeville—people came from all over to go to the drive-in, and on some weekend nights in the summer, it was totally packed, cars lined up in each row.

The Hollywood had two screens, and every Saturday at sundown, they had two current movies in a row on the main screen, but on screen two they did a Creature Double Feature: two classic horror movies. Vi and Eric had seen them all, of course, both at the theater and whenever they were on TV. Vi scoured the *TV Guide* each week looking for horror movies, for anything that held even the hint of a monster.

Tonight the main screen was showing *Harper Valley PTA* and *The Cat from Outer Space*. The Creature Double Feature was *Bride of Frankenstein* and *Frankenstein Meets the Wolf Man*—two of Vi's favorites. She couldn't wait for Iris to see the big screen, the snack bar where they loaded up on popcorn, Junior Mints, Twizzlers, and Charleston Chews (Eric's favorite).

As she pumped the pedals on her bike, Vi wondered if Iris had ever even tasted Junior Mints or Charleston Chews. If she had, she probably wouldn't remember, so it would be like having them for the first time. Everything was new and strange to Iris. Vi was a little jealous of her, experiencing wonderful things for the first time—Rice Krispies, Pop-Tarts, Tootsie Pops ("How many licks does it take to get to the center?" asked the wise old owl in the commercial), Saturday morning cartoons. She didn't even know who Scooby-Doo was!

But she loved watching Iris try new things. She loved teaching her about Pop Rocks that exploded on your tongue, Creamsicles (Vi's favorite—orange outside, vanilla inside!), and how to work a flashlight. She'd taught Iris how to tie her shoes and put her clothes on so that they weren't backward and inside out.

•   •   •

VI'S LEGS WERE burning from the extra weight of Iris on the seat of her bike. They were almost there now, riding across the field, then around the back lot of Leo's Good Deal Autos, where they sold used cars in front and had a junkyard out back. Vi imagined that Leo took pieces from broken-down cars and pieced them together like one of Eric's chimeras.

Just behind Leo's back lot was the fence for the drive-in. They pulled up right on time—the big screen was lit up with dancing popcorn and candy and cups of ice-cold Coca-Cola, inviting everyone to visit the snack bar, where smiling hot dogs were waiting. They laid their bikes down on the ground, and Vi found the loose section of fence, holding it open for Eric and Iris, then crawling through herself. They settled in at their usual spot: a little mound in the corner of the back row. Speakers on poles blasted out the sound.

Bride of Frankenstein started.

Vi loved the beginning, because there were Mary Shelley, her husband, Percy, and Lord Byron, and the men telling her what a great story she came up with, and she saying there's more of the story to tell. It was a perfect night for such a tale, Mary Shelley told the men, a perfect night for mystery and horror. "The air itself is full of monsters," she said.

Vi leaned over and explained to Iris, "That's the woman who wrote *Frankenstein*. She's the one who started it all."

Vi's heart went out to the monster, burned and shot, bloodhounds on his trail, villagers with pitchforks and torches chasing him down.

"He's not bad," she told Iris as they watched. "Just misunderstood. All he wants is a friend."

And Iris nodded and Vi knew she got it, she truly got it, because wasn't she a little like the monster herself? Scared and misunderstood, all alone in the world?

But Iris wasn't alone. Not anymore. Now she had Vi and Eric.

Vi inched a little closer to Iris, and Iris didn't move away. They sat side by side in the dark, their eyes glued to the screen.

They watched the monster, Boris Karloff in makeup and prosthetic forehead, bolts in his neck, as he was captured, tied to a pole, and paraded through town, then set upright on the pole to be stoned by villagers. Vi always thought he was like Christ in this part, but she knew better than to say that out loud to anyone, even to Iris and Eric.

"See," Vi whispered to Iris when the monster cried at finally making a friend. "He's more human than they are."

As they watched, a new monster was created to be a mate and companion for the original. Electricity brought her to life, just like him. Vi loved the laboratory scenes, the machines all pulsing with light and electricity. And when the lightning struck the kite, the Bride's bandage-wrapped body came to life, and Iris scooched even closer to Vi, side by side. Then Iris reached out and took Vi's hand, and Vi wasn't sure if this meant she was happy or scared, maybe a little of both.

It's a fine line between the two, Vi thought, and she wanted to save that thought, put it away in a drawer to take out and look at later, because it felt important.

Vi held her breath, not wanting any of it to end: Iris holding her hand, the smell of popcorn, the crackle of the drive-in speakers, the movie, the link between bliss and fear.

But end it did.

There was always an ending. And in the monster movies, the monster always died. (At least until the sequel.)

They watched the Bride with her amazing lightning-bolt hair reject the monster; she screamed and gave a terrible hiss, and the monster understood then, knew that he would always be alone. Iris gripped Vi's hand tighter. "We belong dead," the monster said, and he pulled the lever to blow them up, setting fire to the tower, killing them.

Iris began to cry, her whole body lurching and rocking with sobs. She made a low moaning howl that was quiet at first but got louder.

"It's okay," Eric said. "It's just a movie."

She was rocking and howling in earnest now, and people in nearby cars were starting to look.

They were not supposed to be noticed. They were supposed to slip in and out of the movie like shadows. Three kids no one saw.

Vi put her arm around Iris, said, "Come on, shhh, it's okay. Let's go home. We'll go home, it's okay."

Iris didn't answer, just kept crying.

A man stepped toward them, a little unsteady. Vi couldn't see his face because he was backlit by the screen playing the intermission clip with dancing popcorn and candy bars, by the bright floodlights that had come on around the snack bar.

"Your friend okay?" he asked. Vi could smell the beer on him.

"Yeah, she's my sister. She's fine. Just scared. Never seen a monster movie before," Vi said.

Vi got on one side of her, Eric on the other, and they walked her back to the fence, murmuring comforting words, and slipped through. The credits rolled behind them, and people headed for the snack bar and playground for intermission.

The man called out, "Hey, where are you going?" He took a few staggering steps toward the fence, and put his hands on the links.

Vi's heart was pounding as they got on their bikes and pedaled hard away from the drive-in, from the man still standing at the fence, watching them.

They pedaled hard and fast until they were on the dirt road, and then they had to get off and push, because the hill was too steep and Vi couldn't do it with Iris on the seat of her bike.

Eric could have kept riding, but he dismounted too and walked alongside the girls, pushing his bike.

"It was a sad ending, wasn't it?" Vi said to Iris as they trudged uphill.

Iris had stopped crying and howling.

"I'm sorry," Vi said. "We should have warned you."

"They burned up," Iris said.

"That's how it is in monster movies," Eric explained. "The monster always dies."

"Why?" Iris asked.

Vi wasn't sure how to answer.

"Because they don't belong," Eric said, voice low.

And Iris started to cry again, not great howling sobs, but quietly, like a puppy snuffling. "It isn't fair," she said.

Vi held the handlebar of her bike with her right hand, and reached out for Iris's hand with her left. Iris let her take it, and they walked like that in silence, all the way up the hill, the moonlight behind them stretching out their shadows, turning them all into monsters.

The Helping Hand of God:
The True Story of the Hillside Inn

By Julia Tetreault, Dark Passages Press, 1980

Helen Hildreth was married while still finishing her surgical residency. Her husband, John Patterson, was a young chemist whom she'd met in a lecture hall. After finishing his dissertation and completing his doctorate at the University of Vermont, he was offered a job at a pharmaceutical company in Philadelphia. The couple moved, and Helen found a position at Philadelphia General Hospital. She was the only female surgeon at the hospital—a groundbreaking role at the time.

There's a photo of the two of them at a fund-raising dinner for the hospital, taken in 1934. They're holding hands and he's leaning into her, as if he's just whispered something into her ear. She's looking back at him with a smile that radiates trust and affection. I don't know if love can be felt from a photograph taken almost fifty years ago, but it is impossible to look at this image and not conclude that Helen and John were very much in love.

A year and a half into their marriage, Helen gave birth to twins, two girls. Although by all accounts her pregnancy was unremarkable, tragically they were both stillborn, and doctors were unable to resuscitate them.

John was a thin man with a history of asthma who tired easily. After the loss of the twins, he seemed to have trouble getting out of bed.

His breathing worsened, and he began coughing blood.

Tuberculosis was suspected, but the cause was mitral valve stenosis, a narrowing of the mitral valve to the heart, likely from scarlet fever when he was a boy. His heart was enlarged and profoundly damaged by the time the diagnosis was made.

He was, quite literally, going to die of a broken heart.

He was dead within six months, making Helen a widow at thirty. According to letters written to her father, she blamed herself for the deaths of both of her daughters, and even more so for John's death. "How could any competent physician miss such a diagnosis in someone with whom I spent so many hours, so many days?" she wrote. "There's no excuse."

She sold their house, gave notice at Philadelphia General, and spent the next ten months traveling in South America.

There are few surviving letters or journals from that time, but I was able to piece together that she spent the majority of her time in Peru and Colombia studying medicinal plants and shamanism. Though a disbeliever in the spirit world and all things supernatural, Helen took a keen interest in the role psychoactive plants played in healing the sick. The trip also, one would assume, sparked her interest in the role the mind and psyche played in overall health.

She returned to the States a changed person. She went back to using her maiden name and returned home to Vermont, where she'd grown up and attended medical school. She left surgery behind and began a residency in psychiatry.

"The tragedies we endure shape our lives: we carry them like shadows," Dr. Hildreth wrote in a paper for the *American Journal of Psychiatry* in May of 1971.

One must wonder how Dr. Hildreth was changed by the stillbirth of the twins, the death of her husband; how much these events shaped her, what shadows she herself carried.

Lizzy

August 20, 2019

SKINK AND I crossed West Main and headed for the long pier that ran along the west side of the downtown area. There were dozens of boats moored there, a little shack selling fried seafood. We passed tables and kiosks selling keepsakes to tourists: jewelry, paintings of Vermont landscapes customized with your name, a guy who made funky animal sculptures out of cut-up old tires—a monkey hanging from the awning of his stand, a dragon the size of a Labrador retriever sprawled on the pavement. As we walked past, the rubber animals all seemed to watch.

At the end of the pier, beside the soft-serve ice cream shop (*Best Maple Creemees in Vermont* promised the sign), three kids were sitting at one of the picnic tables pounding energy drinks in huge black cans and smoking cigarettes: a thin boy with bleached-blond hair and bad skin, and two girls dressed in black with dyed black hair to match.

"Yo," Skink called.

The blond guy nodded at him.

"This is Lizzy, the lady I told you about."

"I've seen you on TV, " the guy said. He squinted at me. "You look different, though."

I smiled. "This is me without a crew to do my makeup and hair," I said, taking a seat at the table.

"Lizzy, this is Alex," Skink said, nodding toward the blond kid. "And that's Riley next to him, and Zoey in the trench coat on the end."

"Hey," they all said, almost in unison.

I guessed these kids were fifteen or sixteen maybe—a bit older than Lauren.

"And you, like, want to interview us? For real?" said Riley. She had a piercing in her upper lip. The skin around it was red and swollen like it had been done recently.

"I'd like to," I said. "If you're cool with it. We don't have to use names or anything if you don't want. But I'd love to hear your stories. Learn more about what you think happened to your friend Lauren."

"So we'll be, like, live on the air?" Alex asked.

"Not live. But you'll be a part of the podcast. People all over the country listen. I can send Skink a link to it when it's finished."

"Cool," Alex said.

Zoey said, "Do you think the TV show might come here? You know, like, do an episode on Rattling Jane next season or something?" Her lips were chapped. Her cheekbones protruded from her face, and she had dark circles under her eyes, giving her a skeletal look. Her dark hair was buzzed short and she wore a trench coat that could have fit two more Zoeys inside it.

"I don't know," I said. "Maybe."

"It would be cool if they did," said Riley. "I mean, maybe we could all be on TV, you know? Tell our stories."

I nodded. "That would be cool," I said. "I know the producers pay attention to my podcast, so who knows. Maybe if they like what they hear. If they think it's intriguing enough for a whole episode." I got out my recorder and set up the two mics, one on each side of the table, and slipped on my headphones.

"It's August twentieth, and I'm here at one of the docks in downtown Chickering Island, Vermont, talking with friends of missing teen Lauren Schumacher." I looked up, smiled at the three kids on the other side of the table. "So how long have you all known Lauren?"

Alex shrugged. "Her family's been coming here for years."

"Just a week or two each summer," Riley added.

"Tell me about her," I said.

"She's a poet," Zoey said, lighting a cigarette. "And she draws too. Pen and ink. She wants to go to college to study art. She's kind of a genius. Literally."

"Like she could get into college." Riley rolled her eyes.

"Why not?" I asked.

"Girl's messed up," said Alex.

"But not really. It's, like, this total persona," Zoey argued. "She acts all tough and crazy, but that's not who she really is."

Alex snorted. "She attacked a kid at school, back in Massachusetts! What about that? In what way is that not messed up?"

"Really?" I asked. "Like physically attacked someone?"

Alex nodded. "That's what she said, and I believe her. She choked him and shit. Got kicked out of school. Lauren's like that. A temper, moody."

Riley shook her head. "Maybe she's moody, but maybe that kid she choked shouldn't have been messing with her. I wouldn't put up with that shit, the things he called her. I say he deserved it. But she didn't deserve to get sent to that place her parents sent her, the brainwashing place, that was messed up."

"Shit like that happens," Zoey said fiddling with the cuff of her trench coat. "I saw a thing on Netflix—people come in the night and get you, kidnap you, take you to a treatment place that's more like a prison.

And your parents okay the whole thing. It happened to that girl who was on TV all the time, the one from the really rich family, what's her name?"

Alex shook his head. "That's not what happened to Lauren. She wasn't kidnapped or anything. *Her parents* brought her to the place."

"What kind of place?" I asked.

"She said it was somewhere in Upstate New York," Alex said. "It's this rehab place for teens that's like a cult or something—lots of meditation and practicing mindfulness—whatever that's supposed to mean. And talking about your feelings and making collages and crap. She hated it. Was there for six weeks. She said she'd rather be in prison."

"Wow," I said. "So this was recently?"

"Yeah," Riley said. "Her parents picked her up from there and brought her straight here to the island for together time. They come every summer. Lauren hates it."

"Lauren hates everything," Alex said. "Literally everything."

Skink shook his head. "Come on, man, not everything, right?"

Alex laughed, ran a hand through his bleached-blond hair. "Right. She loves weed. And trouble. She loves trouble."

"That's totally unfair," said Zoey. "She has an artist's soul."

Alex rolled his eyes dramatically.

"So," I said, "do you have any idea where she is now?"

"She took off," Riley said. She threw her cigarette butt into the water.

"That's what everyone's saying, anyway," said Zoey, biting her lip. "Like her parents, the cops." She wrapped her arms around her torso, giving herself a tight hug, mumbled, "But that's not what happened."

"So what did happen?" I asked.

"Rattling Jane got her," she said. She lit another cigarette with shaking hands.

"That's total bullshit," Alex said. "That's what Lauren wants everyone to think. It's, like, literally brilliant, really. She goes around town telling everyone she met this scary monster lady down by the lake, shows everyone the pebble she got, then disappears. Of course some idiots are gonna think the monster got her."

"I heard they might get a team of divers from the state police to start checking the bottom of the lake," Riley said.

Everyone was quiet for a few seconds.

"How did Lauren first meet her?" I asked. "Rattling Jane?"

"She said it was in the sanctuary," Riley said. "Loon Cove. There's a little beach there, not a sandy beach but a pebbly one. Sometimes we go there to swim and hang out."

"So," I said, "she met Rattling Jane at Loon Cove? Was she alone?"

She nodded. "Loon Cove is kind of hard to get to, and no one ever bothers you there. Like, bird-watchers and hikers show up once in a while, but mostly no one goes. We showed it to Lauren a couple of years ago. This summer she was going there just about every night. Her dad's a dick. They'd have these huge fights."

"Do you know about what?" I asked.

"I guess he'd say shit like, 'I paid money to come to this cabin for family time and you don't even show up for dinner.'"

"It wasn't just that," put in Zoey. "He'd hit her and stuff, too. He was super controlling."

Alex nodded. "That's what she said, anyway. I don't know. Lauren could be kind of dramatic. Anyway, apparently he and Lauren's mom thought that being here would magically bring them all together. It just pissed Lauren off to be dragged to a place with no Wi-Fi, no cell service. Away from all her friends."

I nodded. "I get it."

Riley continued, "Her dad kept threatening to send her back to the lockup psych ward place."

"Guy's a douchebag," said Alex. "Has some fancy job trading bonds or something. He's one of those guys who comes here for a few weeks every summer and walks around like he owns the place."

"Lauren hates him," Zoey said. "She says he represents everything that's wrong with the world: patriarchy, mindless consumption and wealth, total lack of creativity and respect for the planet."

"Right." I got the picture. "So she's miserable, fighting with her parents, and she started walking out to the cove every night? Did any of you guys ever meet her there?"

"Sometimes," Alex said. "But mostly she went on her own."

"She'd walk there along a path from her cabin," Riley said.

"Tell her about the tree," Skink put in.

"There's a hollow tree there," Riley explained, "and she kept her weed and cigarettes and shit there—stuff she didn't want her parents to find. And one day she goes and there's a flower in there. Then another day she goes and there's a coin. Then a piece of sea glass."

Zoey nodded. "Rattling Jane was leaving her gifts."

"How did she know it was Rattling Jane?" I asked.

"She didn't," Zoey said. "Not at first. Not until Jane showed herself to Lauren."

"So she just went one day and found Rattling Jane there waiting?" I asked.

"No way," said Riley. "Rattling Jane doesn't just show up and wait for you! You have to call her!"

"See," Skink said. "Just like I told you."

"So she called her?" I asked.

"Again and again, until she came," said Zoey, still hugging herself, rocking a little. "She came up out of the water all draped in weeds and bones and leaves and shit like that. Lauren asked her where the rock was, if she could get a wish. And she . . . she whispered that Lauren had to earn it."

"Earn it how?" I asked.

"She didn't say," Zoey said.

"But," Riley continued, "she kept going back to the cove, and Rattling Jane would come when she called her. And she kept leaving little things for her in the hollow tree."

"And then Rattling Jane supposedly gave her the rock," Alex added. "The wishing stone. That's what she said, anyway. She showed it to us."

"What'd it look like?" Skink asked.

Alex shook his head, gave a disgusted little laugh. "Like nothing. Like literally just a regular rock."

I looked out at the water, watched the way the sunlight played on the surface, making it glisten and sparkle as if it were really touched by magic; maybe it really was a place where a creature made of sticks and weeds and vengeance dwelled.

"When was the last time you saw Lauren?" I asked.

"The day she went missing," Zoey answered. "She was all upset. Said she'd ruined things by talking to us. That Rattling Jane knew and was mad at her for telling and showing people the stone. She wasn't going to give her her wish."

Skink kicked at the ground. "Man, you don't want to piss off Rattling Jane."

"There is no fucking Rattling Jane," Alex declared, smacking the wooden boards of the table. "It was all just a stupid story Lauren told to get attention. The girl's fucked in the head. Fact!"

"But what if it's not?" asked Zoey. "I mean, what if it's real? If she really did get taken?"

The question hung there. Behind us, a balloon popped, and a little girl screamed.

"Have you been out there since she went missing?" I asked. "Out to Loon Cove?"

Alex shook his head. "Not me."

The girls both shook their heads.

"No way," said Zoey. "I'm not going back there. Not ever again."

THE BOOK OF MONSTERS

By Violet Hildreth and Iris Whose Last Name We Don't Know

Illustrations by Eric Hildreth

1978

MONSTERS ARE UNPREDICTABLE

Monsters aren't like us. They don't think the way we do. They don't have the same sense of right and wrong. They are not empathetic. Many are void of emotion.

A monster lacks morals.

They don't follow the same patterns and rules and moral codes that humans do. They live outside of all that.

Monsters are unpredictable. This is one of the things that makes them truly dangerous and must be remembered whenever you face one. You never know what move a monster is going to make next.

Monsters are full of surprises.

Vi

June 18, 1978

THE GLOWING HANDS of Vi's Timex were both pointed up at twelve.

Midnight.

The hour when all unseen things wake up, come creeping out of the shadows.

She held still, listening, thinking that maybe, if she listened hard enough, she might be able to hear a far-off roar, the gnashing of teeth, or the snapping of twigs.

But there was only the disappointing chirping of crickets, the humming of the big lights outside the Inn, the soft flutter and thump of moths bumping against the lights.

She was by the rear door on the west side of the Inn, her back pressed against the cool brick. She felt like a shadow, a paper doll that could fold in on itself, become nearly invisible.

Eric and Iris were together, watching her, hunkered down along the back edge of the barn—if she looked, she could see their pale faces glowing in the inky blackness. They were lookouts. Their bikes were stashed behind the barn.

Iris seemed to have recovered from her episode at the movies earlier. She'd been quiet but had stopped crying, and by the time they made it to the Inn, she was laughing at stupid stuff Vi said and asking if Eric thought they could take out the rabbit when they got home.

Gran wasn't expecting them back for at least another thirty minutes, and she'd be at home in the living room reading just like she always was when she waited up for them. She read a lot of magazines: *Time*, *Newsweek*, as well as psychiatric and medical journals. She also read novels (never horror, like Vi read, but books that Gran described as well-plotted; books that made her think): her latest was *Gravity's Rainbow* by Thomas Pynchon.

Vi had given Eric and Iris strict instructions: If the lights in the carriage house where Miss Ev was sleeping went on, or if they saw Gran coming, or heard anything out of the ordinary, Eric would do his barred owl call. It was so convincing that real owls often called back in return.

Vi waited by the back door. *Tick tock. Tick tock.* Would Patty show?

Please, please, please, Vi prayed to the God of Miracles, *make Patty come.*

At last came the scrape of a dead bolt unlocking, and the area beside Vi flooded with light as Patty held the heavy door open, whispered, "Come on, hurry. God, I can't believe I'm doing this."

The hallway was so bright and white it made Vi's eyes hurt. She squinted as she ducked into the building and Patty closed the door behind her.

Patty looked up and down the hall, and Vi did too. All clear.

"I'm supposed to be on a bathroom break and I've gotta get back to the nurses' station before Sal or Nancy gets suspicious."

Sal was usually one of the nighttime orderlies—he spent his overnights lifting weights in the exercise room and eating hard-boiled eggs and green bananas, which he said built muscles.

Nancy was the oldest nurse, older than Gran maybe. She painted her eyebrows orange and had thin hair that she dyed black, but really the dye just stuck to her scalp. Vi and Eric called her Mrs. Halloween.

Vi nodded.

Patty thrust the key to Gran's office into Vi's hand. "I'm putting my job on the line. You get that, right?"

Vi nodded more vigorously.

"I'm not doing this ever again, just so you know." She crossed her arms over her chest.

"I know," Vi said, "I really appreciate—"

"Leave the key here when you're done," Patty interrupted her, patting the windowsill. Her breath smelled like bubble gum. "I'll come back in a couple hours, grab it, and put it away before anyone notices it's missing."

Vi held the key tight in her palm.

"Be careful," Patty said. "*Do not* get caught."

"I won't," Vi promised.

"And if you do get caught," Patty said, "I had *nothing* to do with this. You broke into the office somehow and got that key on your own."

"Of course," Vi said. "But I won't get caught. Don't worry."

Patty checked her watch, then scurried down the hall toward the stairs. Vi knew she was heading up to the rooms where the residents were all tucked in for the night.

As she heard Patty's footsteps trotting up the stairs, she turned left, praying to the God of Silence, the God of Invisibility, to help her walk without being seen or heard. She knew there weren't many employees working the overnight shift: usually just two nurses and an orderly. Sometimes Miss Ev would come swooping in if there was an emergency or a nighttime intake. The lights in the hallways and entryway were all dimmed way down, only emergency lighting on so everyone could find their way out if there was a fire. EXIT signs glowed above all the doors. Vi hurried down the tiled hallway, passing Dr. Hutchins's office, the rooms they used for intakes, exams, and therapy sessions.

Gran's office was at the very end of the hall, on the left just before the Oak Room, where they held staff meetings. Its big, dark-wood-paneled door had a brass plaque on it: DIRECTOR'S OFFICE and beneath that, a smaller sign with her name: DR. HELEN E. HILDRETH. Vi slid the key into the lock and turned. A satisfying click. She checked to make sure no one had spotted her, then slipped into the cool, dark room.

She'd been in this office before, but never without Gran. And never at night, in darkness. She looked around, letting her eyes adjust.

It felt all wrong, and she knew that if Gran were to catch her, she'd be in big trouble, the worst trouble of her life, probably.

But she needed to do this.

She needed to do this for her sister.

I promised her.

And it was more than that now. She needed to learn the truth.

The room smelled of lemon furniture polish, cigarettes, and Gran's Jean Naté. A comforting smell, but a little unsettling too, because it made her feel like Gran was right there in the room with her, standing in the corner, watching.

Just what do you think you're doing, Violet Hildreth?

Vi checked the two windows and saw that the blinds and curtains were drawn tight. Still, she didn't dare flip on the overhead light. Too risky. What if Miss Evil woke up and looked out her window and saw a light on in Gran's office?

Better safe than sorry, as Gran always said.

Vi pulled a tiny flashlight from the back pocket of her shorts and flipped it on—a silver penlight Gran had given her, the kind a real doctor would use for checking someone's pupils. Vi used it as a backup on her monster-hunting missions. Now it was her spy flashlight.

She held still, looking around. The ticking of her watch was the only sound in the room.

A huge maple desk dominated the small wood-paneled room. The left wall had built-in bookshelves. On the right wall was a fireplace made of the same yellow brick as the outside of the building. Just to the right of the door stood a large leather chair. And in the other corner was tucked another less-comfortable-looking chair. Sometimes Gran used her office to meet with other doctors or concerned family members. But mostly, this space was for Gran and Gran alone. It was where she wrote her notes each day. Where she made phone calls. Developed treatment plans.

Her framed degrees hung on the wall, along with a silver frame holding a certificate she'd been awarded for all her volunteer work with the criminals and drug addicts at the state-run clinic, Project Hope.

Vi walked over and sat down at the desk, tried to open the top drawer, but it was locked. Feeling foolish, she tried the door key, but wasn't at all surprised when it didn't fit. The big upper drawer on the side pulled open easily, and in it Vi found pencils and pens, rubber bands, empty notebooks and pads of paper. The second drawer held letterhead and envelopes, a roll of stamps. No keys to the basement. No notes about B West or the Mayflower Project or who Iris might be. Nothing interesting at all.

The top of the desk was uncluttered. Gran never left any half-finished work. A black phone with a dial and glowing buttons for reaching each extension of the Inn, a rinsed-out coffee mug, a desk lamp with a stained glass butterfly on it, a heavy glass ashtray, and two photos sat on the desk. One snapshot of Vi and Eric standing together in front of the house, their arms around each other. Gran had taken it with her Instamatic last year: *Smile and say Gorgonzola, my lovelies!* And beside it, in a thick gold frame, a black-and-white photo of Gran when she was young, from back in her med-school days. She was with an older man in a white coat with a neatly trimmed mustache and little round glasses. Vi had asked about this photo before, and Gran had told her the man was one of her professors and mentors. Vi looked at Gran's face in the photo, wearing the half-smile Vi knew so well. The one Gran gave whenever she was asked to pose for a photograph, like a full smile was too much effort.

Vi picked up the photo to look at it more closely, seeking some sign of herself in her grandmother's young face—she thought they looked the same around the eyes maybe. And that's when she saw it: a small, flat brass key hidden beneath the edge of the heavy gold frame.

Vi set the photo down and removed the key, studying it for a second, then slipping it into the keyhole in the top drawer of the desk. It fit perfectly and turned easily.

"Thank you," she whispered to the God of Keys. Then, "Please," to the Clue-Finding God.

What could be in the drawer that Gran felt the need to keep locked up?

Surely nothing that important, or she would have hidden the key better.

Vi pulled the drawer open slowly, carefully, as if she expected a snake to jump out. She angled the beam of her little flashlight down.

Unlike the tidiness of the room and desktop, the drawer was a messy jumble of objects.

Two packs of cigarettes. Cough drops. Matchbooks. A little silver flask that Vi was sure must contain some of Gran's gin. An unlabeled amber plastic vial of pills—Vi picked it up gingerly, saw tiny blue capsules inside.

At the bottom of the drawer was a hardcover book. Weird. Why would Gran keep a book in a locked drawer and not on the bookshelves with all the others?

Vi took it out, shone her light on it.

A Case for Good Breeding: The Templeton Family Study and the Promise of Eugenics by Dr. Wilson G. Hicks.

Eugenics?

Vi didn't know what that word meant, and she felt a little spark of irritation, of failure—she prided herself on her vocabulary.

She opened the book, and there, on the first page, was a photograph of the author.

Vi recognized him instantly—the doctor in the white coat from the photo on Gran's desk. She held the book up to the gold-framed photo, compared the faces under the glow of her penlight. It was the same man, no doubt. Same pinched face, round glasses, thin mustache. Gran's professor. Her mentor.

"Hello, Dr. Wilson G. Hicks," Vi whispered to the man in the old photo. She was solving mysteries already!

She turned a couple pages and began to skim.

Her mouth went dry. There was a heavy feeling in her stomach.

Good breeding of humans is no different than good breeding of chickens, horses, or cattle. It is possible, with proper planning, to weed the population of feeble-mindedness, criminal behaviors, and all forms of physical and mental malformations. Through controlled and proper breeding, we can eradicate all traits that make human beings unfit; perhaps even do away with crime, with the wretched living in squalor, with the howling mad who fill mental hospitals, with the savages and the gipsies, the prostitutes and the half-breeds and the imbeciles.

Vi flipped pages.

Survival and overall success of the species is dependent on those who are superior weeding out the weak and inferior.

We can—and must—control the inferior through whatever means necessary.

A big part of the book seemed to be about one family in the Northeast Kingdom of Vermont, a family Dr. Hicks called "the Templetons." Charts and graphs traced the family back several generations. The Templeton family was full of people arrested for violent crimes, prostitution, gambling, public drunkenness. There was a chart that listed all the "feeble-minded" specimens and "imbeciles" in each generation and how many of the children were illegitimate. Dr. Hicks had created a table showing the monetary outlay by the state, decade by decade, spent on relief for the family, on criminal cases, and on the costs of keeping family members in prison, or institutionalizing those deemed too feeble-minded, insane, or deformed to live at home.

The costs, as you can see, greatly multiply with each generation of Templeton family members, as they continue to pass on, unchecked, their inferior traits and gross deformities. If there was any doubt before, the study of this family shows that idiocy, insanity, and criminal tendencies are hereditary.

It is clear, from a moral standpoint, that families such as the Templetons are an enormous tax to our systems of health care, social welfare, and criminal justice. For the sake of society, compulsory sterilization is both the correct and moral course of action.

Compulsory sterilization.

Vi let the words sink in.

Vi knew what sterilization meant. Cats and dogs had to be taken to the vet to get "fixed" so they wouldn't make more babies.

Dr. Hicks wanted to do that with humans.

Maybe he *had* done it with humans. It made Vi feel a little sick to think about.

What kind of doctor would do something like that?

Vi flipped to the end of the book, where Dr. Hicks had written his acknowledgments. Her eye caught on one line:

I am forever indebted to my marvelous assistant, Helen Elizabeth Hildreth, whose research and fieldwork have proven invaluable—I know she will make a fine physician and a noble warrior in our cause.

The world began to spin. Vi put her head down on the desk for a minute, to take a deep breath.

The Gran she knew only wanted to help people. But wasn't that what Dr. Hicks wanted too? In his own way? Didn't he think not letting this family have any more babies *was* helping them?

It reminded Vi of what she'd read about the Nazis. About how they thought there was only one superior race of humans and everyone else should be destroyed. Shot and gassed and burned up in ovens.

Vi lifted her head up from the desk.

She heard an owl hoot, hoot, hooting.

No. Not an owl. Eric! Eric's warning call.

She sat up, heart jolting.

She shoved the book back into the drawer, hastily tried to arrange things the way she'd found them, slammed the drawer closed, and locked it. She replaced the key beneath the photo frame, stood up, slid the chair back under the desk.

The owl call sounded again: *Hurry, hurry, hurry.*

Vi opened the office door a crack, didn't see anyone or hear anything in the hallway. The lights were still dim. She slipped out, put the key in the dead bolt on Gran's door, but it stuck, wouldn't turn. She wiggled it. Behind her, she heard the front door opening.

She dropped the key, picked it up with trembling fingers, tried the lock on Gran's door again. It turned at last. She pocketed the key and turned the corner just as the lights in the entryway came on. She had about ten feet of hallway to cover before she got to the back door. If whoever had just come through the front door looked to the right, she'd be caught.

Should she go back into Gran's office and hide?

No, the God of Escape told her. *Run!*

She raced for the door, eyes on the red glowing EXIT sign, running on the toes of her sneakers so she wouldn't make a sound. She heard loud footsteps crossing the front hall.

Vi got to the exit door and yanked, praying it was still unlocked. *Thank you, God of Escape.* She stepped out into the night, closing the door quickly but quietly behind her. Then she pressed her back against the brick wall and crept along the edge of the building. When she got to the corner, she ran, head down, in a sprint to the barn where Eric and Iris were waiting.

"Did she see you?" Eric asked.

Vi shook her head, catching her breath. "Was it Gran?"

"Yeah," Eric said.

"What's she doing here so late?" Vi asked. She looked at the building, waiting for the light in Gran's office to come on, but it stayed dark.

Eric shrugged. "No clue, but we should get home so we're there when she gets back."

Vi nodded, and the three of them headed across the lawn, pushing their bikes. They'd made it all the way back to the house, climbing the front steps, when Vi reached into the pockets of her shorts and realized she didn't have the flashlight.

Even worse, she still had the key to Gran's office.

Patty was going to kill her.

The Helping Hand of God:
The True Story of the Hillside Inn

By Julia Tetreault, Dark Passages Press, 1980

INTRODUCTION

This book began as a simple assignment for a journalism class. My plan was to write an article on the eugenics movement in Vermont. During my research, I learned about a man named Dr. Wilson Hicks, whose 1929 book *A Case for Good Breeding: The Templeton Family Study and the Promise of Eugenics* was an important text in the movement.

Having grown up on a farm in rural Vermont, Dr. Hicks had a background in animal husbandry and the efforts to improve the pedigree of dairy cows, horses, and chickens. After medical school, he turned to humans. During 1927 and 1928, he conducted a study of a family in the Northeast Kingdom of Vermont, whom he referred to as "the Templetons." He believed that Vermont could become a modern utopia of above-average people of Caucasian descent.

After completing this study and publishing his book, Dr. Hicks lectured on his theories all over the country and became a leading voice in the field of eugenics. He took an active role putting his theories into practice. He was responsible for the involuntary sterilization of over one hundred people in Vermont hospitals, including at least twenty members of the Templeton family.

And he was assisted in his efforts by his young protégé (and rumored lover), Dr. Helen Hildreth.

Eugenics is indeed a dark part of our history, but it is far from the darkest part of the story I was soon to discover.

Lizzy

August 20, 2019

A FTER LEAVING THE kids at the pier, I hopped into my van and followed East Main out past the winery to a collection of five brightly painted mailboxes with a sign above them: WILDFLOWER COTTAGES.

I slowed down but couldn't see the buildings themselves, just a long dirt driveway.

I pulled in.

It was nearly the end of the season. Most of the summer people would head home after Labor Day weekend. I wondered if the other cottages were occupied—if another family had moved into Bluebell for the remainder of the summer.

I passed a turnoff on the left with a little sign for Daisy Cottage. It wasn't visible; I could only see the narrow, twisting driveway that led to it, thickly wooded on both sides. I passed the turnoffs for Peony, Hyacinth, Buttercup, and finally spotted the one for Bluebell.

Turning right, I followed the gravel drive about twenty feet down toward the water. The cottage was painted a vivid blue, tucked along the shore amid the pine trees. There were no cars parked out front. No towels or swimsuits on the clothesline. No sign of life.

I got out to look around.

A slight breeze rippled my loose T-shirt. I smelled the pines and the lake: musty, tinged with decaying vegetation and algae.

I heard the far-off drone of a motorboat out on the lake, a small animal skittering around in the woods nearby.

Climbing up onto the porch, I leaned over the white-painted wicker furniture to peer into the windows: a kitchen and living room, a bathroom and bedroom downstairs. A loft with what looked like two more bedrooms.

Out back was another deck with a charcoal grill. A couple of canoes were turned upside down, paddles and life jackets tucked under them. And there was a Honda generator and two five-gallon gas cans.

A dock led out to the water and a swimming float a little farther out, the wood on top bleached from the sun, the sides covered with algae.

Thick stands of trees came right up to both sides of the yard, making the cottage feel very secluded, totally cut off from the rest of the world. You couldn't see the other cottages from here.

There were no power lines.

No phone or cable.

I pulled out my phone: no service at all.

It would be utter hell for a teenage girl, particularly one who didn't get along with her parents to begin with. It must have felt like a prison sentence.

Especially after just getting out of a six-week stint in a residential treatment center.

"Poor kid," I muttered.

I followed the shoreline to the edge of the woods and spotted a path thickly carpeted with brown pine needles. Was it the same path Lauren had taken, night after night, heading out to Loon Cove to call to Rattling Jane the way a lonely child might conjure up an imaginary friend?

One way to find out.

I started walking.

The mosquitoes were bad once I got into the thick shade of the woods, and I felt ill-prepared. Back in the van, I had a small backpack for monster-hunting excursions: first aid kit, water, granola bars, fire starters, a silver emergency blanket, my video camera and digital recorder, and bug spray. Sometimes I'd take my gun too—just in case. But here I was, no bag, nothing in my pockets but keys. An ill-equipped monster hunter if ever there was one.

I thought of turning back to grab the bag, but I'd already been walking for a good ten minutes. Best to press on without it, I decided, at least for a few more minutes.

The path more or less followed the shoreline, but far enough away that I stayed in the shadowy woods. The forest was mostly pines here, a few deciduous trees mixed in. The ground was covered with pine needles, fallen leaves and branches, lush moss, although the path showed signs of having been used recently. I noticed the occasional footprint in wet ground, broken twigs and branches. I stopped to pick up a cigarette butt. One of Lauren's?

As I made my way along the path, I tried to imagine I was Lauren, creeping away from the cottage after dark.

It wasn't so hard, really. To remember what it was like to be thirteen and full of secrets, sneaking around in the dark.

◆   ◆   ◆

HOW FAR TO the wildlife sanctuary? Would I even know when I got there?

After nearly half an hour of walking, I was kicking myself for not bringing my knapsack. I was thirsty and being eaten alive by mosquitoes.

Five more minutes, I told myself. If I didn't see anything, I'd turn around, go back, and try again later. This might not even be the right path. Maybe, I decided, it would be best to head to Loon Cove from within the wildlife sanctuary, then try to find the path that led back to Lauren's cottage. Reverse engineering.

Just as I was about to call it quits, the path opened up and I came to a larger trail, more like a dirt road. A painted wooden sign pointed to the right: LOON COVE .25 MILES. The preserve's Silver and Red Trails were to the left.

Another metal sign like the one at the sanctuary's front gate, this one pockmarked with holes—bullet holes—stated that it was open from sunrise to sunset and that motorized vehicles, camping, and fires were prohibited.

I turned right, and the road narrowed to a footpath downhill over rugged terrain: roots and rocks. Eventually I reached rugged and worn stone steps carefully built into the bank. They were old, no longer level and crumbling in places.

I followed them down to the water, stepping carefully. The last thing I needed was to turn an ankle out here—no bag, no cell service.

The cove was small and secluded, surrounded by birch and pine trees—the perfect place for teenagers to come and party. A beach covered in little pebbles showed the remnants of a campfire. The firepit held two empty beer cans, some cigarette butts. A big worn driftwood log was set up as a bench just in front of the firepit. I sat down on it, ran my fingers over the initials and words carved into it.

S.W.

FuK off

Tansy wuz here

No note from Lauren or Rattling Jane hinting at what might have happened here, where she might be. Of course not. What had I expected?

I looked out at the water, the way the light was playing on it, making it dance. I let myself imagine a figure surfacing: a woman made of fish bones and sticks, weeds and mud.

I stood, walked around the perimeter of the cove. It took some looking, but eventually I found the hollow tree the kids had told me about. An old white paper birch with a knothole a little over six feet up, the perfect place for a kid to hide her stash. And the perfect place to leave a secret gift.

I reached up, stuck my hand in blindly, wondering if I'd find a pack of Lauren's cigarettes or a plastic bag of pot.

But my fingers felt something smooth, hard, and rectangular. And beneath it, a little paper bundle of some sort.

I pulled the items out.

An old gold Zippo lighter with a butterfly engraved on the front. A lined piece of notebook paper with three holes punched in the side—the kind we once used for our monster book—folded into a neat rectangle, tied up with a piece of dirty garden twine.

Heart racing, I turned the lighter over in my hands, ran my fingers over the engraved initials: *HEH*

It couldn't be.

But it was.

Gran's lighter.

I opened it up, flicked the wheel, and it sparked, lighting.

It had been cleaned and filled, taken care of.

Carefully, my fingers trembling slightly, I untied the string, un-wrapped the paper bundle.

There was a smooth gray pebble tucked into the center.

And on the paper, a message:

> *The Monster gives the Monster Hunter a stone so she can make a wish.*
> *What does the hunter wish for?*
> *What does she dream of?*

> *What does the Monster dream?*
> *An old dream, a dream of endings and beginnings.*
> *A dream of fire.*
> *Of a lever pulled and a world of bright white light, crumbling ruin.*
> *A single line spoken: "We belong dead."*
> *Do you share the same dream?*
> *Do you dream it with me?*

My skin buzzed with electricity.

Heart hammering, I looked around, eyes studying the trees, ears pricked for any sound. I had the strongest sensation that I was being watched.

That this was part of the game.

Hide-and-seek.

Catch me if you can.

"Hello?" I called out, voice small.

I was sure I could feel it, the creature's eyes on me. I'd never been this close before.

"Are you there?" I called.

The trees rustled in the wind, leaves quaking, branches banging together.

Waves came up and lapped at the rocky shore.

The sound of a distant motorboat.

A loon called, low and mournful, a strange mocking laugh.

I tucked the lighter, paper, and stone carefully into my pocket, made an effort to inhale slowly and deeply. When I felt like I wasn't in danger of fainting, I made my way back up the steps to the trail.

The Monster

I WATCH FROM THE trees, my heart beating so hard I think it might come flying right out of my chest, soar all the way up to the clouds, singing her name.

It's been so long.

So, so long!

But here she is! It's unbelievable, really. Here she is, reaching into the birch, pulling out my gifts.

I knew! I knew she'd find them. She's a clever one, this hunter of monsters.

I bite my tongue to keep from crying out, from calling to her, using her old name, the one she left behind so long ago.

I bite down so hard I taste blood, salty and warm.

"Hello?" she calls out, her eyes moving right over me.

"Are you there?" she asks.

Yes, yes, yes!

And I almost step out, show myself.

The restraint actually physically hurts. The pull is that strong.

Magnetic.

But it's not time yet.

I hold my breath.

Vi

~~~~~~~~~~~

July 7, 1978

"I'M TELLING YOU, I saw it!" Eric insisted, voice squeaky and whis-tling, like someone was squeezing a dog toy in his throat.

"Describe it again," Vi said. She felt like a detective from TV: Kojak, with his bald head and lollipops, or Columbo, with his rumpled rain-coat and cigar.

They were in the clubhouse. Eric had called an emergency meeting because he claimed he'd seen a monster. *A real, actual monster*. And he'd seen it twice! Last night and then again this evening.

Vi was almost thankful for this new monster distraction because she'd been driving herself crazy these last three weeks thinking about eugenics and Dr. Hicks and Gran; trying to make sense of all of it in her mind.

She still hadn't told Iris, Eric, or Patty what she'd found out the night she was in Gran's office. In fact, she'd lied, said there was nothing there—it had been a total bust.

And Patty was still mad at her for taking off with the key.

"I'm such an idiot. You're just a kid," Patty had said, shaking her head. Vi felt like her skin was full of prickers, painful and dangerous.

"No harm done," Vi kept reminding Patty. No one had seemed to notice the missing key. Vi had put it back early the following Monday when she went into the office to talk to Miss Evelyn about making a list of plants for the bird garden. Vi had brought some plant and flower books—and when Miss Ev was sitting at her desk, absorbed, Vi had slipped the key back on the hook. Easy as pie.

The missing flashlight was another matter—Vi hadn't mentioned it to Patty because she knew Patty would flip out completely, flat-out refuse to help with any future missions or share information. Vi had walked the halls of the Inn looking for it. She'd searched the grass around the outside of the building and near the barn where Eric and Iris had been hiding. But it was nowhere to be found.

Gran had never mentioned finding the flashlight in her office. So either that meant she hadn't found it, or that she had and was keeping quiet while she mulled it over. Since Gran had given it to her, she'd no doubt recognize it and know that Vi had been in her office unsupervised. Vi worked the problem over in her mind daily, wondering. It made her think about the chess lessons she'd been given. Gran had started teaching her to play chess a year or so ago; to be good at chess, Gran said, you had to be thinking many moves ahead—not only your own moves, but imagining what your opponent might do.

Then, yesterday, Vi was helping Gran clean her home office, going over all the books in the shelves with a feather duster, when Gran dumped out the contents of her purse on the desk: her calfskin wallet, spare eyeglasses, pens, little notepad, lipstick and face powder, cigarettes, the gold butterfly lighter, and her heavy key ring. Vi's eyes caught on the key ring. She knew the basement key was on there—it had to be.

"Are you all right, Violet?" Gran had asked. "You seem a little preoccupied." That was an understatement. Every time she looked at Gran, Vi imagined her helping Dr. Hicks, and it made her head hurt and her stomach ache. Sometimes, when Gran looked at her, Vi was sure she was just waiting for her to confess, that any second she was going to pull the flashlight out of her pocket and say, "Care to explain *this*?"

Vi forced a smile. "I'm fine, just thinking about Iris. About how frustrating it must be to not remember anything."

Gran nodded, began putting things back in her purse. She lit a cigarette with the gold lighter. Vi focused her eyes on the flame. "Perhaps . . ." Gran had said, letting the flame go out, then flicking it on again. Vi smelled the lighter fluid, studied the yellow and orange dancing together over the butterfly, which seemed to twitch its wings in the flickering light. "Perhaps some things are best not remembered."

• • •

"I KNOW WHAT I saw," Eric said now as they all huddled together in the clubhouse. "It was real." He held his sketchbook on his lap, drawing while he talked. They had candles lit and an old camping lantern blazing, which made the inside of the clubhouse feel warm and cozy and protected. But Vi kept looking out the window, thinking that if there was something out there, having the building all lit up was like turning on a flashing sign outside a motel: *Come on in!*

Eric kept looking up from his drawing at the window, too. Iris was chewing her lip, tilting back in her chair, unable to sit still.

"Last night I saw it at the edge of the woods in the yard." Eric's face was all pinched up and serious. "It had a loping sort of walk. A pale blank face. A hooded cape. It stopped and was just looking at the house, watching. I think . . ." Eric paused, looked up at both of them. "I think it was looking for us."

"For us?" Iris said, her voice higher than usual. She thumped the feet of her chair back down onto the floor.

Eric nodded. "Maybe it *knows*. Knows about the club. About the monster hunting."

Iris gave one solemn nod. Swallowed slowly, like her throat was dry.

"Okay," Vi said, still trying to piece things together. "So why didn't you say anything last night? Or this morning? I mean, you've known about this for over twenty-four hours and you're just now telling us?"

It didn't make any sense.

He rolled his eyes. "Because I knew you wouldn't believe me." His voice was whiny. "I knew I needed proof."

His proof—a Polaroid he'd taken earlier—was sitting on the table in front of them.

"So when it came back tonight, I was waiting. I told everyone I was going to bed early, then I sneaked back outside with my camera. I was hiding in the old rabbit hutch in the backyard."

"Ew!" Vi said, thinking of all the rabbit pee. Had the hutch even been swept out or was it still full of shavings and old fossilized poop? She pictured her little brother there, flat on his belly in old hay and rabbit shit, waiting for the monster to come back.

"It was the perfect hiding spot," he explained. "I knew he'd never see me in there."

"He? He who?"

Eric turned the drawing he'd been working on so Vi and Iris could see it. He'd drawn a humanoid with a blank white face, huge dark eyes, and a heavy black grim reaper–style hood.

"The Ghoul," Vi said, reading the neat block letters Eric had penciled in at the bottom. The creature's eyes seemed to pull her in; *I know you. I'm coming for you*, they said. "So it's like a ghost or something?" she asked.

"I'm not sure exactly what it is. Maybe it's one of the undead. A demon. But it saw me, Vi! When I snapped the picture and the flash went off, it looked right at me."

Vi picked up the Polaroid, squinted down at it. The truth was, it was hard to tell what she was looking at. She could see a form at the edge of their house. If she looked at it the right way, she could see a black-draped figure, a pale face. But it was so blurry, it was hard to make out the details.

"Tell me what it did again," Vi said.

"It came out of the trees and went right over to the house, started looking in the windows. I think it was looking for a way in."

Iris came to stand next to Vi and stared over her shoulder at the photo. She was trembling, her whole body vibrating like a whacked tuning fork. "So what do we do?" she asked.

"I don't know," Vi said. She licked her lips, thinking. Waiting for one of the gods to whisper an idea, but they were all silent. Scared off by the Ghoul.

She felt a headache coming on. She'd been getting them more and more often.

"We need to do a spell of protection," Eric said. He picked up the monster book, flipped through its pages until he found what he was looking for. "We wash the doors of the house with water steeped with sage and thyme, and put kosher salt across all the thresholds, maybe surround our beds with it. Crosses can't hurt, either. Holy water, if we can get it."

"Right," Vi said. "Where are we going to get holy water, Eric?"

"St. Matthew's?" Eric suggested.

"So we're just going to bike on over and tell the priest we need holy water to help protect us from a ghoul?"

Eric shrugged. "I was thinking we'd steal it?"

Vi laughed. Her goody-two-shoes brother wanted to steal holy water from a church?

"Stolen holy water," Iris said. "Doesn't that wreck its powers or something?"

Eric rubbed his face with his hands. "I don't know. I'm trying, but it's hard when we don't even understand what we're up against."

Vi looked down at the Polaroid again. It might not be anything at all, just a shadow cast by the trees, a bright spot caused by the camera flash. Maybe Eric had imagined the whole thing.

But what if he hadn't?

"Okay," Vi said. "We do whatever spells of protection we can. And on the next full moon, we go out and try to find this thing. Hunt it down."

"What do we do if we find it?" Iris asked.

"Banish it or kill it," Vi said. "Do whatever we need to do. In the meantime, we keep our eyes open. We do research. We try to figure out what this thing is and what it wants."

Eric looked scared. "It saw me, Vi," he said, voice trembling a little. "It knows who I am. I feel like . . . like it knows all about me."

"It's okay," Vi told Eric. "We'll put a circle of salt around your bed. Draw some sigils on the floor. Hang a cross on your wall. We'll make sure you're protected, Eric. I promise."

◆   ◆   ◆

"DO YOU THINK he really saw a ghoul?" Iris asked her later. "Do you think it's real?"

They were in Vi's room. Iris sometimes panicked when she slept by herself and often crept in to be with Vi late at night. Gran had figured out what was up, but she didn't seem to mind.

They'd moved a twin mattress in and set it up on the floor in the corner of Vi's room—right across from her own bed. Vi had helped Iris make it up with her own spare sheets—white and clean and smelling like sunshine because they were dried on the line in the backyard. Iris slept every night with the rabbit puppet Vi had given her.

She was on her mattress, and Vi was propped up on one elbow in her own bed, looking down. It was after midnight, and they spoke in low voices.

"I think . . ." Vi chose her words carefully. ". . . that he believes he saw it."

"But is it real?" Iris asked.

"Maybe believing is enough to make it real. Maybe if you believe strongly enough, you can actually, I don't know, *conjure* monsters."

"Do you think so? That they're out there just waiting to be conjured? That there are really . . . monsters?"

Vi looked at her, there in the dark.

Iris had on a pair of Vi's old pajamas, and Vi was thinking about the page on doppelgängers in *The Book of Monsters*. A doppelgänger was a spirit, a creature that looked just like a person, could step right into that person's life, just take her place and no one would ever know the difference. When you saw a doppelgänger—if you happened to pass your twin on the street—it was bad luck. It meant something terrible was coming your way.

She and Iris could really be sisters—they looked so much alike, dark-haired, dark-eyed, skinny girls. Vi found herself thinking (not for the first time) that Iris couldn't be real. That she might be someone Vi had imagined to life, a secret sister.

Could you call a doppelgänger to you? Conjure it just by believing? Was that possible?

Her head hurt. She'd taken some Tylenol from the medicine cabinet, but it didn't seem to be doing much good. She pressed her thumbs into her eyes.

"Well?" Iris said, waiting.

"Monsters are real," Vi told her firmly. "Of course they are. There are just too many people who have seen them for them not to be, you know? Did Eric see a ghoul? I don't know. I believe he saw something. Or thinks he did. And we need to investigate, find out what it is."

"Do you think it could be . . . dangerous?"

"Maybe," Vi said. "If it's a monster, then yes, definitely. Monsters are always dangerous."

"If there are bad monsters out there, do you think there could be good monsters too?" Iris asked.

"I think," said Vi, "that it's more complicated than that." She closed her eyes.

Iris was quiet a minute. Then she asked, voice low, "Do you think there's a God?"

Vi smiled. "I think there are lots of gods. If you listen, you can hear them talking, telling you things, guiding you."

"What do you mean?"

So Vi told Iris all about the gods who guided her, even though she'd never told anyone, not even Eric, not even Gran. And when she was done telling, she said, "Close your eyes and listen. What do you hear?"

"The clock ticking," Iris said.

"That's the God of Time, he's saying something to you. Listen carefully. What is it?"

Iris scrunched up her face. "Hurry," she said. "He's telling me to hurry. That time is running out."

"Time for what?" Vi asked.

Iris listened. "He doesn't say."

Vi nodded. "If you keep listening, maybe he'll tell you more. And the other gods too. Now that you know about them, I bet you'll start hearing them all the time."

Iris lay back on her bed, pulled up the covers nearly to her grungy orange hat.

"You can take off the hat, you know," Vi said. "I've already seen what's under it."

Iris said nothing, just tugged it down tight over her ears.

"I've seen your other scars too. The ones on your chest."

Iris turned away so that she was facing the wall.

Maybe Vi had gone too far this time. She'd wanted to say something for weeks now, but hadn't worked up the nerve. But now, in the almost-dark, she felt like the time was right.

"It's okay," Vi told her. "I've got my own scars too."

Iris turned back toward Vi. "You do?"

Vi sat up. "Do you want to see?"

Iris nodded, and Vi moved to the edge of the bed, started to unbutton her pajama shirt. The bluish moonlight was streaming in through the curtained window. The nightlight on Vi's dresser was on: the ceramic owl with eyes that glowed orange and seemed to watch her every move. She could almost feel the owl turn his head, hear it say, *Who, who, who are you and what do you think you're doing?* The owl's voice was just like Gran's, and Vi imagined Gran the Owl with orange, all-seeing eyes. She knew Gran would not approve of what she was about to do, but the urge to share her secret was more than she could resist.

Sisters, she thought, not by blood, but by something else. Something deeper.

Doppelgängers.

Her fingers fumbled over the last button. She undid it, slipped out of her blue cotton pajama top. The cool air hit her skin, giving her goose bumps. She stepped closer to Iris, got down on her knees so the girl could see, get an up-close look.

"How did you get them?" Iris asked, studying the raised red scars on Vi's stomach and chest.

"Car accident," Vi said. "Eric and I survived, but our parents died.

He was fine, but I had internal injuries. One of my lungs was crushed. And my liver and spleen were messed up. I needed surgery—a bunch of surgeries, actually. I was in the hospital for months."

"Awful," Iris said, but she didn't turn away. She sat up, leaned in for a closer look at the scars.

She was so close that Vi could feel Iris's breath on her skin.

"I don't remember it. Not really. I have nightmares about the accident sometimes, that I'm strapped down in the backseat and I see the bright headlights of a car coming at us. Gran says our car swerved and went down an embankment, flipping. The front of the car crumpled, and the driver's seat came back and crushed me. We ended up in the river, and the car filled up with water." Vi was quiet for a few seconds, could feel the cold water creeping up around her. "That's in the dreams too. Cold, cold water."

"How'd you get out?" Iris asked.

"A man came and pulled us out. He saved Eric and me. I don't know his name. Can't even remember his face. I don't remember my parents, either. Not really. I think I do sometimes, but it gets all jumbled up with the pictures Gran shows us, the stories she tells."

Iris nodded. Then she reached out, touching the scar on Vi's stomach, and Vi let out a little "oh" of surprise. She trembled, the shock of Iris's touch spreading goose bumps all over her skin.

"We're alike," Iris said, running her fingers over the raised scar tissue, the place where Vi had very little feeling, could sense only the pressure of touch. At last she took her fingers away.

Vi stood, then slowly fumbled to do up the buttons of her pajama top, but her hands were shaking, so it was hard. Iris reached for her hand, pulled her down. Vi lay down beside her, and Iris pressed her body against Vi's back, spooning her, wrapping her arm around Vi, holding her tight, so tight Vi wasn't sure she could get away even if she tried. But getting away was the last thing on Vi's mind.

She listened to Iris's breathing, fast at first, then slowing.

She could feel Iris's heart beating against her back, matching the rhythm of her own heart, and it was almost like they were sharing one heart, one body all twisted together; a body of scars and broken memories.

Conjoined twins, separated then put back together, finally whole again.

THE BOOK OF MONSTERS

By Violet Hildreth and Iris Whose Last Name We Don't Know

Illustrations by Eric Hildreth

1978

THE GHOUL

The Ghoul is a humanoid creature. It walks upright, on two legs. It has two arms and moves like a man. It wears a black hood and has a very pale white face with two big black eyes.

We know very little about the Ghoul but believe it to be super-natural. We think it can disappear and reappear.

It's been watching us.

We believe we might be in terrible danger.

Lizzy

August 20, 2019

THE CABIN WAS in sight, a blue beacon at the edge of the shore.

I imagined Lauren making this trip at night, coming home, guided by the glowing lights of the cabin, listening to the loons, the owls, the frogs and toads trilling as she crept along, carrying her secret stone, the knowledge of her secret friend.

I thought about the weight of secrets.

Promises kept.

Dreams shared.

Do you share the same dream?

Do you dream it with me?

Yes, I thought. *Yes.*

But what did it all mean?

Was there a clue in the message? Something that might point me to where I needed to go next? To where the monster had taken the girl?

Did the monster want to be caught?

Did she know what was coming? Could she sense it? Smell it in the wind?

We belong dead.

The lighter, paper, and tiny stone felt heavy in my pocket. I reached in to touch the lighter as I walked, running my fingers over the butterfly etching, over Gran's initials.

Metamorphosis, I remembered Gran explaining, as she held out the lighter, looking at the butterfly. *That's what I think of each time I see this. How the lowly caterpillar turns into the butterfly. How we've each got a butterfly hiding inside us.*

◆ ◆ ◆

I WAS TIRED, thirsty, swollen, and itchy from the mosquitoes feasting. I wanted to go back to the campground, open a beer, put some calamine lotion on my bites, and think about what I'd discovered. I was nearly to the cottage's yard when I spotted a dark blue pickup truck parked next to my van.

And a man sitting in one of the old wicker rocking chairs on the porch, watching me.

A new tenant?

The owner, maybe?

I raised my hand in a friendly wave, came up with a quick cover story: I was a newcomer exploring the island, looking for a place to rent, wondered if that path would take you down to the water, ooh boy how about those mosquitoes? That would do.

But I didn't get the chance.

"Miss Shelley," the man called, standing.

I guessed him to be about my age. He was trim, fit, with close-cropped salt-and-pepper hair and skin tan and lined from the sun. He wore jeans, work boots, a khaki button-down shirt. He jumped down off the porch and walked closer until I could smell his cheap drugstore cologne.

He was smiling, but it was really more of a smirk.

"Yes," I said. "I'm Lizzy Shelley. I don't think we've met?"

"I'm Pete Gibbs. Local constable."

Great. A cop.

I nodded. "Nice to meet you, Constable."

"David tells me you're here to collect stories about Rattling Jane."

"David?" Then it hit me. Where I had heard the last name Gibbs. Shit. "Oh, you mean Skink?"

He seemed to flinch a little at the nickname, but recovered and smiled. "He's my son."

Now it was me who flinched. Somehow Skink had left out this crucial little detail about himself—*oh, and by the way, my dad's a cop.*

"Look, Miss Shelley, I understand you're a big deal—at least according to my son. He seems downright starstruck, to tell the truth. He told me all about your TV show, podcast, and blog. Even made me watch some of the show—*Monsters Among Us.*

"It's impressive, really," he went on, "that you manage to do this for a living—drive around the country searching for bigfoot and his pals."

He looked at me, seeming to wait for some kind of response. I only nodded.

"As impressive as your monster-hunting credentials might be," he said, "I need to ask you to step back a little."

"I'm not sure what you mean."

"Scaring kids crosses the line, Miss Shelley."

"Who have I scared?"

"Zoey Johanssen had to be taken to the emergency room this afternoon."

Zoey. The kid from the pier, the one with the short hair and trench coat. "The emergency room?" I repeated.

"I understand you and my son were talking to her, Riley St. James, and Alexander Farnsworth down by the docks earlier."

I said nothing, knew I was better off neither confirming nor denying.

"The way I heard it," Pete Gibbs said, clearing his throat before continuing, "you were interviewing them? Asking them about Lauren and Rattling Jane?" He looked at me for a long time, his blue eyes turning grayer and stonier by the moment. "Evidently Zoey got shook up so bad she had the mother of all asthma attacks."

"Asthma?" I said with a snort. "Are you kidding? The kid was chain-smoking. I'm no doctor, but I'm guessing that might have had something to do with her breathing problems."

"Look, the thing is . . ." He moved a little closer, speaking more softly, like a friend about to share a secret. In addition to the cologne, he smelled fresh, like laundry hung out on the line to dry. "Zoey is kind of a . . . fragile kid. A history of anxiety. Even some self-harm. Her family is worried. The last thing they want is someone encouraging these crazy ideas that make her so freaked out she can't catch her breath and has to be rushed to the hospital to get shot up with steroids. You get that, right?"

I nodded.

"My son is a good kid, but he has . . . questionable friends sometimes. I've spoken to him and asked him to stay away from that particular group, Zoey especially." His jaw tensed, and he looked out at the lake.

"He seems like a great kid, actually," I said.

He nodded. "He is. I feel really lucky. His mom died when he was ten, so it's been just the two of us for a long time. He keeps me on my toes, that's for sure."

"I can only imagine," I said.

He smiled, shoved his hands deep into the pockets of his jeans.

"So, what are you doing out here at the Wildflower Cottages, Miss Shelley? I'm sure you're aware this is private property?"

"Just looking around. Thinking I might come for a longer stay next summer, rent a little place . . ."

"You looking for Rattling Jane?"

I didn't answer, only smiled in what I hoped was a neutral way.

He gave me a knowing look. "You can do all the ghost hunting you want. I'm sure there are a lot of folks in town who'd love to tell you a story or two about Rattling Jane. And I'm equally sure there are business owners who would love the extra publicity—the idea that your podcast might bring in more tourist dollars, that you might even get the TV folks interested in featuring our little community on an episode or two. But I'd like you to leave Lauren out of it. That includes poking around the cabin her family rented. The owner, Jake, is pretty particular about the area being only for registered guests."

"I understand," I said.

"And I need to know that you're not going to bother the kids in town anymore or add to the crazy stories going around about Lauren being dragged into the lake by a ghost."

I nodded.

"I'd also appreciate it if you'd stop sharing . . . these particular *theories* with my son. He's got a pretty wild imagination. I don't think it needs stoking."

I didn't say anything.

"Do we have a deal?" he asked, eyebrows raised.

"Sure," I said, and started walking toward my van. I stopped, turned back to him. "Can I ask you a question, Constable?"

He smiled. "Please, call me Pete. And sure, you can ask me anything, but I've gotta warn you, I'm not a big believer in the supernatural. I'm afraid I don't have a single Rattling Jane encounter to report despite having lived here my whole life."

"Are you helping with the investigation? Looking into what happened to Lauren? Trying to find her?"

He sighed, ran a hand over his close-cropped hair. "Look, Lauren Schumacher is a troubled kid who ran away. Happens every day."

"You're sure about that?"

He nodded. "According to her parents, this is a regular thing with her—she stays gone a couple of days, crashes with friends, but always comes home. She had a big fight with her dad the day she left. She's just blowing off steam somewhere."

"Is anyone even out looking for her?" I asked.

"It's not really my jurisdiction, but I understand a missing persons report was filed with the state police. But I'll bet you just about anything that she's turned up back at home in Worcester already, tail between her legs."

That told me all I needed to know.

No one was looking all that hard for Lauren.

Just like all the other girls.

Girls everyone expected would disappear.

No one was surprised, and no one looked very hard, and when the girls never came back, people made up stories, said things like *Must have hitchhiked out to California like she always talked about.* Or, *Must have run off with some guy who promised to get her out of this shithole town, her shithole life.*

"I hope you're right," I said, and climbed into my van, shutting the door a little too hard.

Vi

July 19, 1978

I'M TELLING YOU," Patty said, voice low, "there's nothing there. I've looked through chart after chart in that file room, and there's not a single mention of B West or any Mayflower Project."

Vi pushed a shovel into the dirt. Old Mac was dumping a load of rocks at the edge of the garden for lining the flower beds. Some of the patients were gathered around, waiting to help move them. Tom the werewolf was hopping from foot to foot and rubbing at his arms, which were covered in scabs.

Miss Ev, wearing a large straw gardening hat over her wig, was supervising, directing the tractor with the bucket loader full of rocks: "Closer, Mr. MacDermot. That's it. No, too far to the right. Can you back up and come a little to the left?"

Poor Old Mac was going back and forth, back and forth in the old Ford tractor, trying to comply.

"Miss Evelyn," said Tom, "I'm telling you, I could do it. I worked trucking for years. I can drive anything: an eighteen-wheeler, a forklift, even a piece-of-crap old tractor."

"Absolutely not, Tom," she said. "Mr. MacDermot, now you're too far to the left!"

"The records must be somewhere else then," Vi said in a loud whisper. "Down in the basement, maybe."

Working in the garden was the only time Vi could really talk to Patty, and even then there were usually other people around: patients digging and taking in the sun and fresh air, Old Mac laying water lines or delivering piles of mulch and rock with the tractor, Miss Ev in her big hat bossing everyone around.

Patty looked over her shoulder to make sure there were no patients close by. "Maybe there's nothing to find," she said, shaking her head.

"Oh, come on," Vi said. "You don't really believe that, do you?"

Patty scrunched up her face, thinking. "Not really," she said. "But still, I can't help but think we'd be better off leaving it alone."

"Is that what you want to do?" Vi whispered. "Leave it alone?"

Patty hacked at the ground with a hoe. "You know, I used to have this dog, Oscar. There was a spot in our backyard, and Oscar would go out there and dig and dig. The soil there was all rocky, full of shale—it would splinter into sharp edges. Oscar would keep at it in this one spot, getting his feet all cut up. We tried everything: tying Oscar up, fencing that area off, even laying boards over it. But he always found a way back to it. Poor dog. I remember it so well—how he'd be all cut up and bleeding, but he'd keep digging."

"So what happened?" Vi asked. "Did he ever find anything? Dig anything up?"

Patty shook her head. "Nah. There was nothing there. We had to have him put to sleep. He had cancer. The vet said maybe that's what made him so crazy."

Vi shook her head. "I don't get it," she said. "What does that have to do with us? With this situation?"

Patty gave her a long look. "We're Oscar," she said.

"No!" Vi said, a little too loud. Miss Ev looked over, then went back to ordering Old Mac around. He now had the tractor positioned correctly and was about to dump the rocks. "We're not digging at nothing," Vi whispered. "And you know it."

"Everything all right over there?" Miss Ev called to them.

"Just fine," Patty called back. "Vi's just being a perfectionist. She isn't happy with the way I've got the back of the bed shaped."

"It looks good from here," Miss Ev said. "The whole garden is coming along fabulously!"

Vi nodded. The truth was, she was actually disappointed with how well things were going and how quickly the garden was coming together; she was running out of time. Once the garden was done, she wouldn't be able to keep talking with Patty or walking into Miss Ev's office or the Inn without question.

She stood up straight, leaned against her shovel, and looked around.

It was thirty feet from one side to the other, a perfect circle. They'd laid it out by putting a stake in the ground and tying a fifteen-foot string to it, then marking the circumference all the way around. Old Mac and the patients had torn up the sod, marked the areas for the beds and paths with sticks and string. There was a fountain in the center with three cement birds that sprayed water out of their open mouths (Miss Ev had picked it out herself from a catalog at the garden center). Gran thought the fountain was a little tacky, but what mattered, she said, was that Miss Ev and the patients all seemed to love it. When Old Mac first plugged it in and those birds started spitting, everyone cheered and hooted and hollered like they were watching fireworks on the Fourth of July.

Little by little, after putting in the fountain, they'd been adding in beds and lining them with stone.

Vi had enjoyed getting to know some of the patients. Other than the strays Gran brought home from time to time, she'd never interacted with any of them at the Inn before. The thing that surprised her the most was how normal they all seemed. Like Jess, for instance, who'd quickly become one of Vi's favorites. Jess had two kids and a husband who came to visit her twice a week. She talked about her life back at home: her friends, how she was active with the PTA, how she coached her daughter's softball team. She wore cheerful, bright-colored blouses that she'd sewn herself. Vi couldn't understand what she was even doing at the Inn—she seemed so . . . normal. Vi had asked Gran about Jess, and Gran had shaken her head, said, "You know I can't talk about our patients, Violet."

"But she seems fine. Like there's nothing wrong with her at all."

Gran nodded. "Some people's problems are better hidden than others," she'd said. "In fact, sometimes, the better hidden, the deeper they go, the more difficult they are to fix."

Vi thought about that a lot as she worked on the garden with Jess and the other patients for a few hours each afternoon during activity time at the Inn—the time when patients got to choose between working in the vegetable garden, pottery studio, or kitchen. Sometimes there were other special activities, like badminton. One time Miss Ev had even taught patients how to make macramé wall hangings. And now, there was the bird garden.

Each night at dinner, Vi gave a progress report on the garden. Iris kept asking to come help work on it, but Gran had said no again and again.

"You've come such a long way," Gran said to Iris. "I don't want you to push yourself."

So Iris and Eric had been staying home and painting rocks for it:

rocks with ladybugs, butterflies, and birds. They also painted a big sign that Old Mac was going to hang from a post with chains: MISS EVELYN'S BIRD GARDEN. They painted a rainbow with lots of birds flying over it in the background.

But Eric's heart wasn't really in the rock painting or sign painting. He was thinking about the Ghoul. He was determined to find it. It was all he talked about. He wanted—no, he seemed to *need*—to find the Ghoul, just so they'd believe him.

The next night was the full moon, and he had come up with a plan to trap it.

He had this idea that they could lure the Ghoul out and surround it in the clearing by the stream. They'd have a salt circle all set up with just one part missing. Once the Ghoul landed in the circle, they'd lay down the rest of the salt, and it would be trapped. They could try to talk to it, learn what it was and what it wanted. If it gave them any trouble, they'd do the Spell of Banishment.

For Vi, the Ghoul was the least of her worries these days. Figuring out where Iris had come from and what was going on at the Inn was at the forefront of her mind.

Now Miss Ev was arguing with Old Mac about the size of the rocks he'd been gathering—"symmetrical," she kept repeating, and Vi was pretty sure Mac had no idea what that meant. He was adjusting his scarecrow hat, looking down at the rock in Miss Ev's hand—her "ideal size and shape" of rock. "Think about a bowling ball. Not a big one, but one of the little ones they use for candlepin bowling."

He looked at her blankly. "Most rocks ain't round like that, Evelyn," he said.

"That's absolutely true," Jess said.

"He's got a point," said Tom as he scratched at his bare arms.

"It doesn't need to be perfectly round," Miss Ev said, shaking her head like the whole thing was hopeless. "Just rounded. And more or less the same size. It looks funny when you've got a huge boulder next to a little baseball-sized rock, don't you agree? That's what I'm saying about symmetry."

Old Mac licked his lips, adjusted his straw hat.

Vi looked at Patty. "Any other updates?" she whispered.

Patty sighed. "Well," she said.

"What?"

Patty had her eye on Old Mac and Miss Ev as she leaned close to Vi and said in a low voice, "I probably shouldn't be telling you this, but someone came to the Inn yesterday. She showed up and started asking a lot of questions. Got your grandmother and my uncle all stirred up. Did your grandmother happen to say anything to you about it?"

"No." Vi shook her head. Though Gran had been in a lousy mood when she came home from the Inn last night—she'd gulped down two martinis before she even started making tuna casserole for dinner. "Who was she? A family member?"

Gran said sometimes that family members were harder to deal with than the patients.

"I think she was a reporter. Or journalist of some kind."

"A reporter?"

"Yeah." Patty nodded. "She made kind of a scene in the front room, and Dr. Hildreth and my uncle whisked her away to the meeting room."

"But what did she want? What was she saying?"

"I don't know. But I do know it got Dr. Hildreth and Uncle Thad all upset. After she left, the two of them went down into the basement for hours."

"I need to get down there," Vi said. "Tonight. I'll get down there to-night."

"How?"

"I'll take my grandmother's keys." Vi thought of the key ring in Gran's purse—the purse that never left Gran's side.

"You're going to steal her keys and come over and get into the basement without her knowing?" Patty chuffed out a laugh like this was the most ridiculous plan she'd ever heard, and Vi sank a little, knowing she was right. "How exactly are you planning to pull this off?"

"I'll create a distraction. Something to keep her busy." Vi bit her lip, thinking. "How late are you working?"

Patty sighed. "I'm doing a double 'cause Nancy called out. I'll be here till eleven."

"Will you help me?"

"No way," Patty said, voice firm.

"Come on, will you at least be a lookout? I'll have the keys, I'll just need to know the coast is clear." She stared at Patty. "I'm gonna do this with or without you. If you help me, I'll tell you what I find when I go downstairs. If you don't, I'm gonna keep it all to myself, and you'll just have to go on guessing about what might be down there."

Patty shook her head. "You're a little shit, you know that?"

"I know," Vi said proudly.

Lizzy

D O YOU REMEMBER Gran's lighter?" I asked as soon as Eric (Charlie!) picked up the call.

"Huh?" He sounded like I'd woken him up from a nap. He was the sort who took naps. Something I, always wired and unable to turn my brain off, couldn't fathom.

"*Gran's lighter*," I repeated slowly, unable to hide the irritation in my voice. "You remember it, right?"

"Sure. With the butterfly."

"Describe it."

"Lizzy, what's this—"

"Just describe it. Tell me what it looked like."

There was silence, then a long sigh. "Let's see. It was gold-colored. Tarnished. There was a butterfly carved into the front. Etched, I guess. And her initials were on the other side in kind of a curly old-fashioned script."

"Right. Do you remember where she got it? Or anything else about it?"

"No. She just always had it. As long as I could remember."

I was outside at the campsite, sitting at the picnic table, the lighter, note, and stone in front of me. I took a long sip from the bottle of beer I'd opened.

"I found it," I said.

"What?"

"Gran's lighter."

"Wha-at?" he stammered. "How?"

"*She* left it for me."

"She who?" Charlie said.

Who else could it be?

"I was right, Charlie. *It's her.* She's the one! The one taking the girls, using the other monsters. That's how she gets to the girls. She pretends to be these other monsters, she makes contact. And it's not just random. I think she chooses the girls carefully. She must—"

"Lizzy, please," he said. "Stop."

"I know it sounds crazy, and I'm still trying to get my head around it, but I've got Gran's lighter! I'm holding it in my hand right now! It's proof! And she left me a note. I think she—"

"You're right," Charlie said. "It *does* sound crazy. I'm starting to get really worried here, Lizzy. I think you need to see someone. Like a professional."

I barked out a laugh. "You're kidding, right?"

"You need help, Lizzy. Listen to yourself, will you? You're starting to sound, I don't know, delusional or something."

I hung up on him, fuming.

How dare he?

I took a big gulp of my beer, spun the lighter on the table.

I shouldn't have told him. Should have known he wouldn't believe me, wouldn't understand.

"Stupid, stupid, stupid," I muttered.

He called me back, and I let it go to voice mail.

Then he texted: I'm sorry. Really. Call me back, OK? I'm worried about you.

I turned off my phone.

* * *

I WAS STILL sitting at the picnic table in front of my van, working on my second beer, when Skink walked up, a hangdog look on his face. I slipped the lighter, note, and stone into my pocket as I watched him approach.

"Hey," he said.

I was surprised he'd shown up at all.

"Your father is a cop? And you didn't think to mention this little fact to me?"

He shrugged, looked down at the ground. "Constable," he mumbled.

"Huh?"

"He's the town constable. He's not like . . . like a real cop. I mean, he has a day job running fishing charters. The only real constable duties he has are serving papers on people, delivering notices to people who haven't paid their taxes, and cruising around breaking up keg parties and stuff."

"He sounded enough like a real cop," I told him. "He asked me to stop looking into what happened to Lauren, to stop talking about it to people."

"I wouldn't worry about it too much. It's not like he has any real power or anything. He doesn't even have a gun or handcuffs. If he finds any actual trouble, he calls the state police. He couldn't even arrest you or anything."

"Oh, well, that's comforting! All he'll do is call the state police, is that right?" I shook my head. "And I can't believe you told him about the monster-hunting stuff."

"Well, yeah, I kinda had to, didn't I?"

"You made him watch *Monsters Among Us*?"

Skink shrugged. "Just a couple clips. You know, just to show that you were the real deal."

I shook my head.

"I can't believe Zoey caved and spilled everything," Skink said. "My dad is pretty pissed at me. I'm supposed to stay away from that whole group, and from you too."

Me and Constable Pete agreed on one thing, at least.

"So? What are you doing here then?" I asked irritably.

"I came to see if you went out to Loon Cove. That's where you were going, right? Did you find anything?"

I shook my head. "No. I went but didn't find anything. Just some old beer cans and cigarette butts."

There was no way I'd mention the lighter.

I found this lighter from my childhood. I think my sister, who I haven't seen since I was thirteen, is actually the real monster I'm searching for, the one who took Lauren.

"Did you check the hiding spot in the tree? Maybe Lauren left a note or something? Some kind of clue."

"I found the tree, but there was nothing. No note, no cigarettes, no weed. If she was keeping stuff there, she grabbed it and took it with her."

Maybe my brief acting career was paying off—I sounded convincing, even to myself.

"So, what? Now you think she ran away, too?" He gave me a disappointed look.

I took a sip of beer. "Beats me." I was done sharing my theories with this kid. The son of a cop.

He came over and sat down at the picnic table. He eyed the six-pack, like he was waiting for me to offer him a beer. "Are you going back to the cove? 'Cause I could, like, go with you. Do a monster stake-out kind of thing."

I laughed an *are you kidding me right now?* kind of laugh. I was about to tell him to get lost.

"We'd just have to be really careful. My dad's been patrolling the sanctuary nearly every night lately. Ever since the fire in the tower."

The skin at the back of my neck prickled. "Wait? The tower?"

I thought of the message the Monster had left for me:

An old dream, a dream of endings and beginnings.
A dream of fire.
Of a lever pulled and a world of bright white light,
crumbling ruin.
A single line spoken: "We belong dead."
Do you share the same dream?
Do you dream it with me?

A reference to *Frankenstein's Bride*. The movie me and my sister watched at the drive-in so long ago.

That line at the end the monster spoke: *We belong dead,* just before he pulled the lever and blew up the tower.

Could the tower be where she'd been hiding?

"Tell me about the tower," I said, my voice a little too frantic.

"There's this old stone tower in the wildlife sanctuary. My dad's always telling me how it's historic 'cause the Civilian Conservation Corps built it back in the 1930s or whenever. They did work all over Vermont in parks and stuff: built dams, bridges, towers. They put in stone steps in the wildlife sanctuary—you probably noticed the ones going down to Loon Cove, right?"

I nodded.

"They also built this stone tower—it's kind of an island landmark. There's a replica of it on the town green. And my uncle's even got it on the campground sign. You didn't notice?"

"I thought it was a lighthouse," I admitted.

"Kind of a lighthouse-looking tower, I guess? I think it was originally built as a fire tower—you know, to keep an eye out for smoke in the woods around the lake? It's pretty tall—maybe fifty feet or so. But it's in bad shape. They've been trying to get funding in place to rebuild it, fix it up because it's a historic landmark and all that. Right now it's all boarded up. But people still sneak in. My dad goes out there pretty regularly to kick people out. Just last week, someone lit a fire up at the top."

"A fire in the fire tower?"

He nodded. "They must have been setting off fireworks up there or something, because people heard an explosion, then saw flames. They saw it all the way across the lake."

"Where exactly is this tower?" I asked.

"Do you wanna go out there? You think maybe the tower and the fire have something to with Rattling Jane? With what happened to Lauren?"

I shrugged, trying to play it cool.

He thought for a minute, rubbing his chin. "You know, I think the fire was right around the time Lauren disappeared. Like the day before? Or the day after, maybe? I can't be sure."

I remembered working on a page on monster hunting for our book. The two of us writing: *When you look for monsters, there are obvious places: dark woods, caves, old castles and towers. Monsters love towers.*

Monsters love towers.

The words pinged in my brain.

"I'm gonna grab you some paper and a pencil—I need you to draw me a map."

"I can do better than that. I can take you," he said.

I shook my head. "No. If your dad, Officer Friendly, shows up, we'll both be in trouble. And haven't you've gotten in enough hot water with him for one day?"

Skink nodded.

I left off the rest of my thought: *And if she's there waiting, I need to face her on my own.*

Vi

July 19, 1978

E RIC CAME RUNNING, banging open the back door. "Gran! Come
quick! Gran!" His voice was frantic, almost hysterical.

"Whatever is the matter, Eric?" Gran asked, practically running
from her office to the sunroom. They'd had dinner and Gran had gone
over their schoolwork. She'd been alone in her office sipping a martini
and finishing up some patient notes.

In her hurry, she'd left her purse on her desk, just as Vi had hoped
she would. Vi swept into the office, opened the purse, and grabbed the
keys, then crept back out of the office and down to the front door.

"Fire!" Eric was saying from the sunroom.

"What?" Gran asked, voice disbelieving.

"Look!" Eric said. "I was fooling around, trying to make a warming
cage for injured animals with a candle in the old hutch, it was stupid, I
know, but—"

"Good Lord!" Gran cried.

Both the hutch and the old woodshed next to it were burning up.

Vi went outside and crouched under the open kitchen window, listening. Gran's heavy key ring was tucked inside her sweatshirt pocket. A couple moments later, she heard footsteps entering the kitchen.

"We should call the fire department," Eric said urgently.

"We shall do no such thing," Gran replied, voice strangely calm. She picked up the phone and called Miss Ev.

Once Vi knew that Miss Ev and Sal were on their way, she crossed the yard to her hiding spot behind a tree. Her hope was that in the chaos, Gran wouldn't think to ask where she was, would just assume she was up in her room, head in a book, missing out on all the action.

Vi smiled, feeling very pleased with herself. It was all going exactly the way they'd planned. Miss Ev came running across the road into the yard, her wig askew, her robe tied loosely around her pale nightgown, Sal right behind her in blue hospital scrubs.

"Get buckets and the hose," Miss Ev ordered as she moved into the backyard, pointing, directing people, her pink terry-cloth robe flapping.

Gran got a bucket from inside, and Eric turned on the hose and handed it to Sal.

And that's when Iris came outside and saw the fire, moving closer and closer to it, drawn like a moth to flames.

She looked like a moth girl there, light-blue pajamas hanging off her skinny frame, fluttering in the breeze. If Vi squinted, she could almost make out wings pressed against Iris's back, starting to unfurl, delicate and in danger of being burned by the sparks. She had on the orange hat, and Vi imagined soft, feathery antennae hidden underneath it.

"Go inside," Gran ordered when she spotted Iris; but Iris stood, transfixed, and then, right on cue, she began to shriek, a high-pitched, earsplitting scream. Something that you wouldn't think could come from a human.

Phase One of their plan: start the fire, get Gran outside.

"It's okay, Violet," Sal said, stepping toward Iris. Sal had been an orderly at the Inn for years—he was used to people screaming; he knew how to settle them down, and when that didn't work, how to restrain them.

"But that isn't Violet, it's—" Eric started to say, and Gran interrupted, "Take your sister inside, Eric! Now!"

Sister. Our sister, Vi thought. *Our secret sister, the screaming Moth Girl.*

Then, still shrieking, Iris took off into the woods.

Phase Two of the plan: the chase.

Gran followed Iris (as they'd all known she would), with Sal right behind her. Gran turned to Sal and snapped, "No. You stay here and get the damn fire out. I'll take care of my granddaughter."

Once Gran entered the woods, and the others were busy trying to untangle the hose so it would reach the shed, Vi took off running toward the Inn.

She sprinted down the gravel driveway, across the road, then the yard. She slipped around to the Inn's back door. Her heart was pound, pound, pounding, and her whole body was slick with sweat. Her clothes, her hair stank of smoke and another smell, one she hoped no one but her noticed: kerosene.

She knew she didn't have long. She had to be quick. Quick as a bunny. Hippity-hoppity.

She was about to use Gran's keys to open the back door when it flew open.

"What's happening?" Patty asked, nearly breathless, her body silhouetted against the lights behind her in the hall. "Is the house really on fire?"

Vi slipped into the hall, shook her head. "It's not the house. Just the rabbit hutch and woodshed out back."

"But is everyone okay?"

"Of course!" Vi said.

"Did you actually do it?" Patty asked. "Get Dr. Hildreth's keys?"

Vi pulled the key ring out of her sweatshirt pocket. She held up the one labeled B WEST.

Patty's eyes got big. "No way! I can't believe it!"

Vi nodded. She couldn't really believe it either.

"Okay," Patty said. "Just me and Sheila are here now, and I can keep her busy. I don't know how long Sal will be gone, though, and when he gets back he'll probably do his rounds."

Vi nodded, looked down at her watch: 9:17. "I'll be quick."

And she ran past Patty, down the hall toward the Common Room. Once there, she went to the door leading to the basement stairs, took out the key marked BSMNT and opened it.

The lights were already on.

She trotted down the set of concrete steps and found herself in a narrow hallway lined with bricks painted a dull pale green. There was a strong smell of bleach in the air. Long rectangular fluorescent lights flickered and buzzed on the ceiling. To the left was a door marked BOILER ROOM. Vi turned right and reached another door marked B WEST. The door was solid steel, no windows. And instead of a lock built into the door itself, it was fitted with a large metal hasp and a heavy padlock. She took out the key and fitted it into the padlock, felt it slide open, and removed the lock from the hasp. She held her breath, pulled the heavy door open, and stepped through, half thinking an alarm would sound and she'd be caught.

Silence.

More green-brick hallway. More antiseptic smells. More buzzing fluorescent lights. The air felt damp and cool.

Three doors on the left side were all gray metal with little rectangular windows in them. Two doors on the right, no windows.

This felt so different from the rest of the Inn, which had been kept up nicely and felt almost homey—lots of light and windows, warm wood paneling, comfortable furniture. Down here was all dungeon-like cement floor and brick walls, lights that flickered and hummed.

And the doors.

Vi peered through the tiny window in the first door on the left, saw an empty room with a metal hospital bed bolted to the floor, leather restraints attached to the corners. The second room on the left looked the same, but with more equipment: big surgical lights, a metal box on a table with dials and switches and cables leading to two things that looked like microphones. An ECT machine—she'd heard Gran describe such a thing, but had never seen one.

There was a metal cabinet in the corner. Some oxygen tanks. A rolling stainless steel tray. A big metal drain down on the floor.

She put her hand on the doorknob but couldn't make herself turn it.

It felt all wrong, this room.

The gods were mumbling low warnings to her. She couldn't make out the words, just a slow, steady thrum that felt dangerous, like the buzz of high-voltage wires. Everything inside her was telling her to get out, to run. Her stomach was doing somersaults. Her head felt thick and heavy the way it did before she got one of her headaches. Her skin was prickly with sweat.

The air down here felt like poison in her lungs.

Run, the voices called, suddenly clear, louder than ever. *Leave this place as fast as you can.*

But she fought the powerful urge and pressed on, knowing that this might be her only chance to learn the truth.

The window in the third door on the left was dark. She flipped the light switch outside the door, but nothing happened. She stood on her tiptoes, cupped her hands around her eyes, and peered through the window, just barely making out shapes in the darkness: a bed and a table.

She backed away, looked at the doors with the little rectangular windows, just about at eye height.

She'd seen this before.

Iris's drawing.

The day Vi had asked her to draw a monster, and Iris had drawn a rectangle with another dark rectangle in it, and two circles inside that.

It was one of these doors. With someone looking in from outside.

Iris had been down here. This was proof!

But who was the monster on the other side of the door?

Gran?

Vi imagined Iris strapped down to the hospital bed in the middle room. She thought of the scars on Iris's head and chest.

Across the hall was another door, this one windowless. She tried the knob, and it turned easily.

It was some kind of break room, with a couch, a coffeepot, a small refrigerator. A can of Folgers coffee. She opened the fridge, found a carton of milk, some juice, a plate she recognized from their own kitchen at home. The plate had a liverwurst sandwich on it, Gran's favorite, all wrapped up in plastic wrap.

There was a large glass ashtray on the coffee table. A couple of magazines: *Time* and *Life*, addressed to Dr. Hildreth.

Vi left the break room and moved on to the last door in the hallway.

Locked.

She flipped through the keys, found one marked B-OFF.

Be off with you, she thought.

And she should be off. How long had she been down here? Five minutes? More? She looked at her watch. Nearly ten minutes had passed since she'd met Patty at the back door.

Tick tock. Tick tock.

How long would it take them to put out the fire? How long before Sal hurried back and started making his rounds? How long before Gran went back into the house? Before she looked in her purse and saw the keys missing?

Hurry, hurry, hurry, a voice whispered in her ear, one of the gods, but she wasn't sure which one.

Tick tock. Tick tock.

She tried the key. It fit. She opened the door, felt for a light switch on the wall inside, and flipped it on.

She stepped in. B-Office smelled like stale cigarette smoke.

There was an old wooden desk and chair, and a large gray metal file cabinet with four drawers.

"Bingo," she said, heading right for the file cabinet.

She opened the top drawer. Saw file after file marked:

MAYFLOWER

Her heart beat louder; she felt the throbbing pulse in her whole body.

She hesitated a second, suddenly unsure.

Did she want to see?

No.

But she needed to.

She started thumbing through the files.

The earliest records she found were dated more than fifteen years earlier—before she was even born. She pulled out a couple of files and laid them on the desk.

Patients were referred to by letters. Patient A. Patient B. Medical records. Long lists of medications.

Almost all of them had been given some combination of sodium amytal and Metrazol. Vi committed the names to memory, planning to look them up in Gran's drug book when she got back to the house.

There were mentions of experiments with psychoactive plants, lyser-gic acid diethylamide, things with Latin names Vi didn't recognize. She thought of the jars of leaves, roots, and berries in the basement at home and wondered if some of those were hallucinogens; if Gran was making her own mixes and experimenting with them.

The notes contained descriptions: Electroconvulsive therapy. Sen-sory deprivation. Cold water therapy. Hypnosis.

Even surgeries. Vi looked down at carefully sketched diagrams of the brain, of cranial cuts, of areas stimulated, pierced, and cut away.

These were not cures.

These were experiments.

She felt dizzy; things looked blurry. She made herself look away from the notes, all carefully charted in her grandmother's neat pen-manship.

These people had been tortured.

Cut open like the rats in Gran's basement.

Her stomach flipped, and she thought she might be sick.

Was Iris one of these patients? A subject of Gran's experiments?

Had she gotten the scars on her head and chest from surgeries done down here in the Inn basement?

Vi continued to scan the charts, read how Gran tested her subjects' memories, their cognitive abilities and IQs. Again and again, she was disappointed in the results:

Another failure. Memories and sense of personhood are gone, but there are too many deficits. Pt can no longer toilet himself, much less read, write, or have a meaningful conversation.

Vi looked through the first three drawers, frantically searching for something that would help her understand who Iris was. She found a folder on Patient I, but he was a thirty-six-year-old man, a transient with a history of alcohol abuse. At the end of the notes, paper-clipped to the inside back cover of the manila folder, was a photograph. A snapshot of Patient I in a hospital gown, a scar on his shaved head. A scar just like Iris's.

Vi's breath was stuck in her throat. Her heart seemed to freeze, to forget to beat for a second. Because she recognized this man, Patient I.

Patient I was Old Mac.

She closed the file, put it back, looked at her watch. Another five minutes had gone by.

Shit, shit, shit.

She had to get out of here. Had to hurry.

But she couldn't leave quite yet. She was too close. She skimmed through more folders until she got to the last one in the third drawer. There, her eye caught on a line scribbled in her grandmother's familiar handwriting.

> *The project has not shown the results we are looking for*
> *because of one reason: I have not found the right subject.*
> *Until now.*
> *Patient S is the one. I know she is.*
> *The one who will change everything.*

Vi shoved the file back, moved to the final drawer, the one at the bottom.

And there was that funny feeling in her chest again.

Each file folder in the drawer was marked: *PATIENT S.*

It was stuffed full. There must have been hundreds, thousands of pages of records in there, all on Patient S.

She pulled out the first file marked *HISTORY* and opened it:

The Mayflower Project began with a series of simple questions:

Is it possible to take a subpar human being, a person lacking in good breeding, of lower than average intelligence, and—through an experimental regime of surgery, medications, and therapy—turn that human being into something more? Something greater?

Can bad heredity, inferior bloodlines, even a criminal nature, be erased?

Is it possible for a person like this to have a use after all? A greater purpose?

All of our initial experiments yielded disappointing results. Until I realized the problem.

These first patients were too old. Their brains did not have the necessary elasticity. Their bodies were too worn to handle the treatment.

What we needed to succeed, to truly succeed as never before, was a child.

Vi's vision narrowed. She felt the room tilt and spin. But still, she forced herself to keep going, to flip through the mass of records in the file.

The pages ripped a jagged hole in her chest, made her breathing uneven, her head pound in time with her heart. Her tears splashed onto the paper.

A child.

A little girl taken from her home with terrible parents and an older sister deemed a lost cause.

A girl who was the subject of experiments, made to do terrible, unimaginable things.

A girl who had been held in B West for months, while Gran tore her down and tried to rebuild her, make her into something new. It was all there in the files Vi skimmed: records of surgeries, medications, water therapy, hypnosis.

I have, wrote Gran, *given this child a new life. A new beginning. I have taken a doomed soul and created a blank canvas, a life full of possibility.*

Iris's story.

And, Vi realized, also the story of how her beloved grandmother, the brilliant Dr. Hildreth, had created her very own monster.

Lizzy

August 20, 2019

MY PACK WAS sticking to my back, my T-shirt soaked with sweat even though the night air was cool.

This is stupid, I told myself. *Dangerous.*

What was I hoping to find at the tower?

Lauren bound and gagged? The monster standing guard?

The monster who was really my long-lost sister?

And what if I was walking right into a trap? If the monster knew I was coming?

Still, I pressed on through the dark forest, letting myself imagine getting there and saving the girl.

But to save the girl, I'd have to slay the monster.

* * *

"I DON'T THINK you have an evil bone in you," my sister told me once, long ago. "I'm not even sure you'd be *able* to kill a monster if you met one."

"I could so kill a monster," I'd retorted, furious, defensive.

"Tell me," she'd demanded. "Tell me how you'd do it."

"It depends on the kind of monster," I'd said, proving my expertise; proving that I didn't just help create the monster book, I'd memorized it. "A vampire gets a stake through the heart. A werewolf a silver bullet."

"What if you don't know what kind of creature you're dealing with?" my sister asked.

"You make your best guess. You bind it with a spell, with salt and holy water, and you hurt it any way you can. A magic dagger. A silver bullet. And most monsters can be killed if you cut off their head."

My sister laughed. "You make it sound so easy."

"It's not. Killing a monster is never easy."

◆   ◆   ◆

I CARRIED MY monster-hunting backpack, the little revolver tucked inside it, just in case.

My flashlight illuminated the narrow path through the trees. I stopped occasionally to shine the light on the map Skink had drawn for me and his notes. *Take the path from the campground to the Silver Trail. Turn left. Follow the Silver Trail to the Tower Trail on the right.*

I was on the Silver Trail now.

It was quiet in the sanctuary, only the low hum of insects, the occasional call of a loon. I couldn't see the water, but I could smell it, feel it all around me: a dampness in the air, the vaguely ruined scent of decaying weeds, water lilies, and old leaves floating on the surface.

I swept the beam of my flashlight along the trail and spotted the sign up ahead: TOWER TRAIL. I turned right, following it, a narrow path covered with little pebbles that rolled under my feet like marbles.

The wind blew through the trees, seemed to whisper a warning, a warning like the old gods once whispered: *Danger, danger. Turn back while you can.*

Sometimes monsters dwelled in enchanted places.

Was this one of those places?

Had I crossed a veil of some kind?

Yes, the wind whispered.

And your human weapons will do no good here.

You can't win.

The trail took me steeply uphill, my feet slipping on the stones.

I felt it before I saw it, stepped into the thick, dark shadow it cast.

The tower was massive against the moonlit sky, built of stone and mortar; it seemed to be leaning slightly to the left. No wonder I'd mistaken its image for a lighthouse—it was tall and round, slightly wider at the base than at the top.

I heard a soft rustle. Feet against stone.

Had it come from inside?

Was the monster in there, watching, waiting?

I remembered playing hide-and-seek when we were kids, counting to fifty with my head buried in the living room couch cushions, rushing up the stairs to search for my sister: *Ready or not, here I come!*

I could see a yawning doorway and five little square windows, staggered.

I approached the tower, listening hard. No more sounds came from inside. No sound came from anywhere.

It felt as if the whole world was holding its breath.

There were two boards nailed up over the doorway and a sign: DANGER! TOWER CLOSED! NO TRESPASSING!

I shone my light inside, saw a metal spiral staircase, rusted through in places. On the cement floor were smashed bottles, a stained T-shirt, leaves and sticks and candy wrappers. The remnants of a small fire, which was complete idiocy—who would light a fire in there? Old dry wooden timbers jutted out, tied into the metal stairs. And all those old leaves and sticks would go up like a tinderbox.

ENTER AND DIE was written on the wall in red spray paint, with a pentagram drawn next to it. And beneath it, another message sprayed in white paint: *Rattling Jane Was Here!*

I smelled old crumbling cement. Earth. Stale beer. Urine.

And cigarette smoke. Faint, but recent.

I swallowed down the lump that was starting to form in my throat and carefully unshouldered my pack, opened it, and took out the little .38 Special, then shrugged the knapsack back on. I ducked under the warning boards crossing the doorway, the gun in my right hand, the flashlight in my left.

My boots crushed glass, and little sticks and leaves popped and crackled under my feet like tiny bones.

I tested the first metal step with my weight. It seemed solid. I stepped to the second, testing, then the third, which seemed to shift slightly beneath me.

All the spit in my mouth dried up.

I was sure I heard rustling from up above.

Not rustling, footsteps. Dragging, shuffling footsteps.

I shone my light up, saw only the rusting steps, how they'd come loose from some of the metal brackets that braced them to the wall.

Again I thought: *This is stupid. I should turn back.*

There was more graffiti on the stone walls: *SUICIDE IS PAIN-LESS; MARK P SUCKS COCKS; THIS BUD'S FOR YOU* with the out-line of a marijuana leaf.

Then, in what looked like colored chalk, a drawing I recognized: a copy of Eric's chimera from the cover of the monster book. A creature with the head of a lion and the body of a goat, a tail that ended with the head of a snake.

Written under it: *The first thing you need to know is that monsters are real. They're all around us, whether we can see them or not.*

My sister had been here.

Was here right now.

I held my breath, listening.

I was about halfway up the stairs when I heard a noise from outside the tower. A thump and a huff, a little groan.

I nearly called out, demanded to know who was there, but I bit my lip, kept climbing.

The stairs shifted and creaked. Concrete rained down from a spot on the wall somewhere above me. I dropped the flashlight as I instinctively reached out to grab hold of the railing.

The flashlight hit the cement floor below with a crash, went out.

Shit, shit, shit!

Should I go up or down?

Up or down?

Tick tock, tick tock.

I felt it, a strong magnetic pull, one I hadn't felt in a long, long time, drawing me up, up to the top of the tower.

To *her.*

I thought of Frankenstein, of the monster throwing the doctor off the top of the windmill, of the villagers with their torches.

Up I climbed, holding tight to the gun in my right hand, the rusted metal rail in my left. Bits of flaking metal stuck to my hand, jagged edges bit at my skin, but I did not let go.

Ready or not, here I come.

I saw the opening just above me, blue moonlight shining down. I took the last steps as quickly as I could. The element of surprise was gone: If there was anyone up there, they'd heard me. Knew I was coming.

Halfway through the opening, swiveling my head around, pointing the gun in an arching circle, I scanned the shadows for movement, for a figure crouching, lying in wait.

But there was nothing. No one.

I ascended the final steps, walked out onto the wood floor, which gave a little beneath me. The walls were worse up here, the stones coming loose as the mortar failed, the battlements crumbling: eighty years of rain and wind and snow taking their toll.

I searched frantically, walking in a slow and careful circle around the perimeter, testing the boards with each step. They felt spongy, rotten, but they held my weight.

The top floor was empty.

There must be something here, I told myself. Some sign. Some clue.

Another chalk drawing, perhaps?

A message telling me where to go next, like a game, a scavenger hunt.

I was nearly all the way around the circle when I spotted a rectangular object in a nest of leaves. A package? I moved closer, squinting in the darkness, trying to make out the details, wishing for my flashlight.

My breath caught in my throat. My whole body vibrated, ringing like the bell on top of the strongman carnival game. Even my teeth ached.

I knelt on the splintered, rotten wood, reached toward the gift—for surely it was a gift—left just for me.

I picked it up, this old familiar friend—more worn now, cracked and battered—but still, holding it in my hands felt like a homecoming, a reunion.

I ran my fingers over the cover, the title, struggling to make out the details in the dark.

THE BOOK OF MONSTERS
By Violet Hildreth and Iris Whose Last Name We Don't Know
Illustrations by Eric Hildreth
1978

There was Eric's chimera, the bright marker colors faded.

A tear fell from my cheek onto the book, and I quickly wiped it away.

I couldn't bring myself to open it. Instead, I set down the gun, hugged the book, pulling it tight to my chest.

Then I saw something else in the pile of leaves.

A little figure. A doll.

I reached for it, picked it up, trying to make out the details in the moonlight.

The doll was made from white cloth, like the fabric of a T-shirt. It had a stitched face, frowning, with crosses for eyes like a dead character in a cartoon. It was dressed in blue denim shorts, a black hooded sweatshirt. Black sneakers stitched together with pieces of worn canvas made from actual sneakers (I could spot part of the star of the Converse logo). And sewn into the top of the doll's head was a wild spray of blond hair with purple tips. *Real hair,* I realized as I touched it.

Lauren's hair.

The doll's clothes must be made of Lauren's actual clothes.

Then I heard footsteps. Not the wind or the scuttling of a small animal. The metal stairs shifted and groaned, bits of loose concrete falling down as someone started to climb toward me.

THE BOOK OF MONSTERS

By Violet Hildreth and Iris Whose Last Name We Don't Know

Illustrations by Eric Hildreth

1978

Some monsters are born that way.
Some are made.

The Helping Hand of God:
The True Story of the Hillside Inn

By Julia Tetreault, Dark Passages Press, 1980

From the files of Dr. Helen Hildreth
B West, Mayflower Project

PATIENT S

Background and family history:

D.P. was a 38-year-old white male with a history of alcohol abuse and a criminal record. He had been arrested for assault and battery and drunk and disorderly conduct. He worked as a day laborer. His IQ was 84. He had a long, sloping forehead, small close-set eyes, and poor dentition. He had unmanaged high blood pressure.

D.P. was referred to Project Hope, the state-run clinic where I do volunteer work. The underlying mission of Project Hope is to help individuals with psychiatric issues (including drug and alcohol abuse) reintegrate successfully with society after being released from prison.

D.P.'s weekly visits to Project Hope for counseling were part of the requirement of his probation, and he was to continue them for twelve months.

When I began working with D.P., I did background research into his family and was stunned to discover that he was the great-grandson of none other than William "Templeton," the patriarch of the family Dr. Hicks and I followed for years for our study.

Coincidence?

More like a moment of synchronicity, which Jung defined as a "meaningful coincidence."

I am by no means a sentimental person. I do not allow myself to waste time with magical thinking. We cannot change the past. All we can control is this moment. Wishing, longing, and bargaining do no good. I do, however, find myself imagining that Wilson Hicks was alive now so that I could tell him all of this. I imagine him lighting a cigarette, listening carefully, his head cocked to the side in that thoughtful way he had, as I describe the adrenaline rush that came over me when I learned who my new client was, that he happened to come from that same poor family Dr. Hicks and I spent months, years, gathering information on. And I do believe that Wilson Hicks is the only one who could truly understand the significance of all that has transpired since that first meeting with D.P.

I had the opportunity to question D.P. about his family during my intake meeting with him. He never met his maternal great-grandfather, William, who died five years before D.P. was born. The cause was a self-inflicted gunshot wound, shortly after his diagnosis with metastatic liver cancer.

D.P. lived with his wife and two daughters in a two-bedroom trailer on rented land. When I did my home visit, I discovered the conditions were truly squalid. No running water. An outhouse. Windows layered in plastic wrap to keep the cold wind out. D.P.'s wife was an unattractive woman who had not passed seventh grade. She too was an alcoholic and used drugs, primarily amphetamines.

Their older daughter, 14, was a juvenile delinquent. She rarely attended school, sniffed glue and gasoline, drank alcohol, was sexually active, and frequently ran away from home.

The second child was a girl of 8. And somehow, in this child, this girl, I sensed possibility. She was small for her age, quite pale, with filthy hands and face, tangled hair. But in her eyes, I saw something—a spark. A hint of intelligence; of promise.

I instantly knew she was the perfect candidate for the next phase of the Mayflower Project.

There are moments in research, breakthrough moments, where an answer seems to suddenly appear after years of toil. Meeting this child was one of those moments.

I asked D.P. to bring his wife and daughters to our sessions, telling him that family therapy was part of his treatment. After the initial group session, I explained that I felt the younger of the two girls was in need of one-on-one therapy. D.P. complained, said he didn't see the need and that he couldn't take time off from work to shuttle the girl to any appointments. I offered to pick her up on my own and warned that I didn't want to have to take my concerns for the girl's well-being to the state authorities. "An intervention now could make all the difference," I assured him. "And I'd be able to report to your probation officer that you are compliant with all areas of suggested treatment."

At last he agreed. And so I began to pick her up from school weekly, taking her out to get doughnuts—what child can resist a sweet?—building trust.

As I got to know this child, I became certain that she was the one I'd been looking for.

What if I could take her, this poor unfortunate creature, and give her a new self, a new life?

Raise her up from the filth and squalor, reshape her.

I looked at this child with her dark eyes, body too skinny from poor nutrition, and I knew she would truly be a pilgrim of a sort. A traveler entering new and sacred lands.

But first, as with any true pilgrim, she would need to leave her old world behind. To sever all ties to her previous life.

I began to formulate a plan and, in time, to implement it.

Fortunately, the girl proved very easy to influence. I began an intensive regimen of programming and hypnotic suggestion.

•   •   •

IT WAS A fire that killed them. Not technically the fire itself, but smoke inhalation.

D.P. and his wife were too soaked in cheap vodka to wake. The older girl was in her room, most likely too high or drunk herself to know what was happening.

Patient S—the little girl with a book of matches in her pocket and kerosene-stained hands—was never found.

No one looked for her very hard. Not the police or social services.

I was interviewed, of course, because I was on record as having had contact with the family.

I told them that it was my understanding that the younger girl had been sent off to live with a distant relative. A cousin, perhaps? Somewhere out of state—regrettably, I had no more information.

Next came the real challenge of the Mayflower Project: to take this girl who had come from nothing, this girl who had done terrible things—and to wipe her clean. To have her begin again as an empty vessel ready to fill.

Vi

July 20, 1978

V I AND IRIS were alone in Vi's room after dinner—Iris was quiet, glassy-eyed. She sat on her bed on the floor, staring out at nothing. Vi knew that look—Gran had given Iris medicine to help keep her calm after her "episode" at the fire last night.

It was all Vi's fault. If she hadn't come up with the stupid plan and asked Iris to fake going nuts and lead Gran off on a chase through the woods, then Iris wouldn't be all tranqed up. And Eric wouldn't be shut up in his room, sulking, after Gran yelled and yelled at him for setting the fire in the first place. "Idiotic," she'd said. "Honestly, Eric, I'm disappointed in you."

Vi had told both of them that she hadn't been able to get into the basement—that the key hadn't worked. She hadn't been able to face telling either of them the truth. She'd been living with the secret all day, felt it coiled inside her like a poisonous snake.

She looked out the window. She could see the lights of the Inn glowing. The air was damp and the beams of light made a ghostly halo around the building. Gran had said she wouldn't be back until late. They were short-staffed and a patient was in crisis. Vi was glad to see Gran go. Half of her still loved Gran desperately, and the other half hated her with a ferocity she hadn't realized she was capable of. She'd never felt so tangled up.

This was someone she'd known her whole life, who had taught her to read, had nurtured her ambitions to be a doctor, who'd fed her and bathed her and put cool cloths on her head when she was sick, who sang her a lullaby each night. Yet somehow, she was the same woman who'd written those notes, who'd done those horrible things to Iris and all the others.

Iris was obviously Patient S. That meant there had been at least eighteen patients in the Mayflower Project before her. Thinking about it made Vi feel sick and dizzy. She thought of Old Mac—how he always wore a hat, was completely devoted to Gran. But what had happened to all of the others?

"You okay?" she asked Iris for what must have been the hundredth time. She walked over, sat down on the mattress beside her.

"Yeah," Iris said. "Just sleepy." She laid her head back on the pillow. The dingy rabbit puppet was beside her. She slept with it every night.

"I think it's important," Vi said, "that you not take the pills Gran gives you."

With effort, Iris sat up again. She looked at Vi with a puzzled expression, but said nothing.

"Just fake it," Vi explained. "Keep the pill in your cheek—and when she's not looking, spit it out."

For the first time in her life that she could remember, Vi hadn't drunk the special milkshake Gran made for her that morning. She took pretend sips while Gran was watching; then, when she left the kitchen, Vi had dumped it down the drain.

She didn't think there was anything in there besides wheat germ and raw egg, milk and ice cream, but she didn't trust Gran. Not anymore.

"Why shouldn't I take them?" Iris asked now, blinking like a tired owl. "Gran says the medicine helps. It's to help make me better. Make me remember."

"What if it's not?" Vi said.

"Huh?"

Vi picked at a loose string on Iris's quilt. "What if I told you that it's not. That Gran isn't who she seems."

If she told, there was no going back.

But she *had* to tell.

She pulled hard on the loose thread, and part of the quilt's edging began to unravel.

Iris blinked again. "Well, who is she, then?"

"I've got a better question," Vi said, standing up.

"Yeah? What's that?"

"Who are *you*?"

"Me?"

Vi's mouth went dry. She began to pace, going back and forth across the painted floorboards of her room. "Last night, when I went to the Inn, I got down into the basement, into B West."

Iris stared at her. "But you said you couldn't—that the key didn't work."

Vi swallowed hard, shook her head. "I just didn't know how to tell you the truth. I got in and I found things out. Like I promised I would."

It had been a terrible promise to make. A terrible promise to keep. Vi had been wondering all day if she should tell Iris the truth. She'd gone back and forth, back and forth, like a pendulum swinging.

She thought of the movie *The Pit and the Pendulum*. About the man strapped to the table and the pendulum swinging back and forth, getting lower down with each swing, a huge razor-sharp blade on the end.

Back and forth. Back and forth.

Like her pacing now.

Maybe Iris was better off not knowing. Ignorance was bliss, wasn't it?

But then Vi thought of her promise. Promises meant something. Besides, if it were her, she would want to know. She would want to know the truth, no matter what.

Some secrets were too big to keep.

She had to tell.

She had to tell Iris. And she had to tell other people, too.

She had to find a way to stop Gran.

There went the snake, writhing in her belly.

"Tell me," Iris said. She looked more awake now. And more than a little scared.

"Are you sure you want to know?" Vi asked.

Iris nodded.

Vi walked over to her desk, looked out the window above it at the lights of the Inn across the yard. Where was her grandmother? Down in the basement, in B West? Was there a new patient strapped down in one of those rooms?

She had to do this. She knew it. She had to tell people the truth. And she needed to start with Iris.

Vi flipped on her desk lamp, then went back to her bed, pulled the folder of notes she had taken from the Inn from under her mattress.

"You need to read this," she said.

She knew she should be the one to say it, to explain what she had learned. But she felt sick when she thought of having to actually tell Iris the story.

So she laid the folder out on her desk. "Just read," she said.

Vi sat on her bed and chewed her nails while she watched Iris work through the papers slowly. Her finger moved along beneath the words, tapping the pages.

Her eyes were glassy, expressionless.

The seconds ticked by. Soon an hour had passed.

Vi sat still, watching Iris read. She wanted to speak, to break the room's silence, but there was nothing to say.

But what she wanted most was to step back through time, to not have gone down into the basement. To not have discovered any of this. To not be sharing the truth with Iris right now. She wanted to go back to the time when they were just sisters hunting monsters, never realizing how close the real monsters truly were.

◆ ◆ ◆

"IT'S ME, ISN'T it?" Iris said when she looked up at last. Her eyes were glazed over, pupils huge and sparkling, as if they weren't even her eyes at all but the eyes of a doll or a stuffed animal. "I'm Patient S."

Vi nodded.

"I did these things?" Her voice shook. She looked down at her hands as if they weren't her own. "I killed my parents? My sister?"

Sister. She'd had an actual flesh-and-blood sister. A sister she'd killed.

"What Gran and Dr. Hutchins did to you . . . it's . . ." Vi struggled for the right words.

Wrong? Criminal?

Outside, they heard a howl.

They both froze, eyes locked.

Another howl.

"Crap," Vi said. The Monster Club call. "I'll get him to go away." She went to her window and opened it. Eric was down there in the yard holding a flashlight. He'd decided to come out of his room after all.

"Not now," Vi called down.

"But it's time," he yelled up.

Shit. The monster hunt. She had forgotten all about the damn monster hunt.

"We can't," she said.

"What do you mean? What about the Ghoul? It's the full moon," Eric reminded her. "This is our chance."

"We can't," she repeated.

"I did what you told me to do last night. I got in trouble for you!" He glared up at her.

Behind her, Iris stood. She went to the closet, got a dark hooded sweatshirt. "We should go," she said, a girl on autopilot, speaking and moving like a sleepwalker.

"No. We don't have to. Not tonight," Vi said.

"But Eric's waiting."

Vi tried to argue, tried to stop her, but Iris was on her way downstairs and out the door and then it was too late.

• • •

THE MOON WAS a bright orange-red, hanging low and huge in the sky.

It was a damp, cold night—too cold for July. Vi shivered despite her sweatshirt. She wanted to go home. To take Iris home and talk about everything, make a plan for what they should do next.

Eric was telling them that he'd found some footprints down by the creek: footprints that definitely weren't theirs. "I think it's the Ghoul. When I saw him, he had these big boots that looked like they had fur on them. Like animal skin."

He was leading them through the woods, followed by Vi and then Iris last. Vi kept turning back to look at her, but Iris's eyes wouldn't meet hers. They were focused on the ground.

Crunch, crunch, crunch went their feet through old leaves, twigs.

They stumbled and shuffled their way forward, crushing ferns, tripping over roots and stones.

Eric was swinging the light, scanning, always lighting the way up ahead to make sure it was safe, that the Ghoul wasn't there, waiting for them with sharp teeth and claws.

They heard the creek before they saw it, and soon they were right by the bank. In the spring it ran deeper and faster, but at this time of year it was barely a foot in the deepest places. Some years it stopped running altogether by midsummer.

The water was black and sparkling under the beam from Eric's flashlight.

He looked down, shone the beam around in the mud along the edge until he found the strange footprints. "See, they're not ours. These come from boots with a smooth sole. It's the Ghoul."

Vi stepped forward to look at the prints. They were too big to be Gran's. Too small for Old Mac. Who else would come back here?

Eric looked up, shone his light in Vi's face, blinding her. She put her hand up to shield her eyes.

"Eric!" she scolded. "Quit it."

He pointed the beam of light all around her, scanning the trees. "Where's Iris?"

Vi turned to look. "She was right here just a second ago."

But now she was gone.

Eric's eyes got huge. "Do you think . . ." He lowered his voice. "Do you think the Ghoul got her?"

"Iris?" Vi called.

Nothing.

Only the sound of the creek.

"We've got to find her," Vi said.

Eric nodded, still sweeping the area around him with the light. "Iris?" he called, voice squeaky and soft.

They held still, listening.

Vi heard a cracking sound, a branch breaking, from over her right shoulder.

"This way," she said, moving in the direction of the sound. She called out to Iris again, shouting as loud as she could. The trees got thick and closer together as they moved deeper into the woods. She felt everything closing in around her, like a hand tightening its grip.

She heard someone running up ahead.

What if that isn't Iris? she wondered. What if they were really chasing Eric's Ghoul? What if they were heading right into a trap?

She remembered his drawing: the pale face, dark eyes, and black hood.

She pictured those dark eyes staring back at her, black as a starless night sky.

Up ahead, she caught sight of a shadow moving through the trees.

"Iris?" she called.

A branch snapped. Then another.

A grunting cry from up ahead.

"It's not her," Eric said from just behind her. "It's the Ghoul!"

He was moving the flashlight through the trees, but Vi didn't see anything at all.

Then the light caught on a pale face with a dark hood.

Eric yelped.

But this was no ghoul.

It was a girl in a black hooded sweatshirt. Vi's sweatshirt. Vi's twin. Iris was standing beside a tree, a ghostly white paper birch.

"Iris," Vi called. "What are you doing?"

"Go away," Iris said, her voice a twisted snarl. "Leave me alone."

"No," Vi said, moving closer, stepping slowly.

And Iris leaned down, picked up a baseball-sized rock, and threw it at Vi.

She was so surprised, she didn't have time to duck, and the rock caught her on the chin, sending her reeling, her jaw exploding with pain. She fell back on the ground.

"I said, leave me alone!" Iris screamed.

Eric hurried to Vi, dropped to his knees. "Vi?" he said, voice high and squeaky. "You're bleeding, Vi! Oh, crap. Crap."

"I'm okay," she said, sitting up, rubbing at her chin. The rock had barely grazed her. An inch or two up and it might have broken her jaw, cracked her teeth. She got back on her feet, brushing past Eric and moving toward Iris, who was crouched down now, hands wrapped around her knees. And the sounds she was making—deep-throated growls and sobs—were more animal than human. Vi took a slow step forward, hands limp at her sides, trying to look as unthreatening as possible.

"Iris," Vi said, making her voice low and soothing, trying to keep all the panic she was feeling out of it. "It's okay. We want to help you."

Iris stood, and Vi saw she had another rock in her hand. She stepped toward Vi.

"Iris, I—"

Iris swung at Vi, but Vi caught her arm, pushed it back, twisted it until Iris let out a cry of pain and dropped the rock.

Vi was bigger, stronger, but Iris was fueled by a mad rage. She thrust back, surprising Vi with her strength, nearly knocking her off-balance.

The two of them struggled in a strange dance.

"Stop it!" Eric screamed, skittering beside them helplessly, shining his light on their faces, in their eyes. "Please, stop it!"

Vi was holding her ground, but then Iris gave her another hard shove, and Vi slammed her heel against a root and toppled to the ground, with Iris still clinging to her.

The fall knocked the wind out of her, and she felt a searing pain where she'd landed on something hard and sharp.

When she could take in a breath at last, she groaned in agony.

Iris had her wrists pinned. Eric was shining his light in Vi's eyes, and when she looked up, Iris seemed to be glowing, to have a halo around her.

"You know what I am," Iris said, her breath coming in hot bursts, chugging like a locomotive.

Vi kicked up with her legs and hips, ignoring the pain in her back and ribs. She flipped Iris and pinned her.

Put her own face right down in front of Iris's, their lips nearly touching.

"You're my sister," Vi said.

THE BOOK OF MONSTERS

By Violet Hildreth and Iris Whose Last Name We Don't Know

Illustrations by Eric Hildreth

1978

Here's why the world needs monsters: Because they are us and we are them.

Don't we all have a little monster hiding inside us? A little darkness we don't want people to see? The shadow self. The little voice that tells you to go ahead and eat that last cookie, or the whole plate of them, maybe.

And doesn't it feel good when you lose it, really lose it and rip things up, punch a hole in the wall, smash a bunch of bottles to smithereens?

That's your monster self coming out.

The world needs monsters.

And monsters need us.

Lizzy

August 20, 2019

I SHOVED *THE BOOK of Monsters* and the Lauren doll into my backpack. I circled the upper floor of the tower, gun in hand, listening to whoever was climbing the steps coming closer as I frantically searched for a way to escape, a secret door or a ladder. But there was nothing. No way out but the spiral metal staircase, up which someone was coming. I went to the edge and looked over—could I jump? No, too high. There was no way I'd survive it in one piece. And the face of the tower was too smooth to clamber down. I circled around again, desperate.

I thought of the mice running on wheels down in Gran's basement laboratory, how sad and futile it had seemed, those poor animals running in endless circles, never getting anywhere.

Knowing I was trapped, I stopped walking in useless circles, crouched down with my back against the wall, gun pointed at the shadow coming up now through the opening in the floor.

I held my breath.

Would it be *her*?

My sister.

My monster.

My long-ago twin.

Or would it be Rattling Jane, a figure strung together from bits of trash and bone, the little pieces jangling together like wind chimes as she walked?

The bright beam of a flashlight hit me straight on.

"Lizzy?" called a vaguely familiar male voice.

Constable Pete got the light out of my face.

"Let me guess," he said as he climbed the rest of the way up. "More monster hunting?"

I lowered my gun, felt the adrenaline surge begin to wane. My mouth tasted bright and coppery. I'd bitten my lip.

I nodded.

"You thought Rattling Jane might be up here?" Pete asked.

"I was walking around in the woods and saw the tower. Decided to check it out."

"And I suppose you didn't notice the *No Trespassing* sign?"

I shrugged.

"There's a reason for it, you know? This tower is in terrible shape. It's dangerous as hell. In fact, it's kind of a wonder this floor is holding both of us right now."

I said nothing. Pete had the beam of the light pointed down, but it was bright enough to light up the whole space. I could see the bowed and rotten floorboards, the crumbling cement walls around us.

"I assume you've got a permit for that thing?" Pete said, nodding at the gun I still held.

"Of course. Do you want to see it?"

He shook his head. "Not necessary." He looked at me a minute, waiting, then said, "But I was kind of hoping you might put it away."

"Oh yeah. Sorry."

I took off my backpack and slipped the gun into its holster clipped inside the front pocket, careful not to open the main zippered pocket, where I'd tucked the book and the doll.

"Do you always carry a gun when you're hunting ghosts and monsters?" he asked.

"Usually," I said. My hands shook a little as I zipped the front pocket. I hoped he didn't notice but was sure he had.

"Can you actually shoot a ghost?" he asked.

"It's not the ghosts I'm worried about," I told him, shouldering the pack.

He nodded, took a few steps closer. "What were you expecting?"

"I wasn't expecting anything," I said. "Like I said, I saw the tower and decided to check it out. I heard you coming up and I guess I just got spooked."

"Spooked," he repeated.

I gave a sheepish nod.

"I wouldn't think you got spooked easily, considering your line of work."

"I don't usually," I admitted.

He looked at me for what felt like a long time.

"What do you say we get out of here before the tower collapses under us and go talk someplace a little more safe? We can get a cup of coffee and some pie—my treat. There's a diner just off the island that's open till midnight."

"I don't know," I said. "I—" I felt the weight of the backpack, thought of what I had hidden there. I needed to pull myself together, act normal, get him to stop looking at me in that worried, suspicious way. I smiled. "Actually, sure, pie sounds great."

•   •   •

THE HAPPY OWL Diner was one of those old-school aluminum trailer diners, complete with long counter and spinning stools covered with sparkling red vinyl.

We were the only two people in the place. The jukebox looked like it had been there since the fifties. And judging from the music coming from it—Bill Haley and His Comets—it had.

Pete and I settled in at one of the booths. I did my best to hold still, refrain from fidgeting even though my skin prickled and my mind raced. I tried not to think about the monster book and the doll and what finding them in the tower might mean; I tried to put them in a little box in the back of my mind, locked away for now.

Focus on the present, I told myself. There would be time later to think about what I'd discovered.

The waitress came over and said hi to Pete, asked him how things were on the island.

"Busy as ever," he said. "But it'll settle down after Labor Day."

"But then we've got the peepers," she said.

"Peepers?" I asked.

"Leaf peepers," Pete explained. "Tourists here to see the foliage."

"Of course," I said.

"Not a Vermonter, huh?" the waitress said.

I shook my head. "It's my first time in Vermont."

Pete frowned at me. "Really?" he asked.

I nodded, looked at Pete steadily. "Really."

I thought of the monster book: proof of a long-ago childhood in Vermont. And I thought of the doll.

If he knew the doll was there, stitched together from Lauren's clothes, bits of Lauren's hair . . . My palms grew sweaty. I reminded myself to breathe. He had no way of knowing any of this.

Yet he'd given me that odd look when I said I'd never been to Vermont before, like he knew I was lying somehow.

He doesn't know. You're being paranoid.

We each ordered a slice of blueberry pie and coffee.

Act normal, I told myself. *Don't give him any reason to be suspicious.*

The waitress came back with our order. The pie was homemade—the crust buttery and flaky and perfect, the berry filling just the right blend of sweet and tart.

"This is amazing," I said.

"Best pie ever," he agreed, taking a bite himself, then washing it down with a sip of coffee. "So. Do you want to tell me what you were really doing out at the tower tonight?"

I took a bite of pie, thinking. "Like I told you, I went for a walk in the sanctuary."

"At night? In the dark?"

I nodded. "Ghosts and monsters don't usually make themselves seen in the light of day," I said.

"So you went to the tower to hunt for Rattling Jane?"

"I was in the sanctuary, saw the tower, and thought I'd check it out," I repeated. Didn't this guy listen? I looked at him over the edge of the heavy white diner mug. "You know, in all the commotion, I haven't had a chance to ask—what were *you* doing out at the tower tonight?"

"We've had a bit of trouble there lately, so I've been trying to keep an eye on the place."

"What kind of trouble?"

"Kids partying, mostly. Last week, someone was shooting off fireworks and started a fire in there—it's a wonder the whole place didn't go up in flames."

"Did you catch them? The kids who started the fire?"

He shook his head. "Nah. They were long gone by the time the volunteer fire department and I got out there."

We were quiet a minute, both of us sipping our coffee and munching on pie.

"You know, I went to your website, listened to a couple of your podcasts. I watched more of *Monsters Among Us*. I even read some of your interviews and watched your TED talk. It was interesting—the idea that monsters mirror the anxieties of society."

I smiled. "You've been stalking me."

"Just Googling. You've got quite a following. You're kind of a big deal."

I laughed. "In certain circles."

My eyes burned and my head felt foggy. Now that the ramped-up adrenaline surge I'd felt in the tower had subsided, the lack of sleep was catching up with me.

Pete was quiet as he concentrated on his pie.

"It's amazing to me, really," he went on after a minute, "that so many people believe in that kind of stuff."

"And it's amazing to me that so many people don't."

"And you?" he asked. "Do you really believe in all of it? Or is it just for show? You truly think there are monsters and cryptids and ghosts and ghouls out there in the world?"

"Yes," I said without hesitation. "I do."

"Have you always believed?"

I nodded. "Since I was a kid. My brother and sister and I, we had a monster club. We were obsessed: watching monster movies, going on monster hunts, reading everything we could."

He smiled. "Sounds a lot like my son. He was into all that. Still is, I guess."

"Yeah, he told me he'd had a monster club when he was younger."

"Sure did. He'd lead all the kids on monster hunts. Some of them would go home in tears, all freaked out because David had led them into the woods and convinced them there were actual monsters out there. Man, did I get some phone calls from upset parents!"

I smiled. "I think kids especially are drawn to this stuff . . . the un-explained."

Pete put down his fork and wiped his mouth with a napkin. "You're about the same age as me," he said. "Remember that old show that used to be on TV, *In Search Of . . .*? With Leonard Nimoy? Mr. Spock?"

"Of course!" I said.

"Bigfoot, the Bermuda Triangle, ancient aliens . . . I loved all that stuff when I was a kid."

"But not anymore?" I asked.

He laughed. "Guess not."

"You grew out of it? Came to your senses?" I teased.

"You said it, not me," he said, grinning.

"I guess I never did," I said. "Grow out of it, I mean. All my life, I've been drawn to those same unanswered questions that fascinated me when I was young." I took a long sip of black coffee, tried to picture him when he was a kid, sitting on a couch watching *In Search Of . . .* and believing monsters were real.

"And have you found any answers?" he asked.

I shook my head. "Just more questions."

I thought again of what I'd found. I longed to go back to the campground, get a good look at the doll, flip through the book, try to figure out what it all meant. Had the monster left it for me as a clue? Just to taunt me, to remind me that I was always one step behind?

Was I already too late? Was that what the doll meant—that there was no saving Lauren?

I suppressed a shiver, wrapped my hands tightly around my coffee mug.

"Where'd you grow up, Lizzy?" Pete asked.

The most normal of questions. And one I'd been asked over and over throughout my life. But still, each time someone asked it, my body stiffened.

"Pennsylvania," I said, a lie so practiced that it almost felt real. I could imagine a life there, in a cozy little house in a suburban enclave, at the end of a cul-de-sac, two parents who loved me very much, a brother and a sister. "A little town called Yardley, not far from Philly."

He was quiet, nodding. And there it was again, that funny little frown: a look that told me he knew I was lying.

But I was being silly. Paranoid.

How could he know?

The guy's a cop, I reminded myself. It was his business to go digging, to find things no one else bothered to unearth.

If he'd gone to the trouble of Googling me, listening to podcasts and watching videos, maybe he'd taken it further, called in a favor, dug deeper. Maybe he knew who I truly was and was just toying with me.

I finished my last bite of pie, looked at my watch, and stretched. "This was great, thank you so much for the coffee and pie. But honestly, it's been a long day and I'm beat. I should really get back."

He smiled at me. "Of course. Thanks for joining me." He stood up and put money down on the table. "Let's get you back to the campground."

He looked at me across the table, his smile faltering, and a new thought occurred to me: that it was no coincidence that Pete had found me in the tower tonight—he'd followed me there.

I was a suspect.

Vi

V I AND IRIS were in the clubhouse looking through *The Book of Monsters*, not really talking. They'd come here so they *could* talk, because it was the only really safe place where they could say anything, anything at all, but here they were, saying nothing. Just sitting. The God of Silence was standing guard, pressing down over them, heavy as a thick wool blanket. Vi closed her eyes, did her best to will him away. Iris was flipping through the pages of their book, staring down at it, studying each drawing, reading each entry. Vi knew she should speak, but she was waiting for Iris to talk first, to break the terrible spell.

The past few days had been so strange. Iris had been avoiding her, not even looking her in the eye. Vi tried to imagine what it must be like for Iris and couldn't. She just couldn't.

Mostly, she'd been trying to figure out what they were going to do next. Should they run away? But where would they go, two thirteen-year-old girls out on their own with no money, no family or friends, only each other? They'd told no one what they'd learned from the files. Not even Eric.

Should they go to the police? The police would never believe them, even if they brought the notes as proof. Gran was a well-respected member of the community—a famous doctor who people came from all over the country to learn from. The police would call Gran, and they'd all have a good laugh about the crazy ideas of kids with wild imaginations. Then she and Iris would end up locked away in the basement of the Inn, forever maybe. Or maybe Gran would drug them and poke at their brains until they forgot everything and were just walking vegetables. Vi had seen people like that: drooling, nonverbal, shuffling like sleepwalkers or pushed around in wheelchairs, seemingly unaware of their surroundings. No thank you.

Vi had been avoiding Gran whenever she could—if she saw Gran coming, she ducked and turned the other way. She could barely look Gran in the eye, knowing what she had done to Iris. How could Gran— the same Gran who had taught her to read and sew and bake cookies and name every part of the body—how could that woman have this whole evil, secret life?

Did everyone have a secret life?

Vi knew she did. Her secrets sat like stones in her chest, heavy and cold. But her secrets had never hurt anyone.

When she couldn't avoid Gran, she told herself she was an actress playing a role. If Boris Karloff could play Frankenstein's monster and Lon Chaney Jr. could play the Wolf Man, then surely Vi could play her old self—a slightly younger, more naïve self. She practiced in front of the mirror in her room every morning, first thing when she woke up, while Iris was still sound asleep.

There is nothing wrong. My grandmother takes wonderful care of me and my brother, Eric, and my new sister, Iris. I have a clever mind and a strong heart.

The night before, Vi had given her report to Gran just like always. They sat in Gran's home office, Gran sipping a gin and tonic, Neil Diamond on the little turntable—*Brother Love's Travelling Salvation Show*. Vi was perched in the leather chair in the corner by the bookshelves holding the tonic and lime Gran had given her. Quinine was what gave tonic water its bitter taste and it was a medicine—it was used to treat malaria, a sickness you could get from mosquitoes.

Iris and Eric were in the living room watching *The Six Million Dollar Man*, and Vi wished she were out there with them instead.

She lifted the sweating glass in her hand and took another sip of the bitter tonic. "A regular day," she reported, smiling, shrugging her shoulders a little, like an apology. Sorry that the truth was so boring. "We did some reading and math, then watched TV. Went for a walk in the woods. Read a bunch of comic books. Went over to the vegetable garden to get some tomatoes. Old Mac yelled at us for taking too many."

Gran studied her for a long time without saying anything; then she asked, "Are you all right, Violet?"

"Of course. What do you mean? Nothing's wrong." Vi tried not to squirm, though she felt like a worm on a hook. *Caught, caught, caught!*

"You and Iris seem a little . . . tense," Gran said, peering at Vi as she took out her cigarettes and lighter.

Vi shook her head. "Not really. We kind of had an argument, but it was stupid. Everything's fine now."

"An argument about what?" Gran wanted to know.

"Over a game we were playing. Like I said, it was dumb. We made up."

And Gran looked at her like she could see right through whatever lies Vi might tell. Like maybe Vi wasn't the actress she thought she was.

"What happened to your face?" Gran asked.

"Huh?"

"The bruise on your chin, Violet. The one I've been pretending not to notice for days now."

Vi rubbed at her chin. "I . . . I fell down when I was out in the woods the other day."

Gran had stared at Vi for a long time. After lighthing a cigarette, she'd taken a deep drag of it and blown the smoke in Vi's direction.

◆   ◆   ◆

"NONE OF THE monster stories have happy endings," Iris said now, turning the page to the werewolf entry, breaking the silence at last. She flipped to the Invisible Man (Eric had drawn only a hat and glasses on that page).

Vi bit her lip, scrambling for something to say to make it all better. The God of Words was silent. Her head was full of a strange, humming static that was getting progressively louder. Another headache was coming on. She'd been getting so many of them lately. All the secrets piling up, creating a pressure that built and built until she felt like her head might actually explode.

"The monster can try to live among the humans, to act like a human even, but it never works, does it?" Iris asked as she closed the book and stood up. "People always find out the truth." She was crying now, but her face didn't look sad. Her face didn't have any expression at all. It was like a wax mask, except for the tears flowing down her cheeks.

"You're not a monster," Vi said, standing. She reached out and touched Iris's wet cheek. It was cold and pale, like white marble. Iris jerked back.

"Yes, I am." Her voice was high and loud and strange. All wrong for Iris. "You saw the notes. Patient S was a monster Gran created. And I'm that monster."

Vi's chest felt tight, like she couldn't breathe, like her heart might just stop beating. She was scared, more scared than she'd ever been. She stepped toward Iris. Her legs didn't want to cooperate: They were all wobbly, as if they didn't belong to her at all.

"Stay away from me," Iris ordered. "You don't know what I might do."

"I'm not scared of you," Vi said. "You won't hurt me."

"You don't know that."

"Yes, I do," Vi said, putting her hands on Iris's shoulders, looking her right in the eye. "I know you. I know the *real* you."

But Vi wondered how much anyone could really know anyone else.

Had Vi really known Gran?

No. She'd only seen what Gran wanted her to see. One side.

"I know the truth," Iris said. "The truth about monsters. I know because you taught me."

Vi gripped Iris's shoulders more tightly. "Stop it, Iris, please."

Now Vi was crying—Vi, who never cried, who couldn't remember the last time she felt this broken, outside or in. Her whole body throbbed, and her head was full of white noise and static. She let go of Iris, who seemed to waver through the watery lens of Vi's tears, as if she might not be real at all.

"First things first, monsters are real. So real they can reach out and touch you." Iris pressed a finger into Vi's chest, and Vi let out a racking sob.

"There are monsters walking among us." She stalked in a circle around Vi, like a predator sizing up her prey.

Vi was scared. Not scared of Iris, but scared *for* Iris. Scared for both of them. Scared of whatever might come next.

"Sometimes a monster doesn't know that it's a monster"—Iris leaned in, whispered in Vi's ear—"but when it learns the truth, everything makes sense suddenly. At first I didn't want to believe, but at the same time, it was like some part of me already knew."

"No," Vi said, gulping at the air between her own sobs.

"Monsters will always be monsters, and they are always danger-ous," Iris said, quoting Vi's own words, the ones she'd carefully written down in their book.

"It's just make-believe," Vi sobbed. "Just stupid words I wrote."

Iris raised her right arm, flexing all her muscles, her hand clenched into a tight fist, like she was going to hit Vi, but Vi grabbed her arm, twisted it behind Iris's back, shoved her up against the wall hard and fast with a strength she didn't know she had. The whole building seemed to shake: the walls, the floor; Vi worried the roof might come crashing down. Iris let out a little *oomph* as her head hit the wall, her eyes flashing a look of complete surprise and disbelief. A look that seemed to say, *Who are you and where did you come from?*

"Enough!" Vi yelled, her face right up against Iris's, her spit fly-ing, landing on Iris's cheeks, mingling with Iris's tears. "Stop it!" she bellowed, afraid that maybe her voice alone could make the whole building crush them alive.

Just then, *she* felt like the dangerous one. A roaring rushed in her ears, like all the gods were talking at once, screaming inside her. She was filled with fury, fury at what had been done to Iris, fury that her grand-mother could be so wicked and cruel, fury at herself for not being able to fix any of it.

"You're hurting me," Iris said.

But Vi did not let her go.

Her body didn't feel like her own. She'd lost control of it to some-thing else, something that had been sleeping deep inside her.

A current was running through her, and running through Iris too, she was sure: the pull and push of a magnetic field; the motion of elec-tric charges spinning, being drawn together and creating a power greater than anything either of them could produce on their own.

She felt herself pulled forward, her breath on Iris's cheek, her lips moving to find Iris's lips. Their mouths pressed hard against each other, teeth banging together. Vi had never kissed anyone, other than Gran on the cheek at night. And she knew it was wrong—girls weren't supposed to kiss girls, not like this, not like men and women did in movies—but it felt as if everything inside her was pulling her to Iris, and she couldn't stop it if she tried. She kissed Iris desperately, hungrily, as if her kiss alone could save Iris, could pull her back, take away all that had happened; as if her kiss could banish the monsters.

Iris pushed Vi away, her eyes huge with fear.

Vi staggered backward, started to speak: "I—"

She was breathless, heart hammering, unsure just what she was going to say, what words were going to come tumbling out like a random roll of the dice:

I'm sorry.

I love you.

Let's forget this ever happened.

Iris raised her arm, pointed to the window. "There's someone—" she said, and Vi looked in time to see a pale face turn away from just outside the window, a hood over the figure's head.

"The Ghoul," Iris whispered, voice breaking, terrified.

Lizzy

August 21, 2019

T HE BANGING WAS loud, insistent.

"Miss Shelley?" a voice called.

The voice of God, perhaps.

One of the old gods maybe.

The God of Time that's run out.

I opened my eyes.

I was in my van.

"Miss Shelley?" called a voice from outside. "I'm sorry to bother you, but it's Steve. From the office. You've got a phone call."

I jumped out of bed, opened the door. "A call?" I blinked at the bright morning light, then down at my watch. It was nearly ten. I'd slept in.

"Yes, a woman. She said it's very important she reach you. Do you want to ride over to the office with me?" he asked. My solar panels were hooked up, the wheels were chocked. It would be faster to go with him than to disconnect.

I slid on my shoes, didn't bother to brush my hair, just jumped in the four-wheeler next to Steve in my rumpled T-shirt and sweatpants.

Could it be?

Could it be my once-upon-a-time sister?

When we pulled up, I jumped out and nearly ran to the phone, beating Steve into his own office.

"Hello?"

I listened. Turned to Steve, holding the phone out. "No one's there."

He frowned at the phone. "Well, there was. It took me a bit to get you, maybe she gave up. Why don't you sit a minute, have a cuppa coffee? I just made a fresh pot. If it's important, she'll call back."

"Did she give a name? What exactly did she say?"

He shook his head. "No name. But she did say she was family."

"Family?" A knot formed in my throat.

"She said she was looking for you, needed to talk to you. She knew you were here on the island camping, but she wasn't sure of the campground."

"And you told her I was here?"

He nodded. "She told me she was family. And she sounded . . . well, distressed. Like it was urgent that she reach you. Cell service out here is spotty, so a lot of times we get concerned family members wanting to check in."

I poured myself a cup of coffee, hands trembling a little. I waited, staring at the black phone on the desk. It did not ring.

Steve made small talk. He asked me how I was liking the island so far, if I'd had a chance to get out on the water yet, reminded me that the campground had kayaks and canoes for rent. I just stared at the phone. At last, my coffee was gone, and I accepted that there would be no call back. I'd missed my chance. Steve offered to give me a ride back across the campground, but I told him the walk would do me good.

As I walked, my brain turned in desperate circles.

My sister had called, so now she knew where I was.

What next?

I needed more coffee. Then I'd sit and look through the monster book. I couldn't bring myself to open it last night—I'd been too exhausted, and a little too freaked out—so had left it in my backpack with the creepy little doll, deciding I'd look at both with fresh eyes in the light of day. I'd tossed and turned, staring frightened at my backpack half the night, as if the doll might unzip the bag, find its way out, and carry the book over to me.

•   •   •

A FAMILIAR BLUE pickup was parked next to my van at the campsite.

Shit. Now was not the time for a visit from the constable.

Pete wasn't in the truck or anywhere around the site.

And the door to the van was open.

Had I left it open in my haste to get to the call? I jogged the last few steps and climbed up into the van.

"What the hell are you doing?" I demanded.

He was standing in the back by the bed, holding my digital recorder. "Looking for you." He smiled sheepishly, set the recorder back on the shelf.

"You just let yourself in?"

"The door was open, and you didn't answer, so I came in to make sure you were okay."

"Well, I'm fine," I said.

He nodded. "Yeah, I see that."

He stepped forward, his body filling the space. I wasn't used to having anyone but me in the van. Not ever. There wasn't room for two people.

I backed out through the open door, clearing the way for him.

"It's an impressive setup you've got there. Perfect for working on the road."

I said nothing. Then: "Was there a reason you stopped by?" The words came out stonier than I'd meant. His smile faded.

"I talked to the state police this morning," he said.

"Oh?"

"Lauren Schumacher is still missing," he said.

"Is that so?"

He nodded. "They're sending another detective here to town tomorrow morning to interview people. They want to look into this whole Rattling Jane angle." He looked at me. "They'll be wanting to talk to you, I'm sure."

"Me?" I swallowed.

"I think they'd be interested to hear your . . . theories. Among other things."

I forced a smile. "I'm happy to share what I've got, but I'm afraid it's not much."

He paused for a moment. "Tell me honestly, what do you think so far? Do you think there's anything to all the Rattling Jane stories?"

"The jury's still out," I said.

"I don't know, the idea that there could be any truth to them just seems . . . unlikely to me." He looked at me, waiting for a response.

"Sometimes things aren't what they seem," I said.

"Isn't that the truth." He turned toward his truck.

We'd said our goodbyes and I was climbing into my van when he called my name again. I turned, watched as he took a card out of the front pocket of his shirt and left it on the picnic table. "My number," he said. "In case you want to talk."

I closed the door, leaned against it taking deep breaths, listening to him get into his truck and pull away.

Shit.

I put on the kettle, grabbed the jar of instant espresso and my cup. Then, waiting for the water to boil, I grabbed my backpack from where I'd dumped it last night on the floor beside the bed.

I unzipped it, looked inside.

First aid kit. Water bottle. Granola bars. Bug spray.

Panic rising, I turned the bag upside down, dumping everything out.

The monster book was gone.

As was the doll.

And my gun.

THE BOOK OF MONSTERS

By Violet Hildreth and Iris Whose Last Name We Don't Know

Illustrations by Eric Hildreth

1978

CHARMS AND SPELLS TO KEEP YOU SAFE FROM MONSTERS

Monsters cannot cross a circle of salt. Buy a big box of kosher salt. Make lines of it on all the doorways of your house. Make a circle around your bed. Also create a circle of salt anytime you attempt to do any magic, like a binding spell or a spell for seeing monsters.

Other things you can do to protect yourself:

Sleep with your windows closed. Block the space under your bedroom door and your keyholes. Hang a cross and cloves of garlic above your bed. Put mirrors all around your room, facing out of your windows.

Make a charm by filling a small sack of cloth with equal amounts of lavender, dill, oregano, and sage. Keep it with you at all times.

Charge a knife by soaking it in salt water on a full moon. Sleep with this knife under your pillow, knowing that if you need to, you can slay a monster.

Vi

July 24, 1978

HOW LONG HAD the Ghoul been there watching?

How much had it seen?

Had it seen the kiss? Had it heard what they were talking about?

Vi's head raced as she chased it through the trees.

The creature matched Eric's description exactly: black hood, tall black boots, pale face.

It was just approaching dusk, and Vi knew they didn't have much time. If they were out in the woods without a flashlight when it got fully dark, they'd never find it. Worse, they might not be able to find their way home.

Worse still, the Ghoul might tire of being chased and turn around and chase *them*.

Part of Vi worried that they were being led into a trap: that the Ghoul knew just what it was doing, that it had a plan.

Monsters, Vi knew, were clever creatures; some were experienced predators.

They were already far away from any path Vi knew. The sun was down low enough that she couldn't tell what direction it had set in. She was disoriented. Lost. And the Ghoul was fast. Otherworldly fast.

Vi didn't have anything to use for a binding spell—no kosher salt, no holy water, no magic words. She didn't have an amulet of protection or a magic blade.

What would she and Iris do if they actually managed to catch up with it?

She'd started the chase feeling very brave, but was now beginning to doubt herself, to wonder if they should turn and run in the other direction, back toward home.

But which way was home?

The trees flew by. Vi's legs were burning. Her lungs ached. She felt like they'd been running for hours, like the woods had to end soon. At any minute, they'd come out by the highway. At least, she thought that was the direction they'd been running. Maybe they'd come out near the dump or the old Wheaton farm. She looked up at the sky, hoping to see a familiar constellation. Then she might have some idea what direction they were heading. But there was nothing but a thick, dark cover of clouds.

And now it was starting to rain.

The Ghoul was slowing.

It's a trap, a voice screamed inside Vi's head, the God of Caution or her own fear, maybe—she couldn't be sure.

They'd reached a steep hill covered in trees, with a thick carpet of dead leaves and moss beneath them, and the Ghoul kept slipping, stumbling, scrambling up again.

Vi and Iris were closing in.

"Stop!" Vi yelled. "I command you, creature of the night! Leave our realm! Go back to your world! You are not welcome here!"

It was stupid, really, trying to cast the spell without the protective circle of salt, without weapons or any banishing herbs. And she wasn't even sure she remembered all the right words.

The creature ran a few steps up the steep incline, then slipped, fell down on its knees.

"Shit!" it yelped in a high-pitched female voice.

"I am a hunter of monsters," Vi began. "I have knowledge and weapons that could end your life, and I command you—"

"Would you stop already? I think I twisted my damn ankle!" the Ghoul yelled, still down on the ground. "How the hell am I supposed to get out of here now?"

Vi moved closer, Iris right behind her.

Even in the shadows of the woods, Vi could make out the Ghoul on the hill. And it didn't look so Ghoul-like now. It looked like a person in a too-big hooded sweatshirt and a white ski mask. The Ghoul pulled back the hood and peeled off the mask, revealing a young woman with long blond hair.

An imposter. A fake.

Vi was relieved and disappointed all at the same time.

"Crap," the woman said, cradling her ankle inside the big boot. "I really wrenched it. I don't think it's broken, but I doubt I can walk on it."

"What . . . who are you?" Vi demanded, walking right up to her.

The woman looked at her, then at Iris, then back at Vi. "My name is Julia Tetreault."

"Prove it," Iris said.

"Huh?" Julia said. "You're kidding, right? You want ID or something? I left my purse back in my car."

Iris leaned close to Vi. "They can look human, right?" she whispered. "A clever monster knows how to disguise itself. To blend in."

Vi nodded.

"Isn't there a test or something?" Iris asked.

Vi thought. She moved closer to Julia. Touched her shoulder, then gave it a pinch.

"Ow!" Julia shouted. "What the hell?"

"Maybe we should stick her with a pin or something," Iris said. "See if she bleeds."

"No way! No one is sticking me with anything," Julia barked.

The rain was picking up, had turned from scattered showers into a full-on downpour. It pattered down on the leaves of the trees and was quickly soaking their clothes.

"Great," Julia said, looking up at the sky. "Perfect time for a monsoon."

"What are you really?" Vi asked. "I command you to answer."

"You're really stuck on this commanding thing, huh? Like I said, my name is Julia."

"And you expect us to believe you're a human?" Iris asked.

Julia laughed. "What else would I be? An alien from outer space?"

"You've been spying on us," Vi said. "For days now, right?"

"Shit. The little boy saw me. I knew it. And now you two. Are you going to tell?"

"Tell who?"

"Dr. Hildreth."

"Maybe," Vi said. "But maybe not. Tell us who you are and what you want."

"Like I said, my name is Julia."

"And? Why have you been watching us?"

"I'm a journalist. Well, actually, a journalism student over at Lyndon State. And I'm doing this project."

"What kind of project?" Vi asked.

"Look, kid, in case you hadn't noticed, it's raining like hell. It's nearly nine-thirty at night, we're lost in the woods, and I've got a twisted ankle. What do you say we put our energy into getting out of here, and we can talk later?"

Vi shook her head. "Tell us now."

Julia sighed. "Well, it started with me looking into Dr. Wilson Hicks. He taught at the University of Vermont and wrote a book called—"

"The eugenics guy," Vi said.

"Yes!" Julia said. Her demeanor changed completely—she was excited.

"*A Case for Good Breeding*," Vi said. Maybe she shouldn't have said anything, but she couldn't really resist showing off a little to adults, even strangers.

"What's eugenics?" Iris asked.

"It's the scientific study of heredity and breeding and how to improve the human race by making everyone white and smart," Vi explained.

Julia laughed. "Couldn't have put it better myself."

Iris shook her head. "I don't get it."

Julia got up on her knees, pulled herself up by holding on tightly to a tree. "God, that hurts," she said. "Hey, do you think you could find me something I could use as a walking stick?"

Iris and Vi started looking around.

"Did you find him? Dr. Hicks?" Vi asked as she picked up a stick that looked perfect but was actually too rotten to use.

"He died back in the late fifties. Have you read his book?"

"Parts of it."

"So you know about the study of the Templeton family?"

"Yeah."

"Well, that's what I was going to write about for my project, see. I was going to interview surviving members of the family. Templeton isn't their real name, of course."

"Have you talked to any of them? Interviewed them and stuff?" Vi asked. She'd found a good sturdy stick and brought it over.

Up close, she could see how young Julia was. She looked like she could be one of the students at Fayeville High School who worked at the drive-in.

"Some of them," Julia said, taking the stick, testing her ankle by putting a little weight on it. She took a shuffling step forward. "There were some I couldn't contact, though. Because they were dead or . . . missing."

Vi felt the skin at the back of her neck prickle.

"Weird," she said. "So do you think you're okay to walk with that? Iris and I can help you if you need it."

"The stick is great. We'll just go slow, okay?" Julia said. "You think we can find our way out of here?"

Vi shrugged. "I'm not sure. I think we might be near the highway. Or maybe the dump?"

"I can find the way back to the house," Iris said.

"You can?"

Iris nodded. "Follow me."

"I managed to track down Dr. Hicks's research assistant," Julia went on. There was no stopping her now. Vi recognized the excitement in her voice, the pride. She'd been able to follow the trail and uncover what she needed to know. A kindred spirit. "And it turns out she's the one who runs the Inn here, Dr. Hildreth."

"Gran," Iris said.

"She's your grandmother?"

"I'm Violet Hildreth," Vi said. "My brother Eric and I live with Gran."

"And what about you?" Julia asked Iris.

"Her too," Vi answered before Iris could speak. "She's our sister, Iris."

"So Dr. Helen Hildreth is your grandmother?"

Vi nodded. "Yeah."

"Maternal or paternal?"

"Paternal. My father was Jackson Hildreth."

"Jackson Hildreth," Julia repeated, saying the name slowly. "And all three of you live there, in that house with Dr. Hildreth?"

"Yeah."

"For how long?"

"Since our parents died. Like . . ." Vi calculated. "Eight years ago now."

"I'm sorry for asking . . . but would you mind telling me how your parents died?"

"Car accident."

They made their way slowly down the hill as the rain drenched them, and all the while, Vi was thinking about how disappointed Eric was going to be when he learned his ghoul wasn't a ghoul at all but some state college student. Maybe, she thought, maybe it'd be better if he didn't know.

"So why are you spying on us?" Vi asked.

"I'm working on a story."

"By sneaking around in the woods, harassing kids?" Iris asked.

"Listen, I tried the usual route, really I did. I went to the Inn, talked to Dr. Hutchins and Dr. Hildreth, but they didn't have much to say. In fact, they threatened to call the police and have me hauled off for trespassing if I came back."

"That's why you put on the mask?" Iris asked.

"Uh-huh. I didn't want to take the chance of Dr. Hildreth recognizing me."

"Is the story you're writing about eugenics and Dr. Hicks?" Vi asked.

"It started out that way, but things have changed. The story has grown. The Dr. Hicks thing might have just been a door that led me to the true story, the *bigger* story."

"Which is?" Vi asked.

Julia stopped walking and winced a little. Vi wasn't sure if it was because of pain or because of the question.

"I think," Julia said, her voice level and slow like she was choosing her words carefully, "that I've said enough for now."

"You're writing about the Inn," Iris said. "You know there's something strange going on there."

"Shut up, Iris," Vi warned.

Julia turned and looked steadily at both girls. "You two wouldn't know anything about that, would you? About something strange going on over there? Experiments, maybe?"

"The Mayflower Project," Iris said.

Vi grabbed Iris's arm and gave it a twist. "Shu-ut uu-p!" she growled.

Even in the darkness, Vi could see that Julia's jaw had actually fallen open and her eyes were all buggy like a cartoon character's.

"But, Vi," Iris said. "Maybe she can help us."

"No," Vi said. It was too dangerous. Sharing their secrets with a stranger. A college student. Someone they didn't know or trust. A monster imposter.

"I *can* help you, but only if you tell me what you know," Julia said. "Please."

"There's nothing to tell," Vi jumped in before Iris got a chance to blab anything else.

Julia blew out a frustrated breath. "You know what got me into journalism? I've got this idea, this belief, that the truth wants to be told. It's always there, just beneath the surface or hidden deep in some locked-away box, calling to be let out."

"I think you're right," Iris said. "I think—"

"We can't help you," Vi interrupted, giving Iris's arm another warning, shut-the-hell-up twist. "We'll get you back to the road, but that's it. And if we catch you spying on us anymore, I'll tell Gran."

Lizzy

August 21, 2019

TIME TO GO.

Constable Pete had the book, the doll, and the gun. There was no doubt about it now: I was a suspect. Evidence gathered, he'd be returning at any minute with a team of state troopers to arrest me.

I was no good to poor Lauren if the state police dragged me down to the barracks for hours of questioning, for possible arrest.

Where did you get the doll, Miss Shelley?

I found it.

They'd never believe me.

Where did you say you grew up, Miss Shelley? Or is there another name we should use?

I felt the walls closing in.

The monster knew where I was.

Maybe she was watching me right now, studying my every move.

I scanned the trees surrounding my campsite. A few campsites down from mine, a father and son building a fire. A woman walked by on the camp road, a basset hound on a leash lagging behind her.

I disconnected the solar panel, took the chocks from behind the wheels. I tried to move slowly, act natural—just a tourist going out to explore the Green Mountain State.

I quickly got dressed, packed up the inside of the van, made sure everything was tucked away, latched or strapped down. I left the bed unmade.

I reached into my pocket, felt Gran's lighter and the little pebble— the wishing stone.

The Monster gives the Monster Hunter a stone so she can make a wish.

What does the hunter wish for?

What did I wish for?

I wrapped my fingers around the stone. "That I find you before you find me," I whispered.

I settled into the driver's seat, put the key in the ignition and turned it.

Nothing happened.

No comforting hum of the engine, just a sad cough, then nothing.

I tried again.

Shit.

I jumped out, popped the hood, checked the connections. Didn't see anything unusual.

I got back in and tried it again.

My eyes searched the dashboard. Then I saw it: the fuel gauge. The needle was at empty.

It didn't make sense.

I knew damn well I'd had nearly half a tank of gas yesterday.

I hopped out of the van again, got down on my belly to peer underneath, checking for a leak. Nothing.

I pushed myself up, looked around. Had another camper siphoned my gas? Someone who needed a little extra for their generator maybe? It seemed unlikely, but I didn't want to think about the alternatives.

I circled around the van to get the spare gas can I kept strapped on the back rack to use for the generator.

But it wasn't there. The can was missing.

Now what?

I felt panic building.

Trapped. I was trapped.

The monster had done this. I was sure I could feel her watching from the trees, laughing.

Slow down. Think, I told myself, taking a deep breath.

There must be gas at the campground for the four-wheelers and mowers they used. I would head to the office to find Steve, explain the situation, and get enough gas in the van to make it to the nearest gas station and then off this godforsaken "island."

It took me five minutes to jog to the office. As I passed the other campsites, I did my best to look like I was just getting my exercise, not fleeing. The shades to the office were drawn, but I could hear someone moving around inside. I tried the door. Locked. I knocked and heard it click open.

"Hey, my van's out of gas and I—"

Skink was standing in front of the desk.

On top of it sat the monster book, the creepy little Lauren doll, and my gun.

Vi

July 27, 1978

I RIS WAS CHANGING.

She'd grown quieter in the last few days. Not totally mute like she was when she first arrived, but definitely more withdrawn.

Her hair hung in greasy strands from under the filthy orange hat.

She'd started wearing her clothes inside out and backward, as she had when she'd first come.

The night before, Vi had woken up at two a.m. to find Iris standing over her, her black sweatshirt on backward, the hood pulled up over her face. Iris just stood there, arms limp, unmoving.

She looked like she was inside a cocoon, and Vi decided that was exactly right: Iris was undergoing some sort of metamorphosis, and when she emerged, who knew what she might be.

"You okay, Iris?" Vi had asked.

But Iris hadn't answered. She'd just shuffled back to her own bed on the floor, curled up on top of the covers, and gone back to sleep.

Vi was running out of time.

Tick tock, tick tock.

The gods hummed worriedly in her ears, *Hurry, hurry, hurry. Do something. Gran's going to take her away. She's going to take her away and you'll never see her again.*

There was another worry—one that felt even worse. Now that Iris knew the truth, Vi worried that she'd do something terrible; maybe even hurt herself. Or hurt both of them.

She'd burned her family alive.

Vi couldn't stop thinking about it—it was where her imagination went when she let herself wonder what Iris might be capable of.

◆　◆　◆

"REGRESSION," GRAN SAID to Vi. They were in Gran's office. "It's common when a patient is making too much progress too quickly. Backsliding into old ways and patterns can feel like the safe thing to do. But what I'm wondering is, did something in particular trigger this?"

"I don't know," Vi said.

Gran gave her a long look. "You didn't notice anything? She didn't say anything to you?"

Vi shook her head. "She barely talks to me lately."

Gran nodded, but her frown was heavy.

She was going to take Iris away. It was only a matter of time.

◆　◆　◆

GRAN WAS AT the Inn and Vi stood in the kitchen with Eric making lunch when the big beige phone on the kitchen wall rang. It sounded like an alarm bell.

"Hello?" Vi said.

"Is this Violet?"

"Yes."

"This is Julia Tetreault. We met the other day in the woods. I'm the journalism student."

Eric looked up from making a peanut butter and jelly sandwich. "Who is it?" he asked.

Vi shook her head. "No one," she told him. "Wrong number." Then she hung up, slamming the phone down into the cradle a little too hard.

The phone rang again.

"No one's calling back, I guess," Eric said.

Vi groaned and picked up the phone. "What?" she snarled into it.

"Please don't hang up. Just give me one minute."

Vi waited. "What?" she said again.

"I know about B West."

Vi turned her back to her brother. She stepped out into the hall, as far away as the phone cord would stretch. "What do you know?"

"Experiments are going on down there. With some of the patients. You and your sister know about it, don't you? She was telling me the truth."

Vi was silent.

"Have you been down there? Have you seen it?"

More silence. Finally Vi asked, "What do you want?"

"I need proof, Violet. Records, photos. Without those, I've got no story, no evidence."

"That's what this is about? Your story? For some stupid college class?"

"No, Violet. It's much bigger than that. It's about finding out the truth."

"And what good will that do?" Vi asked.

"If there are terrible things going on, and we get proof, we can bring it to the authorities. We can close the whole place down. Don't you see? If what I'm hearing is true, this needs to happen, Violet. We need to do this."

Wasn't that what Vi wanted?

"Do you know how to get me proof, Violet?"

Vi bit her lip, thinking. Could this be her way to save Iris?

"Because if you do, we need to act fast."

"Why?"

"My source at the Inn tells me B West is going to be shut down, all the records destroyed."

"What?" Vi said. "Who? What source?"

"I can't tell you that, but I can tell you that if we want to get any of those records, we've got to move fast. Something tells me we're talking a matter of days here, if that."

"Vi? Who's on the phone?" Eric came into the hall with a peanut butter–covered knife. Vi put her hand over the mouthpiece and ordered him back to the kitchen.

"I've gotta go," Vi said.

"Wait! One more thing," Julia said. "Tell me your father's name again."

Vi paused, watched Eric grab his sandwich and go out the kitchen door to the backyard.

"Jackson," Vi whispered. "Jackson Hildreth."

"And he was a doctor? You're sure?"

"Yes. A surgeon."

The front door banged open.

Gran was home!

"I gotta go," Vi said, rushing back into the kitchen to slam the phone down.

"Violet?" Gran called.

"In the kitchen." She busied herself making her own peanut butter sandwich. "Do you want a sandwich?" she asked cheerfully. "I can get out the liverwurst."

"No thank you, poppet. Do you know where Iris is?"

"Still sleeping, I think."

"I've got something I'd like to try with her. Some new exercises. I think they may help."

Vi swallowed hard.

"Can you go wake her up for me?"

"Sure," Vi said.

"Send her down to the basement once she's dressed and had some food."

"Sure," Vi said again.

"Good girl," Gran said. "I don't know what I'd do without you, Violet." She tousled Vi's hair.

And Vi let herself lean into Gran, let her words make her feel all lit up like the owl lamp on her bedside table. But it didn't last. She couldn't make herself forget what Gran had done.

Gran reached for her wrist. "I feel your pulse."

Vi played the part, wrapped her fingers around Gran's wrist. "And I feel yours."

"You've got a strong heart, Violet Hildreth," Gran said.

Vi pulled away, turned to go upstairs, then stopped.

"Gran?"

"Yes."

"Iris is going to stay with us, right?"

Gran looked at her and gave a forced smile. "Of course, my lovely. Of course she is."

But Vi knew she was lying.

◆　◆　◆

"LISTEN, IRIS, IT'S really important that you act like whatever Gran does today helps you."

Iris glared. "Helps me?"

"You have to pretend. You have to make her think that being here in the house with us is making you better. And whatever happens, you can't let her know we've learned the truth. You can't say anything about the records I took."

Iris said nothing.

"You don't want to go back to the basement of the Inn again, do you?"

Iris shook her head frantically, *no, no, no.*

The threat felt cruel, but Vi was desperate.

"Then you have to pretend. You have to act like Gran is helping you. Like you're feeling more like your old self."

"How?"

"Start by taking a freaking shower. Take that stupid hat off and wash your hair. Put your clothes on right. Act like a regular human being."

Vi hated being mean, but it was what she had to do. It was the only way.

"I . . . don't think I can," Iris said in a whisper.

"Of course you can. You were doing just fine before. I'll help you." She gently took off Iris's hat, got a brush, and started pulling the tangles from her greasy hair. The hair over her scar was growing in. "When you go downstairs, tell Gran that you've been scared lately. Scared because you've come to really like it here, to think of us like your family, but you're afraid it won't last."

Iris nodded.

"Good. And when you come back upstairs, you'll take a shower, put on clean clothes, then go down and ask Gran if you can help make dinner."

"Okay," Iris said.

"And you're not taking the pills she gives you, right? You're faking it?"

Iris nodded.

"I have a plan," Vi told her. "A plan to help you. To undo everything Gran has done."

"How?"

"I'm going back to B West. I'll get your charts. Remember what I told you? A whole file cabinet full of notes was practically all about you and about this Mayflower Project. We'll study them and learn everything that was done to you, then figure out how to *un*do it."

Iris was shaking her head.

Vi continued, "We'll take all the notes—the important ones, at least—and bring them to that journalist, Julia."

"But you said no to that, to her. You told me she couldn't really help us."

"We've gotta try. She says if we bring her proof, she can tell the police what Gran has been doing here. Everyone's gonna find out what's going on here: the cops, the papers, the TV news, Governor Snelling, maybe even President Carter! It's the only way to stop Gran. To not let her ever do this to anyone else ever again."

Iris nodded, but she looked like she was being told a story she didn't dare to believe.

"Now, go on downstairs and tell Gran how scared you've been— how much you love us and how happy you are here."

"Will you come with me?"

"No. You have to do it on your own. I've gotta go figure out a way to get back into the Inn to get those files."

◆   ◆   ◆

GETTING THE KEYS hadn't been difficult, really. As soon as Gran and Iris went down to the basement, Vi found Gran's purse in its usual place on her desk. She took just the keys she needed off the ring—the one to Gran's office, the one to the Inn's back door, and the one to the basement—put the big ring back into Gran's purse, and pedaled her bike into town as fast as she could. Eric was cage-cleaning today, so he was occupied.

"My grandmother needs some spare keys made," she told the clerk at the hardware store. She passed them over, and he cut them without question, making perfect matches. Vi hurried back home—Gran was still downstairs with Iris. She put the originals back on the key ring.

Now, with the duplicate keys tucked into her pocket, she was setting her alarm for one a.m. Gran was usually in bed by eleven. She read for a while and was asleep by midnight.

Iris had showered and was in clean, right-side-out pajamas. She'd told Vi that she and Gran had just played cards down in the basement. And they'd taken out some of the mice and played with them. She told Vi that Gran had hugged her. Afterward, Iris had promised Gran that she was going to try hard to be a normal girl.

"I'm coming with you to the Inn," Iris said.

"No way," Vi told her. "It's too dangerous. Me trying to get in and out of there is hard enough, but two of us? Forget it."

"I need to come with you," Iris said. "To see it for myself."

"I don't think it's a good idea. I'll go in, get all the files I can grab, and come right back."

"If I go with you, we'll be faster. And we can carry more. I need to go, Vi. I need to see where I came from. And maybe being back there, seeing it, maybe it'll help me remember."

Vi sighed and turned out the light.

Iris came and got into bed beside her. "Please," she said. "I did what you asked. I pretended for Gran. Can't you do what I'm asking?"

Vi didn't answer.

"Vi?"

"Yes?"

"Are you afraid of me?" Iris touched Vi's shoulders, ran her fingers over her neck, pressing gently on her throat.

Vi swallowed. "Should I be?"

"Maybe," Iris said.

"And maybe," Vi told her, "you should be afraid of me."

"Why?" asked Iris.

And Vi hugged her. She held her as tight as she could, pushed her whole body against her, melted into her, until she wasn't sure where she ended and Iris began.

Lizzy

August 21, 2019

COME IN AND lock the door behind you," Skink said, his voice cracking a little as he tried to sound like some badass action movie star. He shifted from foot to foot. His eyes were red and blood-shot, like he'd either been crying or hadn't slept.

"What's going on, Skink?" I asked in a calm voice as I stepped into the campground office, my eyes on the monster book, the doll, and the gun on the desk.

Had I misjudged this boy?

"That's just what I want to ask you," he said, moving around to the chair behind the desk. "Sit." He nodded at the chair in the corner of the office by the coffeepot. I walked over and lowered myself into it. He put his hand on my gun but didn't pick it up.

I doubted the kid had ever fired a gun in his life.

"Skink, please be careful. That's loaded."

He jerked his hand away as if the gun had shocked him, but said defensively, "You think I don't know that?"

"Just making sure," I said in what I hoped was a reassuring tone. "So, you went into my van? Took this stuff?"

He nodded, bit his lip.

"How come?"

"You show up here on the island just after Lauren goes missing, asking about Rattling Jane. I *knew* it wasn't a coincidence. I knew you were connected somehow. I just needed proof and now I've got it." He looked very pleased with himself.

Here I was, starting to think that maybe he had something to do with Lauren's disappearance, and he'd been thinking the same thing about me.

"Did you take the gas out of my van too?" I asked.

"Yeah. I didn't want you to get away. Not when I had all this evidence." He reached down, picked up the doll. "This is sick stuff, Lizzy. These are her clothes, her actual clothes, her actual hair! Where is she?"

"I don't know, Skink."

He took out his cell phone, held it like a weapon, finger poised over a button. "I'll call my dad. I probably should have already called him, but I wanted to hear your story first. Maybe it's better if he and I both hear it together."

"I'd like the chance to tell you first," I said, keeping my voice calm, level, friendly. "Then, if you'd like, you can call your dad."

The dark circles under his eyes were like purple bruises. "So start talking."

I took in a breath, wondered how little I could get away with saying while still keeping him happy. "I did come here, to the island, to find Lauren. I'm very sure she didn't run away."

"She was taken," Skink said. "But not by Rattling Jane."

"You're right," I said.

"I read the book," Skink told her.

"This book?" I pointed at the cracked three-ring binder that held *The Book of Monsters*. A child's project dragged from a closet.

I heard Neil Diamond again, one of Gran's crackling records.

I am, I said.

"That's just something my sister and brother and I made when we were kids—it's got sentimental value, but that's it."

He nodded. "I know. I mean, I figured it out. Also that this . . . this *monster* . . . she isn't really who she says she is. She's not Rattling Jane." He paused, chewed his lip. "It's your sister. Your sister who calls herself a monster."

I froze, my body turning to ice.

The truth at last.

"What?" I said. "How do you—"

"It's all here, in this book." He gave me a *well, duh* look. "Haven't you read it?"

"Not for years," I admitted. "I went to the tower last night after I left you. I thought . . . I guess I hoped that maybe I'd find Lauren. But all I found was the book and the doll—left for me."

"Left by your sister?"

"I believe so, yes."

"And she's got Lauren," he said.

I nodded. "She must."

Skink rubbed his eyes.

"You want to help Lauren, don't you?"

He nodded, very slightly.

"I want to help her too. I want to find her and save her. And I think I can."

He sat up straight, staring at me with glassy eyes.

I knew what I had to do, though I hated to do it. I didn't want to involve this boy. But it was too late. He was already in deep; no way he was walking away. "I think I can do it with your help. Will you help me, Skink?"

He stared at me, neither agreeing nor disagreeing. He still held the phone in his hand.

"'Cause here's the thing: if you call your dad, I think we blow all our chances of finding Lauren. I think . . . I think I need to be the one to find her. I'm being led there. It's what the monster wants."

Skink grimaced. "She's playing some sick game with you, using Lauren as bait."

"Maybe," I said. "But it's not just Lauren. There have been other girls."

"Okay," he said at last. "I'll help you." He set the phone down on the table. "But I'm warning you, if you try anything weird, or I find out you're actually more involved in this, then I'm calling my dad. And I want to know *everything*. The whole story. Like, is she really some kind of . . . monster?"

How could I even begin to answer that? "She thinks she is," I told him. "And that's what matters."

"So how do we stop her?" Skink asked.

"First, we have to find her. We know she's on the island. Or she has been in the last day or two, because she left the book and the doll. And if she's here, then Lauren's here. Maybe they're in the woods some-where? Or holed up in one of the cottages?"

"I don't think so," Skink said.

"Why not?"

"I read the book, remember? She's added new stuff to it. She wrote a note to you at the end, and I think it says where they went."

Vi

VI AND IRIS held hands as they crossed the lawn to the Inn. The yellow bricks seemed to glow. It felt like the building was waiting for them, watching them as they ran to it.

For as long as she could remember, Vi had thought of the old hospital as part of her home—ghosts and all. She had looked out at it in every season, from her bedroom window or from the front porch. Had seen it covered in a thick blanket of snow, surrounded by the blazing foliage of autumn, watched it come alive with green buds in spring, and seen it seem to waver like a mirage in the heat of summer.

She had been right all along: The Inn *was* haunted.

Not only by the ghosts of long-ago Civil War patients, but by the things Gran was doing down in the basement. Terrible deeds and actions caused their own kind of haunting. Vi believed that it held memories of every terrible thing that had happened inside its walls. The building felt angry and sick to her; it felt dangerous.

The summer rain pounded down, soaking their clothes, their hair.

They slipped in the wet grass, holding each other up. Thunder boomed in the distance, a low grumbling roar. Lightning struck, and the world flashed bright and blue and brilliant for one second, as if God were taking a picture. The sky was electric, alive and humming, and Vi felt like they were tapped into it, feeding off it, the current running through them, turning them into live-wire girls. She felt that if lightning came down and struck them right now, it wouldn't kill them or even hurt them.

It would just make them more powerful.

They reached the building and crept around to the back door. Vi's heart was pounding, partly from nerves, but also because with Iris she felt like so much more than herself. She couldn't let Gran take Iris away. This was their only hope. It was the only thing that could save Iris, save them both.

Vi slipped her copy of the key into the lock.

"I'm afraid," Iris said, stepping back.

"You don't have to do this," Vi told her.

"Yes, I do. I need to see where I came from."

"What we find in there," Vi said, "we're going to use it to fix things."

"Promise?"

Vi nodded. "We're going to find out who you really are," she said. "We're going to learn your real name. We'll get the papers that prove everything Gran did to you, and we'll bring them to Julia and the police. The whole world is going to know what happened here."

And what will happen then? she wondered.

What would Gran do?

How would she react when she learned what Vi had done?

She couldn't think about that. Could only think about the next step.

She pulled the door open.

They peered up and down the hallway before they entered. All clear. She took Iris's hand again, and in they went. Each of them had on an empty backpack to help them carry more files.

The building smelled like disinfectant spray, old wood, and brick. It smelled like ghosts.

They turned right, creeping down the corridor into the Common Room. Vi led Iris to the door marked BASEMENT and quickly unlocked it, and Iris followed her through. They went down the stairs to the basement, took a right, and approached the heavy metal door. Vi pulled out the key she'd marked B WEST.

"Are you ready?" she asked Iris.

Iris nodded, gave a weak smile.

Vi thought of the months, the years maybe, that Iris had spent down there, locked in that room. While the whole time, Vi was right across the lawn. She could have come and rescued her. Saved her. If only she had known.

She unlocked the door.

They stepped through, looking and listening. It was quiet.

"These three rooms on the left," Vi said, "that's where they keep the patients."

They peered through the little window into the first room. It was empty, holding only a single bed.

"No one," Vi said. Iris nodded, looking relieved.

They moved on to the next room, opened the door. The same size as the first, but in addition to the bed with the leather restraints, this one held big metal lights, like in an operating room, and a metal table with a metal box on it.

"Is that . . ." Iris reached for the box, touched one of the dials.

There were cables leading out of it to two paddles.

Vi nodded. "It's for shock treatments."

Iris pulled her hand away. "Is this where they did it to me?"

"Maybe," Vi said, all the spit in her mouth drying up. "Probably."

She went to the metal cabinet in the corner, opened one of the drawers.

Surgical tools. Scalpels. Forceps. Curved scissors. Retractors. Suturing kits. A small silver saw. She slammed the drawer shut before Iris could see.

The next drawer held vials of medication and needles. Vi picked one up. Thorazine. She put it back, saw several bottles full of ether and chloroform.

"What's in there?" asked Iris.

"Medicines," Vi said.

The green-painted concrete floor sloped slightly to a drain with a rusted metal cover.

"I don't like this room," Iris said.

"Me neither," Vi agreed. Again, she took Iris's hand and led her back into the hall.

They moved down to the final door on the left.

She reached out, tried the switch. The light inside did not come on. Vi turned the knob, pushed the door open, and stepped into the room, with Iris following her.

Vi let out the breath she'd been holding.

"I know this room," Iris said.

Vi nodded, feeling like she knew it too, though she couldn't have, not really. She'd only imagined it.

Like the others, it held a metal-framed hospital bed with restraints. And to the right, a deep tub.

Iris closed the door. They were plunged into darkness. Iris was squeezing Vi's hand so hard Vi worried her fingers would be crushed.

Vi felt the walls closing in. She needed to get out, away from the darkness. Her breathing got faster, more frantic. "I—I—" she stammered. *Need to go. Can't stay. Please.* But Iris was speaking.

"I always knew when something bad was going to happen because

I could see them coming. Most of the time, they covered the little window so that it was totally black in here. When they were about to come in, they'd open the little window and look in at me. All I could see was their eyes."

It felt as if Vi remembered too; her own memories were mixed up with Iris's. She looked at the little rectangle in the door glowing with light, and it became the headlights of an oncoming car. She was in the backseat of the car with her parents. Her father was driving. He swerved to avoid the car, the oncoming lights filling their windshield, impossibly bright.

"And I couldn't move," Iris went on. Her voice was quiet. "Couldn't sit up or even lift my arms or legs because I was held down to the bed with leather straps that left my wrists and ankles raw."

Vi felt herself strapped tightly into the backseat as the car plunged into the water. She struggled to get loose and couldn't. She was going to drown down there, the car filling with water, the seatbelt keeping her trapped.

"Sometimes they put me in the tub. The water was ice-cold. They'd strap me and leave me there in the dark. I'd stay in that water until my whole body was numb, even my brain," Iris said. "They did other things. I can't remember details, just lights and sounds. The smell of medicine. A buzz. Voices. But it was like I went someplace else."

"Yes," Vi said, because she knew about going someplace else, someplace other than where you were. She closed her eyes and she was back in the car, only it was a bed she was strapped to, and someone was talking to her, someone was counting backward, and she wasn't sure who she was, if she was herself or Iris.

10, 9, 8, 7 . . .

"And then Dr. Hildreth came and released me," Iris said. "She undid the bindings. She took my hand. Asked if I was ready to go home."

It was Gran's voice counting backward in Vi's memory, Gran undoing the seatbelt, pulling Vi from the wrecked car in the water.

Vi was so cold. She couldn't move. Couldn't feel anything but Gran's arms around her.

You've got a strong heart, Violet Hildreth.

The world spun. Vi felt a headache coming on, one of the bad ones.

"Come on," she said, seizing Iris's hand. "Let's get out of here. I'll take you to the file room. We'll grab what we can and go."

She'd had enough of this place.

She was worried that they were too late. That Gran and Dr. Hutchins had already destroyed all the records.

Too late, too late.

She flipped on the light in the little room with the file cabinet and desk.

"I've been here before," Iris said.

"You have?"

"This is where Dr. Hildreth—Gran—took me before she brought me home. I sat right in this chair, and she told me all about you. She said I had a family waiting to meet me. A brother and sister who'd been hoping for a new sister of their own. Someone to come and make their family whole. A family who would make me whole again. Make me well."

Vi nodded. A lump formed in her throat.

She shouldn't have brought Iris here. It was all too much. She remembered what Gran had said about regression. Wondered if this would trigger it, make everything worse.

She walked over to the file cabinet. "The entire bottom drawer is full of files on Patient S. I only took the first one. There's so much more. We can't take it all—we'll just have to pick the stuff that looks most important."

She pulled open the heavy gray drawer. Iris crouched beside Vi, their hips touching.

We're conjoined twins, Vi thought.

We share the same heart, the same memories.

I don't know where I end and she begins.

Iris pulled out a file and started reading some of the notes out loud: "'Sodium amytal . . .'"

"I looked that one up," Vi said. "It's like a truth serum. When the military needs to get the truth out of a prisoner, they'll dose them up with that."

"Why would she give me that?"

"To get inside your head. To empty things out. To control you."

Iris went back to reading. "'Metrazol.'"

"Gran gives it to her rats. It gives them seizures. Sometimes it kills them."

"But why would she give it to me?"

"I think it kind of scrambles your brain."

"The rest of this is notes on ECT?" Iris said, looking down at the paper.

Vi nodded. "Electroconvulsive therapy. Shock treatments. They put these paddles on your head, and—"

"And a rubber thing in your mouth," Iris said. "I remember. I remember the taste of the rubber, biting down on it, knowing what was coming." She looked at the paper. "'Subject underwent daily sessions this week.'"

"Every day?" Vi said, looking down, reading the notes. "I think they normally do, like, two or three a month? That's what Gran's told me, anyway. That many . . . it's a miracle you've got a brain left."

Iris flipped through the pages. "But why? Why do all of this to me? Hypnosis. Sleep deprivation. The drugs. The shocks. Leaving me in that dark room, in that cold water for hours. Why?"

To wipe everything clean, Vi thought. To take a human being that Gran thought was inferior in some way and remake her. Tear her apart, erase everything so that she could build her back. "Well," she said. "'Start with a blank canvas'—that's what she wrote in her notes on the Mayflower Project."

"So who am I?" Iris said, looking up from the notes. "If she's taken everything away—all my memories? Everything I was when I first came here?"

"You're you," Vi said, her voice breaking a little when she thought, *You're her monster.* "She can't have taken everything away. And there have to be clues in these files about where you came from, who you were before you got here. The papers I took earlier said your parents were members of the family that Dr. Hicks and Gran studied. And Julia has been researching the family. She's had contact with remaining family members. She can help us figure it out. We can look through the files for more clues."

"But my parents are dead!" Iris said. "That's what the notes said. I killed them! Them and my sister. I started the fire."

Vi shook her head. "Only because she made you. You were brain-washed. Programmed."

Iris was quiet for a second. "What else have I done? What else might I be capable of?"

Vi put her hand on Iris's, resting on top of the open file. "I know you. And I'm with you all the damn time. There's no way you're doing anything bad."

"Promise?"

"I promise," Vi said. "Now, come on, let's quickly look through these and see what we can find. We'll grab what we can and get out of here."

Iris reached all the way into the back, took out the last folder.

"Bring it over here," Vi said, standing up and going over to the desk. "You go through that one. I'll get the folder before it. Pull out anything that seems important. Anything that might help us. Look for stuff with names. History. Where you might have come from. We need lots of documentation."

Iris nodded as she started reading.

"Vi," she said a minute later, her voice higher than usual. "Vi, come here."

Vi set down her own folder and walked back to the desk, looked down at the paragraph of scribbled notes that Iris was pointing at.

The experiment has exceeded all expectations. Patient S fully believes that her parents were killed in a car accident that she and her brother survived. She does not question that this boy she lives with is her brother. Patient S believes in this fictional version of herself so strongly that she is able to tell me about early memories she has of her parents, of the accident itself.

Vi's mouth went dry. The room began to shift and spin.

No. No. No.

She was shaking her head.

Can't be. Can't be. Can't be.

She was back in the car at the bottom of the river. The water was so cold, and she couldn't move.

10, 9, 8 . . .

This wasn't Iris they were reading about.

This was . . .

. . . 7, 6, 5 . . .

Iris flipped the pages to the back of the file folder. A photo was attached to the back with a description below, penned in Gran's messy handwriting:

Patient S, 11th birthday.

And there was Vi, smiling as she leaned in to blow out the candles of her favorite cake, the one Gran made just for her every year: angel food with strawberry-and-peach whipped cream filling.

"Vi," Iris said softly. She sounded strangely far away.

"It's me," Vi said. "It's been me all along."

Her voice was high and airy, a balloon at the end of a string, floating up, up, up.

. . . *4, 3, 2, 1.*

And then the world went black around her.

THE BOOK OF MONSTERS

By Violet Hildreth and Iris Whose Last Name We Don't Know

Illustrations by Eric Hildreth

1978

Dearest Iris,

Do you remember when we thought you were the monster?

You, my secret sister.

My truest love.

My twin.

I used to picture us that way sometimes. Not just sisters, but twins, curled around each other in the darkness of the womb, then later, in the darkness of my room. Entangled, both of us unsure whose limbs were whose.

Shadow sisters.

Doppelgängers.

I loved you so much I thought my heart might explode.

Do you remember when I gave you lessons in being human?

Walk upright. Brush your hair. Wear your clothes right side out. This is how we tie our shoes. This is how we smile and say please and thank you.

As if I were an expert.

Learn to blend in, I told you.

I can help you.

I can save you.

And you did need saving. But not from yourself.

All along, you needed saving from *me*.

Lizzy

~~~~~~~~~~

August 21, 2019

S KINK PUT ON a pot of coffee while I sat at the desk in the camp-ground office reading *The Book of Monsters*. The pages sucked me in, sent me tumbling back through time.

Back to a time when I was a girl named Iris.

A stitched-together girl whom a strange old doctor ("Call me Gran, dear") brought home and introduced to her grandchildren.

"Children, this is Iris. She's going to be staying with us. Iris, these are my grandchildren, Violet and Eric."

They were standing over a wounded rabbit, and I was terrified, but mostly at the way my heart ached with hope.

We are your family now, Gran told me. *We've been waiting for you.*

And the children taught me things.

All the normal things I'd forgotten how to do: how to dress and brush my hair and tie my shoes.

They taught me about Scooby-Doo and Captain Kangaroo. About Count Chocula cereal and candy that sizzled and exploded on my tongue. How to make lemonade and Kool-Aid by mixing powder with water. How to do Spirographs and box with plastic robots.

They played me records, Neil Diamond crooning out love songs, songs about loss.

They took me to the movies, to a secret clubhouse in the woods.

They taught me about monsters.

About how to spot one.

How to be one.

How to act human even when you are sure you're a monster.

I turned the pages, revisiting all the old monsters. It felt a little like a forgotten family album; the figures were that familiar. There was the vampire, teeth dripping blood. And the werewolf, the full moon behind him almost as menacing as the monster himself.

The images and words pulled me back to the clubhouse with the cracked window and the wide pine boards on the floor, Eric and Violet at my side. I could smell the old wood, the musty scent of the building.

"Write down your favorite monster," Vi told me that first day, handing me a paper and marker. The day they'd invited me to be part of the club. I still remembered what I'd drawn. I flipped through and found it now: my drawing of the door in B West, of Gran's eyes looking through. *MNSTR.*

"Are you at the end yet?" Skink asked, and for half a second, I was unsure where I was, *when* I was.

It could have been Eric standing next to me, hurrying me along because we were late, late for a monster hunt.

I blinked and looked around to remind myself that I was still in the Chickering Island Campground office, sitting at the desk. Skink was bringing me a cup of coffee, and together we were trying to work out what to do next. Whatever it was, I wished like hell I could leave this boy out of it, but he was already in it. And he'd made it clear that there was no way I was going anywhere without him.

"Not yet," I said, turning to the next page—Dr. Jekyll and Mr. Hyde—soaking it all in.

I read the last lines:

By taking the potion, Dr. Jekyll awakened the beast, his dark side, and in the end, the dark side is stronger. The dark side wins.

And because the monster takes over, they both must die.

Skink perched himself on the edge of the desk, leaning down to read over my shoulder.

"So this girl," Skink said. "This girl you wrote the book with, she's your sister?"

"Yes," I said.

He flipped the binder closed and pointed at the cover. "Are you Violet Hildreth or Iris?"

"I was Iris."

"What was she like? Back then, I mean? I mean, did you know that she had this . . . this evil inside her?"

I shook my head. "No. I was supposed to be the broken one. I was the monster."

*   *   *

I REMEMBERED THAT final night, together in the basement room at the Inn, how Vi closed her eyes, slipped down to the floor on her knees.

I dropped down, shook her shoulders, called her name, "Vi! Violet! Wake up, Violet!"

But when she did wake up, did open her eyes, she was not the same person.

She never would be again.

Violet Hildreth was gone.

The monster looked back at me from icy-cold eyes.

• • •

NOW I TURNED back to the book, flipped to the final entries, the new pages—so much whiter and crisper. The pages the monster herself had added in.

> *There are so many kinds of monsters, are there not?*
>
> *Like Eric's chimera, I am many-faced.*
>
> *I contain multitudes.*
>
> *For years now I have roamed the country, much like you, dear sister. Haven't we always been each other's shadows? Bound inexplicably.*
>
> *But are we really so inexplicable, when you look at where we both came from?*
>
> *We may not be sisters by birth, but the way in which we were reborn in that basement binds us more strongly than shared blood, don't you agree?*
>
> *Like you, I'm always moving, always on the run, always SEEKING. Seeking the girls.*
>
> *You know about the girls.*
>
> *I seek the girls while you seek the monsters.*
>
> *But do you know—have you guessed—why I do what I do?*
>
> *Because we know every monster has a motivation, a driving force. Every monster has a HUNGER, a need it must satisfy. Do you remember our lessons?*
>
> *What do I do to the girls?*
>
> *I SAVE them.*
>
> *I save them because . . . because . . . because . . .*
>
> *Because I could not save you.*
>
> *Each time I transform a girl, it's YOU I'm saving.*
>
> *You, my sister.*

My brave hunter of monsters.
My other half.
My missing piece.
Come find me.
Come home.
I'll be waiting.

"Do you know what she means?" Skink asked, pointing at the page. "Where home is?"

I blinked down at the page, the world around me flickering and wavering, the past and the present entwined. The past I'd been running so hard from, yet chasing after, for all these years.

"The Inn," I told him. "She's gone back to the Hillside Inn."

"Wait," he said, eyes wide. "The Hillside Inn? From *The Helping Hand of God*?"

I nodded.

"Holy shit! That's why the name Hildreth sounded so familiar. You two are from there? You were like . . . that crazy doctor's experiments? No way!"

I stood, my legs shaky.

And just like that, the die was cast.

I was going back to the place where both the monster and I were created.

I was going home.

The Helping Hand of God:
The True Story of the Hillside Inn

By Julia Tetreault, Dark Passages Press, 1980

From the files of Dr. Helen Hildreth
Patient S files

The process I have outlined and perfected in the Mayflower Project is a unique combination of medications, ECT, hypnosis, cold water therapy, and sensory deprivation.

When done correctly, as with Patient S, the subject is wiped clean of memories, of any sense of his or her past self.

But the final and most crucial step, the key to making it all work, is to stop the patient's heart with either an electric shock or a high dose of seizure-inducing medication.

Then the heart must be started again by the practitioner, either by electrical or manual means.

This process of dying and being brought back to life is ancient. There are stories in every culture of the travelers who have made this journey. It is the most profound physical and symbolic act of transformation a human body can endure.

While the subject may be brought back by a defibrillator or cardiopulmonary resuscitation, my own preferred method is open-chest cardiac massage. I place the heart on my left palm, which is held open and flat. With my right hand on the anterior surface of the organ, I squeeze at 100 beats per minute. The heart must remain horizontal.

When the heart begins to beat on its own in my hands, I replace it in the cavity of the chest.

It is a moment of, dare I say, transcendence, for both the subject and myself.

I have given this person a new life. A new beginning.

Dr. Hutchins says it is a bit like playing God.

But I don't entirely agree with that assessment.

I tell him, "It is like being the helping hand of God."

The Monster

August 21, 2019

I COME FROM THE belly of the snake. The dark side of the moon. From my grandmother's gin still: juniper berries, coriander, orris-root. I leave a bitter taste on your tongue.

I am poison.

I am, I said.

I come from the electricity in the air, captured lightning in a bottle. From a rabbit shot and brought back to life again.

I come from the loneliness of rain dripping down a windowpane, a little girl looking out from it, wishing for a friend, a sister she could share everything with.

I come from the Templeton family: a long line of drunks, imbeciles, and inferior specimens of humanity.

I come from the voices of the old gods and the new ones. The voice of Neil Diamond, full of the crackles and skips from Gran's old albums. I am Brother Love. I am every monster in the old black-and-white movies. I am the mice in the killing jars and the one who puts them inside those jars; I am the cotton ball soaked in chloroform. I am the squeak of metal wheels the mice run on, going round and round, round and round.

Wheel of life. Wheel of creation.

Wheel of going nowhere fast, stuck in a cage.

And me, I know about cages and locks.

And I know how to be freed.

I come from the Hillside Inn.

From the dark room in B West where I was held down to a bed with leather straps, given 150 volts right in the head; shocked to death, then brought back to life again.

You've got a strong heart, Violet Hildreth.

I have been to the other side.

I have been there and back again.

Do you remember? Do you remember?

Oh yes, I remember. I remember all of the things my grandmother taught me. The lies she told. The invented life she gave me: with imaginary parents who never existed, a car crash that never happened, a brother who wasn't really my brother, who was a stranger.

She taught me the parts of the body from the tiniest cell to the largest organ (the skin). She taught me to memorize the scientific names for the things we see every day: for the maple tree at the edge of the yard (*Acer saccharum*), for the mouse (*Mus musculus*), for juniper (*Juniperus communis*).

She taught me to draw medicine into a needle, to make a surgical incision, to stitch a wound.

She taught me how to make a killing jar.

To put a sick creature out of its misery.

To be the God of Rodents.

To hold my head up high.

You're special, Violet Hildreth.

She taught me how to live among the humans, a monster hiding in plain sight.

THE BOOK OF MONSTERS

By Violet Hildreth and Iris Whose Last Name We Don't Know

Illustrations by Eric Hildreth

1978

HOW TO KILL MONSTERS
   Vampire: Stake through the heart
   Werewolf: Silver bullet
   Fairy/goblin: Bind it in iron
   Demon: Holy water, crucifix, exorcism
   Ghost: Cast a circle and send it on to the next world

If you don't know the type, there are other things you can try.

Fire will almost always kill a monster, and so will chopping off its head.

Sometimes it's as simple as saying the creature's name backward.

There are as many ways to kill monsters as there are monsters.

Vi

<hr/>

July 28, 1978

THE GODS WERE roaring, screaming in her ears. Their voices like thunder, like waves crashing. Car crash voices. Sounds made of broken glass and screams.

She tried to scream, but when she opened her mouth, no sound came out.

Everything she knew, or thought she knew, was a lie. A carefully painted backdrop that pulled away to reveal a vast nothingness.

There had been no car crash, no brilliant surgeon father, no mother with the beauty of a movie star.

She had no brother.

This was where she came from. This basement, these medications, treatments, hypnotic sessions, surgeries.

Can't be, can't be, can't be: The words were a wishful train chugging in her ears. *Can't be, can't be.*

But it was.

And hadn't some part of her known all along? Hadn't some part of her been preparing?

Vi was down on the ground on her knees, and Iris was shaking her shoulders. "Vi! Violet! Wake up, Violet!"

But Violet Hildreth was a made-up name. A character.

Who am I? Who am I? Who am I?

She opened her eyes, and they were no longer Violet Hildreth's eyes.

She stood up on shaky legs and walked to the file cabinet.

"Vi?" Iris said. "Talk to me, Vi."

She began to pull the files out, not even looking at the contents through her tear-filled eyes, just throwing the papers all over the floor.

I am Patient S.

And she felt it in her chest, blooming, the words sure and strong:

I am a monster.

This she knew how to be.

The pages were scattered around the room now like a strange fallen snow. She tipped over the heavy metal cabinet, letting the scream that had been building inside her out at last.

She'd give them a monster.

She'd give them the worst monster the world had ever seen.

And wouldn't Gran be sorry then?

She'd *make* Gran sorry.

Sorry for everything she'd done.

Vi picked up the wooden chair and smashed it against the wall, breaking its back and legs. She was amazed by her own strength, by the power and fury flowing inside her, lighting her up, making her crackle and glow.

THIS is who I am, who I am, who I am!

"Vi!" Iris was calling, "Violet, stop!" but her voice sounded far off, a voice at the end of a long dark tunnel.

Vi felt a hand on her shoulder, gentle at first, then firm, turning her.

But it wasn't her shoulder anymore. It was the shoulder of a girl named Vi, a paper-doll girl who no longer existed.

"It's okay," Iris said, pulling Vi closer. "Shh, it's going to be okay. Please talk to me, Vi."

Iris petted at Vi's hair, touched Vi's face, looked at her with such love, but also a trace of pity. It was an *I'm so sorry* look. Iris was crying, tears running down her pale face.

The girl named Vi—what was left of her—loved Iris, loved her so much her chest ached and she could hardly catch her breath.

But the monster was full of hate and scorn and fury.

And the monster was stronger.

The monster was winning.

"Let go of me," she ordered.

"No," Iris said. "Vi, I—"

"Let me go!" she roared, but Iris held tight.

The monster reeled back, making a fist with her right hand, swinging her arm through the air. It seemed to happen in slow motion, and what caught Vi most off guard was not her strength, but Iris's expression of pure bewilderment and disbelief.

Vi's fist made contact with Iris's temple, and Iris went down, sprawling backward, hitting the back of her head on the edge of the desk with a sickening crack. She crumpled to the floor on top of the scattered notes.

The monster roared louder, ripped at her own hair, her clothes, tore her shirt, scratched deep red welts into her own chest.

Her voice became a furious, deep growl.

Her vision sharpened as colors brightened and sound intensified.

She heard footsteps rushing down the stairs, coming to see what all the commotion was about.

She heard the mad patter of rain on the roof, the crack of thunder, the sound of Eric sleeping softly in his bed, the squeak of the metal wheels going round and round in the basement.

She heard it all.

She felt it all.

And she understood, just then, what it meant to be a god. The voices of the gods who spoke to her, told her what to do, guided her every day were just her own self all along.

And now she didn't need the gods.

She knew what must be done.

It was the only thing left to do.

She let out another roar, stepped around Iris moaning on the floor, went down the hall to the procedure room. She smashed the ECT machine on the concrete floor. Pulled bottles and vials of medicine out of the cabinet and threw them down, stomping on the broken glass and spilled liquid, dancing her own strange monster dance.

No more, no more, no more.

"Violet?" Gran was there in the doorway, hair mussed from sleep, clothes thrown quickly on.

Sal lurked behind her, a great gargoyle in his blue scrubs, a man solid as stone.

"What the—" His voice trailed off.

Gran scanned the scene, saw the smashed electric-shock box, the glass bottles and vials of medicine crushed in damp puddles.

Sal took a step toward Vi.

Gran put up her hand in a *stop* gesture. "You may go, Sal."

"But, Dr. Hildreth—"

"I can control my granddaughter on my own. Leave us."

"But—"

"Don't come down here again. And keep the rest of the staff away too." Her *I'm the boss* voice, edgy as a knife, the words annunciated with perfect clarity, perfect calm.

Sal slipped away looking regretful, as if rounding up an out-of-control teenage girl would have made his night.

Gran took a step closer to Vi, her shoes loud on the cement floor. *Click clack*, like the hooves of an animal. A monster.

"I remember," Vi said.

The worst sort of monster: the kind who hid in plain sight.

"What is it you think you remember, Violet?"

"I remember *everything*."

"Do you?" There it was, that sly forced smile, which wasn't really a smile all, just a loose facsimile of one. It was all wrong. Grotesque, even.

"I remember the sound of your shoes on the floor down here. *Clip-clop, clip-clop.* How I would wait for you to come, watching for that little window to light up, for you to pull back the cover and look in at me. How sometimes, you'd bring me candy. And sometimes, you'd give me shocks, shots, put me into the cold tub and leave me there for hours."

It was all coming back. And the rage was building. Rage not just over what had been done to her, but over what had been done to the others.

"And it wasn't only me you did this to. It was Iris. It was all the others."

Gran said nothing, just stood, playing with something in her hand. What did she have?

A needle full of tranquilizer? Something to manage the monster back into submission? An amnesia drug of some kind?

Forget, Vi. Forget all you've learned. Let's go back to the way things were. Wouldn't it be easier? Isn't that the way things are meant to be?

Part of her longed to go back.

"I think," Gran began, her words slow and calm, "that you're very shaken up right now, Violet."

"I read the files. I know what you did. And you can't do it anymore."

Gran twirled the object in her fingers.

The lighter. The gold lighter with the engraved butterfly and her initials.

Vi thought of the butterfly, of metamorphosis. Of how once she was a lowly caterpillar, an ugly thing. But now she'd been transformed. She'd crawled out of the chrysalis and unfurled her black, wicked wings.

"If you read the notes, then you know I did you a favor, Violet. I rescued you. I took you away from a doomed life, a dreadful situation. I gave you a second chance."

Vi shook her head. "You turned me into a monster!"

Gran held up the lighter, flicked it once, twice, three times.

Vi felt her head swimming.

Gran reached for her, wrapped her hand around Vi's wrist, feeling her pulse. A loving gesture she'd done a thousand times.

"No!" Vi cried, pulling away, scuttling backward. She got behind the bed and held tight to its metal frame, keeping it between them.

Gran flicked the lighter again, began counting down, her voice drawn-out, slow and drippy like molasses. "Ten, nine . . ." She paused.

"Shut up!" Vi ordered.

"I gave you everything, Violet. You're the best thing I've ever done, my masterpiece. The thing I'm proudest of in all the world." Gran frowned, then resumed the countdown and flicked the lighter again. "Eight, seven, six, five—"

Vi's eyelids fluttered.

I am all the gods rolled into one, she told herself. Hypnosis might have worked on the lost girl, Vi, but she was not Vi anymore.

"I. Am. The. Monster," she said, firmly but not loudly. Her own kind of hypnosis.

And it worked.

She shoved the bed as hard as she could, and it slid, hitting Gran just above the knees. The lighter went skittering across the floor, the butterfly spinning drunkenly. Gran went down with an *oof* and a clatter, her feet flying up, heels off the ground.

Vi ran to the metal med cart, rummaged through what was left in the medicine drawer.

She snatched a brown glass bottle of chloroform. Moving to the bed, she pulled the clean, starched white case off the plastic pillow and crumpled it up, then dumped some of the bottle's contents into the center of the folded pillowcase.

Gran was starting to sit up. Vi pushed the bed again, slamming it against her until she went back down.

Vi tracked back through the broken glass, the bits of circuit and wire and metal, and crouched behind Gran's head. She slapped the pillowcase over Gran's mouth and held it in place with both hands. Gran stiffened, struggled, so like the rodents she had euthanized over the years. She was screaming, saying something over and over, but the words were muffled. What Vi heard (or thought she heard) was *please*.

"You did this," Vi told her. "You made me."

At last, Gran went limp.

Vi released her, dropped the pillowcase.

Then she dragged her toward the bed.

Gran was small, but Vi was surprised at how easy she was to move. She didn't even stir when Vi lifted her onto the bed like a sleepy child to be tucked in for the night. Her breathing was slow and soft. She smelled like gin and cigarettes, like clean laundry and Aqua Net hair spray. Like the Jean Naté cologne she always put on after her bath.

Vi slipped Gran's wrists—so slender, the skin so thin—into the leather restraints attached to the bed, then did her ankles. She'd lost one of her shoes, abandoned on the floor. Next to it was the butterfly lighter.

Vi picked up the lighter. It was still warm from Gran's hand.

She flicked it, and the flame jumped to life, the familiar smell of lighter fluid filling her nose.

She stepped around the bed. She felt so light she was almost floating, as if she was not even in the room where she'd spent hours, days, weeks, months, years even, chained to that same bed, being made to forget everything she once was, then made to believe she was something entirely new.

Where she was put to death, then brought back to life with a new name. A new identity.

Vi looked at the lighter in her hand, the flame still burning, guiding her like a torch, the butterfly sparkling.

Did the butterfly remember what it meant to be a caterpillar?

Sometimes, Vi thought. Sometimes it did.

That caterpillar was still inside but transformed, now so much greater than itself.

Vi left the room without looking back, shut the door, and turned out the lights.

Lizzy

August 21, 2019

W E WERE NEARLY there now.

  I could feel an electric charge, a thrum building as we got closer.

A storm was settling in over the valley. The sky darkened and opened up, heavy drops of rain thumping on the roof of the van.

The air felt thick and heavy.

The inside of the windshield fogged.

I slowed, squinting at the highway. I put on my turn signal and got off at exit 10, where the green and white sign said: FAYEVILLE.

"So you're saying your sister is Violet Hildreth, Patient S? Like *the* Patient S?"

I gripped the wheel tightly, eyes darting from the road to the GPS map.

The windshield wipers were slapping back and forth, back and forth, the defroster blasting air to try to clear the glass.

I had spent most of the nearly two-hour drive so far telling Skink

about the Inn, about how I was once a girl named Iris, and about Vi
and Eric and Gran.

"Yes," I said. "She's Patient S."

"Wow. I read the book, like, a hundred times. And I've got a DVD
of the movie. I know all about it. What Patient S did—killing her family and everything."

I shook my head. "You know what Julia wrote. But she left a lot
out, and some of what was in there was wrong. Just guesses."

"But she used Dr. Hildreth's papers, right?"

"She only had one file. The only one left. The others were all destroyed."

"How'd she get it?"

"I gave it to her," I said.

"No way!"

I nodded. "I packed it the night the police took Eric and me from
the house." I looked out the windshield at the rain pouring down in
sheets, making it look as if the world itself were melting.

"Wait." Skink frowned. "So if she's Patient S, then where did you
come from? Did you ever find out?"

"No," I said. "Anything that might have told me who I was was destroyed."

I squinted into the rain, eyes on the two lanes of rural highway in
front of me. It was getting dark.

I knew we should wait until morning, make a better plan and go in
with daylight on our side. I knew we should wait—but if we waited, we
might be too late.

"In the movie," Skink said, "there's that scene near the end, all
those children escaping the rooms in the basement at the Inn. Did that
really happen?"

I cringed a little. I'd never been able to make it through the whole
movie, but I'd seen enough to know it was a loose interpretation of the

truth—a Hollywood version with lots of special effects and pretty girls in makeup playing the patients.

"No. Violet and I were the only two kids in the Inn that night. It was just us."

Skink was quiet for a while. He had *The Book of Monsters* balanced on his lap and was looking through it as we drove.

I kept my eyes on the road, slowed when I came to a sharp curve.

Skink, lit by the reading light, was tapping his fingers on the book. "What does she mean when she says she 'transforms' the girls?" he asked.

"I don't know."

He nodded, closed the monster book, and looked around.

"So this is Fayeville, huh?" We were passing by a grocery store and a Dollar General. "I've actually never been here. Some friends and I in high school, we talked about coming down here and looking for the Inn, but my friends chickened out, said it was haunted and cursed."

I forced a smile. "I'm sure it is."

"In the movie, Fayeville looked bigger than this. A little more cheerful too."

I shook my head and sighed.

We passed a gas station, the post office, Fayeville General Store. We drove by another gas station with a Dunkin' Donuts attached. A vape shop. A sign for the town dump and recycling center.

At a bend in the road, I slowed. There, on the right, was a falling-down sign for the Hollywood Drive-In.

One giant screen was mostly intact, but big squares of it were missing, showing only wooden scaffolding behind. The screen on the other side had completely collapsed. The ticket booth was boarded over with plywood tagged with graffiti, the driveway chained off.

"How much farther?" Skink asked.

"We're almost there."

Passing the drive-in, we continued down Main Street for another mile, then turned right onto Forest Hill Drive. At least, I thought it was Forest Hill Drive. The GPS told me it was, but no street sign marked it. The trees had grown, nearly overtaking the entrance to the dirt road, making it hard to spot.

The road was in terrible shape: hardly a road at all. More like a dried-out old riverbed. The van bumped slowly over the rocks, and I swerved around the worst ruts and a fallen tree partially blocking the road.

"Are you sure this is right?" Skink asked.

"No, I'm not sure of anything," I said irritably, peering through the pouring rain, trying to make out something, anything familiar.

I slammed on the brakes, sending Skink jolting forward, stopped by his seatbelt, hands braced on the dashboard.

"No worries," he said. "Just a little whiplash is all."

A heavy rusted chain drooped across the road. An orange and white sawhorse with a faded ROAD CLOSED sign was on its side beneath it. There were NO TRESPASSING signs posted on the trees beside the road.

"Guess we walk from here," I said.

I pulled the van over, turned the engine off. Then I stepped into the back, grabbed my backpack, and checked to make sure it had everything I might need. I grabbed my rain slicker from the little closet, then got the holster for my gun and slipped it on over my shoulder before putting on the rain jacket.

"You don't think you'll actually need to use that, do you?" Skink asked as I clipped the gun into the holster. He'd gone pale and looked much younger. Strangely, with his face so serious, I saw his father in him for the first time. They had the same eyes, the same worry lines on their foreheads.

For half an instant, I wished Pete were with us. Then I thought of the shitstorm that would ensue when he learned I'd taken his son into such a potentially dangerous situation.

"Maybe you should wait here," I suggested. "If I'm not back in an hour, call for help. Call your dad, then 911."

Skink shook his head. "Uh-uh. No way! I'm coming with you. We had a deal!"

I nodded in reluctant acquiescence, then reached into my backpack, pulling out the extra sets of keys to the van I kept there. I handed them to Skink.

"What's this for?"

"In case you need to make it out of here on your own."

"Lizzy—"

"You know"—I gave him a weak smile—"like to go for help or something."

"You and me and Lauren are walking out of here," he said, clearly doing his best to sound action-hero-ish. "That's the only way this is going to go down. Agreed?"

"Agreed," I said, hopping out of the van and into the rain.

I was soaked to the skin in five minutes. The wind was blowing the rain at us from all angles, coming in through my sleeves, up through the bottom of my coat. My jeans and sneakers were waterlogged. And Skink was worse off in his heavy work boots, jeans, and cotton hoodie.

The road was muddy, full of ruts that had filled with water, turned to miniature rivers. On we trudged, uphill. At last, the road leveled and I saw it: what remained of Gran's old house. All that was left was part of the front porch, a cellar hole, and piles of debris: charred wood, broken glass, a rusted bathtub. It amazed me, really, to see what little remained.

The house had been intact when I'd seen it last. This fire must have happened after it had been abandoned.

I looked across the overgrown field at the Inn. The carriage house and barn had been leveled, but the Inn itself was still there, looming like a broken-backed thing, a monster all its own. Part of the front wall had crumbled away, the yellow bricks lying in heaps amid charred wood and indiscernible debris. The roof had caved in, but most of the old slate shingles remained. The windows were either broken or covered with pieces of plywood, which had weathered and buckled and were covered in graffiti.

I could almost smell the smoke still, though it had been over forty years.

We stood in the rain staring at the Inn, neither of us moving. It was getting dark, and late-season crickets were chirping.

"Is that a light on in there?" Skink asked, squinting and raising one hand to shield his eyes from the rain.

He was right. There was a soft glow coming from the lower windows.

"She's waiting for us," I said.

For me.

She's waiting for me.

"Come on," I said, leading him across the road and over the grass. I was pulling him along, and just like that, I was thirteen years old again, running across the yard with Vi, slipping and sliding as we held each other up, alive and giddy. Two girls setting off to learn the truth they thought would save them.

Stop! I wanted to scream to those girls.

Turn around!

Go back before it's too late.

But there was no changing what had happened. No reaching back through time.

The light in the window flickered, jumped, and twitched, giving off a soft orange glow.

Flames.

"Hurry," I said, starting to sprint. "It's on fire!"

Vi

I AM, I SAID.
 I am, I cried.

The voices (hers! all hers!) were singing in her head. Singing in golden, crystal-clear tones.

With a flash, she understood her lifelong obsession with monsters. With the old movies and stories and legends. Part of her was preparing. Preparing herself for the day when she'd wake up and realize what she truly was.

   • • •

VI FOUND IRIS still on the floor of the office. She was sitting up amid the mess of papers and file folders.

"Vi?" Iris said.

Vi went to the papers on the desk, the final file they'd found.

She began by ripping off the back cover with the photograph stuck to it.

She looked at the girl, Patient S, the smile on her face, the contentment. She had been taken care of and loved by her grandmother, who was smart and clever and kind, the best doctor in the world. And her grandmother had baked her favorite cake, so sweet it made her teeth ache, but light and fluffy, truly the food of angels.

Lucky girl, lucky girl, the God of Birthdays sang.

Make a wish, urged the God of Wishes.

What had she wished for?

A wish that seemed to come from nowhere, yet everywhere. A wish that had been inside her all along but had just worked its way up to the surface of her conscious mind.

She'd wished for a sister.

Someone to share everything with.

She looked down at this girl in the photograph, this pitiful know-nothing girl, and hardly recognized her.

She flicked on Gran's lighter and touched the tip of the file folder to the flame, watched it catch.

"Vi?" Iris called. She was up on her feet, swaying slightly as if the room were spinning. She put her hands on the desk to steady herself. "What are you doing?" Her face was pale and sweaty, her eyes focused.

Vi shook her head.

Not Vi. Not anymore.

Call me by my true name, I dare you.

And what was her true name?

Patient S?

The Monster?

She must have had a name once before, when she was some other girl with real parents and a real sister.

She searched her memory for a name, for some flash of an image of that past life, but nothing came.

Only darkness.

It didn't matter. Not really.

She wasn't that girl anymore.

Nor was she Violet Hildreth.

She was someone—something—else altogether.

The folder was fully engulfed now, the edges of the flames burning her fingers. Pain pulled her back into her own body.

Whose body, though?

She dropped the burning folder onto the other papers on the desk. Then she gathered more files, more papers, and added those to the little pyre.

Iris came closer. "Stop! What are you doing?" Vi pushed Iris away, ordered her to stay back.

Smoke and ash and blackened curls of burned paper drifted up, then fell to the floor, burning on the carpet, sending up a hideous chemical stink.

She threw the broken chair parts onto the flames.

Let it burn.

Let it all burn.

The desk itself had caught fire now, and the flames shot up, up to the low drop ceiling. The plastic cover over the flickering fluorescent lights was melting from the heat. The bulbs exploded. The room went dark.

Iris screamed.

And the monster laughed.

She laughed and laughed until she was choking, the thick plastic-scented smoke filling her throat and lungs.

Iris was coughing, choking.

The room was so thick with smoke that Vi could hardly see her there, a pale figure standing just behind her. Her shadow, her doppelgänger.

Vi took her hand, and Iris fought against her, tried to pull away. But Vi held tight, tugged her away from the fire toward the door.

Lizzy

August 21, 2019

*T*OO LATE, TOO *late*, I was thinking as I got to the crumbling front steps.

I touched the outside of the door, feeling for heat.

The door was cool and wet.

I put my hand on the knob.

Please open. Don't be locked.

I could feel Skink behind me, hear him breathing fast.

The knob turned in my hand.

I took a deep breath, stepped in, and let out a relieved sigh.

Candles.

Candles were lit around the main reception area: two on the floor on either side of the door and three more farther in. The flickering light made a path that led to the basement door.

The building smelled like mildew, rotten wood, wet plaster, and smoke.

"Guess she's expecting you," Skink whispered, stepping into the room.

I nodded, pulled out my gun, and moved slowly forward, following the candlelit path to the basement stairs.

The floor was covered in chunks of fallen plaster, the mildewed remains of rugs, pieces of broken furniture. The floor gave a little beneath my feet. In places there was no floor at all: just burned-through timbers.

I turned back and whispered to Skink, "Careful where you step."

He nodded, cautiously moving forward. "So do you have a plan, or what?"

I didn't answer.

What *was* the plan?

I had to stop the monster. Save the girl.

Would I kill the monster?

That was how it worked in all the movies and what we'd written in our book: The monster had to die.

Beneath the raincoat, a slick sweat covered my body. The gun felt heavy and cold in my hand.

I paused at the top of the basement stairs. The door stood open, and candles lit the stairway.

I had the feeling I was walking right into a trap. I'd been led here. My sister was down there waiting.

I remembered the old hospital beds, the restraints, the ECT machine.

I started down the stairs, slowly.

Skink followed. "I don't like this," he whispered.

Me neither, I thought. But what choice did I have?

The only person I'd ever truly felt kinship with was waiting for me down in the basement.

My sister.

"Quiet," I told Skink. "Get behind me."

The walls and ceiling down here were intact, but had been spray-painted by vandals. Smashed beer bottles littered the floor, along with empty bags of chips and fast food cartons. I spied a condom wrapper and shivered—what a strange place to have sex.

Someone had outlined a pentagram with red spray paint on the steel door leading to B West. And written beneath it: *The Devil Lived Here.*

True enough, I thought.

Holding the gun in my right hand, I pushed the door open with my left.

More candles lined the green cement hallway. The walls were stained black from smoke and mildew. The place smelled like rot and ruin with a tinge of smoke like a ghost, even after all these years.

"I've got a bad feeling about this," Skink whispered. He stopped walking. I flapped my left hand back at him: *You stay here.*

I crept slowly down the hallway, trying to keep my feet from crunching too loudly on more broken glass, crumbled cement, bits of charred wood and plaster, melted plastic.

I heard voices. A shriek.

A girl in pain?

My heart jackhammered.

I wasn't too late! Lauren was alive!

There was still time to save her.

I wanted to run but knew I had to move slowly, carefully.

I passed the first door on the left, spinning to look inside it, gun out in front of me like some TV show cop.

The room was empty, dark.

But the door to the procedure room, the room where Gran's body had been found strapped to the bed, was open, candlelight flickering inside.

It's a trap, it's a trap, screamed a voice in the back of my brain. *Run! Get out while you can!*

My feet froze, not wanting to go any farther, not wanting to know what awaited me.

"Hold still," a woman's voice ordered from inside the room. "Or I'll cut you."

I took a deep breath and stepped into the room, gun raised and held steady with both hands.

The room was full of candles, their flames flickering, dancing. An old camping lantern was set on an overturned table, emitting a bright glow, throwing huge shadows on the wall.

The girl was sitting in a chair with a sheet wrapped around her so that all I could really see was the back of her head.

And there was the monster: my long-ago sister, standing by the girl's side, the glint of a blade flashing in her right hand.

Vi

~~~~~~~~~

July 28, 1978

THE BUILDING WAS in flames behind them.

The fire alarm was ringing, the bells deafening. The sprinkler system had gone off. They were both soaked. Soaked from the sprinklers inside the building and soaked from the rain that was pounding down on them.

Iris was sitting up, leaning against a tree. The back of her head was bleeding, the rain mixing with the blood, making it run down her neck. Her face was pale, and her lips had a bluish tinge. Her hat was gone, and Vi could see the scar that ran along the front of her head under her stubbly hair.

From somewhere around the front of the building they could hear Miss Evelyn screaming, "Where is Dr. Hildreth?" as the thunder boomed. Patty and Sal were there, by the side of the building, counting the patients, who were half-asleep, medicated, staggering around in their hospital gowns, the rain pelting them.

Miss Evelyn kept yelling for Dr. Hildreth, her voice more and more shrill, more and more frantic, but no one seemed to be able to answer.

"What have you done?" Iris asked, looking past Vi to the Inn—the smoke pouring out of it, flames now visible from some of the lower-story windows.

Vi thought she could make out shapes in the smoke writhing and twisting as it rose: the ghosts escaping. Ghosts that had been there all along.

"I did what needed to be done."

"The records, the files—" Iris said.

"Are all gone now."

Iris looked as though she might start crying again.

"I'm sorry," Vi said. "If there was anything in there about who you were, who you used to be, it's gone."

And she *was* sorry. She'd broken her promise: She never had found out who Iris was, where she'd come from. And now she never would.

But really, Vi believed she'd saved Iris in some way. Now Iris didn't need to know the terrible things that had been done to her; the terrible things she might have done to others.

Iris leaned her head back against the tree, looked up at the sky through the canopy of leaves. Vi looked too. There were no stars. Only darkness. The occasional bright flash of lightning.

Vi turned to see a shadow moving quickly toward them across the wide expanse of lawn, running, past the lost-looking patients, past the night staff trying to maintain control.

It was Eric, his wild curls flying out, his pajamas pale and soaked, his feet bare.

"What happened?" he asked, panting to catch his breath. He looked at Vi. "Where's Gran?"

"Eric—I—" she stammered, unsure what to say, where to even begin. The power and confidence of the monster was fading. She looked at the building in flames behind Eric and knew she had done it. She remembered setting the fire, yet somehow it felt like it had been someone else. Like it was a movie: a monster on a rampage.

She wasn't sure who she was now, a monster or a girl or some combination of the two.

Miss Ev—in her robe, her wig crooked—was standing next to the building, staring at the flames, shouting, "Dr. Hildreth!" She rushed toward the east side door, like she was going to go right in, but Sal grabbed her, pulled her back, which proved to be more of an effort than he'd expected. They tussled, and Miss Ev nearly got away, but Sal got behind her, wrapped her tightly in his arms, and walked her back away from the building.

"You're not gonna do anyone any good going in there, Miss Ev," he said. "We need you out here. The patients need you."

"Dr. Hildreth!" Miss Ev sobbed.

Eric looked from Vi to the Inn, his face lit orange from the glow of the flames. "What did you do to Gran?" he demanded.

Vi pitied the little boy she'd believed was her brother. She wanted to shelter him from the truth. But she knew the truth would come out. And it was best that he hear it from her.

"Gran," she began, voice unsure, "Gran isn't who you think she is. And I'm not who you think I am."

He stared at her, his mouth opening a little. His eyes narrowed in anger. "I know who you are. I know all about you."

"Eric," Iris said, "I think—"

"You're not my sister," he said. "You're a *stray*"—he spat out the word—"like Iris."

Vi felt something collapse inside of her.

She forced the words out through her too-tight throat: "How long have you known?"

"Since Gran brought you home."

No. Vi shook her head.

"She gave me a special job," Eric said. "To keep an eye on you. Give her reports."

"Reports," Vi repeated. The rain was so loud, so cold. She was shivering, shaking all over.

It shouldn't have surprised her. Not after everything she'd learned tonight. But still, it did. He'd been giving Gran reports on Vi just as Vi was giving Gran reports on Iris. If they'd waited long enough, surely Iris would have been giving reports on some new kid.

Eric nodded. "Gran said to treat you like a sister. That I had to go along with whatever you said, whatever crazy beliefs you had. I shouldn't ever tell you your ideas weren't real. She said . . . she said you could be dangerous."

Vi felt the rage roaring up again, the monster taking hold. "You knew! You knew and you never said anything?" Her tattletale brother had kept the biggest secret of all. "How could you?"

"I promised Gran," he said. "I promised her I'd be the best brother ever. And I'd *never* tell you the truth. No matter what." He was crying now, looking at Vi. "And you know what? I actually kind of forgot. That you weren't really my sister." He rubbed at his eyes, looked back to the burning building. "But Gran was right. She said one day you might do something bad. Something awful."

Sirens were coming up the hill—they could hear them in the distance, faint at first, but getting louder. Soon the whole yard would be overrun with men in uniforms and fire coats, men wearing masks and air tanks on their backs. Men asking questions.

"I'm going to tell them," Eric said, rubbing his nose with the back of his hand. "I'm going to tell them what you've done. I'm going to tell them all about you." He looked so brave just then. So angry and defiant. Vi believed that whatever happened to him, wherever he went from there, he was going to be okay.

"Go tell them. Tell them the truth," Vi said. "Look under my bed. There's a file there. Show that to them. It proves what I am. What I've done." Eric turned and ran toward the police cars and fire trucks that were coming up the road, red lights flashing in the rain. He was waving his arms frantically, yelling to them.

"Eric, wait!" Iris called, getting to her feet to chase after him.

"Let him go," Vi said, watching him disappear around the corner of the building, thinking that was it—the last time she'd ever see her brother. And even though he wasn't really her brother, even though he'd lied to her, her chest cracked open to see him go.

"They'll come for you," Iris said.

"Yes," Vi replied, watching the first fire truck pull up in front of the Inn, followed by a police car. Then an ambulance and another fire truck.

"They'll lock you up!" Iris said.

Vi smiled. "They'll have to catch me first."

"But—"

"Come with me," she said.

Iris shook her head, looked away from Vi. Her eyes were full of tears. "There's no way. We'd never make it. We're just kids! Where are we supposed to go? What are we supposed to do?"

You're my clever girl, Gran had always told her.

She was clever. But she was so much more than that.

A thirteen-year-old girl might not be able to get by in the world on her own.

But a monster could.

"Trust me," Vi said. She looked down at the road. Eric was there, talking to a policeman. "Please. We have to go now."

Vi touched Iris's chest, just above her heart, running her fingers over the scar, the scar that she'd once longed so badly to touch. The scar that made them twins, bound them together.

"We belong together," she said. "Don't you see?"

Two broken girls who together made a whole.

Iris flinched, stepped backward, shaking her head. She looked at Vi as if she didn't know her at all, her eyes frantic and full of fear.

And Vi understood then.

She truly was a monster.

And like any monster, she'd always be alone.

She pulled her hand away, then turned, took off running into the woods.

The Helping Hand of God:
The True Story of the Hillside Inn

Julia Tetreault, Dark Passages Press, 1980

THE AFTERMATH

Dr. Thad Hutchins took his own life with an overdose of barbiturates one week after the fire at the Hillside Inn. Many dark secrets no doubt died with him. He was able to tell the police a few things in his first interviews.

According to Dr. Hutchins, the boy who had been raised as Dr. Hildreth's grandson, Eric, had been born at the Inn in the fall of 1969. He was the child of an eighteen-year-old young woman with a mood disorder and a drug addiction—a long-term patient at the Inn. The child's father is unknown. The young woman went into labor early. Dr. Hildreth delivered the child and told the mother her baby was stillborn—as her own twin girls had been so many years before. Dr. Hildreth believed she could give this child a better life than his mother could. He was, according to Dr. Hutchins, an experiment in nature versus nurture. The boy was raised to believe he was Dr. Hildreth's grandson, that his parents had died. At this writing, he is in foster care and doing well with his new family and new identity. Any record of his biological mother's identity was destroyed in the fire.

The girl known as Iris is also in foster care. Attempts to learn about her background have been unsuccessful. Dr. Hutchins reported that Dr. Hildreth brought her to the Inn herself. He claimed he did not know where she'd come from. Although whatever documentation there might have been about Iris was destroyed, it is clear she was part of the Mayflower Project. The child bears scars of both open-heart surgery and brain surgery. She has no memory of her life before the Inn.

Patient S—a.k.a. Violet Hildreth—disappeared without a trace. The last time she was seen was the night of the fire: July 28, 1978.

Where does a thirteen-year-old girl on her own go?

No real records remain that could tell us who she truly was. No proof that she even existed at all. No paper trail.

The police put little effort into finding her.

Using the few notes I had from Dr. Hildreth's surviving files and my own research into the remaining members of the "Templeton family," I believe I have identified Patient S.

Here's what I discovered.

On October 3, 1974, a small mobile home in Island Pond, Vermont, burned down, killing Daniel Poirier; his wife, Lucy; and their older daughter, Michelle. Their younger daughter, Susan, was never found. It was reported that Susan had been sent to live with family out of state. I tracked down her birth certificate and second-grade class picture. I am convinced that this girl, Susan Poirier, born September 3, 1965, in St. Johnsbury, Vermont, is Patient S.

I am also convinced that she is out there still. That she may, one day, hold a copy of this book in her hands.

•   •   •

Susan, if you're reading: You are Susan Poirier. Your second-grade teacher, Mrs. Styles, remembers you as the smartest girl in the class, bright and cheerful and full of questions. You have family in the Northeast Kingdom still—aunts, uncles, cousins. None of them blame you for the things that happened. All of them hope that you will one day come home.

Lizzy

August 21, 2019

"DON'T MOVE," I ordered, my voice a croak.

The monster turned toward me, not looking very monstrous at all.

And the girl turned too, swiveling her head around, the hair on one side cut short, the other long.

"Hello, Monster Hunter," Vi said, smiling. She had short, dark hair flecked with gray, a few wrinkles around her brown eyes. She was trim, muscular beneath her green T-shirt. She had on jeans and leather boots. She looked so . . . ordinary. And so much like her thirteen-year-old self that I was startled.

"Drop the knife," I ordered, aiming the gun right at her chest.

The monster continued smiling and held up the pair of scissors she had in her hand to show me before dropping them. They clattered to the floor.

I looked down at the floor, covered in wisps of blond hair with purple tips.

She'd been giving Lauren a haircut.

"Step away from the girl, Vi."

The monster gaze me a quizzical look, took three steps backward, her hands raised in the air. "I haven't heard anyone call me by that name since you did last, right here."

"Lauren!" Skink cried from behind me, running for the girl who was standing now, taking off the sheet. She was wearing yoga pants, a T-shirt. Other than the funky half-finished haircut, she looked absolutely fine.

"Skink?" She stepped forward and embraced the boy. "Oh my God! What are you doing here?"

"I came to save you. Well," he said, smiling sheepishly, "Lizzy and I did." Then he demanded, "Did she hurt you?"

"No," the girl said.

"Drug you? Hypnotize you?"

"Um, no. Nothing like that."

"I don't get it," Skink said. "What did she do?"

"She saved me."

I still had the gun pointed at Vi. "Skink, I'd like you to take Lauren out of the room, please. Go back upstairs and wait for me there."

"Really," Lauren said, "there's no need for all this. I'm fine. Better than fine, actually. I mean, I'm sure my hair looks a little ridiculous right now, but that's kinda your fault, right?" She laughed.

"Take her upstairs, Skink," I ordered. "Now."

The two teens left the room.

"Down to you and me, Iris," Vi said. "Just like old times."

"No one calls me that anymore."

"I'm sorry. Lizzy, then. Lizzy Shelley. A beautiful name. I'm happy to see you. I've been waiting a long time for this."

"For what, exactly?"

"To show you. To show you what I've become. Isn't that why you're here? Why you've hunted me down? You're very clever, you know. Catching on. Following me around the country. And now we've come full circle, haven't we? Back here, where it all began. Really, it just seems perfect."

"Were you going to kill her in front of me?"

Vi laughed. "Is that really what you think?"

"I think at least ten girls have gone missing, never to be seen again," I said. "If you're not killing them, then what—"

"Some monsters," Vi interrupted, "use their powers for good. Please, come sit. I have something to show you."

She bent down to reach into the pack beside her, and I yelled, "Stop! You need to keep your hands where I can see them."

Vi put her hands above her head. "Fine. Will you please get my laptop out for me, then? I don't have any weapons."

She shoved the pack toward me, and I peered in. Yes, a laptop. Some apples and granola bars, a first aid kit and a flashlight. I pulled out the computer, handed it over.

"May I sit down?" Vi asked.

I nodded. Vi took a seat on a pile of blankets on the floor, opened the computer on her lap, started typing.

"Here," she said. "Look."

I stepped closer, just behind Vi, and looked down at the screen.

Vi had opened to a page showing a woman in business attire, a profile page of some sort. Claire Michaels. Forty-four years old, executive at Livewire Multimedia in Burbank, California. Married with two kids. All her contact info.

Vi flipped to another profile page, another woman. Jessica Blankenship, thirty-six, a nurse midwife in Akron, Ohio. Single.

"What is this?" I asked. "Some kind of dating app?"

"Look at the bottom of the pages," Vi said. She flipped back to Claire Michaels. I leaned closer. There, in little letters at the bottom of the page: *FKA Jennifer Rothchild.*

The name pinged in my brain. I looked at the photo again of the woman in the white collared shirt and blazer, frosted hair, full makeup.

Jennifer Rothchild had been the monster's first victim. She'd disappeared in the summer of 1988 after claiming to have met a bigfoot-type creature in the woods of her little town in Washington State. She was never heard from again.

"Look," Vi said, clicking to another page, showing a photo of Jennifer Rothchild at thirteen. The one they'd circulated to the media and put on posters when she went missing. Vi tapped again so that the photo of thirteen-year-old Jennifer Rothchild was next to forty-four-year-old Claire Michaels. Same heart-shaped face, same blue eyes, same little dimple in the left cheek. The same person.

I put the gun back in the holster, dropped down to my knees on the floor beside Vi, took hold of the laptop with both hands, using the track pad to click through one profile after another. All the adult versions of girls who'd been taken. Each profile had the FKA name and photograph: Vanessa Morales, Sandra Novotny, Anna Larson. I knew those names, those photos so well—those ten missing girls. I had a whole folder stuffed full of information on them—cataloging my desperate attempts to find out what had happened to them. But there they were, all found. All living good lives with new names: an executive, a doctor, a marine biology professor, a filmmaker. And there were more than ten, girls I didn't even know about. Girls who'd wandered away from their teenage lives and shown up as successful adults with new names.

"I don't understand," I said.

"It's what I do," Vi said. "What *we* do. Take girls in bad situations:

girls who are being abused by family members or boyfriends, girls with drug problems, girls who've made terrible mistakes, even girls who've killed people. The girls other people call *monsters*," she said, emphasizing the last word, then pausing to let it mingle with our own shadows in the flickering light. "We give them a second chance. We transform them. Teach them that the anger they feel inside, the thing that makes them different, can be a source of strength and power. We show them how to slip away from who they once were and start again."

I blinked at her, still not believing what I was hearing. "Who's *we*?"

"I have benefactors, collaborators. Mostly women I've helped who've reached out to me, who want to do what they can for other girls. Claire Michaels, for instance. She sends money every month and has a carriage house behind her home where she can host girls who are starting over. Nearly all of the women I've transformed contribute what they can. The money goes to getting the girls set up in new lives. New schools. College, even. It's a network—a monster club, sort of."

I thought of what Gran had done, the lives she'd ruined trying to wipe people's old selves away. Vi was giving these lost girls, girls like we had once been, second chances.

"You're not killing them. You're not hurting them. You're saving them?"

Vi tilted her head. "We're showing them how to save themselves," she said.

I was quiet, taking it all in.

"And now I need your help," Vi said.

"My help?"

"I need you to walk away from all of this. To not draw attention to the monsters and the girls."

"So you're asking me to stop hunting monsters?"

She laughed. "No. Not all monsters. Just me."

"How will I know that it's you?"

"You'll know. You'll be able to feel it, won't you? Isn't that how we ended up here?"

I looked at her. Here she was, the monster I'd been chasing for so long.

"Are you disappointed?" Vi asked. "I'm not what you expected?"

"No . . . I just . . ."

"Do you ever think about it? About what might have happened if you'd come with me back then?"

My eyes burned with tears. "All the time."

"Me too." Vi nodded. "You broke my heart that night."

I opened my mouth to say something, but didn't know what: *I'm sorry? I'd do things differently if I could go back?*

Lauren and Skink returned. "Just making sure no one's shot anyone yet," Lauren said.

"Lizzy," Skink said, "we were all wrong about this. Lauren's been telling me what's really going on. She was in some serious shit, like scary bad stuff I didn't know about—"

"And I've been given a second chance," Lauren said.

"I still don't understand," I admitted. "Why not just go home and start over there? Why leave everything behind?"

"Because that's the way it has to work," Vi said. "My rules. To be reborn, you have to die. Cut all ties. Let go of your old life and the hold it had over you. It might seem extreme, but it works. Time after time."

"What if the girls don't want to change?" Skink asked.

"Then they go back home. It doesn't happen very often. I choose the girls carefully. Only the ones in truly dire straits make the cut. The ones who really are out of options. The ones who already feel like there's nowhere they belong."

"Like we were once," I said.

Vi smiled. "Exactly."

AFTERWORD

Lizzy

September 5, 2019

"HOW'S THE WENDIGO hunting?" Skink asked.

"No sign of it yet, but I interviewed an eyewitness today. A reliable woman—works at the town hall. Swears she saw this creature grab her dog and carry it off when she was out jogging a couple of weeks ago. Not a small dog either, a husky."

The story had unsettled me: a pale humanoid creature nearly ten feet tall, half skeletal with huge black eye sockets. "And it stank," the woman had told me, "like putrid, rotting flesh."

"Yikes," Skink said. "Sure you don't need any backup out there?"

I laughed. "You've got school. Your dad would kill you if you got on a plane to the wilds of Wisconsin."

Skink laughed too. "I don't know. I kinda think he'd want to come with me. He talks about you all the time. He's been checking your blog every day and listening to all the podcasts. I think he's listened to some twice now."

"That's a lot for a nonbeliever."

"He wants to know when you're coming back to Vermont. He says to remind you we've got lots more monsters here for you to investigate. He says he could take you out to Lake Champlain on his boat, go hunting for Champ."

"Sounds like a plan," I said. "Maybe next summer."

"You still heading out to California after Wisconsin?" Skink asked.

"I'm gonna stop in and see my brother for a little while first. Then, yeah, I promised Brian I'd at least meet with him and the team and hear about this new show they've dreamed up."

"I think it's an awesome idea: *Lizzy Shelley, Monster Hunter!*"

"God, I hope they've come up with a better name than that!"

"You'd be an idiot not to do it, you know?" Skink said. "If your mission truly is to educate people about monsters, you've gotta do what gets the most sets of eyeballs on you. Plus, you're good at it. People loved you in *Monsters Among Us.*"

I sighed.

I was in my van camped at the edge of the Point Beach State Forest in Two Rivers, Wisconsin. It was dark now, and when I glanced out of the windows, I saw only myself reflected. The van was full of the cozy glow of LED lights and my laptop screen.

Skink was quiet.

"So how are you doing, really?" I asked.

"Okay," he said, blowing out a long, slow breath. "It's weird. Not being able to tell anyone that Lauren's okay—not even my dad. And I just worry about her, you know?"

"She's fine, Skink. She's in good hands."

"I know. I just wish . . ."

"That things were different?"

"Yeah," he said.

"I know," I said. "Me too."

I wished I knew where Vi and Lauren had gone. I wished we'd made a plan to meet up again, like normal sisters might.

Instead, Vi had warned me off, asked me not to follow them, not to try to find her.

"But what if I need you?" I had asked.

"If it's an emergency, you can email me." She'd written down an email address that began with MNSTRGRL.

"There's something else," Skink said.

"What is it?"

"I heard my dad and that state police detective talking today."

"About Lauren?"

"Yeah. Apparently the cops in Worcester found . . . evidence."

"What kind of evidence?"

"Lauren's diary. Her father had been abusing her for a while. The cops said it was pretty awful. According to this diary, she was going to tell. About to go to her mom and the police, tell her therapist— everyone. She'd already told a couple of friends."

I felt a knot in my throat. "We knew all that, didn't we?"

"Yeah," Skink said. "But the police think maybe her dad found out she was about to tell and did something to her, something to keep her quiet."

"Okay. Have they arrested her father? Brought him in for questioning?"

"No," Skink said. "They can't find him."

"Huh?"

"Looks like the guy ran. Disappeared."

"Guilty much?" I said.

"Yeah, I know. I get why he'd take off, but it's still weird."

"What do you mean?"

"Well, he disappeared the night *before* they found the diary, for one. His wife, Lauren's mom, said he went to take the trash out and just never came back. He left his car, his phone, his wallet. His bank account and credit cards haven't been touched. The dude disappeared without a trace. And get this—he was in his pajamas and barefoot when he went out with the trash."

"Okay, that *is* a little weird," I agreed.

"Can you, you know, like, email Vi?"

"Skink, I—"

"Please," he said.

The Monster

September 5, 2019

THE AIR SEEMS to crackle and hum, the last light of sunset through the windows an explosion of colors. We're waiting until darkness.

Here, in the near dark, the girl and I wait, our hearts pounding, our claws and teeth ready.

She's ready, this girl. Ready to go the rest of the way, to complete the transformation.

Death is always part of the rebirth.

Gran taught me that. It's part of my origin story. My own DNA.

Death and sacrifice.

It makes me feel so alive, almost giddy, my heart racing beneath the scars on my chest as I take it all in: this spectacle of the dying light, the live-wire feel I get when I know what's going to happen next.

The gods are whispering, saying: *Soon, soon, soon.*

The cycle will be complete.

• • •

"HE'S WAKING UP," the girl says now.

And I feel it: the thrill of what will happen next.

She smiles down at him, strapped to the bed. "Hey, Dad."

His eyelids flutter as he comes to and brings her into focus, his face a look of complete surprise. "Lauren? What the hell are you—"

But she's not Lauren anymore.

She raises the blade.

And she is so beautiful: her eyes glittering, her teeth bared as she howls; her monster self fully realized.

The transformation is complete.

No going back now.

•   •   •

LATER, AFTER WE'VE cleaned up and are prepared to move on, I see Lizzy's email and write a reply.

I know she might come after me again, try to pick up my trail.

It gives me a little thrill, to know this. We'll play hide-and-seek, catch me if you can. We will be drawn together and pushed apart and drawn together again. It reminds me of the push and pull of magnets, of the North and South Pole. We are that strong, that powerful.

A monster and a hunter of monsters.

Once upon a time sisters, linked not by blood, but by something much deeper.

You've got a strong heart, Violet Hildreth, Gran used to say, and on this one point, she was absolutely right.

Acknowledgments

MANY THANKS, AS always, to the most amazing agent in the world, Dan Lazar. To Kate Dresser, who helped shape this story from its earliest stages—working with you was true magic. To Jackie Cantor, your keen insight never ceases to amaze me and this book is so much stronger because of you. To Jen Bergstrom, Jessica Roth, Bianca Salvant, Andrew Nguyen, and the whole team at Scout Books—you guys are the absolute best!

To Drea and Zella—thanks for talking me out of giving up when things got hard, and for watching a whole lot of classic monster movies with me! I love you both and couldn't do this without you.

To everyone at the Trapp Family Lodge winter writing retreat, where this book really started to take shape—thanks for sharing beers with me, and listening to me read and talk about my vision for the story.

And last, to Mary Shelley, because as Vi says: *She's the one who started it all.*